A DISCRETE PASSION

James R. Nichols

ISBN 978-0-6151-4076-6

a narrative, told by a son who has lost a father

a reminiscence, told by a daughter who has lost a grandfather

a history, told by a sister who is lost

a love story, of a man and a woman

And your young men shall see visions...

Acts II: 17

This novel began as the letters of my grandfather to my then-to-be grandmother. Most of the events, stories, and myths herein are still extant in the folklore of northern New York State. The events, places, and times of this narrative are actual, by and large. The names have been changed to suggest a more stable reality. The narrators and people are fictitious--but real.

CHAPTER I
PORTRAIT I

THE FATHER

It was like I told you--Remember?

He lived all his life upland, away from the city, in a country that was clean and cold, hard with the crackling shiver of ice in winter and warm only with the reflected sunlight off blue mountain lakes in the summer. His father, your great-grandfather, had lived there before him and his father's father for countless generations.

He was a real mountain man: tall, sturdy, and quiet. He had shocking red hair that never grayed, even when into his sixties he could no longer grub potatoes from sun-up till sunset and come into the house muddied from his shaggy, blonde brows to the caked bottoms of his torn, scratched, Montgomery Ward boots. Then, there would be fifteen barrels in the cellar and a smile of pride and satisfaction on his face which was seldom displayed even among his own family.

He had ice-blue eyes, and if he never stared a treed coon to death, there is at least the legend that at eighteen, by then over six feet tall and as broad across the shoulders as a saw-horse, he killed a bear one winter with only his axe when surprised away from his rifle while felling timber. Reports have it that the bear was crazed with hunger from waking early to a false spring and came upon him in a clearing some three miles from the farmhouse where he was wont to cut and draw wood in the winter for the local school house and neighborhood merchants,

The bear clawed him up right good, evidently, before he finally killed it with a clean stroke of the axe across the top of its neck at the skull base after they'd both rolled off a rock outcropping and fell together some ten or twelve feet onto hard slate. I've often wondered. his arms and neck ripped raw as they were, how he held onto that axe throughout the fight, much less drove it down through all that hair and muscle. I've often wondered if the bear didn't fall first and crack its head at the bottom. but then....

There's no doubt, though. 'bout the dead bear. Folks saw it. And he carried the scars till his dying day, one from just below his left ear, across his jaw and deep into his chest, stopping at the tit. He always said that hurt the most, and he was never known to lie.

And there was no arguing either that the axe cut clear through to skull and spine. A bloody mess, that bear was, cut up in the snow, staining the pristine glare of winter with the thick globular purple of its misspent rage.

The bear'd scared Dad's team off and he, torn up as he was, could not walk home. So he'd done what you often see in the movies these days and slit the gaunt, black bear down the belly, pulled half its empty gut out onto the meadow and crawled inside the cavity to wait for help. It was a lucky thing he had such sense too because it snowed a blizzard all that night, and it wasn't 'til the next morning that they found him, warm, if not very happy, weak but still clutching his axe, "waitin," he used to say later, "for the next ole bear to come along."

"A man, even a good one, spends half his life waitin'," he'd say with an astringent mountain charm in which he always wrapped his clichés. "Anything good is worth waitin' for," he would add. And we believed.

Yes, he was a man made for the woods--and farm. He grew up toward the sky, and he finally looked like a mountain at 6 foot 3 and over 200 pounds. He had lungs like an ox, and at Christmas he could burst balloons in three, great puffs and send us all squealing across the room only later to sneak back around his rocker while he pretended to snooze from dinner and beg him to do it again.

He walked five miles a day every winter and spring on his maple sugar route. He did that after the morning chores and breakfast, and he was still at home by ten to take care of the dogs and stock, feed the hens, and check for eggs before lunch. Then he'd hunt with Minnie all afternoon and make the rounds of his

6

traps. There was never a winter we didn't have venison once a day. After the state put a limit on deer, he saw to it that each of us kids got a license. I shot my first deer at fifteen, Martin his at eleven, though I doubt the Albany fellows ever knew that.

He was always right proud of the sixteen-point buck of his he took back in '17. Its stuffed head hung outside for the longest time, to one side of the porch door, across from the bear--Mom wouldn't have either in the kitchen. When he later moved them inside to the front hall, folks used to joke that they didn't know whether to hang their hats on the antlers or the teeth, and it was true those two heads almost blocked the foyer as they hung across from one another, the soft, proud eyes of the buck staring with miraculous calm into the open-jawed, maniacal rage of the bear.

His skin, always tender and milk-white beneath his clothes, was wind-burned in the winter and sun-burned in the summer. At the end of baseball season his face and neck and arms would be seared crisp between freckles and beneath a pure wash of blond hair along his shoulders and arms.

Strong? I've never known a man stronger, and yet I can't remember a single time, outside of hitting home runs in every game he played, when he really showed off his strength. He could hay all day in a sun that would make other men wilt by noon. In eight hours he could plow an entire field that would take other men a week. He could pick twenty quarts of berries in the time that the rest of us could pick five.

But I remember him most in a boat, sitting still, seemingly idle on a cold, late fall morning out on Long Lake, waiting for the fish to come up and feed along the shore. He'd sit there, the fog rising slowly off the lake, sometimes so thick you couldn't see to the other side and always cold. But none of us kids would say a word to scare away the fish. And then the bobber would dip once, twice on the lake's misty sheen. At the third dip, he'd give his pole a short jerk and begin to reel in. There was never a vain move. We always came home with fifteen or twenty fish. Bullheads, pickerel, sunfish, even a bass or two, sometimes a walleye.

He was a man for all seasons. He strode endlessly the long untilled acres which his father gave to him. And which he conquered. Then he died and gave it all to us. Those days.

7

****

the younger daughter

      yes, I've read about them often--very often, a dozen times at least. it must have been a good life to have known him as you did.

      in these dusty attics of ours full of cobwebs spun between forgotten antiques, i sometimes get confused--we have only his letters; that's all. a picture here and there. like this one in he box, taken when he was at mount union. he is quite clearly a handsome man. his arms crossed, standing a head higher that all the rest, that long square face and deep eyes, the closed straight lips and firmly set jaw. such straight shoulders too.

      no wonder grandma couldn't resist him even if he was poor. and he gave it all up--the education i mean--to come back and marry her--their letters are irreplaceable.

      he was kind. kind and gentle it seems. his letters show it all. reading them, i feel often that i know him almost better than you. at least as well. here's one of my favorites. it's his first letter to grandma during the year i told you about--remember? of their courtship. listen!

* * * *

Dunedin, N.Y
Dec. 5, 1912

Dearest Katherine,

      We arrived home at half past twelve. Agnes was almost

froze. It was the coldest night we've had all winter. Even I felt it, and Agnes did not get out of bed 'til noon today.

No such pleasure for me. Father was in more of a hurry to get to the barn and do the chores than he was on Saturday. I got five hours sleep, and I really slept you can bet as I did not have any ring to keep me awake (ha, ha). That is some joke now but before I understood what it meant it was no joke at all.

I'm finishing your letter at ten o'clock now that the pests are all in bed. They all came in the front room where I was writing, and I thought I did not need so much help.

Agnes poked around and saw the heading of my letter and then yelled out to mother and father, "Dearest Katherine-is that the way you begin your letters?" She told all she saw while she was down to Hawk's Farm with us. She said that if she had counted our kisses she would have done nothing else.

Mother got after me and said that she guessed she would have to scour up the old knives father found over at the Meyer's place or perhaps I would like her silver ones when I get married.

I got mad and told her that when I got married I should not ask her; that I should be able to keep my own wife well and would need no help.

Father, he started in then. "Oh, he is in love so he can't go to school anymore." It seems it is not enough that I stay at home through mother's sickness and help keep father out of debt.

--But nonsense, what do you care of our family problems. I do love you enough to stay home from school, or anywhere else for that matter.

Agnes told them I was going to buy you a locket. She said you told her and Lillian about it when the three of you were upstairs last night. I said I guessed I would not tell you when I was

9

going to buy anyone a locket anymore.

Oh say! You have not found anything of mine down there have you? My heart perhaps? I have been trying to find it for the longest time now, an hour or more, but can't. If you find it and do not want to keep it, please send it back in your next letter. But if you keep it, I will be satisfied with yours instead of my own. Please don't keep both.

I wish I were coming down in place of the letter, for all the pleasure I get nowadays is when I am with you. Katherine, I would give a great deal for one of those kisses which troubles Agnes so much. It is some pleasure though, even without a kiss, to know that I am not forgotten by the girl I can't forget.

I hope this letter is long enough. It took long enough to write it. But I would write all night if by doing so I could please you.

I am and hope ever to remain your most loving cousin.

Arthur Countryman

* * * *

See! now how could any little edwardian maiden resist that. 'oh say have you found my lost heart?' i couldn't do that even if i was paid. what a fool i'd feel. --- i wonder why?
he talks a lot about that locket elsewhere too, and the ring i guess was someone else's. grandma was, after all, a bit of a flirt, and i can't say it didn't serve him right.
i worry a bit about the 'cousins.' the family was awfully angry about their engagement. you've often told me how much, and

10

just how against them everybody was. agnes must have been terribly bitchy. there's a note here, somewhere, from her to grandma. here it is at the bottom of the pile.

* * * *

My Dear dear Dearest darling Kathy,

How are you? Are you well? If you are not too busy tonight please write. I am getting lonesome to see you. Do you like your place. I hope so. How is Lillian getting along with her work? Mamma sends her regards to you, as best she can.

Well, now for business. Arthur said you said for me to kiss your foot. Well, you suck my tongue.

Please excuse me if I have been mean to you any time when you have been up here. Do you suppose you'll ever be able to come again? Albert is talking of moving to the Centre.

Well. I will have to close with love to you my pet.

Your Cos,

Agnes
P.S. Answer soon

11

* * * *

they are, aren't they, the mysteries of love? and i remember
aunt agnes as fat and old and jolly, surrounded by half a dozen kids
in a farmhouse kitchen with no running water. i mean, before she
moved.

CHAPTER II
History Lesson I

THE OLDER DAUGHTER

The story goes, apocryphal no doubt, but true enough in the folklore of the northern New York hills, passed on from generation to generation, farmer to his son, mother to her daughter, hollow to hollow along the old Taconic Trail and down along Champlain, like seed cast carelessly upon the rocky glacial earth, a few blossoming with wanton persistence from decade to decade until all the Adirondacks knew--held it--made it true--that Anne Boleyn had three bastard sons (although where she found the time I'll never know).

Love is, after all, at least unpredictable, its consequences momentarily unthought of--the heat of passion being what it is, in this case was--in spite of our more public protestations to the contrary. Three bastard sons are not too high a price to pay for one Elizabeth, and after all, poor Anne probably could not help herself, or at least did not, thus, if the story is true, justifying Henry in his cuckolded rage to delimit the height of her passion at exactly her pretty, if probably largely unwashed, neck.

The Gallia and Helvetii and Germania had peopled fully the cockpit of Europe (among other parts), and as the seers tell us, not only Welsh (legend has it) bastards fled the moral decay of millennial, Christian Europe, but from all over the Continent flocked tens, then hundreds, then thousands, then tens and hundreds of thousands to freedom's bright, untrammeled shores. The rhetoric, now quaint, was much the real thing a-way back when. The facts of the matter much another. When Anne had finished her prodigious task (the historian must admit the possibility for argument's sake) the magic isles were still muddy little England, not yet (or no longer) a giant among the growing profusion of nation-states still dominated, indeed created, molded, and fashioned from fire by an aristocracy which had, marvelously unknown to itself though not to others, been steadily decaying for over four-hundred years and was to continue that inexorable process for another benighted four hundred. Poor England--poor France, poor Austria or the Papal States, but certainly not the Prussians until they stubbed and broke both their toes with one too many blank checks (a peculiarly distasteful modern metaphor) in 1914.

Anne's three bastard sons, however, were quite different, not between (or among) themselves but from the aforementioned and luckless mass of peasants who lacked the gumption, perspicacity, or money (or luck) to flee the dilatory effects of landed wealth and an unnatural class system and follow liberty's shining flame. For so the three Welsh brothers did, amazingly enough together, and settled somewhere in Quebec, probably due to the latent effects of a Norman ancestry. Their father, the myth goes (having engendered them over a period of years I assume as no record exists of Anne birthing triplets, but then she had so little private time) a damnable Norman, Nicholas Countryman de Giullaume, whose great, great granddaddy ad infinitum, with William ate up the 'pure' English line in 1066 and later moved northward and westward to claim his ancestral rights of ravage below Shrewsbury, the town, as it turned out, a perfect appellation for his Welsh wife whom he courted and won against her will but with her heart (so the story goes), thus effectively terminating for generations to come the western marches of Norman power; the wife claiming ever thereafter until a very old and much awaited death, that she, her children, children's children, and their children unto a thousand generations were Welsh.

For most of their lives, however. Anne's Welsh bastards spoke French in Canada, and although we don't find their given names in any literature, there must have been about ten generations by fair thumbnail calculation before Nicholas Countryman de Guillaume's wayward and often removed progeny finally brought forth on their chosen land of the brave and free across the wide St. Lawrence a person of latter historical significance (we can find his name in the birth records) Jebediah Countryman, having lost all recognizable traces of his French cognomen and claiming, of all things, Shakerdom, luckily late in his life after the family's regeneration was assured not just by himself but by Jebediah's only son (recorded) Ebenezer Countryman who followed his father south across the wide expanse of first river then mountains to Lebanon and thence Albany before, thirteen years later, deserting the continent, carrying with him only the memory of straight-backed chairs and austere oaken chests of drawers, again across water, this time the Hudson to Stephentown, where on a farm of his own in what was then and now Rennselaer County, he began the verifiable Countryman line (which is our present interest) by producing for himself two sons, not bastards and certainly not Shakers, William Clarke and David, good Baptists both as was their mother. Out of such a milieu grew Arthur Terrence Countryman (his mother Esther Schoonhoven of good Albany family once removed and although not well traveled, yet of landed Dutch parentage from the city and thus a lover of the classics, if read to her, well-educated enough for her station, and good with a needle). His father was Martin, son of Alexander Washington, the latter a man too young to enlist in the civil war but who lied about his age in '64 after being bought by a desperate draftee from Kingston and so found himself sitting in Libby Prison for 7 months 'til war's end, an experience from which he never recovered being 6'1" and 210 pounds when he went away and 113 pounds when he returned, sick and bed-ridden, never to weigh over 150 for the rest of his moderately long life and dependent upon Martin, his later born son, from a very early old and scarred age.

Alexander's father was the aforementioned William Clarke who moved to Perrysville up near the Taconic Trail and set about trapping, killing the few remaining bears and mountain lions in the place, and generally making his wife Ruth Ann Turnbull from Poesenkill miserable with his wild way about the village. He loved her though, among others. At least she inscribed it so upon her headstone, and history thus was sanctified, or transmuted, or mollified by grand design and the first fruits of freedom.

Arthur, the letter writer, was of another ilk, or else we know more of him and so are the more confused. He was no wencher, though he evidently liked a good poke at least in thought if not in deed. He married a cousin Katherine Terrel related to him not through the massive flux of Jews, Slavs, Irish, and Germans who arrived at New York City during the 1850's and 1880's to join the sons of liberty but by Suzie Campbell who married Thomas Terrel, son of Joe Terrel and Sarah Cook, who was daughter of Arnold Cook and Becky Countryman two generations removed from David Countryman, William Clarke's brother, who married an Irish girl from Berlin, New York while her father and his good-for-nothing Irish immigrant friends, safe from starving for lack of potatoes, built the great plank roads of New York State, and Massachusetts, and Pennsylvania, Ohio. and Connecticut that readied the nation for Mr. Lincoln's war.

Those were titanic days, or relatively so. At end of century, by 1900, a million immigrants a year were passing through Ellis Island, and the stream flowed strongly until 1917 when Congress passed the Registration Act, and we lately arrived Americans became suspicious of foreigners in a more 'formal' way. We all do, of course, love, but usually only ourselves and those strong enough to command our love. Passion, such an invidious form of self-protection, allows slight room for real altruism. How many among us can afford to love the weak, being so strong in ourselves? Even d'Crevecoeur distrusted the Irish and entertained an abject passion for the Germans, Anglophile that he was.

Arthur Terrence Countryman, too, had a sentimental dream, which he loved, of a farm, upland, much like dilettante farmer d'Crevecoeur's Pennsylvania paradise. Contrary to our popular traditions, it took lettered men to conquer the frontier, men of character and stability, who clasped to their bosom the more cherished lies of civilization and were willing to suffer to make them real. Not the settlers, but the real estate agents built the towns and cleared the forest; the Dutchmen left their deliciously droll octosyllables all up and down the best land along the Hudson, and

16

finally the English and Scotch passed beyond them onto the Mohawk and into Cherry Valley, scattering rocks behind them like Ducalion and Phyrra.

And from this passion for land, which brought strength with it, whole nations died before Arthur and Katherine could bide in simple bliss upon their one-hundred and ninety acres of woodland given by a joyful father out of his bounty, passed on from generation to generation since originally stolen, through legal recourse, by William Clarke whose superior and lasting vision it was that Arthur should live so.

Not only the Dutch and French fell, the latter to Queen Ann's stubbornness and Marlborough's brilliance, but the Mohicans and Mohawks, original owners of the land after beaver and mastodon and wooly mammoth and diplodicus. All fell and passed away as the American frontier raced west from love of sex, money, and the evil city. All this, of course, accomplished long before Arthur and Katherine made their dozy, cozy, little home outside Dunedin, but nonetheless accomplished, and Ann Boleyn's penultimate generation read William Dean Howells and dared to steal a kiss.

* * * *

not so! you must allow some balance in your structure. dreams are dreams after all, and we cannot forever live under the sins of our ancestor. such are, i suspect, always in the past, sins are our luxury. life is not structure but feeling, i feel it so. and observing, so do you.

what is, after all, sentiment? and who are you to name it? there are some things that people believe which believing itself makes true. there's a poem in the letters. you'll hate it, but that

doesn't alter the lines one bit. it's dated the chicago daily news
1910. he must have saved it for her as a tease. listen.

* * * *

Sister's nervous and flustered the whole of the day,
an' she gives funny answers to what you may say,
She's apt to forget what she ought to have done,
And she'll never half finish the job she's begun.

She will sugar her meat and put salt in her tea,
And eat soup with her fork just as calm as can be
Why, I reckon she can't do a single thing right
When her beau comes to see her on Saturday night.

She is good to us kids, just as pleasant as pie--
And she laughs when I never can figger out why.
She gets red as a flower at nothin' at all
Then our pa says he wonders if some one won't call.

Then our ma says, "you stop that! Don't mind him my dear,
I won't have the girl bothered, John Jones, do you hear?"
And then sis will run off and she'll stay out of sight,
When her beau comes to see her on Saturday night.

Sister goes to her room with her hair all in crimp,
And She'll primp and she'll primp and she'll primp and she'll primp.
It's a couple of hours before she'll come down,
And then she's all dressed in her best Sunday gown.

And she's fixed up with ribbons and fixed up with lace,
And I'll bet you a nickel she powders her face.

I can't tell you no more, for they turn down the light
When her beau comes to see her on Saturday night.

* * * *

that's a world less fragile than our own, and who's to say it's neither
real nor right. certainly not a priggish, unapproachable liberationist
among the kitchen tins and a broken coffee grinder, who fancies
herself less an historian than a writer of history.

      invidious moralist. i like to laugh, and so would you without
your liberation. he sends a letter with the poem.

* * * *

Dunedin, N.Y.
Dec. 26, 1912

My Darling Katherine,

      Agnes, Lillian, and I arrived home just in time for dinner. It
was rather cold from Stump's Corner up. The wind began to blow
and it snowed a little before we arrived.

      Father was a bit mad that I stayed over and did not get back
so he could go into the woods this morning. It stormed so late this
afternoon that we could not do anything. I took a nap and when
mom woke me it was five thirty and father had all the chores done.
When we sat down to eat he told Lillian to tell your father to kick
me out when I came down again. He says now that if he had just a
girl at half past nine in the morning he would certainly let her go
one day before he wrote.

19

I sometimes wonder if father ever knew what it was to love anyone as I love you, Katherine. I should not be surprised if we met with much opposition to our plans, but I will love you just the same. Nothing matters except that we love one another. Of that I am sure. You must have faith in me for you are too sweet and too good for me ever to fail you.

The girls have just finished doing the dishes and are pestering father to play dominoes with them. I suspect I will have to play very soon. The two of them seem to get along well together. They talk a continual stream. Agnes sends you these verses. She has signed Lillian's name to them. Lillian says to tell you she had nothing to do with it.

Katherine, you have made me the happiest of men. It will be a great inspiration over this year to know that I am working for the sweetest girl that ever lived. I know I can live happily with you. No other girl could ever satisfy me. I close with love stronger than life itself. Your loving and devoted cousin.

Arthur

* * * *

darn, i had forgotten that agnes sent that poem. she must have been an insufferable child. well, it doesn't alter my point. the letters remain, and they are truer history than yours. truer because they give us history itself, naked and unreduced--felt, not told. he loved grandma, and he wanted this farm we now may sell. he wanted it, and built it. wrested it from the forest and made a good life for his children. his may be an age gone, but it is not and age lost.

+ + +

History misunderstood is always history misapplied and thus an end to history. The circularity may be obvious to most, but it nonetheless defines the danger. Let me read from my own books; the records of the place and Jeremiah (Martin's brother) Countryman's uncompleted history.

There were bears in the trees when these hills were first visited by western man come north from the east, and the original settlers of Dunedin slept in lean-to's the first winter while they cleared forest and surveyed boundaries before bringing their families from Albany the following spring. Within twenty years there were some 159 souls abiding the Baptist mass, such as it was, of which 44 were adult males, 37 females, and 68 children, the latter being 30 males and 38 "females unmarried and under the age of sixteen." The census records are models of probity.

There were also 2,971 1/4 "acres of improved land occupied;" 2,111 "neat cattle owned;" 136 horses, a bit fewer than the number of Baptist souls but no less essential; 875 sheep; and 471 hogs. The figures here also note the number of yards of cloth manufactured "in the domestic way in the family;" the number of grist mills--one; saw mills--one outside of town; distilleries-none, not surprising; and idiots--1 male supported by his son-in-law.

The town's first library was established in 1810 in the meeting house of the Baptist church with 135 volumes donated by the "good householders of the township." Wolves were still considered a menace in the area and the library was only open on the weekends, closing before dark. It was suggested children carry clubs with which to fend them off.

21

The railroad never came to Dunedin, but the village grew, albeit slowly. Trees were planted along the main street, which was then as now old highway 4 out of Athens and through the Centre to Perrysville. In 1859 they elected a dog catcher. There was by then a county assessor. The high school was private, an innovation of the Methodists earlier in the century. An agricultural society was founded in 1861, the fairgrounds bounded and established at their present site the next year, and a volunteer fire department organized, belatedly it seems, 3 months after Richard Forsgate's general store burned to the ground in 1863.

The records of Jeremiah's hotel, the town's only, off Lewis Road fronting the highway, suggest a regular and marginally profitable traffic over the mountains into Massachusetts and Vermont. Jeremiah and his two daughters, sempiternal virgins both, attended to the place and lived there to a ripe old age while entertaining the township's freemasons twice a month in the second floor ballroom. Sewers and a waterworks didn't come to the town until the 1890's and were "frightfully expensive," old Jeremiah notes. Among those things listed for sale at the auction in 1891 is a "silk wedding dress used once" by Jessica (Bailey) Countryman and saved for her granddaughters Theresa and Louise, neither of whom took husbands. Today we might feel a certain affinity for their actions if not their ending or possible motives. Anne the magna mater of us all would understand.

Jerry's place wasn't sold at the auction and eventually passed from Theresa and Louise to Joseph, oldest of Arthur's three sons, who married Abigail, a pretty little Jewess from Niskayuna, and took carelessly but manfully upon himself the harsher but simpler judgements of the old law, moderating his family's despair somewhat by choosing the slight, doe-eyed, black-haired beauty after violently breaking off an affair he had carried on for three years with an Irish Catholic from Lathams near Schenectady, the advent of the auto and his father's two townhouses presenting to Joseph more modern methods of courtship by making distance a more negligible factor than it ever had been for his father.

Chapter III
Portrait II

I remember Grandma--Mom--most, as she stood on the porch in front of the screen-door calling us to dinner, the late afternoon darkening into an early evening thunderstorm, the great rosebush in the middle of the front yard with its blood red flowers bending before the quixotic wind, the great, haggard rope which was our swing waving capriciously from a limb of the large oak beside which Grandpa had insisted upon building the new house so many years before.

She was fat even then, fat and old and tired from overwork--worn down by bearing seven of us, six of whom lived. But she was forever. And we knew it.

She had always been, and would always be there, on the farm, ringing the large, black, school bell which grandpa had affixed beside the door so she need not lose her voice while calling us from all over creation. We would come dirty, skin-kneed, smelling of hay and manure. After school I always played in the crooked apple tree which had somehow wedged itself into the great boulder behind the hen house. Her voice would always reach me in the uppermost limbs. I would stop, look anxiously around to see if she'd come out back, then scramble down, thanking my stars that I had gone unnoticed. Still, in the summer I would get stomach-aches, and then she would know that Sarah could climb too. Sis hardly ever had a dress or pair of drawers which were not torn.

"Sarah Ann, you get down from there this instant! Do you hear me? A regular tom-boy! A tom-boy! That's what you are," she would admonish Sarah when she caught us, repeating the phrase in the kitchen over supper so Gramps would hear.

"A tom-boy! She plays with Joseph in the trees. You ought to be ashamed of yourself. It's no way for a proper young lady to act, let me tell you. You gonna' climb trees all your life and show off your back side to every Tom, Dick, and Harry!"

But Sarah wouldn't blush at all, and I'm sure that frustrated Mom more than anything else. Sarah would just sit there straight up, eating, staring at her plate as cool as a cucumber, bringing her fork up to her mouth as ladylike as could be and acting for all the world like little Miss Astor or Vanderbilt. Gramps would grunt and ask if we older ones had finished our chores. He never spanked the girls. Never touched them.

Then after dinner I'd go with Dad out to check the dogs and see to the barn. Sarah would be the first to start cleaning the table and putting the dish water on the stove to heat. By the time we got back, it would be coal black outside with a cold wind coming up over the mountains. Grandma would be in the living room, sitting in the rocker with a resigned purse upon her face, mending clothes. Lillian and Sarah would be at the dining room table doing homework and pulling the folds of their long woolen night-gowns about them to keep warm. Alex and Jessie, and even Martin, I mostly remember playing in Grandma's skirts or wandering off into a corner and picking up slivers in their feet. How they would howl. But for all of that, only Grandma could take the sliver out with that blackened needle they knew to be red-hot but which, after it was over, miraculously never hurt.

I remember Grandpa on his knees stoking the small fireplace, candles and oil lamps flickering tenuously through the long silent evenings, and the crisp rustle of Granpa's newspaper as he turned and straightened pages, or the more muted whisper of Grandma's skirts when she got up to bring in tea and cookies from the kitchen, the shrill wind which buffeted the window-panes forgotten as everyone stopped for the treat. Gramps was first and then the youngest. The older kids waited till last - and finally Grandma. Those were nights, too, which never ended. I never remember falling asleep.

Because she grew fat, I remember Grandma as a big woman, towering over us in the broad sunlight of a spring morning, waiting for the milk to come up from the barn. She was never a patient woman, and thus she was forever waiting.

But fact is that she was extremely small, only five-foot-one, and when she stood next to Gramps everyone would call them Mutt and Jeff. Gramps towered over her, and as he grew older his face weathered, taking on the long scarred red gashes that slashed across his forehead and fell down his cheeks from the deep wells of his eyes to alongside his nose. He grew even more fiercesome looking that when he was younger. A regular bear he was then.

Grandma was always in awe of him. Once, one December when he had shot three squirrels that morning for dinner, Grandma failed to get all the buckshot out of a cooked thigh. Grandpa bit on it and cracked a molar. He swore seldom, good Baptist that he was, but swear then he did.

"Damn be it, woman, am I eating stones?" he roared when he discovered the shot between his fingers.

Suddenly he remembered the four of us at the table, and he stopped yelling. He tried to eat three or four mouthfuls more, but the pain was too great, and he had to spit it out on his plate right in front of us.

Finally he pushed back his chair, stood up, picked up the shot and threw it across the room. He walked out, leaving us to eat alone and Grandma to shiver in her chair. Tears began to streak her face and her nose ran so badly she had to leave the table in order to blow it.

For the next two weeks Grandma was as timid as a mouse, even with us kids. The house became a tomb, the two of them speaking to each other only when it was absolutely necessary.

Grandpa would bring up the milk in the morning and wordlessly leave it outside the back door. Grandma would have his oatmeal, bacon, and eggs ready for him when he came in, and they would both eat in silence, he with his coffee steaming in the still, chilly kitchen and Grandma with her small, chubby hands clasped tightly around her oversized mug of tea.

Gramps would then leave to peddle milk in Athens,

Grandma silently getting him his muffler (which he always forgot purposefully because he hated its loud orange stripes and which she just as purposefully wound around his neck every morning for the long, cold ride into town), the two of them kissing wordlessly at the door. And then there was only the sharp clop of Billy's hooves on the frozen gravel together with the rhythmic creak of the wagon as it lurched and swayed under its load toward the road.

Gramps stood the pain for a full two weeks before Grandma finally called the dentist in Hawk's Farm and made an appointment for him. Then the two of them finally talked to one another.

"Arthur," she said to him next morning in the kitchen, "you have got to get your tooth seen to."

When we heard that Lillian and Sarah and I all squirmed in our chairs. Grandma had always called Gramps "husband" when she addressed him, emphasizing the curiously antique quality of her usage by looking straight at him, her eyes never wavering, as if she expected him to deny the fact if she didn't fiercely hold him to it. When she used his given name, we all knew something big was about to happen.

"Ayup," he replied through his coffee. "Just like you've done yours these many years."

Grandma had false teeth by then, the best of what she'd had being taken by Lillian and Sarah before I arrived.

"That's of no concern, Arthur. The tooth hurts and it's come to bother us all."

"I expect you think we're still getting' 1914 prices for our crops, too. Don't you woman." Gramps was not about to give up without a fight.

"And you'll be better able to tend them if you can't eat and get sick on us all, I suppose?"

"I eat," he mumbled. We could tell he was losing.

"You suck and swallow like an old sow is what you do. I tell you, husband, I don't want any sick man on my hands come plantin' time. I got enough troubles as it is."

"And where do we get the money? Damn, woman, think! You're talking' nonsense. Now be done with it."

Grandma had him, although none of us were positive of it

26

yet. She took a tied handkerchief from under the folds of her dress, laid it on the table, and pushed it brusquely towards him

"There. Take it and stop your complainin'. It's more than enough. Five dollars and forty-seven cents."

"I'll not take your pin money, girl. What do you take me for?"

Gramps wanted the money. We could all tell. His tooth had not let him sleep for a week. But he had to put up an argument just to save face. Confused, he reached for a piece of toast and smeared a thick layer of strawberry preserves over it. Then, just as he was about to eat it, he stopped in mid bite and sheepishly put the bread on his plate.

Grandma looked at us all, even winked at little Alex in his high-chair. She was triumphant, flushed with her victory.

"And I suppose you'll just go along wastin' what little we do have, huh? I imagine that's just what a man would do."

Gramps reached out, took the handkerchief, and stuffed it without ceremony into his shirt pocket. He left later that morning behind Billy for Hawk's Farm and returned at supper time with a shiny silver-like cap for his molar which we all insisted upon inspecting again and again right up to bedtime.

The incident was never spoken of after that. Grandma could be as feisty as a banty hen when she needed to be, but her victories were always hard-fought and short-lasting. Thereafter, whenever we had rabbit I was always fearful, on the chance that another shot would go undetected until it, too, broke Gramps' shiny new cap.

Those were good times, I think. At least they seem so now. Grandma was always with us, always fat and cheerful, picking roses from the huge, red bush in the middle of the front yard or clipping lilac sprigs from the two bushes that Gramps allowed to grow over twelve feet tall so that most of the flowers were always out of her reach. She would trundle a step-ladder out of the house and desperately clutch the bushes as the ladder tottered this way and that as it sank into the deep, precarious loam beneath the grass.

But those lilacs! How good they smelled, their clean, heady scent washing through the house on a late spring evening after dinner. How good it was to wake to flowers on a crisp June morning and listen to Grandma bustling about downstairs as she stoked the old wood-burning stove and beat pancake batter for a Sunday breakfast.

We all liked that, the long, slow breakfast at eight o'clock. Only the necessary chores were done on a Sunday. The sheep and cows were tended-to late Saturday afternoon, and we never checked for eggs in the hen house until Monday morning. We fed what had to be fed, slopping only the pigs in the afternoon after dinner and caring for the horses.

The rest of the time was church at ten, Bible reading before and after church, and long, deliciously mindless walks up the road to visit the Bannisters and Kendalls who lived on the neighboring farms. When we returned from playing among the large granite boulders and glacial rock faces in the pasture, she was always there. Play on our meadowland cliffs, which in summer were always alive with a luxuriance of bramble bushes, poison oak, and poison ivy sprouting from every fissure, always left us dirty, tired, and desperate for food, with the passion of dusty faces.

Remember Grandma's sour cream chocolate cake? It, too, covered with wax paper in the middle of an austerely scrubbed kitchen table, was always there when we arrived home. Either it or strawberry short-cake, or blueberry pie, or--or all those fascinating and bewitching desserts that were your Grandmother's special glory on a late Sunday afternoon with the crickets beginning to chirp and the evening taking on the hint of a chill in the hushed semi-pink of sunset as we sat down at table for soup and crackers before night belied the still, unmoving balm of the hour.

I remember her too, no longer fat and ample, but wizened and small, her hollow and pale face sunken down into the cavity between her shoulders where her neck had once been, the humped curvature of her wizened spine protruding like Quasimodo's above her head as she rocked back and forth in front of the TV, watching Saturday night wrestling from Pauley Arena in Chicago, year after year with increasingly somnolent eyes. For her, the ritual battles between good and evil, the black-masked monster against Thor, the wonder-child, were always real and rock-like, the symbolic yet vivified consummation, I imagine, of those fierce some Old-Testament wars she had been so fond of reading to us.

"Arthur," she said, "Arthur! Husband Arthur," when she

died, lying beneath us there in the sallow yellow of the hospital light.

"Arthur, Husband Arthur."

CHAPTER IV
Love Story I

here is a letter from grandpa to grandma. i think it explains the family's particular sensitivity to their engagement. it does seem odd though that they never mention genetics.

* * * *

Dunedin, N.Y.
Jan. 18, 1913
My Darling Kathy,

So there is a storm coming. Well, I've seen many a thunderhead in these parts, and I am as well prepared for it now as later.

Oddly enough what your family said only excited me and made me angry. Surely God would not have given us so great a love had he not intended us to care for one another, cousins or no.

What does it matter? I have gotten along without others before. I can do it again. Now that I have cooled down a bit I am rather inclined to smile at the part I will play in the coming tempest.

I do not think any of your family will hurt you. They know me too well, even if I have been away for two years in Connecticut. If anyone should lay a hand on you he will have to answer to me.

You can keep your ring out of sight. They need not have that to excite them.

If bad comes to worse, we may have to change our plans. The only thing gained by waiting till next year to marry is that we could start keeping house in better style. In either case the land will be mine and it will supply us with what we will need.

If they get too mean, I can arrange it so that you can stay up here. By partly falling in with my father's plan, I believe I can get him to help us. I am inclined to think, though, that your father will not be so bullheaded after he finds out that he cannot stop our keeping company. If he should mistreat you, do not be afraid to come up here. You will always find the door open if I understand my parents right.

Perhaps a little opposition will only make us the dearer to one another. You are, Katherine, your own woman, and I am certainly my own man. If we choose to care for each other, I do not see how anyone can hinder us. I know for sure that I will fight for what is mine, even though I am as peaceable a man as the next. No one will stop me from seeing you but you yourself, and I hope never to hear those words from your sweet lips.

I will be down Sunday as usual and we can talk things over more carefully then. But let everyone know my dearest that now that I know you to be mine only you can ever send me away, and I will protect you from all who try to hurt you. I know my own mind on this matter.

They say there was a large crowd at the Presbyterian Donation. There is to be another at West Dunedin a week from tomorrow. It will be held at Parker Avrey's. That is the second house past the school house as you come toward our farm. I wish you could be here for it. There would be more fun at this one than at the Baptist one.

Tell Willis I have not been hunting this week. I am waiting for him to get his t--l up here.

Mother said to tell you Mrs. Rawlins--the one who was in the hospital with her--was up to visit today.

I must leave now. It is always so good talking to you that I do hate to go. May the love which is yours always prove ever true.

Your Most Loving,
Arthur

* * * *

here is another that i remember from a few months later. it has my note on the envelope, 'cousins marry?' he protests to love her selflessly. i wish we had her letters too.

* * * *

Dunedin, N.Y.
April 11, 1913

My Darling, Darling Katy,

33

I washed the wagon today after visiting you yesterday. The wagon box was spotted as a leopard from where the mud had frozen onto it. I guess it will be ready for the paint shop by the time the roads settle.

Don't worry so. I bet your father will forget his prejudice against cousins marrying and will come to see us often.

I suppose you have kept house for him so long that he has begun to think of you as part of the furniture. I think he believes you have no right to leave him for anyone else. I cannot blame him. I should be jealous of so precious a jewel as you. I know I shall be all my life.

I do not think, though, that your father harbors any ill-will against me personally, other than that I am your cousin. He holds on to that as many others do. Katherine, if I thought there was anything wrong in my caring for you as I do, nothing could make me marry you. The very love which brings me to you now would then push me far away.

But I do not see the harm in it. Generations separate us. Love brings us together. I know that I care for you as I never have anyone else, and I could never be happy without you. I should not live were we to separate. There would be no joy in life, no light. Surely God could not give me so great a love and make it wrong. Such wrong could not come from so much that is good.

I tapped a few maples today. We are boiling the sap down on the stove. If the season is good, perhaps I can sell some and fatten our bank book. As it is, I will not be able to write again until I buy some paper.

I   don't suppose you mind if I use our money to buy writing paper. If I know you, you will think it better than drinking and gambling it away as Jim has done. Such actions never better things. It may be Jim was the cause of his own trouble. I don't know.

Whoever started the first wrangle in his home is to blame. The first opened the way for the second, and each one was that much easier. I hope and pray that we may never have such a beginning or an end.

Do what you will, you will never drive me to drink. I would not cut off my nose to spite my face. You have asked me to promise you that I will never touch any strong drink. I should like you to promise never to offer me any first.

Darling, don't think I uphold Jim in his drinking and gambling. I uphold no man in those things which destroy body and soul. Jim has a wife and his two boys to take care of. He needs every cent he can earn for them.

I do not blame him, however, for not wishing to say in a home where he cannot find a moment's peace. Your Aunt Lillian can be good when she wants to be, but that is not often. If the two of them did not have children they would have parted long ago. I feel sorry for them all, but I do not believe in divorce, "What God has joined together let no man put asunder." If a man and woman get each other, then let them keep to one another. If they get stung, well, then grin and bear it. Divorce will not make them happier for they have made their own unhappiness to begin with. If a couple cannot bring themselves to be content and happy, then they will be miserable wherever they are.

Oh, let me come down next week with you to have your molars fixed. I will furnish the money, but you are to have them all fixed. You might as well have it done now as later. It will cost no more now and hurt as much later. I will come down on the stage so if I have to stay over I will not have a horse to pay for.

Call the Hill's Dental Co. the day before you want me to come and don't worry, my time is my own to use as I please. Being with you will be ample pay.

It is past two o'clock now, and everyone is in bed but me.
I'm almost dozing at the table. Good night my love. Sweet Dreams
and all my love.

Your loving Arthur

* * * *

agnes, gramps' sister, wrote an undated letter which seems
to touch on the same subject. although it is vague enough to leave
some doubt as to family motives and desires.

* * * *

Dear Carrie,

How are you? I told Arthur to tell you ma was mad at you.
Did he? Well, there is one of you I am not mad at and that is your
dad. He is a good relative.

Ma said to tell you pa was going off for a week around
Christmas so we will have to keep Arthur here or else you would
have to send up somebody from down there for we could not stay
alone.

We are having a wind night. Tomorrow school closes for
two weeks vacation and I am glad. I have not been to church yet
but am going Sunday. I am having a new dress made for Christmas
by Mrs. Barker and am going to get it tomorrow.

Pa says for you not to get any more girls' fellows away from them and ma says not to disgrace your family and Arthur by such a thing. You did not know I seen your ring did you. If you did, I didn't say anything.

I have a favor to ask you. Can Arthur take me to the Christmas tree Friday night in Dunedin? Have you any objections? If so I suppose I will have to go alone. I am in a temperance dialogue. The name is "The Best Time to Stop." There is one girl besides me and three boys. The two of us girls have to be sewing.

Say, you tell Lillian it is all up with her. Everybody knows. Say you know the whole house is full of cranks up here. If Edgar were back with us up here like he was when I was down there last Saturday, I would have to send some of them down to you.

I would keep pa tho, because he is the best.

I will have to close now, but since I can't close with love I will just say good night.

Agnes Countryman
P.S. answer soon

* * * *

I remember a time, way back, when we were at the seashore, and i had run away from you and mom and sis. the sun was golden, warm and fierce in a noon sky, and the wet sand shimmered far away to the north, so far that i could not see to the beach's end. it seemed to go on forever. the waves rolling huge out to sea and then breaking in great, white confusion upon the beach! they must have only seemed huge for i was little and ran from them, not wanting to get my new swimsuit wet with its scalloped skirt

37

that fell over the pants. it was a two-piece, the first swimsuit i had ever worn that had a bra, and i felt myself very big and kept looking down and smoothing the little skirt. i played a game with the waves and ran before them, teasing them and always running in to shore before they could get my suit wet.

then i saw a bird up the beach. i noticed it because it was large and black, almost as large as the sea gulls although small when compared to the pelicans which dived al at once into the clear blue waters and came up big pouched and riding so easily upon the waves. the bird was strange to me, and as i walked closer i realized that it was not a seabird like the willets, pipers, and gulls scavenging around it, but a land bird, awkward and slow with a short, thick beak, bluntly pointed. it was, i decided, either a crow or a blackbird, the last word was my general catch-all for any bird black in color for which i had no other name. and here that bird was, picking carrion from the sand.

as i watched, the awkwardness of the bird became apparent, so precious it seemed. the bird was slow and was constantly interrupted by the waves because it had no sense of the sea's rhythm. he (i decided that) had no mate and must have been desperately hungry to have been driven to the beach. but when the bird got lucky and found a large morsel of jellyfish or some such rotten amoeba-like flesh, he was attacked viciously by a nearby gull. i became scared and almost ran back to you all, but i was also curious and so merely backed away a few steps.

i didn't follow the bird, but i watched him move past me, scarred and feather-rent, and then he limped down along the beach past you, and then further until i couldn't see him anymore. he was harassed and reviled all the way, especially by the gulls. once his weakness was exposed, even the smaller birds would rush in and steal from him; they were so much quicker. i don't think you ever saw it.

the bird must have gone hungry, and yet he never left the shore. i remember wondering at the time whether he had a home of his own or anybody to love him. now i realize that it was a full-grown bird, adult and very unlovable in its weakness. perhaps it was the first black-bird of its kind to hunt the shore, the ancestor of what a million years from now will be a million black-birds with long beaks, and wider, webbed feet, and more nervous rhythms in their bodies that will command the shore and defeat the gulls.

more likely he was without a mate because he could not master one, without a home because he could not conquer or defend a territory, and the revulsion and hatred of his fellow birds was natural and good, ensuring, as it might, the survival of only those fit enough to escape, for a short period, the consummation of their weakness.

oh, i should not try this. i don't like it.

*****************why is vulnerability so endearing?

CHAPTER V
History Lesson II

If we are useful we are loved, or, to state the proposition more accurately if a bit less forcefully, we are loved only when we are useful. The proper Socratic premise (and conclusion) would be: if and only if we are useful will we be loved. Love, then, does indeed lack altruism, our own hidden greed often unseen by others and always unrecognized by ourselves, even in our most reflective moments. I state the fact but decline to argue its merits with Socrates, Plato, or Aristotle. Such insights are tautological and admit to little profitable discussion, the ordering of the world and cosmos being more man's retrospection than the cosmos' achievement.

Anne was beloved of Henry because she sated his lust. She was useful to him and used him in return (her own lust being what it was) on balcony, in great halls, and in and on the bed. Henry ignored his stately duties; the archbishop knew he was not loved and frowned and died. More's love was great but unrequited at the last, and so for love he (and John the Baptist) offered up his head, required of him by love for greater love and thus he lusted no more, if ever, leaving these lesser appetites to gross and syphilitic Henry who lusted long after feeling was only thought, and vain at that.

The mind, as well as the body, travels strange and queer roads. To Acquinas lust was the antipathy of love, thus to Henry it should have been so also. But who, once loving, has not lusted,

either before or after the fact and so often both? These are
meddlesome reflections, but Arthur and Katherine as surely as
Jessie and Alexander, and Ruth Ann and William Clark, and Anne
and Henry, bound Prometheus to his rock, and out of lust came
man's certain knowledge and the God's destruction by Power and
Violence. Who loves us most; what is it that we love?

* * * *

how vain you are. you know, in spite of all your
protestations you're still one of us. here's the eleventh letter in the
group. he calls her 'my darling kate.'

* * * *

Dunedin, N.Y.
January 9, 1913

My Darling Katy,

This has been a blue old day. I have not known what to do
with myself.

I have heard some bad news about you since I came home. I
have been told that a lady down Albany way told someone in
Dunedin that Katherine Terrel had a bad name in the city. Lord

42

knows you've stayed little enough in Athens and less in Albany.

I could not find out what you have done to give you a bad name nor could I discover who said that of you.

Don't think, though, that I care what people say. I love you too much to let the rumor, which I know in my heart to be a lie, turn me from you. You are all that I could wish in a girl, and I love you for what you are to me now. I shall never ask for more.

I don't know why I speak of this. I will tell you all I have heard when next I see you, and you may judge for yourself. Someone told mother and she told me. She said that she did not know whether to believe it or be angry with the one who told her. If I knew who started the story, I would trim him good, you bet. Someone might have talked about you just to be mean because you prefer me to him. I don't know, but I had better not learn his name.

Did it rain down there last night after I left? It poured like the devil on my way up through Stumps Corner. Luckily, it rained and snowed together, so I did not get overly wet. The water ran down unto the carriage seat, and I had a wet ---. but that was the extent of my dunking.

By the way, the Dunedin Centre school teacher lost her locket and chain at the party the other night. I know I have a girl who will take better care of what is entrusted to her.

I miss you so since last week. The Baptist Donation is the 7th of February. You will have to come up to go with me. Father's cold is very bad. He coughed so I could hardly sleep the night out, so I got up early this morning to do the chores and passed your room of last week. I even had to go in and look at the bed in which you slept before I could come downstairs.

Oh Katy, stay away from the city. The two of us have ever been ill-treated by those people. Even when I was in Pittsfield I felt awkward and tied down. Now that we have our love, let us be

43

niggardly about it and stay here, spending it among our friends. Write soon. Without your letters I die a little each day.

I will close now with my love, true love from a true heart.

Your loving and devoted Cousin,
Arthur

* * * * *

i remember once when dad and mom had left us on the farm during the war, we were in the living room one night after supper. it was spring, and the evening air was heavy with the lingering humidity from an unusually warm day. i could have been no more than three or four at the time, and yet i'm sure i remember it. you, sis, were doing homework in the kitchen. aunt jessie was doing hers at the dining room table next to an open window. i was playing under the table at jessie's feet and every once in awhile she'd kick a little and complain that she couldn't work with me there. i remember the sounds of beetles and crickets coming through the windows. now and then the dogs would howl or huff once or twice. the sheep had settled in the near pasture, but occasionally old nanny would bleat commands, and i'd hear her bell clear and sharp over the night air. gramps, his belly straining against his worn coveralls, was dozing in his rocking chair and gramma was crocheting flower doilies near the bricked-up fireplace.

uncle martin put the book he'd been reading on the table and knelt down underneath to play with me. you remember dad, how easy he always was to love. uncle martin was the youngest of you, and so I guess the craziest. we played a while. jessie complained about the noise. we stopped, and i leaned back against the center post and rested.

then uncle martin grinned at me and took two wooden matches from his pocket. he motioned to me to play again and make some noise, and when i did he pushed one match, he must have especially prepared it, into the seam, between sole and shoe, of jessie's oxford. it took time, but he was patient, and as i scooted out from under the table, laughing as he told me to, he lit aunt jessie's foot.

it didn't take long, but uncle martin and i both made it to the other side of the room before jessie let our a yell, woke gramps, bruised her knee on the underside of the table, knocked over the chair and fell down herself while hopping on one foot as she tried to pull off her shoe.

uncle martin and i laughed until we cried. for the longest time, gramps and gramma were at a loss as to what had happened. i don't know what you did, sis.

jessie, angry as flame, finally got her shoe off, stared at martin and swore through tears. gramps, who'd by now deciphered the mystery and was smiling behind a day's stubble of sun-whitened beard, stopped his rocking.

"that's enough of that, jessica," he said. i'll have no cussin' in this house." gramma never stopped crocheting, i'm sure, while jessie, seated on the rug, began to bawl, rubbing her knee and pushing down her skirt to keep us from seeing.

"it was him, paw, it was him," she snuffled, pointing to uncle martin and me. i remember being afraid, but i could not stop laughing.

for a long time gramps just looked at us. he said something to martin about not teaching the child such. uncle martin said yes, and i think he apologized to jessie who turned away in a huff.
 then gramp's voice boomed and he began to laugh. "jessie, stop your sulkin' and next time kick his behind if he bothers you so. as for you martin, since you like fire, i don't imagine you'll mind a mornin' at the woodshed layin' in a stock of kindlin'."

uncle martin looked up. "but pa, we got enough kindlin'," he protested, "and besides, winter's over."

"it'll come again, son. don't you fret non," gramps admonished.

"but pa, i was goin' to go with ya."

"don't know how that'll be possible seein' as how you've got that kindlin' to chop."

"pa!" uncle martin was suddenly desperate and hopeless all at once.

jessie couldn't help herself. she sniggered so through her tears, she sounded just like a pig. gramma laughed too, then me, then all of us, even uncle martin.

we all had strawberry short-cake later that night, fresh strawberries and real whipped cream like only gramma made. you could never stay mad at uncle martin. no one could, not even aunt jessie. he was so easy to love.

some years after that gramma moved to town for good, because of her heart condition. gramps stayed on at the farm and came down on weekends to see the family. it must have been a lonely life.

* * * *

Memory, the most unreliable of historical tools as Herodotus should have known, plays tricks on all who suffer its intrusion--Martin, the youngest child, being Jessie's senior by at least five years. He fought across the Pacific, enlisting in early '43 the day he turned 18, at his father's behest who saw all three of his sons, Joseph and Alex too, go off to war and, with unaccustomed luck, was able to welcome them home in '45, all three, two from Japan and one--Joseph--from France (though Navy too) having fought (with fury, he insisted) through the African invasions, Sicily, and Normandy. Probably not possible. Jessie, at the time of their return, was still a junior in high school.

The aforementioned incident most likely happened, if it happened, not in the dark days of '42 when Hitler marched to and back from the gates of Mother Russia only to make the same hegira the next year, equally as fruitless, and the boys on Bataan marched only once, needing no more to convince them of their co-ordinate mortality, but in '46 when fun-loving Martin was out of the Navy and out of work, having brought home his booty, before he took over his father's milk route in Athens. Also, high summer is a more likely time for the fabled hot-foot since fresh strawberries suggest June at the earliest. That would make Joseph's young daughter a full seven years and probably visiting "the folks" on summer's vacation, her elder sister ten. The city was far away where Alex and his good wife Dorothy, two rolling stones, worked and saved for their Athens' cottage and two kids, all lately gained by '51.

But the graveyards were peopled then, overrun anew, with those who suffered and sacrificed for man, gaining a secure if not too cozy place among the calm and quiet flowers as the scruple of their savage love. Dunedin's church is rent through with them: David Matteson, Edgar and Elizabeth's son born to them early in '17 who went to Athens Institute in '36, graduated, barely, but with a good job in sight downstate, only to volunteer December 27th, right after Christmas so as not to disappoint the folks, and die on a bloody ridge on Guadalcanal. The battle, he was sure, he said in his last letter, would never be remembered. Carl Burdick, Victor's son who . . . . but the list is unimportant here.

Suffice it! There are twenty-one who rest there, out back of the Methodist and Baptist churches, eleven and ten respectively, so there is little to dispute, except that the toll is disproportionately high for so small a village. Of the towns nearby only Perrysville boasts more, twenty-three, and Perrysville was larger than Dunedin by twice as many at the time. Jake Snooks keeps the records and he testifies to it. Testifies, too, to the absence of Countryman stones in either yard: Arthur being buried with Katherine at Hawk's Farm, her town; Martin with Esther in Albany, Jeremiah and Theresa and Louise with them; Austin in New York City; Edgar at the Centre; and Agnes in Athens. Some of Arthur's kids may still live in the town, Joseph at the hotel and young Martin at the farm, but none are buried there. Lillian and Sarah, Alex and Jessie have all moved to Athens and the shirt factories, and ballbearing plants, and steel mills across the river.

Dunedin remains a rock though. It is the Countrymen's town. All around know it, a Democratic flaw upon the otherwise unsullied surface of the craggy Republican hills, not by much, mind you, and always a precarious position won only by hard work and endurance in the face of defeat. Once won, maintained by stubbornness and mountain pride.

In the hills traditions grow slowly, live long, and die hard. In 1912 few would admit they voted for Wilson, but he almost carried the town. Arthur, the ardent Connecticut socialist, helped. The town meeting records list the results of his "liberal" education. In 1921 he stated for all to hear:

In the matter of land tenure, we are slavish followers of the British. All life, all wealth and sustenance comes from the soil. To deny anyone access to the soil, Nature's own bosom, is to require of them their manhood, their very soul and livelihood. Whoever champions private ownership of the land must be willing to equally defend private ownership of water, air, and the gentle dew from heaven itself.

But these are given to all men. So long as any neighbor can say to me, 'you shall not grow the food you require upon this land, so long shall poverty, disease, hunger, and social inequality exist. I dream of a life for us all, a good life here, no matter where we have come from. The privations endured by the pioneers of Dunedin were for a small strip of land, each of his own, from which bounty the wants of a family could be assured.

Land monopoly is as odious as hell itself, as the trusts and bankers of Albany. Our land is ours to use well and protect carefully. Together!

The lumber company never got the rights it wanted down near Wilson Reservoir, and Arthur and his family lived for over five decades upon his ninety acres, well-respected, much loved, and regularly elected by the village's voters.

CHAPTER VI
Love Story II

'memory is often without necessary order,' that's your phrase, and when so, always trustworthy. we have no letters of hers, as i have said before, but she is within his. hard as their life was it had about it a stability, a continuity, and expectation fulfills. so little was looked for. it was quick with animate things, life precious because it was, so to speak, so casually given and taken, so often tottering on the brink of the grave. people died by "turning up their toes" or "kicking the bucket" or "hopping the twig." and when you were dead, your were "dead as a nit" of "doorpost" or "herring" or "doornail." killing, to grandfather, was very normal, a necessary, near, and lively part of his life. should not his own death be the same?

oh, i don't know! philosophy doesn't come easily to me and i feel embarrassed now, before so much that has already been and is therefore "real" beyond fact alone. isn't it in our imaginations that we are all most comfortable, loving and being loved? now we destroy ourselves with greed, wanting not only what we cannot have but what is not worth the having.

perhaps we are loved too much, like some narcissus afloat upon a crystal sea. who can ever reject love except one who has an excess of it? whoever wants it most except those without? and who may suffer himself the chains of loneliness except the social man?

49

we are too greedy with all that's good and simple. we want
too much.
here's one of the last letters.

* * * *

Dunedin, N.Y.
Nov. 22, 1913

My Darling, Darling, Darling Katy,

    I have been hunting today, though not for what you accused
me of last week. If it's true that only the rich can afford to be stingy
with their goods, then I must be marrying a wealthy woman indeed.

    Don't be mad at my joke, now. You know how I love to
plague the most wonderful girl in the world.

    In spite of the weather my throat is alright. I think there was
something in it. Don't know what but it felt that way.

    It stormed here nearly all day yesterday, and I stayed home.
Today I hunted and shot a rabbit, a partridge, and a quail. I should
have had a back load of rabbits, but I guess my nerves are going, or
my eyes, for I missed a dozen of fifteen chances. I always feel it is a
shame to kill them until I think about what they do to our garden in
the summer. Besides, I do love rabbit stew. As you'll soon find out,
Hey?

    I saw one of the largest buck deers I ever saw today. He
must have had at least twelve points if not more.

    I was down to our house yesterday and finished burning up
what paper there was on the floor from the packing boxes. I also
cleaned the straw out.

I signed a dollar's worth with Gertrude Bonette on her soap order, too.

I suppose Mrs. Poultrie is making you work overtime now that you're leaving so as to get everything possible done before you go. Bet you never knew she liked you so well, heh? I guess you can stand it as long as she works alongside you, but don't overwork yourself when she gets tired out.

How is Eddie doing? Did he get another girl? He and Edgar always make me laugh. Eddie's such a big wind. If you see Edgar, tell him to be sure to come up Friday if he wants to go hunting.

I guess I will have to go down and see Miss Howard tomorrow and finish putting the wood in the schoolhouse. Boy, was that a help to us this year. I may go and set some traps, though, for I have all my work nearly done and I don't want to loaf like some lazy bachelor. Loafing would not pay as well as trapping.

But Albert's dog that Oliver is keeping for him came down to us again last night. He is here yet and shows no signs of leaving. It's very sad. I guess he must get used better here than he does up at Oliver's. It's probably a good thing Albert doesn't know.

I guess you are going down and have Pearl make your wedding dress. Maybe she will have your Aunt Lillian help. It would be fine if she would. Would it not?

When are you and Ida going to Athens? You'd better go before you are finished at Poultrie's. You might even get out of a day's work. They wouldn't have the nerve to dock you just for going to Athens.

Mother made our feather tick the other day. She said we should have gotten the heaviest material we could, and she was afraid the feathers would work through this. I was sorely tempted

51

to tell her that we'd manage to keep warm, feathers or no, but I thought better of it. Was I right?

I will get the rest of our furniture and things undone so you can see how they look when you come up, again.

Dear, you cannot imagine how I miss you. With you gone this house is barren, and I hate to stay in it. With you here, I should never wish to leave. Oh, will the day ever come?

All my love and kisses. Don't worry about my throat; it is better now, and trapping will make things easier for us next year.

Your loving, loving, loving

Arthur

P.S. I may shoot some ducks by the reservoir if I can find any.

* * * *

that was a relatively late letter in the group, written not long before their marriage i guess. but i always wonder what a chase she led him and why. if so pretty and urbane, did she ever consent? love, i suppose, is without logic. it pleases me to think so.
yet how often trapping comes up in the letters. singularly appropriate for his line of work. listen.

* * * *

Dunedin, N.Y.
January 29, 1913

--- I got two rabbits today and I already have one frozen.

How many do you need for Sunday dinner? I will send them down on the stage so you can get them ready early.

I will come down as soon as I get around to my traps. I did not get back from them until noon today, and I expect to set some more tomorrow if the weather allows.

So I will not be able to get down very early. I went to the centre yesterday to get some scent for mink. They seem not to like my bait for I have not gotten anymore this past week.

I am glad, though, that it is only mink that avoid my traps or else I should not be able to put up with these long cold months.

* * * *

get that? he's glad it's only mink. a very real literary sense there. look at the way he speaks of great uncle albert's dog, "better used here." sometimes the letters are very painful. remember great uncle albert's admonition, "it ain't ever easy, and it gets harder and harder."
life, he meant. i half believe him now, and when he told us

53

that, his red, grizzled face bending low over the birthday cake we'd all brought for him, i'd wanted to cry. later i thought it spiteful and wrong of him to spoil such a nice day.

now, i don't know. his children gone, his wife a loveless hulk who would settle monstrously into her over-stuffed armchair in the living room and fall asleep in the middle of company. she could do it in five minutes. once she farted in her sleep and it never woke her. i remember i laughed, and mom shut me up with a withering look. then everyone ignored it even though the smell penetrated the entire room, each person in order turning first their head, then covering their nose as unobtrusively as possible, then finally shifting position in their seats to try and avoid the thick dog-like stink of it. "but mom," i said, and then she sent me outside while all the while uncle albert sat there in a straight-backed kitchen chair, elbows on his knees, leaning forward and talking animatedly with aunt sarah about cows and the proper way to clean stables. aunt sarah was blowing her nose when i left and leaning over the side of the couch in a vain effort to avoid the smell.

i remember, too, catching a last look at the dirty, purple flowered wall-paper and the great brown stain which had appeared over the chimney. it was cracked and beginning to peel back in places.

how good it was to open the front door to raging sunlight and escape the dark, curtained gloom of chipped, edwardian furniture and that dusty imitation oriental rug which covered the bare floor. uncle alex never missed a breath.

that and his birthday, i remember most. i wonder now when he stopped going to bed with her. she was so gross. i still feel sorry for him, even though i know he would hate me to do so. he was very brave. still, even love does not last forever. though it should.

oh, how nice it would be if the sun always shone as hot and as fierce as on that day when i left that room. i wanted to kiss someone so badly that i hugged myself on the front porch and became weak and dizzy so that i had to lean against the rail to keep from falling down. it wasn't fair.

how easy it must be to destroy love?

but the letters. they are our main concern. they tell the story. here are some early ones.

* * * *

Dunedin, N.Y
December 15,1912

My Dearest Katherine,

How kind it was of you to write such a long letter. I should have written a longer one Monday night but father built such a hot fire before he went to bed that I thought I should roast before I ever finished what little I did write.

Seriously, though, your letter was short but very sweet.

I do not know if I will be able to get down Sunday. It has snowed all this afternoon and is still snowing and blowing so you can hardly see out of doors. If the roads allow, you may count on me. I do not know what I should do if I had to stay away from you for two weeks.

Agnes has just written you a letter which she is going to send down. I have been reading it, and I asked father and mother what she could mean when she said for you not to disgrace your family and Arthur with such a thing. They said they did not know. Mother said that she had never mentioned any such thing. I'm afraid that you will have to figure out what Agnes means by yourself.

You must not let Lillian bother you with what she says. You know what I think of you and that is all that should be necessary. If you do not know, I do not mind telling you again that I love you and only you. There is no place in my heart for any other nor shall there ever be if you prove to be the sweet and loving girl I believe you are. I shall always think you the purest, dearest little girl who ever lived. I think I have a right to say this, knowing you as I do.

Father just joked that you had better get that fellow to stay with you that I found there when I came down last Sunday. I think not! If you ever need anyone to stay with you, you know who to ask. If your father is going away, I will come down the Saturday before Christmas and stay over Sunday.

Make your father get you glasses before he goes on his vacation. The longer you go without them the worse your headaches will get, and I know they cannot be much fun.

I will be down by ten Sunday if I can get Mom and the folks up for breakfast in time. You must not get discouraged though, if I do not get there at exactly ten. Be patient. Father is going to send Frank a rooster, so I will have lots of company on the way down.

We have been in the woods every day this week. Today, I worked only in the forenoon. It stormed so that I could not chop firewood this afternoon.

Say, that was a corking letter you wrote to Mother. I thought I should split when I read it. She has to have one of us read her letters for she says she can read only certain hands. Your writing is as plain as it can be, but she complains that she cannot make it out. So I read it. What fun.

You are indeed, your own woman Katherine, and I am glad of it. No, mother could probably not have traced the maternal line, but I warrant she can now. What I marvel at is that you said it all with such grace and delicacy. You are a wonder.

I don't know whether I could have resisted the temptation to read the letter anyway, knowing that it came from you and was with my letter. Next to the promises of God, I prize most anything that is of you. That is, I believe, all you can ask for.

I wonder if I will ever know enough to come home when I get to where you are again. I feel as though I could squeeze you to death, and one kiss from those ruby lips would be paradise.

With my truest love and most affectionate kisses, I am and ever shall be, your willing and most loving cousin.

Arthur

* * * *

there is a streak of bitchiness in our family. i wonder who it comes from. a few days later this follows.

* * * *

Dunedin, N.Y.
December 23, 1912

My Dearest Katherine,

How good it was to hear from you, and hear about your new glasses too. That's really a fine Christmas present. Good for your father.

What was the trouble Monday? You said you were in bed when the grocery boy came, but you never explained why.

I have asked Dr. Hull to see if he can get me a job in Perrysville. He said that they were taking new men in the laundry over there. Do not worry if I go to work. I can come and see you as often as I do now, and after I learn to iron well it may be that I can get a job in Athens. An experienced man has more chance of a job in one of the Athen's shops than a green hand.

Whether I am in Perrysville or Dunedin or anywhere else, my heart shall always be with you, and I shall come some day to claim it.

Never worry about losing my love, Katherine. I don't see why you should doubt me so. If you truly think God has taken my love in order to punish you, what can my friendship with others be? Hell -- most likely? I don't understand that last sentence of yours, and I shall ask you to explain it Sunday.

I do not believe I ever had a friend who can say that I turned him down, and God knows that for every time I think of others I think a hundred times of you. Lord, I wish only that I were in a position to show you my love and that I am sincere.

I suppose I will have to take Agnes to the West Dunedin Christmas tree Friday night and to the Dunedin tree Saturday. Be sure, it will be simply to please her and not for any pleasure I shall receive myself. Without you to share it with me, all the world is but darkest night.

Do not let my coming down hinder you from taking part in any New Year's entertainment, for I should be as pleased as anyone to hear you recite. All Agnes has done this week is to learn Christmas pieces. She has six, I think.

Father has been sick this week and not out of the house. I hope he will be able to do the chores Sunday if I come down.

I had been wondering how to get some rabbits for your father. It has been so cold they are hard to find, and I did not know if he would let me stay for Christmas should I not bring some down. Now I will not have to worry, for I think you will not find any fault with me should I fail to bring rabbits. Or would you?

In any case, I will be down Sunday and stay past Tuesday if you do not kick me out.

Mother has written you a letter, and I suppose she has been as mean as she knows how. She and father were in the front room all night trying to discover how they could make you mad at me. We were talking about my going to Perrysville to work last night, and Mother said she did not care where I went as long as I did not make the same mistake Albert did when he tried to learn shirt ironing. As if with you I ever would.

Father said he was not afraid of that as I would not have to come home every week to see Ma, but he supposed I would have to go and see Katie quite often.

Mother began to cry and said, "Well, if he can find anyone who will mend his shirts as often and clean his underwear any better then let him go, I shan't say a word."

I said, "For heaven sakes, Ma, are you getting jealous too? Is it not enough for Agnes and Lillian to be jealous without you too?"

Then she protested that she was not jealous. Father spoke up and said, "She is not jealous, son, only mad.--That is the same thing she told me once when she got jealous of my mother."

Well, we all had a good laugh over that. You will want to tease her when you write about being jealous and crying over it.

Father said that it must be his concern who you got to stay with you while your father is gone for you are trying to get his best man away from him at a time when there was lots of work to be done and he was laid up.

I'll have to close with that. The rest are all in bed now and the fire is almost out. Its embers are deep red beneath the ashes, and there is little heat left. I have had a sore throat most of the week and my trousers are wet where the snow soaked through them today. If I sit here much longer I fear I will become as sick as father and then no work will get done around here.

Write me again this week. Remember, you promised to write twice.

Love to you my darling Kathy, a love of such a kind as one has who has never known love before.

Your loving and most devoted cousin,

Arthur

* * * *

the world may not end with love, but it must surely have begun with it. hell is its absence, i'm sure.

CHAPTER VII
History III

Unfortunately, and I suspect demonstrably so, fine sentiment is the moral equivalent of nothing--nothing at all. Black (and white), although fraught with quite obvious social, political, psychological, and economic, connotations, all frightful realities no doubt, more or less, according to local custom, bias, state of the art, habit, and habitat, is not in itself a thing, substance, or quality of extraordinary note. True, to those who have a certain courage which often borders upon a vertiginous amentia, it is obvious (local galaxies, nebulae, and red giants accounted for) that the essential characteristic of the universe is darkness; black and unyielding it enfolds the frenetic agony of the lesser stars with infinite duration. They're right. But what is that to Gotoma?

In the beginning there was only darkness upon the face of the deep.

Whether such a statement is or was descriptive fact or ethical judgment I insist upon leaving to greater, or lesser, minds interested solely in the theoretical presumption of useless and forever sectarian conjecture. Raw energy is lacking between discrete cosmic explosions by any standards, and my own peculiar hagiological supposition is that black holes are probably the more convincing powers by which life, both physical and sexual, has been, is, and will be forever judged upon this terrageous globe. Mea culpa, mea culpa.

The poor black-bird was not alone, regardless of the tender ministrations of guilt with which an embattled Caucasian female might want to sooth her always aching heart. The world accepts both our good intentions and purified emotions equally for what they are and so ignores them absolutely. I dare say there have been more white slaves than black in the world with brutality, by varying standards, their also constant master.

Broadtail grackles, for such was the bird in question, are not likely the momentous beginning of a sacred chain of natural selection. We are too Bible-bound.

In the beginning God created . . .

As there is no end so there was no beginning. For the possibly wise, it is only the finite which is impossible to comprehend. Grackles are the end product of evolutionary art as well as the substance for continued growth all at a time.

There are no magic moments.

The string is never cut.

Like the vulture on the road, grackles gather carrion along a more golden strand, their passion dictated solely by their stomach, saved from Henry's gross and vulgar obesity only by the comparative poverty of their environment and their blessed inability to control it as completely as the kings of light. But then, even "Le Roi du Soleil" found his own especial stygian umbra, didn't he? "Apres moi le deluge."

The vaults of heaven enclose no mcgacosm, but megacosm there is. It is tautological once more. Those who love strength survive. Therefore we, the survivors, love strength, and few, if any, of us can bear with selfless equanimity the weakness of our protectors. Christ was right, love saves.

Katherine loved strength. There can be no doubt since Arthur bore upon her vigorous body seven fine children only one of whom, William, died unexpectedly, no more than two days after birth, his quiet leaving being unforeseen by his parents and doctor both and thus all unwarned--of nothing--nothing at all; although Katie always afterward contended, and she was not contradicted by Arthur, that said leave-taking was an act of God to save from pain and mortal abuse a child that had not sucked upon first being presented the tit and, therefore, had it lived, would have grown increasingly sickly and unfit to make his way within this vale of tears.

"Hard work needs hard folks," she would often say when child or grandchild would interrupt her while sweaty, working over a hot stove in August or September, hair in long, wet strands which stuck to her forehead and cheeks as she canned tomatoes or made jam, "hard work on a farm, and it's never finished."

So if a man can't suck a tit, he'll never be strong, and who are we to argue with such forceful logic, in spite of Katherine's protestations, often voiced, that her first-born Lillian, named after her older sister, had been the hearty one, so in love with life that she calloused both breasts for a year in her furious greed and thus maybe what Katherine presented to the luckless man-child was unfit and therefore unused, Arthur for years wordless on the matter, for thirty-five long years until his death, alone upon the farm, now deserted by Katherine who had moved to the city to tend a heart condition and the kids.

By the time of the Countryman's marriage, however, out of strength good old Teddy Roosevelt had already given his excess of love to hovering Howard Taft, a man particularly drawn to strength as his sizeable girth, and staying power proved.

"Oh goodness, I must go thank Teddy for this," he said, or something to that effect.

Atalanta, Jason, Bellerophon, Alcestis--all attest to the efficacy of good friends in high places and the necessity of circumspection for the relatively weak. If we cannot command than it is best to obey joyfully, as Katherine seems to have increasingly learned.

Who deserves to be loved? The question needs no answer and should abide no asking.

All those who live, said Christ. All those who survive, said Darwin, his choice of verbs implying with oracular certainty the fragility of cosmic order, the inevitability of competition regardless of our moral suasion, and the dread black hole that is the beginning and the end, which never was and isn't, and always will be.

Oh Thomas, Thomas, dumb ox Thomas that you were, save

us from our own dear feast of life. I bled, I fell upon the thorns. The order does not matter, egg or chicken. A poke solves all our problems in feverish, recreative genius by burdening other generations. And we are never alone--except in obstinate and sentimental vanity.

The farmers of the '90's thought themselves the inheritors of a hard lot. Yet, by necessity, self-love must blind us all (except the non-survivors), and the Jeffersonian wonderland of cash crop politics had given way (if it ever had been in those waning years) to backwoods and plainsman entrepreneurs and real-estate speculators. 1900-1914 were good years for farmers, and Arthur and Katherine were hardly poor folk all through the war which he so fortunately avoided because of Baptist birth and a lordly distaste for corrupting city life.

"Have I answered the charges? Have I defended myself?" pleaded Roosevelt years earlier from his Pleiadian chair.

"You certainly have Mr. President," expostulated Root with a sage brush of his chin. "You have shown that you were accused of seduction and you have conclusively proved that you were guilty of rape."

Strong-willed, heroic personalities these pioneers. No softness here, no preacher's timidity, and just so much love. What's a girl want if not six good pokes and squalling brats in order nine months later, Jessie and Martin being premies, and so the couple took care to avoid any more in Katherine's old age.

The love affair between Teddy and Howard was, after all, unnatural and born out of both silver and gold. And so was fated to end.

Unnatural love from silver and gold, there's what's fair for you. Old Alex, bless his still breathing soul, thought himself no vain man and would, more out of fear than pride, never have thought once about jealousy and God, yet he sacrificed himself upon the cross of gold in 1854 barely learning, if ever, to sing a more chaste devotional before the altar of his own dearly chosen god, the tones of "Onward Christian Soldiers" or even "Battle Hymn of the Republic" having never been heard to cross his lips those last forty-two odd years after his return to the just, and thus he saw his grandson born, and he knelt, if only briefly because of his back, in

64

silent and soulful appreciation, thanking God once more for this his second deliverance from death and sin unto the third generation.

Of course Martin, the father, knelt too, as did crotchety, even then, brother Jeremiah and his two decorous and continent daughters Theresa and Louise born much earlier to a young father but under the wrong stars which failed to interrupt the concinnity of their thus sexually mellifluous lives with any equally mopsy event suggestive of lechery and fornication no matter how discreet. Are we jealous of our God's superior delight? What a deliciously tantalizing question, especially since to God all manner of actions bespeak delight, even the cross--indeed, most profoundly the cross if acceptance and intention be considered. Easter is, after all, a moveable feast being moved originally by fear and hate and greed, all of which speak of endless love.

In 1890 there was one car in the continental United States. By 1920 two million and coming. Before the war Arthur still rode a buggy and often defined the limits of his love upon the hard bench seat of a country wagon. Old Nestor would have understood.

There was a fire in Athens in 1861. Old Alex was privileged to witness the certain passion of it. It was noon, and he stood not 20 yards away in the small stock pen near the mid-river island rail yard which lay across the Hudson from the city proper. He'd just sold three worthless cows which had run dry on William Clarke and, happy with an unusually good price from a foolish buyer, he was kneeling down amidst dung and chips to tie his boot. Finished, he looked up in time to see sparks from a nearby locomotive which was crossing the river set fire to dry and aging timbers.

A stiff wind was blowing east across the channel and soon the bridge became an inferno. The flames spread to wooden buildings on River Street from thence to 507 gracious monuments of Athens' prosperity. All in all, 75 acres of the city's pride were ravaged by six o'clock that night. Viewed from the surrounding hills which penned the city in, Athens was a mass of flame twenty blocks along the river and eight blocks up the bank side.

Alex hardly moved, too small he knew to be of use, but settled himself upon the shore of the island some feet away and watched the increasing pyrotechnics bathed increasingly in their own general calidity. He loved it all and told the story over and over to his father who, terrified and unable to get to the island from the 1st National Bank where he had gone to negotiate a loan, had raced around the city endlessly till after eight that night searching for what increasingly he feared would be the charred remains of his "little boy." William Clarke's indisposition later became a favorite tale of his son's, Alex never tiring of regaling his own children with the event every time he took them into Athens.

But the city rose from its ashes and built new bridges too, although the island bridge was once again destroyed by fire in 1920 before a steel structure was finally erected. "Fire. Man's born of fire," old Alex would state most unctuously, "and he'll die of fire. You mark my words."

The Populists lost in 1896. Later, even Arthur knew that was a dark day in American history. Skidmore's philosophy, if ever he had one, lay not dead to be sure, but the courageous critic of Malthus had brought with him no living body with which to continue his lonely journey. After the Civil War, farmers knew themselves an oppressed people, but free education, cheap land, and class equality proved neither real answer nor fantastic dream. Group agrarianism could no more save the farmer than the silver he had so dearly clasped to his bosom in an unwarranted, showy, and vainglorious attempt at cultural manipulation.

Esther's wedding dress was used over and over again out of necessity more than tradition, as Agnes well testified before her corpuscular demise in Athens, now many years long past. The railroads ruled a prospering nation and in doing so made Mr. Sears and Mr. Montgomery the happiest of corporate wards.

And Teddy won because he expropriated (an act largely done for him by others somewhat less astute in seizing the day and hour) the Populist issues. The Progressivists moved from country to city, forgetting Martin and his sons Arthur, Albert, and Edgar (though they didn't know it at the time), and appealed there to a more heterogeneous public. After 1900 the sons managed to consume their fathers, Martin only one of the many, while the much acclaimed status revolution among professionals effectively left the farmer, eastern especially, alone and unwed, his grief and despair an increasingly peculiar and antique testament of what had been, before Mr. Jefferson's agrarian democracy ran head on into Mr.

Lincoln's war and the modern industrialist.

Thank god for wars, sisters! They, of all things, truly liberate in savage and inhuman conjunction.

CHAPTER VIII
LOVE STORY III

the letters continue. here are three early ones. he mentions the laundry in one for the first time, but it seems gratuitous. neither one seems initially to have wanted to remain on the farm. how much some of the letters remind me of dead alcestis brought back from the grave, so greatly he comes to fear the city.

the parallel fails, of course. they all do. there is no love that is not unique. a tilted nose, a flirting eye, a word spoken or unspoken, all accident combines to fashion us.

and tragedy must play its necessary part. alcestis died for love, mother and father, friends, and servants refused her. yet she and he both were born of tyro. i sometimes question the lesson but never the desire. love so often gives what more often cowardice requires. a shame. and what of love that fails because we love too well? what of that?

* * * *

69

Dunedin, N.Y.
December 19, 1912

My Dearest Katie,

You must not expect too long a letter from me tonight. I have just had a row with Agnes to keep her away from the table while I write. I did not feel like staying up tonight until all the family was in bed.

Father said he would finish the chores and let me get some rest early as he warranted I had not gotten two hours' sleep in the last 48. I finished the chores, though, and then told them all that I had it in mind to write to you. Mother asked if I could not write tomorrow night so she would have time to write too. I told her I could not wait but that she could write next time if she chose. So maybe you'll get a note from her when I write at week's end.

Albert came over later this morning to go in the woods with me, but I wasn't home yet and he had to go in alone. Albert hates to go in the woods alone. He's always afraid of bears and the like. I try to tell him there are few wolves and fewer bears left hereabouts but it doesn't do any good. I think he's more afraid of himself than the bears. The old blackies left around here would run away from their own shadow.

I went in after dinner and we cut logs until dark. It must have been six or later when we got back to the house, so you see I have been bushed since I arrived home.

Mother says to tell you she is coming down whenever I get so's I can stay at home long enough for her to make the trip.

I suppose Lillian has been telling you that I do not like you again. As long as you and I know, who cares what she says?

Did you know that your father tried to steal my horse this

70

morning while I was in the house bidding you goodbye. He had him driven in where old George keeps his milk wagon. When I saw that he was gone I thought I was to have the fun of walking home. I suppose he had a great laugh on me when he came in the house.

I spoke to father tonight about going to Perrysville to work, and he said I should take the twenty dollars he owed me and go off to Athens to learn a trade. Then, he said, I could go where I pleased to work. If I went to Perrysville I would have to sign a contract to stay a certain length of time in the laundry after I had learned the business. In either case, I guess I will not have a very hard time in getting away if I should take a notion to go.

Do not worry, I shall not go for a while yet if I go at all. I want to help get what logs and timber I can out of the woods first. It's good and profitable man's work and I like it. Although I fear sometimes there will be few woods like ours left soon. Out in Michigan I'm told they level whole miles at a time.

I wish I could go to Athens, especially if you decide to work there. Then I could see you more often than I do now. That would be a greater pleasure for me than seeing the Green of England.

Katie, you are continually before me, in my mind's eye and heart, but nothing can replace my holding you close and feeling your sweet lips on mine. I never knew a man could love as I do, and I have laughed at many another fellow who was in love, never realizing what I was doing.

Now I know what love is for the first time. And this must, too, be the last for nothing could ever be as sweet again. I could never tell you or write of my feelings, but every thought of my life is tied to yours. Albert wanted me to chop with him today. "For company's sake," he said. I guess I was that. But I have come to care for no other company than yours. Of course at times I must seem rather poor company when I am so inclined to let you do all the talking and me the listening.

I saw Willis on the way up this morning and he gave me a broad smile when he said good-day. I do not know if it was a smile of pity, fun, or contempt, nor do I care. As I was passing the White Church, I heard someone say hello. I looked up and your grocery boy stood there smiling at me. He must have thought that you kept me pretty late. I wish I could have stayed forever, but I suppose your father would have something to say about that.

Well I must end now as I am very sleepy. Your loving and devoted cousin who hopes someday to be much more.

Arthur

P.S. Tell Lillian not to be jealous. Raymond does not like jealous girls. And I cannot listen to Jimmy Hardy sing anymore.

* * * *

at the time he must have been visiting her every weekend and staying over. at christmastime, too. can you imagine her father's wrath? i wonder if the whole perrysville business wasn't just a ploy. love, after all, can be crafty.

* * * *

Dunedin, N.Y.
December 28, 1912

My Dearest Katie,

Your letter came Tuesday night, but I could not write until I went to the Centre and got paper and envelopes.

Lillian nearly cried when I told her what you said. She and Agnes have been having a fine time over the holidays. She would not believe it until I let her read the letter herself. She had been teasing me to know if it was true. She was going to write but decided she would not get an answer before Friday so she might as well wait until she got home to see you. She has been making eyes at Albert some, so Raymond had better watch out. Albert eats his dinner here when we work in the wood, and she and Agnes are impossible.

I don't know when you will get this letter. If it keeps snowing and blowing so, maybe never. The stage may not be able to get up tomorrow at this rate.

I have not heard from Dr. Hull yet so I don't know if I will get a job in Perrysville. I think I will write Jim and have him keep his eyes open in Athens. He would have more of a chance of finding me one there than I have out here.

You need not worry about me killing myself with work. If I were to work myself to death before I got you, I think we would not enjoy it much. So I will be very careful you can bet.

If you make me work myself to death after you get me, I shall be ready to go. But I do not think there will ever be any danger of me dying from overwork; it is much too healthy a practice.

I think, Katie, that since Christmas you now understand me. You said you did not last Sunday, but you should now. We are, true, still young, but every year we are obliged to live apart will be a century to me.

Lillian and I were talking after father went to bed last night and he got up later and drove us to bed. He said if you were coming up next week, probably he would be kept awake half the night

73

every night for two weeks, and he did not care for the thought.

If your father comes home and says anything about me, write at once. Don't fear that I will stay away on account of anything he says. I merely want to know what to expect.

I think I will ask him why he objects so to my coming down. If he has anything to say to me, I might as well let him say it.

Also, don't talk to me about my having a chance to do better. I want what I have. No more, for I already have the world. I would never marry for any reason but love even if the girl were worth millions.

You are the only girl in the world for me Katie, the only girl I have every loved, ever could or ever would. I am satisfied that you love me enough to marry me, and when that time comes I shall be the happiest of men.

Jim has a good home even if he does have to work hard for his living, and he started with no more than I. He might even have been wealthy today if he had not turned to drink.

You need never fear on that account for me as long as you are true. I love you too much to ever let drink turn me away. I was able to break away from it when I had no one to help me. Surely, I will not forsake the love of the truest and sweetest girl in the world for mere rum. I stand in no fear of drink anymore. I have tried it once and that is enough.

Supper is ready. Lillian has called me. I have written until father has all the chores done I guess. We are expecting you next week so do not disappoint us. Oh, just think, a whole week when I can see you every day.

Now Agnes calls me too, so I must go. Agnes and Lillian have gotten along wonderfully. Agnes said she was glad there was school next week if you were coming up. I hope it will storm every day for her while you and I say home together.

Albert never mentions your name. I don't know why. He may think it will make me angry if he speaks his mind of you.

I believe I can talk better than I can write so I will close your loving and most devoted cousin,

Arthur

P.S. Lillian told me last night she had read three of my letters. She found them wrapped in a sheet in your bureau. Find a new hiding place for them.

* * * *

another demon rum letter. it must have led to the april one where he admonished her never to give him a reason to drink. how vulnerable we are when we love. we must all be very, very lonely to risk it.

i wonder if later in his life when he lived at the farm and she in the city for her heart condition -- i wonder if they truly loved each other while so far apart. for all the songs about it, love is not often very strong i suspect. distance breaks, and does not temper, the blade. what a strange image. why did i use it? there are enough hints here that she was a sharp and wilful girl. they couldn't have all disliked her so just because they were cousins? could they? she could have hurt him so easily. he offers no defense. how brave the letters show him. here's the third.

* * * *

Dunedin, N.Y.
Jan. 16, 1913

My Darling Katie,

I wish I had stayed down to your house all night. It has been so cold here that we have not worked all day. I suppose if I had stayed, though, father would have found something to do so he could find fault when I got home.

It was certainly a beautiful night and if you had been along in the wagon I could have enjoyed the ride greatly.

I think it was as cold this morning as it has been all winter. I carried Agnes to school and came near freezing my fingers. We can hardly keep warm in the house tonight. The wind blows through every crack, and it is icy cold. I guess I will stop writing for a while and warm my ----side, hey?

Dr. Hull was up today and there does not seem to be any work down that way. I guess I am doomed to lay idle just when I should like to be at work.

Don't worry though. I think I will speak to father and see what he will do if I stay at home and help him. I might accomplish more at home in a year if I struck out by myself. I can think of nothing that will help me in any way to get a job. I will have to keep looking if father will not give me enough to stay. I will speak to Charlie Fouks when I come again. By then I will know what father will do.

Albert asked me this morning if I was going to the donations tomorrow. I said, "No." He did not ask me why. They say Ida is going to show her face for the first time since the

Stephentown affair. I should think by now she might want some public entertainment. I know I should not.

Tell Edgar to sell his skunk skin if he can get over two dollars for it. I asked Victor Burden what he was paying and he said $2.10.

Mother asked me what excuse I made to your father for coming down Sunday. I told her I did not make any. What did he say to Lillian for bringing Ray in? Some dig I'll bet.

Katie, how can I tell you of my love? I feel I write so awkwardly that I am ashamed. It is good that actions speak louder than words for I am not one of those fellows who can give vent to his feelings in pretty phrases.

I have a girl worthy of much more than I can give, yet money is not all. If we can be happy that is enough. Only happiness brings true joy. I can only give the truest love of man's heart, and I receive, I know, no less in return.

I think I have shown you that I wish to take nothing back. My promises are my love for you. And for heaven's sake don't ever think I distrust you. If I thought any such thing I should not be backward about speaking. That I know I can trust you is the very thing that makes me love you, and I trust you with that love which has never been anyone else's.

If I have said anything here to hurt you, forgive me. I know I often speak unthinkingly in my letters. I can say no more.

All the rest are in bed, and I must soon join them.

I close with love and a prayer that you will always abide in my love as I in yours. Your loving and devoted cousin,

Arthur

CHAPTER IX
History IV

Happiness is joy? A happy thought, and true enough since joy, at joyful times, waxes indistinguishable from its more sensate neighbor and leaves us all savoring the warm glow, the unstoppable snicker, the welcome tears, the shaky stomach, and the goose-pimply skin of good times. Ah, we are so vulnerable and love it so, indeed if not in thought.

"Help me! Help me! Love me more," we all cry from dumb mouths, all the while loathe to admit, implicit in the argument, "I need! I may be hurt."

Happiness is joy? Why not? Andy Carnegie (patron sanctus?) would agree and certainly good old J.P. Teddy knew them all, the patron saints of our joyful centennial mercantilism. The public be damned and full speed ahead, and America was loved by Ford, Swift, Pillsbury, Armour, J. Rockefeller, Vanderbilt, Havemeyer, and how many more who deserve mention for their diurnal affection. The woods were full of such devotionaries, and bears, as Mr. Weyerhauser attests.

There is no altruism greater than the love of money.

"I would marry only for love," states Arthur; a noble thought most nobly expressed. But then he adds, "you'll get me, and I'll get you," and love, that pure draught which makes a great heart greater, which spurs us on to glorious deeds, and renders crass materialism naked and limp beneath our feet, love is itself reduced to getting, having, holding, and poking, to possession and its associated grunts and groans.

In loving one is either very brave or very ignorant, but in either case it is not the act which so illuminates the scope--expanse and depth--of our moral world as it is the object upon which our love is placed. Strong men marry pretty women. Beautiful people are intellectually as well as physically superior to the masses. Such biological as well as sociological facts have been well-documented over the ages, our own century affording them empirical and statistical proof in addition to the witness of our sight and senses. Pimply people, the fat and chronically depressed, the old and genetically malformed, the shy, the timid, those with cleft chins and palates, the weak and foolish, stupid and naive; they wait for each other and seldom are granted the comfort of superior action.

For these, only vision is left, apocalyptic often, always Utopian and forever moral. By 1912 the American rural mind had been confronted, painfully and through exacting scrutiny, with urban life. Between 1860 and 1910, those years when Alexander Washington and his son Martin Countryman were hewing out their precious stake to the west of the Little Hoosic, the number of cities in these United States counting over 50,000 inhabitants rose from 16 to 109. Rural population doubled in that time but the urban boom was seven-fold. Commodity prices for our poor, poor farmer rose steadily from $447,000 in 1897 to $2,382,000 in 1911. The totals are accurate, but I forget for what.

And out of love, professionals flocked to the cities, thus assuring Arthur and Katherine of their pristine isolation in the woods, more truly untainted by urban corruption than a hundred years before since now the heroic freedom fighters were moving inward and eastward rather than outward and westward.

The doctor wished to practice his tender ministrations upon the deserving urbanites, though not upon the then some 13,000,000 foreign-born ghetto dwellers of New York, Chicago, Philadelphia, Baltimore, St. Louis, and Detroit who paid even worse than Dunedin folk. The preacher, too, saw the divine light of ministering to an urban church full of wealthy, articulate, well-intentioned parishioners; all willing, albeit eager, to alleviate, through dollars and a distancing piety, the suffering of an industrialized poor. To a man, or more properly to a proper woman, professionals and their newly, by casual affluence, half-educated mates forsook the sacrosanct and fructifying conservatism of their latter days and regaled themselves beneath the more chaste banner of social welfare and trust regulation, of women's rights and the class struggle, of labor justice and death to the monopolies, of municipal reform and, of course, the proper way to conduct a deep finesse.

And if populism-progressivism moved into the cities from the country to appeal to their more diverse and happy human conjunction, then what about the poor (himself admitted), poor farmer?

History becomes all too often, if not always, what we assume it should have been. Our particular canons of satisfaction determine our understanding by also determining how we observe the world about us. Old men justify themselves only to young boys. And since we can only look back, never forward (no matter what the white, upper, middle-class protests), history, as we can ever know it, always is what we wish it to be. And there's an end to it, individuation being what it is.

Arthur of the great heart lived in the fading days of participatory democracy. His love, thus, could afford a careless purity. But, all unbeknown to him, corporate growth had united with political machines and, fed by the clotted, sickly masses of an immigrant population, would leave him feckless before the century's more common whores.

In 1912, the essential year in question, old J.P. Morgan ("a man who's got money can use it as he damn well pleases") could peruse a kingdom of 341 interlocking directorates in 112 companies with 22 billion dollars of capital worth, at that time a figure three times the worth of all New England and twice that of the thirteen southern states. Or was it that a little Boston railroad could have 18,000 employees, pay its top executive $35,000 a year, and gross revenues of 40 million a year, such figures thrice and twice respectively the annual outlay of the said respective, and respectable, governments? Exact figures escape me and, after all, are of minor importance. 'Tis within a buck or two. The fact remains that the governor of Massachusettes at that time made only

$6,600 per annum.

Life on the farm was left behind us. The city man, a magnificent apparition, entertained himself with burlesque, melodrama, and vaudeville. There were band concerts in the park (oh, delicious Sunday afternoons upon the beach at Coney) picnics, baseball (the national sport for a deserving populace), church socials, and (that most dangerous, wild, and wooly of all sports) bicycle riding. Sadly, or gratefully, according to individual preference for long baseline rallies, tennis was not yet Big Bill Tilden's game.

Canals, railroads, and the Grangers had all grown up into big boys. Jim Fisk, Dan Drew (not McGraw), Jay Gould, Jim Hill, and Cornelius lived well (and once in awhile not so) off of what was good for the country-- late in life, engaging in the general penchant for the new and bigger and better.
Father Martin began in rebirthed Athens a milk-route, the Diamond Rock Creamery on 8th Street North eventually providing him over a period of years with the necessary additional milk (and buttermilk, and cream, and yogurt blend, and butter, and heavy cream, and ice cream) which his own small herd of twenty cows found it inconvenient to produce at exactly the proper times.

He did well and was greatly rewarded by the greatness of his estate which passed onto Arthur (largely), Albert and Edgar having moved to the city-- New York and the Centre respectively--and Agnes being, after-all, a girl and duly protected by her looks which early in life acquired for her, through careful husbanding, some style, and much ambition, a Dunedin laddie who later moved to Athens when the farm gave out and discovered, just in the nick of it, a treasure trove of monies across the river in the great furnaces of Allegheny-Ludlum where he worked until his accidental death by drowning in a running stream of hot bessemer steel when he tripped over a cold bar accidentally mislaid. His wife received no pension and remained in a three-story walkup in North Athens, much beloved though seldom visited by her newly grown children, until she succumbed to grief and loneliness and a heart attack brought on by overweight and little exercise, her will directing that her remaining funds be spent upon a lavish, final processional from Havermeyer's Funeral Home on 2nd Avenue to the Brookgreen Cemetery in the hills above the valley overlooking the Hudson-Mohawk river conjunction, her progeny and abundant relatives attending the funeral in hordes so fulsome as to block the cemetery entrance, the lawyer having not yet told them about the will.

But most of this was long after the days of our present interest and certainly long after the power of economic decision and then political action was expropriated from the landowners by the money moguls (supposedly). By 1912 Taft was through, his obstinacy being what it was (his girth too), and Arthur had come back from the Lebanon school, healthy, strong, but love-sick, having run track, played baseball and football (the latter at that time averaged forty deaths a year), and ready now to forsake the bottle and demon rum for the good life (revitalized) upon the farm.

To conclude the cultural bias: movies were popular and available to a general public by 1905. The Great White Fleet had sailed in 1908. James Dewey, blessed philosopher, had discovered the quintessence of modern man (much like Rousseau) when he casually noted that the truth of a belief depends upon its value to the individual, a statement, we must be quick to observe, of which Arthur, as yet, was blissfully unaware.

Abroad, it was all Teddy's favorite wet dream (a gentle vulgarity). The Marines (and Navy) intervened in Cuba in 1898, created Panama in 1903, saved Nicaragua in 1909, and (I had forgot) had aided in the annexation of Puerto Rico in 1898. Haiti and the Dominican Republic in this peaceful little American Lake were to come later, excepting 1905 another banner year, and all the while Sigmund Romberg was singing desert love songs to Victor Herbert; Robinson, Masters, Frost, and Lindsay were discovering the true American spirit; Whistler's mother continued to rock in black and white; and the Armory Show (1913) set New York ablaze with artistic piety and the urge to create, an urge which Flanders, the Marne, and Belleau Wood would soon, and one day, with functionary and funereal eloquence, sate in the grotesque and misshapen surrealistic pall of battlefields with blackened, stick-stump, summer trees and rotten, rat-filled trenches from the Alps to the Atlantic Ocean.

No greater love!

CHAPTER X
PORTRAIT III

"Love is as love does," Gramps would always say, and though the cliche was as old and worn as these hills, he meant every word of it. Of course he would say that about anything. He was a man of simple tastes. Simple tastes and direct living. He always meant what he said.

He never fought Johnie Poultrie as far as I know, but there is the story of an Athens police sergeant whom he met one day upon the milk route while running a stop sign at four-thirty in the morning. It was a terribly cold morning, in December I believe, and Gramps was buttoned up tight with the bulk of Ma's long muffler wrapped down about his neck.

The policeman was a red-headed, Irish giant--maybe Pollock too, I'm not quite sure--and all of six foot three or four, which in those days, before frozen foods and public school dieticians, was quite a stature. It made the policeman fully an inch or two taller than Gramps and caught him unaware when he had to look up into eyes equally as blue and a mite more laughing than his own.

McKenney, the Policeman, was all for giving Gramps a ticket despite the early hour and the absence of any other vehicles upon the streets.

"The law's the law," he smiled at Gramps, displaying a large gap between his upper front teeth, "ya flaunt it at yer peril."

"True enough" judged Gramps sententiously, "but laws are made for a purpose, and this serves none at four o'clock in the morning."

"Four-thirty," the Irishman corrected with a broader smile still and handed Gramp the ticket which he had been making out on the side of his Model A. He grinned across the street at Grandpa's horse and milk wagon, then quipped as he got back in his car, "At least ya'll never be caught for speedin' now, will you?"

That rankled Gramps, but he took the ticket, stuck it in his old, torn black steer-hide wallet and showed up at the Athens courthouse two days later fully intending to plead not guilty and "test the justice of the law" as he put it.

He never got that far. The wild Irishman was at the far end of the hall as Gramps passed through, and he yelled down the corridor, "Hey, old farmer, how's yer mule."

It was not a friendly joke, and Gramps was in no mind to be generous.

"Not as able to kick you to Albany and back as I were I a mind too, young feller," Gramps called back.

The challenge caught McKenney by surprise and momentarily his eyes opened wider than his mouth. But he quickly squinted them again and then marched down the hall toward Gramps.

"Ya challengin' the law are ya, Countryman? Ya'll want anither ticket fer that, I'll warrant."

"Not a'tall," Gramps said as contritely as he was ever able, "I spoke to the man not the badge, and if you'll ever stop hiding behind it, I'll be glad to meet you man to man for a friendly demonstration."

No sooner said than done, and a dozen witnesses attested to it before they died.

Quite forgetting himself, McKenney threw down his badge on the hall floor, and motioned to an empty pleas room off the end.

"Well now, man, I'm glad to oblige a friend. That I am," he offered as he bowed Gramps through the door.

Gramps walked in, a hair shorter than McKenney, only a few years older, and slightly wider through the chest and biceps.

Both were taller by four inches than any man around them. McKenney followed him, smiling broadly back toward the dumbfounded onlookers in the hall. Gramps just glowered straight ahead, beneath the brush of his blonde eyebrows. The door was heard to lock, there was a short silence, and then the fight began.

Except for the first few minutes of grunting, they say the sound was frightening, echoing as it did up and down the hall. Chairs were thrown and benches broken. No one could get in, not even old Judge Privet who stalked out of his office and ran quickly down the hall to the gathering before the locked doors. When Privet discovered what was happening he beat on the doors so hard, yelling at the top of his minister's squeal, "come out you vandals! Desist and come out, I say this minute, you ruffians, or I'll have the law on you!" that he split the heel of his right hand clear to the bone and had to leave for the doctor's office across Federal Street.

The fighting continued for a full half hour, its pace never slackening, they say. Three great windows were stove out and a great deal of wagering went on throughout the courthouse. Then finally the chatter and banging stopped. Ed Matteson tried the door but it wouldn't budge. Everyone was breathless to know who had won. That either man might be dead never occurred to them. The bets were on the line.

All was silent, the courthouse like a church for the first and only time.

It was a full fifteen minutes later that the doors opened and Gramps and McKenney staggered out arm-in-arm. It was the only way, Gramps later said, that they could still stand. The fight had been a draw. Gramps had lost his left earlobe to McKenney's skillful teeth, and McKenney's nose was never again as straight after Gramps taught him a boxing lesson at the beginning of the fight. There was blood everywhere, even on the bottom of their boots, and neither man had a good stitch of clothing on. The pleas room wasn't used for six months.

Privet fined them both $50, doctor's costs, damages, and court fees. McKenney was suspended for a month, and two weeks more when the chief of police learned he'd given a ticket at four in the morning. Privet laughed and eventually charged Gramps five dollars for the ticket.

"The law's the law," he said from behind the bench.

The fight was told all over town for years, and it really didn't cost Gramps that much. He was well-known in town and county politics, and most of the bettors decided that in a draw the money went to the contestants. After that, McKenney and Gramps were ever the best of friends, and when Uncle Martin married a Catholic, it was McKenney who stood up for him. I never knew a man not to like Gramps sooner or later.

Like the home-run for another instance. It was only one of many. Gramps was a great long-ball hitter. But I went with him to that reunion years later, and he never once brought up the subject. It was everyone else who wanted to remember it for him, as though through him they found themselves again, and in his deeds lay a portion of their own.

But there is another story, more clever yet equally as true, and it too, involves old Judge Privet, the toughest old bastard on the bench everyone used to say.

Seems one winter's morning after a fierce three-day storm had blown itself out two days before, Gramps was making his rounds on the milk route. He was being careful to have his horse follow the previous day's ruts which he had broken, because the storm had layed a thick coat of ice atop the snow and he didn't want young Billy's legs all cut up on him.

Well, Gramps is moving down Fourth Avenue when along comes this taxi that passes him and slips into the ruts three or four houses ahead. The driver gets out, walks up to a big white house, and bangs on the door. Seems he's got a drunk in the cab and can't find out where to put him. The cabby makes a a hell of a racket, waking up half the street with lights going on everywhere. Then Gramps comes up behind him and can't get around without risking young Billy's legs.

Well, the cabby comes back to the taxi, mad as a wet hen, and the drunk still lolling in the back seat singing "I got sixpence." Gramps finally gets the taxi driver's attention and tells him what's wrong. After all, he made the ruts yesterday and couldn't the taxi pull off the street a bit to let him by.

"No! It's a public street. I got troubles of me own," the

cabby yells.

OK. Gramps goes back to Billy and carefully leads the horse, breaking a new path around the taxi, all the while the driver going from house to house banging on doors and shouting like a wild man, and the drunk getting louder and louder.

Gramps goes on about his business up the street a few blocks and doesn't think too much about the whole thing until he comes out of the Mahan house and finds that the taxi has gone around him again and is parked a house or two up from Billy.

That made him mad, and he walked up to the cabby and explained about the horse's legs again, but the cabby wouldn't listen.

"Hey guy, I had to go around you, didn't I? Tough luck."

So once again Gramps went back and broke a new trail through the ice only to find ten minutes later that the cabby was once again ahead of him. And that was the cabby's first and last mistake.

"Hey bub," Gramps yelled from behind the taxi, "I've asked you twice, now I'm telling you. Get off my path."

Like a flash the cabby was out from behind the wheel, fists clenched. His second and last mistake.

He races toward Gramps. Gramps trudges toward him, and Pow! Gramps cold-cocks him out, flat in the snow. Then he leads Billy, lovingly, for the last time, around the cab.

But that wasn't the end of it. About two hours later Gramps was making his way down Seventh Avenue when up pulls a patrol car and out jumps two policemen and the cabby, his jaw all black and blue and his lip as big as a balloon.

"Got to take you in, Arthur, says one the police, "this man's sworn against you for assault."

"Oh that," says Gramps, still pulling milk out of the wagon, "No need. I reported that to central station 'bout an hour and a half ago. Said a hearin'd be set for next week sometime before old Judge Privet."

The cabby was dumbfounded. "I'll get you, Countryman," he yelled, shaking his fist. "You can't assault an honest citizen and get away with it."

And he didn't. The next Thursday Gramps and the cabby appeared before old Privet.

"Is this the way it happened, Countryman?" Privet asked, pounding the palm of his hand with his gavel.

"Yes sir," Gramps said, "you can ask most of the neighbors on the street. They all saw it."

"You had no cause to hit him, Countryman. It was a public way."

"Well, Judge," Gramps was all contrition, "I saw him come at me with closed fists and felt I'd better get the first shot in."

"Twenty dollars and cost," banged the judge. "Next case."

Gramps walked a step or two to the clerk and dragged twenty dollars out of his milk-money satchel that he wore on a strap across his shoulders. It was a whole lot of money in those days, but he paid it and turned to go when he saw the cabby just behind him, white-toothed and grinning like a beat-up alley-cat.

That was enough. Gramps turned around reached into his satchel and slowly, ever so slowly, counted out another, and his last, twenty dollars in bills.

"Judge," he says sententiously staring at old Privet for a long second, 'I think I'll have another go at it." Then he turned slowly back to the cabby.

No such luck. The cabby faded white as a sheet, spun on his heels, and raced up the aisle, hitting his head against the courtroom doors when he tried to open them. The whole place broke up. Everybody was laughing, even Privet.

"That's contempt, Countryman," the old Judge called down to Gramps. But take your twenty dollars back. It did my heart good."

That story's told more often than the other two, I guess. It and the first Privet story are my favorites. Funny, I always said your grandfather was slow to anger. It's the remembrance I have of Gramps, and all his friends told me the same thing. Slow to anger and terrible in his fury, like some giant among pygmies. Those stories don't seem to suggest it, though, do they?

How he loved old Billy, and young Billy too. I don't think I ever saw him strike an animal in anger, not a tame one. He loved that old hound Minnie more than most people, I suspect. She was the best rabbit dog in the county, and he was never the same after she died. He kept her outside all year long though. Can you imagine that? He didn't want any soft house dog, and Minnie and all her pups stayed outside come rain or snow in that specially made shed he built for them. Better made and warmer than the house, I sometimes thought. With three or four dogs in it, there wasn't much of a chill in even the dead of winter, and those dogs always got fed before we did--every morning.

He lived on the farm with Millie's grandson until he died. He wouldn't come into the city to stay, even when Doc White told him his heart couldn't take country life another six months.

"That's enough these days," he said to Doc. "I've got little left to do, and I'm in no great hurry to do it."

He'd tried to live with Gramma in the city for a year and had to give it up when he got too nervous. It must have been lonely out there those last months, lonely and frightening. They found him smiling, though. Dead four days and smiling.

CHAPTER XI
Love Story IV

not only canals and railroads were built then but reservoirs as well. it must have been hard changing the land like that, but he doesn't act as though it bothered him. mainly, he's concerned with gramma's health and her letters. which is, i guess, as it should be.

* * * *

Dunedin, N.Y.
April 7, 1913

My Darling, Darling Katy,

I have received only one letter as yet. I suppose you have all you can handle if they are all sick at your house. I will not get scared if I don't receive another letter. Who knows where Grant may leave them this time.

93

Mother's pigs are all dead. The last of them went last night. It was a shame, but there was nothing we could do.

Wilbur is up. He brought us a can of maple syrup. I hear he is after some young lady in Berlin, so I guess Matilda is going to get left at the church after all.

Good news, I hope. The contract has been let for the building of the Wilson-Pepper Dam. If I get a job on that with the team, I guess we will not need to worry about money anymore. I will be able to do much better than we expected.

If I do not get down early Sunday you will know I am stuck in the mud along the way. The roads are worse up this way than they have been in years.

Oh! Darling, I can hardly wait to see you. It seems a month since I last held you close. I do so want you near. I know I should have more courage to work harder were you with me.

Let nothing happen to you. Be careful and do not work hard. Take care not to get sick like the rest of the family.

A good hug and lots of kisses. xxxxx

Your loving sweetheart,

Arthur

* * * *

it didn't work out though. listen to this.

* * * *

Dunedin, N.Y.
June 22, 1913

My Darling, Darling Katy,

Boom! Bang! The dam job has proved a d--m failure.
Edgar has tried his hand. Tuesday one horse got his foot bruised
and was lamed. Edgar was not heavy enough to handle the job so
Father said he would put Billy to work and drive the team himself
Wednesday. This would have taken the only driving horse on the
place, and I would have had to see you as best I could on Sundays
because we could not drive Billy after he had worked so hard
through the week.

I told father he could not stand to drive a team, but he
thought he would. So Wednesday morning he started off with Billy,
and Edgar and I worked in the garden in the forenoon. In the
afternoon I cultivated potatoes with the lame horse and Edgar dug
worms for fishing.

Then about four o'clock Father came driving up. I came
down to the house and asked what was the matter. He said the
other old horse could not stand the dam work, and so he had
thrown it all up. They could get along as they d--n well pleased
with their dam job. He was through.

Well, I came near turning inside out, I was so tickled. I had been worrying all day about how I was to see you. When I heard Father had given up the job, I knew Billy was mine. I know we could have had more money in the fall, darling, but I would not have seen much of you. I don't think that I could have stood that.

Edgar and I caught three fish all last night. A big haul, hey? We are going for an all-day fishing trip tomorrow. We'll leave before breakfast so when you get this letter we'll be fishing.

I am going to Athens on the route Saturday. The Dunedin Boys are going to play ball at Hawk's Farm Saturday and want me to play with them, so it is me instead of Father to Athens. I will take my ball suit down to your house and leave it, then come back and change. Edgar is going with me.

I do admire Dick's grit and wish him great success as a married man. He certainly had an uphill fight to win the girl he loved, against hope most of the time. It is hard enough to wait when the girl you love loves you, much less to have the one you love say she does not love you.

It would kill me if ever you said such a thing. I don't think it would be lucky for the man who stood in my way if I caught him alone. But I don't have to worry about that anymore do I?

Can't you come over to the house for a while Saturday afternoon. If you do not, I will drive over and see you after the game. You will not care if I play ball first will you? You know how I like to play, and the Dunedin boys really need me.

If you cannot understand all this I will translate it for you Sunday. OK? All my love is yours, and I will never, never distrust you again, if you choose to call it that.

Edgar is waiting to go to bed, so I must close. Good night my love and let nothing worry you.

xxxxxxxxxxxxxxxxxxx Your loving Sweetheart, Arthur

* * * *

      lame horses? for some reason i have always thought they
were shot.
there are, somewhere, more letters about the dead pigs, and about
this time katherine was off gallivanting to berlin, much to arthur's
distaste. here's a letter i note--'horse lamed, teasing.'

* * * *

Dunedin, N.Y.
August 21, 1913

My Darling, Darling Katie,

      You will have to excuse me for writing short letters if I
must write five this week. It seems funny to address them all to
Berlin. I had one all addressed to Hawk's Farm before I realized
what I had done.

      I would like to know where you are tonight and what you

are doing. If it is possible, you want to enjoy yourself while you are away. I suppose you have a headache (am I right?) so I will not get a letter from you Wednesday.

How do you like Berlin? Would you like to stay there?

Don't forget to write me while you are down there, or I will not come after you on Sunday. I hope you will not get angry with your sister and have a fight with her. You should be able to live without fighting for one week if Lillian did for four.

You must be careful dear and not get hurt in any way while you are down there. I want you to enjoy yourself, but don't be reckless.

It is nine o'clock, and I have just come home and had supper. I think we will finish the field tomorrow if nothing happens.

I lamed another horse today, or rather he lamed himself because of me. I left him tied while I raked hay this afternoon and when I came to get him about four o'clock he was down and had rolled over a heap of stone. His feet were sticking up in the air and the halter was drawn tight around his neck. When I saw him I thought he was dead. Was I scared! Oh! No! I thought. When I got him up, he was lame in the same leg he was earlier when Edgar had him down. Thank God it was me no more. Father did not like it very well, but I guess he had heard me rave about not driving Billy in the woods, and he did not say anything about it when I hitched up this morning.

Mother says to tell you that your lace handkerchief was out on the toilet shelf--up in a book. Agnes found it after you went away.

Darling, I hope you will not think the less of me for what I confessed last night. It is nothing I can help now, and there is no danger of my trying anymore. Once, and a failure that time, proved an effective cure. I believe now, and I always have, that the hand of

98

God saved me. If I had gotten started, there is no telling where I would have stopped.

You know dear I never had anyone to love me until you did, and if I had gone wrong it would have harmed no one but myself. Now, you know I would not think of such a thing.

You little goose! You must not cry when I plague you a little. You know I don't mean anything when I talk as I did last night about Hattie Benchman and Edith. One of the hairs on your head is worth more to me than either of them, hair, head, body, and all.

I must close now or I will be writing a long letter. All my love is yours. Don't forget me while you are down there. Your loving sweetheart,

Arthur xxxxxxxxxx--

P.S. Don't get homesick until Sunday.

* * * *

how about that? he must close or else write a long letter? and hattie and edith too?

this wasn't the letter i was thinking of, however. the right one got lost in the pile. the lamed horse here was another incident. the date should have told me that.

notice the berlin thing? he's quite obviously worried and jealous. that, to some degree, accounts for hattie and edith, but i still wonder who was there.

the confessional bit is a little hard to understand but very endearing. it could have been a sexual conquest, just to let her know he doesn't come begging.

however, i doubt it.

men don't admit to failure, no matter what the kind or who the man. we won't let them. ever! more likely its a drinking episode again, the favorite sin of the teens and innocuous enough in moderation.

two later letters talk some of that, and one i especially like speaks of marriage and trust, no matter what the situation. it is, after all, possible. i'll read the temperance lectures first. they're short.

* * * *

Dunedin, N.Y.
October 26, 1913

My Darling, Darling Katie,

I will try to write tonight, but I was in Athens yesterday, and when I got back and finished the chores late, I found I had no stamps, and so I couldn't write. I intended to get stamps today, but it took all morning and afternoon for me to finish digging the potatoes. I dug fifteen barrels and picked them up today. It was the last for the year.

Father was all but up the flue today, and he did not help me one bit. It was seven before I got the chores done again, and I am tired enough to drop, so father will take this letter in the morning and mail it for me.

I got your postals Monday and Wednesday, but I thought you must be mad at me when I received no letter Tuesday. The other two were peaches though, and, yes, I will go to the temperance lecture.

Say, why didn't you tell me Sunday was my birthday. Twenty-three, imagine? I didn't know until I got your postal. None of the folks up here thought of it, so I did not get a licking. Some luck huh? It was the first time I've had so much on my mind that I forgot.

Hey, tell Mr. Johnie Poultrie I may be a tramp, but I am no bum. On second thought, it still has to be proven that I'm a tramp. I'll leave that to drinkers like himself.

If he or Mr. Wagner have anything else to say about my stopping under a public shed to get out of the rain last Sunday, I would thank them to say it to me. I don't care how many officers they bring out. I have friends enough in both Dunedin and Athens to prove that I am a peaceable citizen and not a public nuisance like some drinkers around these parts. Tell Johnie to put that in his pipe and smoke it, and if he is man enough to come to me, I have two full fists to hand him or anyone else who fails to mind his own business. The cuss of it is that I can't tell Johnie from Eddie unless I see them together, and I would not like to punch Eddie's face for what his good-for-nothing brother said.

Sears and Roebuck answered me yesterday. They got the money and will send us our furniture when it is packed.

I will get some stamps tomorrow night and write again when I return from the temperance lecture.

If it rains this Sunday excuse me, but bed will be my place. I do not care to be kicked out at seven o'clock and spend the night under a shed for any Poultrie living.

Your loving, loving Sweetheart,

Arthur

* * * *

lord! i've never had a birthday forgotten. can he really be serious?

* * * *

Dunedin, N.Y.
October 27, 1913

My Darling, Darling Katie,

You must not expect a long letter tonight for it is fifteen after eleven, and I have been up since half past four.

I just got home from the temperance lecture. It was simply a plain talk based on fact. Rum will ruin not only a man's life but those of his loved ones as well. I guess it's going to be a hard fight to keep liquor out of town this fall, but I know one vote the liquor men can't count on.

I wish you were here with me eating apples like we used to. Now, I have no little mouse to eat the seeds and so must throw them away.

I suppose Mrs. Poultrie will be back by now. If not I don't suppose you will leave to go home Sunday, so there will be no use in my coming down. I will be sad to break my record of not missing a Sunday though. I shall be glad when you are here with me, and I need not travel so far to see the only girl I do, or ever will, love.

Don't talk to me about staying over at your house anymore. Your father acted at though I bothered him last time. I would not do it again were I to die on the road.

Possibly it would be better for you and my folks if I did, for you all have to bear with me all too often. There are times when I am very tired and cross. Then I would just as soon fight as eat. You must make me good, for it hurts me to think that I might hurt you. I have no wings though, and you are not getting an angel.

Let people talk if they wish. As long as we love one another it cannot hurt us. Without our love, life would have no meaning.

I shall be glad when you are done at the Poultrie's. Then when I come to see you, I shall not have to leave so early. I was not getting the worth of my traveling when I had to leave so soon, it seems.

If you could not stand to have anyone speak ill of me, how could you stand and let a bum refer to me as a tramp? I suppose it was a good joke, and you laughed too.

It is now after twelve, and I must close. Your loving sweetheart,

103

Arthur

* * * *

      and the earlier letter on trust. it seems more appropriate
now that i remember the poultrie incident. i wonder just how much
she really hurt him? or did she?

* * * *

Dunedin, N.Y.
January 23, 1912

My Darling Katie,

      I arrived home at two o'clock. I walked from Stump's
Corners to the Ashokan Dam to keep from freezing. The cold took
hold of me more last night than ever before. It seemed in my very
bones. I did not drive very slow from Ashokan you bet for when I
got Billy in the barn he was nearly as wet as if he had been dunked
in a pond.

      Do not think me mad about the postals. I was just unable to
state my feelings about them. I had to wait awhile and think about
them all. It's not that I did not trust you. What hurt was my lack of
power to hold all of your thoughts, to make you love only me.
Nothing hurts a man more than to discover he is not the all-in-all to
the one he loves.

I do not care to send Mabel a postal. You know why I sent the other. I was a fool to send it under those circumstances. She is the last girl in the world I would ever care for. I never sent Mabel one postal because I felt anything for her. I sent them to please Agnes and plague mother more than anything else. I should never have let you know how I cared, but it seems I am unable to hide my feelings. I would have given anything in the world, save your love, to have hidden my hurt. But I could not. It cost me much in the end.

You little know how it felt when you said, "get mad if you please" and walked away from me. If I had died right then, it would have been welcome relief. I thought that you were disgusted with my selfishness. If you had let me leave feeling as I did then, it would have been a dear lesson for letting you see that I cared in the first place.

But you still loved me in spite of the fact that I had proved myself unworthy of you. You had done nothing to be forgiven for. If I had been the man you expected of me, neither of us would ever have been hurt.

Katherine, I love you just as much as ever, and trust you more. Nothing could ever turn that love, not even if, as I feared the other night, it had separated us forever. How fragile love is and how frightening. If you had allowed me to leave as I was last night, I am sure that neither you nor any of my friends would have looked upon my face again. Our love would have driven us apart. How strange.

Father and Mother got after me today. They asked what I was going to do. Father said I could stay home and have half of the profits next fall. Then, if I did not care to stay longer he would sell off the stock and farm and move down off his place. I could then go where I pleased.

If I wished to stay at home, he thought he could do well by

105

me. If I got married I need not be afraid to bring my wife back.

I told him that if I did get married, I should not like to live right in the family for Agnes and you would not get along very well.

He said that he would purchase furniture enough for us and we could have the house where the family now lives when he moved the first of April. I told him I guessed I would stay at home but did not know about getting married right away.

What do you think? I do not see what we can gain by waiting out the full year as we had planned. I wanted enough money to start keeping house in style, but if father will furnish the house, why wait? We certainly are not happy when we are apart. Every day seems a week to me. I don't want to press you, so if you want to wait the year just say so. I can stand it if you can. I want to please you more than anything else in the world so do not fear to speak your mind.

I am glad your Father did not speak to you about our tiff. I hope he will not. Let him say what he wished to me. I have your love. You have told me so, and that is enough. Any less would be too little, but no more is necessary.

Oh Katherine, I dream of a love which is forever, where people are not afraid, and there are only smiles to make you happy.

Tell Lillian that I guess she intended to forget my pencil but no matter. I will write as many letters as you, even if it is one every day. I will not be outdone in my love for you. I will do anything for you, and I will never question you again.

Do not lose sleep thinking that I will change from loving you. I could not change even if the world stopped moving.

Your loving, loving sweetheart,

Arthur

* * * *

    it seems almost absurd that he would apologize for so little, what does shakespeare say about lovers being fools?

    I wonder what it is like to be alone after you have been together for a long time? what is it like to give love and not receive it? and why, being loved, do we so capriciously refuse it?

    great aunt mattie was alone in that old house in berlin for so long after grandma's mother died. she was farmed out because grandma could barely take care of herself and lillian. i wonder if she felt that anyone loved her, both motherless and fatherless as she was.

    death, i suspect, is preferable to rejection.

CHAPTER XII
History V

Few, if any, ever care. How committed, how dedicated we are hardly depends upon how much we are loved. How much we are given, what's in it for us, is more usually the subtle compassion of our altruism.

Loneliness is the black hole wherein nothing escapes, and we cannot see ourselves because we are so totally ourselves without space between. It is variety, not love, for which the body lusts.

In sympathy (for our own dear flesh), we want not good pokes but different ones and would crucify our gentler loves upon the cross of self-content.

What dreadful punishment dear Anne suffered so that she might not suffer. There is no love so strong as the caprice of boredom. Given what he desired, Henry stopped loving. Katherine, properly regaled in loving Arthur's devotion, found Berlin a proper, nay, exquisite place in which to display herself and her superior position to the more impoverished society of a long absent sister.

Once satisfied, vanity has no need of love and will gladly lose it for entertainment's sake. Anne lost her life, Henry his health (among other things), Catherine her virtue (foolish Henry's foolish girl), Jebediah his lechery (if seldom thought of), and Katie and Arthur their simple trust, if ever it had been. All for the sake of a greater passion.

When is love ever true? Whenever has it ever, been so?

Wilson was elected in 1912 but hardly out of love, which causes equally both pain and joy, and thus there is neither justice nor discernible order in the way within which it is dispensed and accepted. Taft had been loved in '09 but failing a proper humility and gratefulness in later years, Teddy's passion withered upon one vine only to blossom upon another, only seemingly, more commodious stock. Wilson won, and would again. And thus the 'poor' farmer (Martin also thought himself so, although he owned one farm; rented one, had mortgages on two others, one rented, one unoccupied; was negotiating for the last stage route from Perrysville to Athens, a contract which he later won and lived well off of for most all his fading years; was executor for cousin Sarah's, on Katie's side, estate; and counted 5 horses, 12 milk cows, 47 sheep, 12 pigs, 53 chickens, 3 good hunting dogs, and 7 cats upon his occupied 125 acres of 'good?' up-country land; not to mention a wife and four children, sometimes present after their late teens). The poor farmer was thus abandoned by his century, a perceived fact he had long since decided upon, although he was not to feel the reality of its more lasting effects until the late '20's and even then had to share the virtues of his misfortune with the often superior suffering of the urban dispossessed throughout the thirties until Mr. Roosevelt's war (and Hitler's too and Atlee's too, etc.) saved all the world equally from love, boredom, and hunger in the exciting and colorful fantasy of American farmers (and mechanics, and shoe salesmen, and insurance agents, and soda jerks, and dime-store attendants) traveling to the far ends of the earth, not this time to save the world for democracy but to discover too late the remains of six million Jews, help the commies eat up half of Europe, learn to sing good German songs and feel gemutlekeit, and keep the chaste emperor (a biologist of sorts at heart) upon his throne even when all Japan was changing around him.

A prodigious task but not too great for American know-how, and even though Arthur failed to make either, prodigious fighter that he was, his sons contributed a full measure in the 2nd, if not the greater, war.

Death is indeed preferable to rejection except in those most common instances where hate rescues us from the appalling consequences of our previous vulnerability. We die for love in letters but hardly ever in the flesh. Love is ever where the action is, at least in this century. And who was the man who could not give up all and follow the master? Action, too, needs careful definition.

Arthur wished forgiveness for his untoward jealousy, but there seems no need for apology unless the love, so freely given in manner and consequence, was unreciprocated, Katherine's greed being not for love as much as for worship, if not that then at least to be left alone and not bothered by the lesser demands of love and lover.

"Trust me," said Kate.

"I do," begged Arthur in blissful submission.

"It doesn't suit my purpose," said Henry to Anne, he as king being accorded a terrible generosity of time and power which enabled him to speak the truth even when love and the superior deception of self-pity and shame would have denied such callous facts.

Unfortunately some loves must die. Others never do that never should have been. In either case, tragedy and heartbreak accounted for, we most often ignore what is freely given, it coming too cheaply and thus going unnoticed, depending upon its certain security, while vainly clutching to that which suits our lesser (or greater) vanity. Middle-aged men of forty or so are famous for such escapades, until now women (because of their peculiar environmental prohibitions) being unable to display themselves as fatuously and with such vainglorious self-indulgence.

Teddy R. came back from Africa in 1910 only to find Howard unworthy of his trust. If so great a love fail, what had Katie done to deserve poor Arthur's abject devotion? There'd been little trust in Harrisburg, Haymarket, and Homestead twenty odd years before. I often imagine Dionysus being torn apart by the lovers of Demeter, of all people. So the little New Jersey governor won, no Dionysus on the field to command the maenads, and Arthur showed himself the true and contrite heart before and beneath his pedestaled beauty, a position which she seems to have neither liked nor deserved. Such was the custom of the day.

Arthur, on the other hand, seems fully worthy of such

marginal prominence, at least at this point. A bully boy, Teddy would have loved him too; democrat of sorts in northern New York; and a sportsman of note; his humility was freely and honestly given. In 1910 (Teddy's camping sojourn) he socked a homer (the old cowhide was dead then) 635 feet, by fair measure of the Mt. Union boys, from the home plate of the new baseball field just off the college commons to the foundation stone of the then only partially constructed library annex which was in later years to house one of the finest collections of books, magazines, and scholarly articles devoted to animal husbandry to be found anywhere in the northeast, decades later the faculty still protesting "the country" when a raft of land-grant, mid-western, cow colleges had rendered them obviously mistaken.

In later years, too, the boys were all to come back in early summer, Arthur with his oldest son, the girls left at home with the old lady to can blueberries and the like, and all swore once more, attesting with due deliberation, each singly in solemn remonstrance, to the accuracy of their previous judgments, the unchanging nature of factual history, and the much-lamented, decline in the quality of modern ballplayers.

Arthur never played pro-ball; Katherine would not let him, competition being what it was and her teeth going bad (although not where it showed). In truth Arthur himself was probably not good enough, although the boys (then 45 and 47, and some even 49) all knew better. Six-hundred-fifty feet if the truth be known, they insisted, since Arthur always stood far back in the box, left foot far forward of the right and pulled the ball a country mile, its flight along the 3rd base line (if extended outward) stopped dead by the unusually high cornerstone before the ball could fairly touch the ground. Six-fifty at least. No doubt!

O, Teddy would have like him, and Gentleman Jim, too, and Diamond Jim, and Black-Jack, and Andy, and J.P. and the Babe. He was the kind of stuff old American was made of. The Fatherland's true spirit, but he never quite got his chance. A pro prospect for sure, if he'd gone to the city.
But Arthur wouldn't hear of it, and, out of love, Katherine was glad. No laundry, no stage-route from Perrysville to Athens (twice weekly at the end) which Martin cozzened so craftily and ran with

hired help those last years before he, too, old and tired, his wizened shoulders hanging slack and gaunt beside his always spare and sunken chest (but his eyes still burning as fiercely as ever), finally gave up the ghost to a second heart attack (the family curse) in '33, two years after his wife more peacefully found eternal rest in her own sleep, saying no good-byes, letting no one know, not even her husband who since '27 and his first attack had slept beside her only in another bed, so peacefully she left.

Not so with husband Martin who cursed the farm and its glacial stone-filled fields with every failing shudder. There was the milk route, and the stage line, and the odd sixty acres west of Dunedin near Long Lake, and "yes God almighty," the farm itself, Alexander's farm given by him not to be lost, even though Albert and Edgar might desert it. But not Arthur, not his first-born, while Arthur and Katherine sat in the drafty, old kitchen listening in caged silence to Martin in the bedroom (and remember what was happening in Germany in '33) as he fought the inevitability of his death with pop-eyed ardor. Arthur always remembered it. He had left all the children with Lillian, the oldest, at the south farm. Now Martin would not give up, lying there on the old, wooden, four-poster bed of Alexander Washington's, his father having, strangely enough for all his business success, been a man who forever spurned the Sears' and Wards' catalogues. So much, old Martin loved his live.

The old man did die, of course, and Hitler eventually did, in some way or another, and Henry too. All power has its limits. After all, syphilis follows power. It is the price the great pay for their various lusts, the secret gift the weak and timid offer up, out of love, so silently, as due recompense for the superior protection afforded them in their humility and obeisance.

Ah, just reward! And Arthur, as far as we know, remained faithful to Katie through forty years of storm and sun. One of the lucky ones?

CHAPTER XIII
Love Story V

      he really did have to be a fighter in order to marry gramma. sometimes, i think, we forget just how much. the courtship was very hard--for cousins i mean. to just admit that they loved one another, you know. and somewhere i've heard that they might not have been fifth cousins, but second or third. that close.

      here's another early letter. he must have had to put up with these things a very long time.

* * * *

Dunedin, N.Y.
December 12, 1912

My Dearest Katherine,

      I arrived home at half-past one this morning. It was cold. Cold as the devil, you bet, but I did not freeze thanks to your old, red-head stocking.

Mother would not take the kisses when I arrived. She said that she did not take kisses second-hand. Then I got mad and said that I did not give them so to anyone and that she did not have to, as I should like to keep them all for myself.

Mother wanted to know if your father asked me what I was down there for once again and what I would have told him if he had asked. I said I would have told him I came down to bring him some rabbits. She asked what my excuse would be next Sunday. I told her we were going to Jim's.

I told them about Lillian seeing a ghost, too. Now Agnes says she saw one last night because she sent you word she did not like you.

I needn't have told them anything, but I should not have been afraid to tell them everything if I had been of a mind to.

I showed them my cuff-links and then closed the box and sat it on the mantle. Some time in the forenoon Mother thought she would like to see the initials on them, but when she took the box down she found no cuff-links in it. When I came home from the woods she asked me what I had done with them. I said they were in the box. She looked again to make sure, but they were not there.

Then I knew that Agnes had done something with them, and I was some mad, you bet!

Mother was afraid that I was going to lay it to her for losing them, and she began to cry. I went back in the woods, though, to cool off, and sometime in the afternoon Aunt Net came over and found the cuff-links upon the mantle in a ring box where Agnes had put them. They are in their box again now, and I think it is understood that they are to stay there until I get ready to use them.

Katherine, you little know how lonely it is up here for me since you went home to stay. It is a great satisfaction, though, to

116

know that your love remains with me, and I cherish it above all the rest of the world. I know that I can love you always even though you are far away. You are with me always. I do not forget to think of you even when I am asleep. You are my dreams at night, and I wake myself saying "Katie" every morning.

Oh, if I could only be with you again every day, it would be near to heaven for me.

My love, my love, all my love is only for you my own darling Katherine.

Your devoted cousin,

Arthur

* * * *

here's another short one. i really should have read it first.

* * * *

i remember once a little boy loved me. or at least i call it love now. i was very mean to him. he would come around the

house every afternoon at three-thirty, right after school, stopping
only to change into his play clothes and leave his good, green
corduroy trousers at home. he was so funny. he had a nose too big
for his face, and when he was shy, as he always was, he would
follow me about the yard and play tag with me without ever being
brave enough to catch me. when he came close, and i never ran fast
for i knew him to be afraid and delighted in teasing him, he would
slow down for fear of bumping me and stare at the ground,
scratching the back of his ear and turning red as a beet.

"come, come, catch me" i would cry and stop still in my
tracks smoothing my skirt so that he could see the pretty lace
fringes on my slip.

but he could not. he would stop, too, look at the ground,
shuffle his feet and make snorting noises through his big nose that
made him look and sound for all matters like an old sow in the barn
pen.

i didn't like him, but because there was no one else, i never
chased him away.

"scat you piggy, scat," i would laugh at him and chase him
in turn back across the yard, slapping his shoulder or head just
enough that he would come back the next day. he was the only
child nearby my own age, and it was so lonely on the farm then.

one day, though, i remember it was summer and the
hollyhocks were in magnificent bloom down near the road, he came
by in the morning when i was out reading near the big lilac bush
that mother had to cut back the next year. since i was not expecting
him, he stole up on me from behind, then he bent down by me.

"trish," he called sharply near my ear, and when i turned
around in surprise, he kissed me quickly, hard upon the lips, then
ran a distance away.

i was so embarrassed. he had no right, and i pulled up my
skirt over my face and wept in it. i couldn't look at him, but i yelled
out, "billy bordlowe, you shouldn't. you're mean, billy bordlowe,
and my daddy'll get you for this. you'll be sorry."

"no he won't," billy called back, "my dad says kissin's all
right and nice, and that's what you've been wantin' me to do
anyway. i asked. you're just a little tease, dad says. like all girls. i
know, but i don't want to chase you no more. you don't make me

feel very nice, and it's too hard.

then he stooped and cocked his head and grunted like a pig again, his nose red and his eyes just narrow little slits, "i guess i'm sorry," he snorted, "it wasn't nothin' to ya, was it?"

we played many times after that, for years until he went away into the army, but billy never chased me again, and never kissed me, even when we were old enough that it mattered and he'd lost his baby fat and was much handsomer.

now i wonder--why did i treat him so? i think he truly loved me, and he gave me so much happiness, once.

of course i was only six--or seven--as i remember it, and he eight or nine. one can't be a bitch at seven.

can one?

listen to this letter.

* * * *

Dunedin, N. Y.
Dec. 8, 1912

Dearest Katherine,

For Heavens' sakes and for the love of one who never knew what love was before you, why do you not write? I have been to the Centre two nights now looking for a letter. Two nights!

It was the same old story both times. No letter.

It may be that you did not receive my letter. I left it on the table with two others to be mailed. When I came downstairs next morning all three were gone. I supposed that father had mailed

119

them. If you do not receive it by Sunday, I shall ask father about it.

No such chances with this one. Upstairs with me when I go to bed, and I shall rise early enough to mail it myself.

If you are sick, why have you not had Lillian tell me so I could come down? I worry much about you and do not know what to think. It may be you think I would not care if I did not hear from you. If you have any such thought get it out of your head. Is it not bad enough to go a whole week without seeing you? Now, am I not to hear from you?

I have not given up all hope. I shall go to the Centre tomorrow night. There must be something the trouble with you or you would not let me go so long without a letter. If I have done anything wrong, please don't punish me like this. You little know how I feel receiving no letter tonight.

I shall be down Sunday whether I receive a letter or not. If you can get Mr. Dunley to let you use his telephone, call me up at McCheney & Rifensburger's store at eight p.m. I will be there waiting. The store may be in the directory under Rick Cathari's name.

I will close now, hoping there's better luck for me tomorrow. If I were away at Mt. Union and you failed to write me when expected, I think I should go wild.

Your most loving and devoted cousin,

Arthur

* * * *

the poor dear. what a sad, cute letter. oh, she must have
been a cut-up. i mean, she was a seamstress at one time wasn't she?
well, anyway, listen to this next one a few weeks later.
women had much their way even then, i think.

* * * *

Dunedin, N.Y.
January 25, 1913

My Darling Katy,

    I am glad that you were not disgusted with me for having
made an ass of myself Sunday night.

    I did not think I would care if you sent other fellows
postals. It seems I did not know myself. I don't suppose I had a
right to care anyway. It was purely selfish on my part, now that I
am able to see it more clearly.

    Katy, I never cared for anyone the way I care for you. That
was why I acted so. If you want to send postals, don't let anything I
have said or done stop you. I may as well be broke of my
selfishness now as later. I will always love you. Nothing could keep
my whole heart from that.

Father keeps asking me what we are to do. I will not give him any answer until I see you. The matter will rest in your hands entirely.

We have had a little lamb and expect more soon. I have been cutting up firewood this week while father watches the sheep. I do not know what kind of a shepherd I will make when father goes to Athens.

You must not think ill of Tommie for what he says. He has so much trouble of his own that he finds it hard to watch anyone else enjoy themselves. I will be down to see you before Sunday afternoon. There is no danger of my waiting. I would come down in mid-week if it were possible. Look for me early.

People are anxious for me to attend the donation Saturday night, but I have sent all my good laundry to Athens and so have a good excuse to stay home. I would not wish to go without you. Going out and staying up half the night would be tiresome without you, but I would dance the night away in your company. What am I saying? You've known all this since Christmas night.

Agnes is a bit under the weather and groaning in my ear. She says to tell you that if she keeps on failing she will be dead by morning. I guess there is no danger of that. She has been to school all week.

I had an accident last night just as I was going to bed. I bumped my nose on the bedpost and peeled a piece of skin. You would have thought I'd been fighting if you'd seen me this morning. I won't tell you what I said when I hit the post. It was not my prayers, you can bank on that.

I'm sending you all the love and kisses that I would waste on someone else were I to go to the donation. It is more pleasure to me that I have only love which will always be true than a mob of girls to waste my attentions on. I have always dreamed of only one love, enduring and forever. If you were to be angry with me now, I should not care to live.

With my love, it is all that matters,

Arthur

* * * *

how blessedly simple. it's hard to believe these days that he really means what he says. it all sounds so hokey. and grandma just a little suffragette seamstress from the city, or at least she became one for a while after they were married.
mattie was part and parcel to the shirt-waist fire in1911, wasn't she? how like a good mystery it all is.
there is a letter here most like him. it's so convincing.
"god," yes, i put "god" on the outside of it. can you imagine that today? a man lost between earthly love and his god, like some old medieval morality. i can almost hear the gregorian chants now, rising from the moss-covered stones in some cobwebbed corner of lincolnshire or york.
but he was baptist, wasn't he? square, one-room, wooden chapels for him, and white-washed shingles.

* * * *

Dunedin, N. Y.
February 22, 1913

My Darling Katie,

I hope this letter will find you well again. I should like to have come down to see you today, but business before pleasure. I have been on the go since six o'clock what with the morning chores and working in the woods.

Albert helped me yesterday and this afternoon, but he had to help Aunt Jessica's folks this forenoon. One of the girls has the pink-eye and the other is too lame to walk.

We have another lamb. Old Bess dropped a little George Washington today.

I have my brown suit home again, but I do not think I have a clean collar to wear with it. Can I come in a dirty one or shall I stay home? It will do you no good to refuse me. I would come anyway. It is hard enough to stay at home when I have to. I hope you will be well enough Sunday to take a ride if nothing else. But if we ride, there will be more for me I guess.

I suppose Angie and Ray have been over to see you every day. It would be just payment, seeing as how you help so when they are sick. I hope no one saw me acting as nurse the other night. I do not wish any more stories to be told about us. I should like to be your nurse always as long as you would not be sick.

Don't let Lillian take that temperance book to church until I finish reading it. I meant to fetch it home with me but forgot.

I did not get the grip from being down last week, so don't worry. Did you finish eating your pickles? I'll bring some more if you like.

Katie, I do love you so. I feel many times that I do not love you as much as you deserve, but if I do not, it will be forever impossible for me to love anyone else more.

It almost seems as if I am placing you before my God. You insist upon my being with you when I should be in church. I do as you wish of me instead of my duty to my God. What else is that if not pleasing you first.

I love you enough to do anything you wish. And I will do so regardless of all else. You asked me if I did not pray. I do, but God says if you break one commandment you break them all.

Do not be angry or hurt. I find no fault with you. Before my eyes you are faultless. I only say this to make the position you place me in clear to you. You wish me to be good and to pray, still you insist upon coming first. I do not begrudge it, but when I said I should attend Sunday school and church you acted as if I were doing it to avoid seeing you.

You must know better. I said nothing then because I wished to prove my love by doing whatever you asked. I will be down Sunday as usual. I do not wish to offend you and would rather lose anything than your love. But there are things you must not continue to ask.

I know you have meant no harm in your requests of me, but we do not see alike on spiritual matters. You only ask me to come down early Sunday mornings because you love me and want me near you as long as possible, which is short enough. I agree.

The time is coming, though, when we can be near each other always. Then we must make up for our present mistakes. I will pray if you wish. There is need enough for it. I hope that you will not forget to pray for me.

Gosh, it is eleven-thirty already and I must close now. I wish you were here. Hug yourself for me. I will take kisses enough when I see you Sunday.

Your loving, loving sweetheart,

Arthur
xxxxxxxxxxxxxxxxxxxxxxx

* * * *

    the lecture is as unlike him as a farmer might be. it suggests something of the grandfather i remember, so strong, red-faced, and stern. but he, too, was a gentle man. those were, i think, gentler times in some very absolute ways, and then too, love often makes fools of us all.

    he's very practical about sin, isn't he? 'later,' he says. but later he really did start to have things to repent. love does such.

    remember great-aunt jessica, how much she suffered and how much she willed it? we can't take happiness when it is offered. and we accept little weakness in others.

    but that's really not so, is it? all people possess within themselves their own salvation. It is only when we forget to touch one another tenderly that we fail to hold it. isn't that right?

    he wasn't greedy, not really, nor was she. he seems quite wise for his age.

    here's a last letter on the subject, at least for the time being. it was written much later in the year. do you think it lacks tenderness?

* * * *

Dunedin, N. Y.
August 16, 1913

My Darling, Darling Katie,

I received both your letters. Two letters! You must have
had a writing fit. The more the better though. Just don't write two
days in succession and then forget about me the rest of the week.
Alone up here, your letters are like life to me, and I am so greedy
that I want to be in your thoughts all the time.

I can come down Sunday, but I'll be driving Tom. Billy's leg
is a little better, but he will not be in shape for work for at least two
weeks.

You must come back with me or I will be angry (and I
know you wouldn't want to chance that). Why can't Mattie and the
children stay overnight here? They would not have such a long
drive the next day. I should think it would tire the little ones half to
death to ride all the way from Hawk's Farm to Berlin in one day.

Dear, I really am glad you are going to take a vacation. It
will do you good. There is little more than four months left to me in
which to prepare for you, and so I will not be able to vacation.
Since you are going away, I think I will go to the picnic Saturday
though. I know you will not mind. I didn't care such about the
picnic, but the Dunedin boys play ball with Perrysville that
afternoon, and they want me with them. It may be I can regain
some of the popularity I lost by doing as you bid me and thus
disappointing the team. If father thinks he can manage in Athens

without me Saturday, I will be with the boys. Perrysville has defeated Berlin in a series of seven games, and we are anxious to see what we can do against them.

I don't see where I am to get much rest this winter (I suspect you'll see to that if I don't). It will be work for me then as in the summer. It will take all I can get these next months just to start keeping house, and then most likely I will have to be sparing with our money. I will have to work hard if we are to live at all decently for as much as we might like, we cannot exist on love alone.

I don't care. As long as I can see you every day and be with you for the rest of my life, I will work without stopping if need be.

Mother and Agnes went to the picnic today. They said Esta West was asking about me. Mother told her I did not go out much anymore. She said that I was mostly attracted toward Hawk's Farm these days. Mother was right.

I guess Esta would not mind if it were somewhere else, but she had her chance and threw it away. Now there is but one girl in the world for me, and you know who she is.

All my love to you. Will I be good? Yes. But only if you come up to visit in September.

Your loving Sweetheart,

Arthur

* * * *

128

he will be good? but only if he's given the chance to be bad. how sweet. how like him. only one girl in the world, but esta could have made two. and then how many more?

what happens when we stop loving? to love only one person and never another must be a great privilege. so few are capable of it, especially nowadays.

then to have the dream taken from us? how terrible: not to have lost the love but to be denied the dream; to know that love can never be the same again not because we no longer dream but because time and space conjoin against us all, and callouses cover the soul with an adamantine hardness that no amount of future tenderness can soften.

each act is singular in itself and once committed is immutable. isn't it?

i wonder how much he really cared for esta, or if he might have really loved her?

how are the lucky ones lucky? or do we punish lovers and ourselves and so reap only the just harvest of our own self-indulgence? i know very little and know few who know more. i would have said yes to him too. the price was little to pay.

CHAPTER XIV
History VI

Of all things important and necessary to man, most specifically modern man, most absolute, are love and money. Of these two dispensations, more or less according to definition, the most essential is love. And money assures its continuance.

By love, of course, we must denote something more than just sex--pure, or pure sex (both phrases fail to depict with absolute accuracy the empirical nature of the act and wrap about themselves a certain moral or ethical ambiguity which often descends to no more than cultural etiquette and aesthetics). A certain redundancy in human affairs, naive of course, but necessarily so if order is to be discovered out of chaos (that is to say, pattern traced where before there was none), a certain redundancy assures us that we are human. Indeed the nature of sin being what it is, we must not only endure but verily enjoy and lust after it if ever we are to gain heaven. Which, of course, we may not, quite rightly, attain.

"Oh, happy, happy sin." And God, himself, remains our silent, meek accomplice in this never-ending cycle of pleasurable damnation.

It is natural for man to lust, as Anne surely knew, or found so at a very early age. It is, too, quite natural for women to lecherously fornicate, although, culture-bound as they are and without the real power (both physical and economic) for overt, aggressive action, they have more often sold themselves as wives and whores (the accepted epithet is 'mistress') to the drinkers and gamblers, thus breeding passion out of bed and lies in it, in and out of the act proper.

The courtship structure of western-man provides an excellent, if somewhat shabby, case in point. Poor Arthur, dear Henry's none-to-royal and many-times-removed relative, had not the prerogatives of uncircumscribed authority. In her need and most absolute dependency, Anne had found it necessary to give of her passion unreservedly. Katherine could be, and was, more chary of her favors. Arthur thus suffered with his little, latter-day suffragette and found, or made the best of his situation as we all do by castigating himself quite righteously and rightly, the covetous nature of his own greedy love.

Katie was a seamstress, or at least had been so earlier within her as yet still young life (remember the Shirt-Waist Fire of 1911). She was thus, if purely out of academic passion, much beloved of Samuel Gompers, a knight and chivalrous man of labor who came not riding out of the Golden West but marching and trudging up from and upon the sewers, gutters, pavement, and streets of the East, loving and giving with loss of self for those he believed, indeed, knew to be, downtrodden and oppressed. So he was, if unknown by them both, a comrade in arms to farmer as well as seamstress, Arthur all along wishing fervently for Katie to quit her job, whichever one it might be at the time, and cultivate the more seemly (and comely) habits of a country matron.

Genteel Esta, notwithstanding, ran off in '21, quite happily as it turned out, with a Florsheim shoe salesman from Castleton (on the Hudson) who failed to visit upon her all-to-willing body six kids and forty years of backbreaking servitude to ninety acres of upland glacial rock and balky milk cows. Rather he took her south to Poughkeepsie and then to Nyack and Tarrytown, growing with the company, and spending as he went, to Esta's all too evident delight, avoiding wars and lasting out the depression, sample-case in hand, until he finally retired with Esta, not old and fat but slim and trim and lovingly by his money-padded side, in '49 before the boom, to cheap land in Florida on the west coast where he made a killing by dabbling in real estate just to keep senility at bay, his three hundred thousand being snug and secure in G.M., Con. Ed., W.R. Grace, and other traditionally high yielding stocks that provided a modest hedge against inflation.

Hubert and Esta had no kids--ever--and died, seemingly happy, in their bed one night in '73, he of a stroke and she of an arrhythmic heart, after making love (i.e.: sex) on their king-sized bed (or so it looked), one last time -- just for the fun of it.

Arthur knew his women, however, and mention of Esta never failed in later years to get Katie's gumption up (so he would put it) like a banty hen. She was a fighter too, as should be obvious, and did not deny him the kisses which a jealous mother horded to such ill-effect.

There is a picture of Esta, standing seriously, but open-mouthed, beside her Hubert. The hat is white, wide brimmed, and gracious, decorated with feathers on top. Her dress, equally white and wholesome, fulsome too about the bosom with intricate crewel work around the neck and down between the breasts, is classic Edwardian, bell-shaped or hour-glass (as suits one's fetish), hip snug but billowing, only slightly, just above two well-turned ankles. So comely and of genteel deportment she was.

But all is lost with time. Hubert sits heavy-jowled, laden with the sententiousness of post-Edwardian reflection. The chair is quite too large, and his clothes envelope his all-too-slight body in leaden wooliness. He seems uncomfortable, his hands hanging loosely, disjointed and cumbersome above his baggy knees. Already, his hair recedes far back over his brow and his eyes peer outward with hardened wisdom from beneath a lined and deeply furrowed forehead. His eyes will never move from that camera center; they are fastened to it equally in fear and rage. His trousers, easily four sizes too large, drop straight without folds along his absurdly short calves, allowing only his half-unshined, high-top, work boots to show beneath their voluminous cuffs. He is all in gray, save for the high, starched, white collar within which his neck roams freely.

Such as this was loved--and forever at that--by a wide-hipped, thin-waisted, large assed belle-of-the-Dunedin-ball in

1916 and 17, just before and after the war bore all our brave young boys away to greater passion and midnight rendezvous' with an even more inevitable mistress.

The calloused soul is hardly so out of love that it cannot love itself and those that render it service. We sit and wait because we fear the consequences of a possibly more importunate act. Thus conscience does indeed make cowards of us all in love as well as hate: or lust or greed or envy or covetousness or any other of the several ungenerous venialties with which we amuse our fearsome spirits.

Arthur never did go to the picnic or any of the profusion of spring and summer donations which dotted the land before planting and harvest and so brought to both seasons a somewhat more difficult redemption for the true and faithful. But many times thereafter, in the years that came (and went, he said, all too quickly), he stood, horse-shoe in hand, pitching from the open end with slightly more than half a turn for a ringer every time, or every other time, or every third time but certainly more often than Mark Stringer or Harry Gateswell, both of whom tied way behind for second best in the county, horse-shoe pitching being one of the few manly arts which a proud and garrulous Katie, sitting proudly over her needlework, allowed her faithful and so fortunate Arthur.

The years were good to them. The courtship ended with a modicum of success, if seven children, six finally raised to adulthood, is any sure and accurate measurement. Arthur cherished dear Katie's love and came to love her all the more as she grew fat and tired and heavy-bosomed. The rose bush in the front yard was planted, and it quickly outstripped the little wire fence that Arthur placed around it to keep away the dogs. After that, no fence was needed since the bush could produce more shoots faster than the animals could urinate them away.

Dunedin grew too, like Arthur and Kate, out of jealousy and self-indulgence and an impassioned, if less private, love of its own god. The stage line died, eventually, the rolling stock growing old, the boys leaving for town or elsewhere. The inevitable decline of its importance, even in the hinterlands, was due to the railroads as the New York Central ate up the Hoyner Spur and ran a new track from Athens through Hawks' Farm and Perrysville thence under (in a miracle of modern technology) the more benign parts of the Taconic to Williamston and Adams, all this before the war, the war's end and sizzling (if not roaring and they did) twenties eventually making the venture a bad bet as upstate farming increasingly proved unprofitable in a big way, and the Central wrote off the line early on after its completion thus gaining an immediate tax benefit with which it happily brought about the last rites of the Erie Canal (and subsystems) in Ohio, Indiana, and Illinois.

Dunedin, itself, like Athens after the great storm of '17, ceased to grow as quickly as the boys might have wished. Athens--the "Whore of the Hudson" some said, and who would not have believed it what with the shirt factories strewn up and down the river's shore, dirty and grimy amidst the increasing blackness of smokestack and sewer discharge.

"A whore's a whore and the more honest woman at that," old syphilitic Henry once gasped between greasy chicken legs and green hock, "and in her honesty, my favorite sport."

Well said! And thus a lack of conscience does make brave men of us all. All the more-so was corpulent and towering Henry who, brave to begin with, having had the luck to be born into it, ate men and women up alike just for the fun of it (in conscience) while Saturn turned only slowly on its monumental exis, a necessary act in space if a body is to keep its way, yet necessary only for those of us with the courage (and ability enough) to defend our own small piece of it.

"She sells her favors by the pound (a pun)," he continued, "and so you must stick to it (another pun, the age being inordinately fond of them) or lose your way by inches, long enough" (he pressed his luck).

Whore or lecher-like both, the city knew or learned soon enough its own worth, a certain advantage afforded the profession and its more certain rewards. One hundred thousand souls plied Athens' streets by 1920, after the war when the boys were home at last, "God Save em." One hundred thousand! That was twenty thousand more than in 1900 and two thousand more than in 1950, the mid-century census delimiting with poignant objectivity the unduly and tragically protracted climax of a once increasing but soon parochial mid-river civilization.

Jews had come, after the Dutch and English a century before, and Irish and Italians (the Catholics overwhelmed the place with icons and "Holy Mary's") and eventually Negroes, who were all right as long as there weren't too many and they remained in their place which was conveniently in South Athens, along the river, down with, but not among, the countless Italians who built large, ornate Gothic churches which soon dirtied to a stolid liturgical gray and so shepherded with prudent and monumental love the rickety, wooden two-storied, slate-roofed apartment buildings all around them in which their ever-faithful parishioners choose to abide during those hours when the women were not at prayer and their husbands (during the 20's) were not running liquor in from Canada or the coast.

Across the river, like a good whore, the city fostered more diversity. Ball bearing plants and steel mills, coke factories, catalogue warehouses, more shirt factories, and later even an RCA record-pressing plant sprung up in due rabbit fashion as fast as supple thighs could hop from one century to another. But by the turn, the old Erie Canal had seen its best days, and Schenectady had gotten G.E., due to the shirt mills' fear of losing their cheap labor. Athens calcified into a seemingly vigorous old age, saved from early senescence by the tendency of New York boys to come north for a vacation when the heat was on in the Big Apple.

The social order remained stable, its pattern blessedly clarified and reinforced by the spiritual geography of the place: Niggers and Wops on ten blocks of flatlands, south along the east bank of the river from 1st Street to Constitution in the midtown business district, a total of fifty six blocks north-south; Micks from Constitution north to 101st Street, the ten blocks width remaining steady until the hills cut into it at 86th where the Perrysville Road began and chopped two whole blocks off the habitat until restored in North Athens at 126th Street, there widening to fourteen mellifluous blocks of Welsh and Yorkshire Protestants, not rich but good Methodists and Presbyterians, all of whom lived in simple harmony above the factories and grime but still below the hills which housed on their steep and rutted flanks, from Constitution to 118th Street, the less fortunate of white protestants who were neither able to afford their own small cottage in the north along the east bank nor climb higher to the top of the hills where doctors, lawyers, college teachers (an allowable dignity), pharmacists, shopkeepers, bankers, upper-management personnel, politicians, the Jews (kikes), and one small pocket of mixed Irish and Italian Catholics (two blocks from Perrysville Road north) held sway, and so they lived in rented circumspection, dreaming of the day when Stallings Avenue and North Lake Lane might be theirs, a halcyon event which all six of Arthur and Katie's living children were to claim to a greater or lesser degree, their older, country kinfolk never achieving such distinction, Arthur's two townhouses on 110th Street and 4th Avenue, usually rented and always at least with boarders, being as far up on both vertical and horizontal planes as the old folks ever got.

Oh, the old place is there yet Teddy boy. Bully for you and to hell with Woody and all his be-spectacled good intentions.

CHAPTER XV
PORTRAIT IV

Of the girls, Sarah Anne and Jessie were the wildest and Lillian the luckiest. Dad loved them all, although sometimes it might not have seemed so. Maybe often it didn't seem so. But then, he was never one for being easy on a body.

Lillian never got much of a tailing, but then, Lillian was the oldest and minded well, and like Martin the youngest, she was her father's favorite for a good many years.

I remember him often on warm summer evenings, the crickets chirping so loudly you couldn't hear yourself think and the sun having just set behind the shimmering hills in a blaze of furnace red, him walking out onto the front porch, being careful not to let the screen door slam and startle Grandma who was still doing dishes, and sitting himself down in his old straight-slatted rocking chair to wait for Lillian's appearance. She would come--after Ma had finished the last of the flatware and let her go--fifteen or twenty minutes later, the lap of her gingham dress soiled with dish water and her wet curls smoothed back behind her absurdly tiny ears, come almost carelessly out the door, she too never letting it slam, and plop herself down on the wooden deck with an exaggerated nonchalance, her feet hanging, but for an inch or two, almost to the ground.

Maybe that's why Sarah Anne and Jessie turned out so

obstreperous, they never had Lillian's cleverness abut them and in later years would invariably come home wearing lipstick even after Gramps had told them "never in his house," and they had been scrupulously careful about leaving early in the evening without any on.

Lillian never wore it until after the old man died, and she always knew how to get what she wanted out of him.

Gramps would wait for her, rocking back and forth, making out like he didn't care, but eventually the minutes would get him and he'd call out to her.

"A penny for your thoughts young Miss Priss," he'd say, still leafing through the old Farmer's Almanac and not looking at her as he rocked.

I'd scrooch back into a corner and continue to whittle as I listened to them.

"And why not a nickle, Paw?" Lillian would say staring straight out past the rose bush which was in full bloom, its pungent redolence invading the house on the moist night air. Then Lil would kick her feet against the side slats of the porch and give a real long sigh while leaning back on her elbows.

"Those shoes'll last a darn sight longer if you don't use 'em fer hammers," he'd say.

"Sorry Paw," and Lil would stop.

Then in a bit Gramp wouldn't be able to take the tension. "And ain't you got anything better to do then just sit there on your rear and stare at the dark?"

"Ain't dark yet, Paw-----and besides I'm jus' dreamin."

That always got him, and Lil knew it. She'd always wait until just the right moment for that one. "Jus dreamin," as if he didn't know, and she already waiting for him to ask.

"Bout what?" he'd say, finally. Pa never gave up easily, and the rocker would creak back and forth at the same steady pace.

"Things"

"Things?"

"Jus things."

"Like what?"

"Oh, like nothin. Jus things."

Then Pa would have had too much of it all. "Damn you Mis

140

Smarty Britches." If I have to get up and come over there before you answer me with a civil tongue, you might find a tailin for your troubles." He always said it like that but never stopped the lazy motion of his rocker, and Lil always knew when to quit. It was her genius.

She'd stop kicking and turn to look at him with that smile on her face she always knew worked. "Oh, I was only kiddin Paw," she'd laugh, then hold her legs up high, clasp her knees and turn round on her butt to face him. "I was only funnin."

Well, you'd try the Lord's own patience," he'd growl as if hurt by how lightly she'd taken him.

"But I can't tell Paw. Not here." And she'd stretch her neck around, look cute at me and Sarah Anne, and stick out her tongue when Paw couldn't see.

"Not even your own father, I suppose?"

Then the game was over. She'd captured him?

"You want me to Paw? Really?" Lil would look slyly back at him, purse up her lips and make eyes. "I could whisper it Paw, couldn't I" Would you like that?

Pa wouldn't answer but just keep on rocking. He always maintained some dignity even in defeat. But soon Lil would get up, tip-toe over to him softly, and then crawl up into his lap. Pa's arm would somehow drop down over her shoulder, and she'd pretend to whisper in his ear even though we all knew she had nothing to tell him.

And there they'd stay, rocking deep in the rhythm of the day's last waking, Sarah and me staring sleepy-eyed at the two of them, the purple sun a smaller and ever deeper bruise among the darkened hills - until Ma came out and would wake us all and make us hightail it into bed, 'cause work came early the next morning.

CHAPTER XVI
Love Story VI

some letters remain forever unopened or at least unread, or at least should be so.

* * * *

Dunedin, New York
April 10, 1913

My Darling, Darling, Darling Katie,

I arrived home at half past two after a delightful ride.

You should have seen the wagon. Father asked me if I had left any dirt on the road, and I was like to admit he was more right than wrong.

I got about four hours sleep and would not have got up but for sending that skunk's grease. Mother sent about half of what we had. I told Grant to put it on the back of the stagecoach and leave it in the mail box. If the Poultrie's didn't get it, it was not my fault.

Mother thought the cloth very nice, and Agnes said you would have to collect your five cents of me.

Say, don't spend anymore money this week! I have your purse in my pocket, so I guess there is no danger. If you think it is not safe with me, I can send it down by the stage. I do not expect to go to Athens this week, so I could not spend it even if I wished to.

We have been having a wash day here today for fair. We got all the colored cloth washed and dried, but it will take another day for the white.

I went and laid down for a nap after dinner. I had just got fairly sleepy when I heard Father and Mother quarreling over who would empty the last wash water. Mother wanted it emptied right away, and Father wanted it left so he could mop with it later. I thought I would have to get up and keep them apart, but at last Father gave in and emptied the water. I heard him slam the pail in the house and yank the washing machine across the floor before I fell asleep. By the time I woke, he had hitched up old Billy and gone to Ed Hill's.

I don't know but what he was real mad. I went to bed. If he doesn't like the way I do things, he will have to get someone he does like. That is all there is to it and all I ask of any of them.

Katie, I don't know how you are going to make a bad egg good. I guess you will find me a hopeless case. The better I intend to be, the worse I am. So what is a fellow to do?

They say what is bred in the bone can't be beat out of the flesh. I guess my trying to be good is like a man trying to stop drinking. You'll have to make allowance for me.

144

I know I can be good though. But by now you would think I acted mighty strange if I was, wouldn't you? Perhaps you would even think I didn't care for you anymore.

If I must, I will be good. So don't think me odd if I am a changed man this Sunday. I shall love you just as dearly as ever. Nothing could stop that. Don't ever fret about my love. It is and will be always yours.

I shall never stop coming to see you until you tell me to. And when you do that, you will shut the door to all my happiness. My whole world is you and my one desire is your happiness. If that is what you want of me, I will be good to make you happy.

I will do any thing for you my own true love.

Your loving, loving

Arthur

* * * *

Dunedin, New York
April 14, 1913

My Own True Love,

I am not worrying about your being true. I know if such is possible for anyone, you will be so. I must have been the one that has been such a bad egg. Were you surprised to find me so bad? Did you think I had wings started before I let you know how terrible I had once been?

Never mind, though, I have never been any worse than I

145

have told you, and I have something to be good for now. You are all the world to me. You already have my promise not to drink, so I suppose you will not worry over that anymore.

I guess you would not have had a very big time last night. Everyone did not get back until midnight. Agnes just laughed this morning at the table and would not say a thing about "my day in Athens." I told her I had not asked about it and that it seemed foolish for her to ask her own questions and then refuse to answer them.

I have sent the two hind wheels of my wagon down to the blacksmith shop to be fixed. If they are not done by Saturday, I don't know how I will get down to see you Sunday. If it is fair weather though, I will come even if I must walk all the way to Hawk's Farm barefoot. I will be ready to go to Athens any time you are.

Susannah sent you a postal. It's up here. She wants you to save her a piece of wedding cake, I guess she expects things to happen early. I only wish it were so.

Anyway, another month of this long, long year is half-gone. So we will both live in hope.

Agnes' birthday is tomorrow. She will get hers I warrant. I wish you were here to help. Then I would have hugs and kisses to spare.

We have two more lambs. One is for you. She's the prettiest little thing. She is red and white and spotted like a calf. In the line of lambs, she must be the funniest thing I've ever seen. And she's all yours.

Hoping to see you Sunday. With all my hugs and kisses. I remain, and hope to forever be, your loving loving xxxxxxxxxxxxxx

x Arthur xxxxxxxxxx

* * * *

Dunedin, New York
June 16, 1913

My Darling, Darling, Darling Katie,

xxx----xxxx-----I think I will write you a short letter. I'm all
tired out, and I know you will not expect another after those two
long ones last week.

I suppose you have been to Athens, so I will have to excuse
you if I do not get another one of your letters this week. If you do
write...well, I won't say what you should do, for you will not get
this in time for it to do any good.

The old sow had ten pigs last night. They were all alive--for
all of the old one being sick. She has however, already, lain on two
and killed them. I guess we will be able to save half-a-dozen if
nothing new sets in. I hope so, for I have let them worry me enough
that I should get at least three pigs as a reward.

Until today, I have not been able to plow since Monday.
Tomorrow, if it does not rain, I will finish plowing for this year.

Yesterday, Agnes and I took the dogs and drove up in the
woods on our old place to see if the strawberries were ripe for
picking yet. We got enough berries for a short cake, and the dogs
caught four woodchucks.

147

Wilbur is married at last. He was out here this forenoon and got his heifer and calf. Matilda was with him. Mother said that when they got ready to go they should come in the house first for tea. Then Wilbur said he would kiss all the girls before he left. He began with Matilda, and Mother said it looked too comical for anything to see them so. She is so small and he is too.

I guess it's not really so bad. Anyway, here are some verses that have been written about them. I don't know how they will sound to you, but they ought to make Wilbur smile when he hears them.

There was a man, both tall and great,
Who had long been looking for a mate,
And to the people's great surprise,
There came a Miss Peckman before his eyes.

The roads he rode to and fro,
And didn't know which way to go,

For he was lingering near to hear,
An answer from his dear sweet dear.

At last she gave her consent
And to the parson's at last they went.
The blushing maid and ironer, gay,
After the ceremony hiked away.

Now at last the dread deed is done,
And they are looking for a son
Content, we hope now, he will be,
And live in peace and harmony.

I told Wilbur what you said. He said thank you, but he thought the first would be a girl for he felt sick to his stomach this morning.

Hey! You said two weeks ago that we would go over to Sullivan's Sunday. But you have said nothing about it since. Should I come down? If you had told me earlier I would know whether to come down before or after dinner, to go or not to go if you could get away. As it is, I don't even know what to do. I guess I will come as usual, and we can go there or wait until another time.

Flint, the city engineer has moved up to the Centre. There is a hired girl but I guess you need not be scared for she is not like Web's daughter. Rotten luck!

Now don't be mad. You need not be afraid as far as I am concerned for you must know you are the only girl for me. I could never love another no matter how you used me. It's strange, but I have had a feeling for quite a while now that something was going to happen to make trouble between us. It may be just my imagination. I hope so.

If anything should ever happen though, remember that you are the only girl I have ever loved and would ever marry. If you should ever turn from me, I would never trust another. You are the only girl I have ever trusted. I have always had a fancy that women in general could not be trusted, but I believe I have found one in you. If I am not right we will both be losers, for I believe you care for me as much as I do for you.

I know I have disappointed you in more ways than one. In some ways I could not help it. In others I could have but did not. I do not know myself. I would like to please, but sometimes you seem perversely inclined not to be so.

I know you must have seen all this. I wish you hadn't. After this I will try and put aside more fancied slights and foolish pride and the like. I will be myself to you even if to no one else.

I would give a good deal to be as fine as I felt myself two years ago. I seem to get worse every day. Won't you help me instead of hinting that I must shut my eyes to things I know to be

149

wrong? Bad as I am, I will never consent to your doing what I know many are. If you marry me, you will have to be content to let come what may. If you think I will ever consent to you doing what Lillian came near doing you are mistaken. It must never come to that. God grant that we never have occasion for it. If you ever thought I would remain dumb as did Tommie, you were mistaken.

I must speak plainly for this must not be dallied about. It has been the cause of more trouble between us than any other thing could have caused.

Katie, we must settle this once and for all, before all is lost. I told you my mind once and you chose to have attacked this thing in different ways. We must settle it and never bring it up again. Either that or part forever.

The grave awaits us all, and if it must come to the last, the quicker I reach it the better. Better that than add a sin greater than any I have ever committed.

I know this letter will cause you grief. It cannot be helped. It is much better to speak now than to wait until it's too late. I don't know why you take the stand you do, but Heaven knows it's caused me enough pain to kill a dozen. You tell me not to let it trouble me, but how can I not?

I can say no more. I have said too much already I know. Let come what will I shall love you till the end of life itself. But please don't try to put this off any further. The end can only be the same one time or another.

I guess this letter is long enough. I wish I might send only the first half, but I can't. It will cost us too much to try and settle this thing in years to come.

I have half a notion to throw this letter into the stove, but that would not do I guess.

I don't know if you will want them after reading this letter, but if you do all my love, and hugs, and kisses are yours forever.

Your loving, loving, loving

xx Arthur xx

P.S. Please don't get angry at anything I have said. I might have been wrong in my thoughts.

* * * *

Dunedin, New York
June 26, 1913

My Darling, Darling Little Katie,

I had a hard time keeping awake last night. It was half past twelve when I arrived home. I guess I caught cold for my nose is stuffed up so I can hardly breathe. It was cold as the deuce before I got here.

You do not want to let worry you what I said about collecting for eggs and butter. You know you can trust me. If I wanted to be bad, I could be bad here as well as in Athens. I can be good and am when I am away from you. I know I am to blame for your weakness, but if we don't do anything worse than tease each other I guess we will live through it all. I am, always, just your foolish old bear. You know that.

I said what I did just to see if I could plague you. I know I promised to stop such things, but I can't help it at times. It seems just natural for me sometimes. Yesterday I did not plague you much though, for you know you can trust me anywhere, and I would not be apt to go cutting up when I have the love of the best little girl in the world. I have behaved myself before.

If you wish to go to the park on the Fourth, we will go. I told the Hawk's Farm boys I would play ball with them then if they wanted, but they can get along very well without me. They have enough men of their own. Let me know for sure if you want to go. If you wish to visit Sullivan's on Sunday, write and tell me.

By the way, I have your pocket book again. I guess you will not need it this week.

I found some more strawberries today and picked enough for two quarts after they were hulled. I wish you had been here tonight to eat shortcake. If I were coming down tomorrow I would bring enough for one.

You said that I should decide upon what I was to do before long. Actually, I will not know until after the heifers are sold. If I sell everything, I have enough to start keeping house properly. I hope to have enough so that I will not have to sell the sheep or the calf, but if I have to get rid of everything I will try to get a job in Athens I guess. If I come to Hawk's Farm to work, I should think it will not be on a farm if I can help it.

I will close now for Len and Ruth are over, and I cannot think when they are talking. I will go right to bed.

Goodnight my Darling. Sweet dream. I will write more next time.

Your loving, loving, loving,

xxxxxx Arthur xxxxxx

* * * * *

a last and later one follows.

* * * * *

Dunedin, New York
September 14, 1913

My Darling, Darling, Darling, Katie,

I guess this will beat all previous records. Two letters written in one day is going some. Hey?

I received your letter tonight when I arrived home. We didn't start out for Athens until nearly eight this morning and so it was after seven when we got home tonight.

I could not go to the prize fight because I had promised Herb Rawley I would work for him as soon as I could. He came for me yesterday, but I told him he would have to wait until Wednesday because of the Athens trip. If I had gone to the fight, I would have lost another day's work, so I thought it best to come home. I will have another chance to go with Edgar, so he can see one before the winter is over. I will have more time in November.

I thought I would not have much to do after a day's haying, but I don't see any difference. I work all the time and still there seems to be just as much to do as when I began. Oh well.

Our silverware came tonight. It is the same as mother's. It came by express and so cost forty cents more. I had not expected it for another month since I had not received the register receipt back yet.

Darling, you must not take it so to heart because you are a little naughty at times. I know you try to be good. I do too, but it is as you say. The more I promise positively to be good, the worse I am. It does seem that we ought to be good when we have such a little while to wait, but it seems that the nearer the time comes, you should be disgusted with me for not being able to be good and making you be good also. Especially when you have told me so often how I hurt you when I am not good. I am always ashamed of myself after I leave you for using you so.

It seems that if I love you as I believe I do, and knowing how you love me, that I could somehow keep from doing anything that could possibly harm you. And I do love you so! I will try, even though both good and bad seem to be born out of the same love for you. I will try.

Aunt Susannah has been sent for from New York. She is leaving next week, and she said I would have to come down and help her one day soon to get her things packed and stored so that we could put ours in the house once we get them. She will not be able to get the chamber ceiling fixed now that she has been called away on such short notice. I guess we will be able to manage somehow, though, won't we?

I would be content with just you and a place to sleep. Wouldn't you?

I guess we will have all the room we need, at least for the first three months. I bet those three will not be as long as these next three will be. My Darling, the nearer the time comes for you to be mine the more time seems to drag. If I did not have so much work to keep me busy, I think I might go wild.

I was up to the Democratic Primaries last night and guess what? I got nominated as a delegate to the Assembly Convention at Sand Lake. The caucus for the nominations of town officers will be held a week from Saturday night. I think I have a chance for Justice if not something better. I could have been appointed Inspector of Elections if I had taken the job. That would have barred me from running for office, however, so I declined. I don't suppose the Democratic ticket has a ghost of a chance to win in Dunedin, but we can at least give them a hell of a scare.

I wish you were going to Sand Lake with me. It will be some lonesome if I cannot get other delegates to go along. There are four of them so I might get lucky.

Mother got ten cans of tomatoes from those Edgar picked. She finished them today.

I found Lillian to bed when I arrived. She had the screen door hooked and I just slipped my hand through and unhooked it. When I got in the front room I found her just crawling out of your father's bedroom. She had a wash on the line and gave me a call down for breaking her slumber.

Then I got the jar and teased her about when she was going to pay up. "Eggs and butter and milk's expensive," I said. She said she did not have any money. Ha!

I guess she was not the only one in such shape for I did not have but thirty-cents and father would have been broke except he borrowed a dollar on the way down. I guess we took in about $10.00 today besides the five or more we trusted out.

155

I must close now Darling. I will have to get up early tomorrow morning to get up to Victor's by seven o'clock.

All my love is yours forever. After this I will see if I can be good. I know we should be. Love and kisses.

Your loving, loving, loving Sweetheart,

Arthur

xxxxxxxxxxxxxxxxxxxxxxxxxxx
x Love and Kisses x
xxxxxxxxxxxxxxxxxxxxxxxxxxx

CHAPTER XVII
Love Story VII

    remember gramps once saying, to you dad when he didn't know i was around, "joseph."

    you were the oldest boy, and i remember he would always be formal with you whenever he was teaching you about "family" business.

    "joseph, if you're old enough to get a girl in trouble then you're old enough to own up to it and take care of her."

    he never spoke about you, of course, old married man that you were, but of martin, the youngest--yes, i know, and of the boys, the most lovable too--which was forever getting him into trouble. i never found out which one gramps was talking about that particular time, but it really didn't matter.

    if you're old enough for one you're old enough for the other. i remember sneaking away with the rhythm of those words all around me. i whispered them in the hallway and then after i'd carefully cracked the big front door, just enough to squeeze out with only a small tear on the seam of my dress pocket when it caught on the latch, then i ran and jumped all across the front yard and into the near meadow.

    "if you're old enough to get a girl in trouble then you're old enough to own up to it."

    i was much too young to understand what gramps meant,

but he had said it so sententiously, with such gravity and adamantine seriousness beneath the thick, sunburnt swarth of his face that i knew it to be very important. it was as if the lines had been written upon the weathered furrows of his forehead and along the deep, scarlike creases of his cheek and jaw.

i became entranced with the sound, with the careful artlessness of grampa's speech. and i set out, all across the field to my favorite clump of rocks and seared birch trees; to improve upon it.

if you're old enough to , you're old enough to .
if you're old enough to talk, you're old enough to listen.
if you're old enough to play, you're old enough to work.
if you're old enough to sing, you're old enough to dance.
if you're old enough to run, you're old enough to fly.
if you're old enough to lie, you're old enough to be whipped.

and how many more? it was just like gramps. to sit you down, i mean. and to make you not only listen to, but repeat the catechism of his experience and wisdom. he knew his country to be great because it was good, and he felt that always. deep in his bones. old j.p. and john were not his friends, and the choice was his to make. teddy would not have been his friend had he known all there was to know. the country was the land--the trees and hills, the hard, unforgiving glacial rocks that would not surrender their sentinel stations to even the most sedulous and backbreaking attempts to remove them.

i'll always remember that mighty old rock (in the middle to the north corn field) i used to play on. it sat there, right in the middle of seven acres of corn, an enormous field for a new york hill farmer like gramps. and it always seemed to me a huge, dark, foreboding god, protective, possibly threatening, yet supremely huge and quiescent, there beneath the one small tree that had spouted out of its middle and was slowly growing taller, cracking the sovereign boulder into three distinct pieces as it did so.

until i found the birches, it was my haven, my refuge, in spite of all the times that gramps would chase me out of the field for ruining his corn. within those three great pieces of granite (i at least thought them so) i was secure and impregnable. i could even climb my tree to the lookout and search the horizon all around over the rustling stalks of corn. there was forest to the north, the curling ribbon of the old state road to the east, the farmhouse, barns, pens, and chicken-coop spread across the south and south west with old minnie and her pups forever scratching around the outhouse and garbage pit off the driveway, and finally to the west the cliff that dropped directly into the wild raspberry patch. i was impregnable within the crevices of my rock. no one could approach me, and i never felt lonely.

of course, i eventually outgrew the rock. i'll always remember how terribly disappointed i was to come back to it after four years of college and seven or eight, (all-totaled) of suburban life. at most it took a few minutes to walk across the field to where the rock lay short and dumpy. even the tree, not as tall as when i had known it, protruded hardly much above my head. i believe i found the boulders in the east field next to the birch woods when i became older--nine or ten--and discovered the unquestionable superiority of secrecy over clearly manifest power as a protection. no one ever knew where my sun-seared, pure-white birches were. and i never told.

uncle martin did marry not long after that, a matter of months i'm sure. her name was susanne, although he never speaks of her anymore, and he smiles less i think. at least at private times he does or when, as so often happens, the conversation swings away from him. and uncle martin, his gray hair straggling down over his ears, and the mustache he grew after his second marriage, untrimmed on his lip, will lean back almost imperceptibly into his chair, let his long, thin arms dangle over the bulky, squat arms of his overstuffed rocker and stare, rigid and frozen, for only a few moments, at the bare far wall of the living room.

there was a letter like that somewhere.
i remember it. here! on the envelope i have written "crying and incompatibility. feels himself poor."

* * * *

Dunedin, New York
September 4, 1913

My Own Darling, Darling, Darling...
 xxxxxKatie,

I came near freezing before I got home last night. It certainly makes a fellow think of winter. You don't know how I dread those Sunday night rides to come, all alone, when every minute I think I might fall asleep and not wake up until I find myself frozen stiff.

But Darling you are worth many such rides. I would make them every Sunday night for another winter if I had to.

It will be much pleasanter though to snooze by your side then to ride from Hawk's Farm to Dunedin every week with only Billy for company.

Dear you must not think any less of me because I cry once and a while. I've never cried over anyone else before. You have made a regular, big bleating calf of me. I could stand to have others speak ill of me but not you. It does hurt so Dear, even when at times you don't mean to.

It seems to me that often I am a nuisance to all around me. That I am always making trouble or hurting those that love me the most.

I try to do everything you wish of me. But there are times when you insist upon things I just cannot do, and when I say no, you get angry. I know how you love me, dear, and I love you. But there are times when I wish we had never known each other.

It seems to me that we may not be happy, and I would

rather be dead than make you unhappy for the rest of your life.

If you had never known me, you could have found someone who was in a position to do all the things I cannot. Then maybe you could have enjoyed your life.

I know you are not enjoying it now, and if we do not care for the same things, I cannot see how you are going to enjoy them after you are joined to me. I think the only thing we ever were united on is our love of flowers. I am glad you are going to have some, for they make home life more pleasant. But have you stopped to think of how many little pleasures you may have to sacrifice if you marry me? It drives me mad to think of all the many things you will want and not be able to have. I know you do not want to turn your back on me, but it is better that you know now and count the cost beforehand rather than wait until it is too late and reap only unhappiness.

I hope in time to be able to get you everything you want, but I can see only many long years of hard work before me in order to accomplish that goal.

I could be happy though, if only you were happy with me. Although I know I could never forget you or love another, I could go away where no one would ever hear from me again.

But I know that if you love me as I do you, you would only mourn for me and would not take the chance to get someone who could furnish you with horses and wagons and all the nice things that go to make life happy for a woman. I know I have no right to let you make yourself unhappy for me and without me. But would you be more unhappy with me and thus without all those things you want around you?

Katie, do you want a city man who can give you money and jewels, costly furniture, and a great house or a poor farmer who has to give only an undying love and a desire to make you happy? Oh, I wish you could be happy with me and not want what I cannot get for you. They say in the song "sometimes the silver cord will break." Sometimes, I think the cord will break that ties me to this world, and I will not have to fear anymore that you will not be happy with me.

Oh, this all seems muddled and distressed. These ramblings make no sense even to me, and I could cry now if I did not know how upset it would make you.

You need not come up next week if you don't want to--I mean if you cannot get away easily. I can take time to help mother do what is to be done, and what I cannot help her finish we can give to the pigs. I know you have to work hard, and I would rather let all my labour in raising these crops go down the pig's neck rather than overtire you and make you sick with a lot of unnecessary work.

I will not be through up at Herb Rawley's until Thursday. Then I will take the rest of the week to do whatever Father wants.

I got a half bushel of plums up at Herb's today. They cost me a dollar. I would have gotten half bushel for your father, but I knew it would only make more work for you, and then I did not know if he would want to pay 50 cents a peck. Herb told me where I could get some more blackberries. If Mother does not feel like bossing me around for a few days, I may get time to go for some more this week.

Well, I have written for an hour and a half. It is now nine o'clock. I got only four hours sleep last night and have worked hard today so you will have to excuse me from writing any longer.

Oh, Darling look before you leap and tell me of what you decide. If you think you can be happy with me and wait for time to bring the things of this world to us, you can rest assured of my undying love. You have all that, no matter what you decide. Don't count the cost to me. I can bear anything rather than see you unhappy.

My love is ever yours in life or death. Thank God I have a right to love you even if I cannot hope to have you.

Your loving sweetheart,

xArthurx

* * * *

crying! i can't imagine grampa crying. it's much to out of character. really! except when he laughed, i don't think I ever remember seeing him cry.

certainly their love affair didn't run smoothly, but why would anyone dare love as he does? it seems much too painful, and i wonder if she's worth it. he is only a farmer, and she must have made ridiculous demands to put him in such a state.

funny? i remember once, just after mom and dad moved to 114th street in athens, i was playing hopscotch down the block with patty hansen. i was new in the neighborhood and on my best behavior. patty was winning, so i didn't want to leave and seem like a bad sport even though i had to go to the bathroom very badly. every time patty would throw her stone i'd wish her to make it, and i'd crouch down, pull my skirt over my knees and hug my legs together hoping patty would go all the way.

she finally did, though it seemed like forever, especially the three times i deliberately missed my jump so that patty could finish and let me hurry home. then i excused myself, saying i'd be back soon and very jealous of patty winning because i knew that normally i could beat her easy. i ran down the old crumbling, slate sidewalks to the big brownstone where our apartment was.

163

i was horrified when i pulled on the big brass latch and found it locked. i called, but no one answered. then i jumped up and down, rubbed my knees together, and banged on the door with all my might. no one was home, even mrs. kilmer downstairs was out and she was the only grownup i knew as yet. then i didn't know what to do and started crying. grampa's was two blocks down the street and i knew i couldn't make it. i banged on the door some more and tried hard not to think about it, but it was no use. there were no bushes anywhere where i could go without being seen, and i was too old to go into the alley and hope i wasn't noticed.

I walked, and jumped, and squeezed my legs together. i sat down and stood up, and yelled for mom and dad, and cried some more. it all did no good. eventually i just sat down on the dirty stone steps, tucked my green plaid dress between my knees and tried hard as i could to hold back. i couldn't, of course, and i peed all over my dress and down my legs onto my white knee-highs and into my shoes. i felt wet and miserable, and i scootched up under the stone bannister, holding myself and hoping no one would ever see me again in all the world.

i don't know how long it was before gramps came, but when i heard him i just pressed myself harder into the brownstone and began to cry all the more. i was so ashamed. of all people i didn't want grampa to see me.

"good lord child, what's the matter?" i remember him saying, and then he reached down to pick me up. I cried even louder, kicked my feet, and pushed at him but it was useless. he picked me up in his thick, red-haired arms and discovered what was wrong without saying a word. then he began to laugh. i was mortified.

"don't laugh," i screamed, and kicked at him.

"but trish," he whispered, all-of-a-sudden very tender, "why didn't you come down to gramma's?"

"it was too far! and i don't know anybody here. and mommy and daddy and liz have left me. and mrs. kilmer was gone, and the alley was too bare. and i waited too long with patty hansen," i blurted without looking at him. "oh grampa i'm sorry. i won't do it again."

grampa began to laugh again, this time in big belly laughs

that joggled me in his wet arms and made me even more ashamed.

"don't laugh! don't laugh!" i screamed. "why are you laughing?" it's not funny," and i buried my head even deeper into his rough, red wool of his jacket.

"why trish," he said to me, very tenderly with tears streaming down his face and onto my hand which had been pushing him away. "i'm sure you'll do it again, and quite often at that, with great satisfaction. and i'm laughing because i love you so."

he carried me down to gramma's and she got me some dry clothes, and the three of you came back a few minutes later from the grocery. i knew you had told me you were going, but i'd forgotten.

i remember that bumpy, joggling, wet ride, safe in grampa's big arms, pressed close into the thick, red wool of his shoulder, and i thought i'd never be as safe as i was then. ever again.

CHAPTER XVIII
PORTRAIT V

I'll always remember Dad and Lillian! Remember how tender he could be. Remember it, I guess, as much as Jessie's strapping. Lord that was a day, and Pa no moon-eyed lover then.

Jessie was full nineteen and staying on the farm with Grandpa to keep him company long after Grandma had been forced to live in town because of her heart condition. Fifteen years, and mostly apart, there's a love story for you. Grandpa coming in almost every day at first to see her. But in the end he couldn't abide the city and left it for good, except on holidays.

Well, Jessie was a young colt if ever there was one. headstrong and pretty, and if the two ever went together it was only to make dynamite more explosive. Jessie loved Dad, but she hated staying all alone up on the farm with him, cooking his meals, doing the housekeeping, canning for the winter, slopping the pigs, and all the other chores Grandma had always done as just a matter of course.

Yes, Jessie hated it, and she made no bones about it. She insisted upon going out after supper even on week nights, and in spite of all Gramp could do, the boys came calling for her night after night all that summer.

"God damn hounds sniffin around here again are they?" he would mutter whenever he heard Art Wickendom's Ford pickup bouncing over the rutted gravel driveway. He'd never like Art, and he liked it even less when Jessie up and married him a few years later. It was '44, near the end of the war, and the two of them together convinced Dad that Germans, "the huns" as he and Winston Churchill were fond of calling them, were not to be trusted.

"Aw, Pa, leave me be will you," Jessie had evidently hollered this particular night as she rushed out the door. Whether she ever heard Dad's admonition that she was to damn well have his breakfast ready no matter when she came home has been bandied about for years in the family. Dad always insisted that it was a rule of the household and that no daughter of his was going to ever ignore her duties to her own flesh and blood and get away with it.

As it turned out, he meant every word. Jessie got home real late. "Again," Dad always insisted years afterward. "About one in the morning," Jessie said, and that was late for Dad who was always in bed by ten and up by five.

Dad heard Jessie come in but said nothing until the next morning when he got up and there was no breakfast on the table for him. That was the last straw. He turned and marched through the parlor and up the hall stairs to Jessie's room. When he opened the door after no one answered his knocking, he found Jessie sprawled, half naked across the bed, "bare-assed and broad-beamed, like some Centre whore" he swore later to Grandma, though Jessie always insisted that she'd had her underwear still on.

"I was decent Ma, I really was," she blubbered later that night, "God Almighty, I was too drunk to take it off when I came in. I had to be decent."

That didn't matter none to Dad though. He stomped over to the bed, threw some bedding over Jessie and told her to have breakfast by the time he finished with the dogs.

"Aw, Pa, leave me alone," Jessie moaned and evidently rolled back atop the bed clothes.

"What? What'd you say girl?' Jessie said he'd already walked to the door when he heard her, and he stopped dead beneath the arch.

That should have been enough, but Jessie was still asleep, really, and she didn't take much notice. She just grabbed the pillow and hunkered into the bed some more. That was the very word Dad used "hunkered down." I can't much see her doing it, but that's what he said.

"God damn, Pa," Jessie whined through the pillow, "I ain't gonna get any damn breakfast. Just leave me alone will ya."

"Well, I'll be switched," Dad whispered. He had to have been shocked because there weren't any of us that ever had the courage to talk back to him like that except Jessie, and it didn't do her any good that morning.

Still, Dad might have said it, but Jessie was the one to get it. He stood in the doorway getting madder and madder, and when Jessie didn't move he just got more to fuming.

"Girl, get my breakfast!" he finally roared.

"Aw hell Pa, get it yourself," Jessie moaned back.

With that Dad unbuckled the wide black belt he always wore when working, even though his suspenders held up his trousers and he never needed it, and he walked over to Jessie's bed again. Without another word he doubled the belt over, grasped the buckle end, raised his arm, and let fly all over Jessie's all but bare back.

Well! Jessie screamed a lot and tried to get away. And well she might have too for the looks of her when we all saw her later in the day. Dad laid three or four good ones on her before she was able to get out of the bed, and then he chased her all over the room, grabbing a hold of her when she tried to run for the door and laying his belt all over her. Head, arms, back, legs. Dad beat her everywhere and didn't stop until Jessie was tight-up in a little ball on the floor just sobbing for him to stop.

He did. Eventually. But she was half dead by that time. Then he went over to the chest of drawers, pulled them open, snatched some clothes out, and dressed Jessie like a baby while she lay on the floor crying out every time he touched one of the ugly, red welts that were growing all over her.

After that Dad half-dragged and half-carried her out to the truck and drove her into town. By the time he arrived at the house on Fourth Avenue, Jessie's bruises were fire black and tender as raw meat. When Dad walked around the truck, opened the right hand door, and pulled her out, she screamed bloody murder. She either wouldn't or couldn't walk, I suspect a little of both, and he had to carry her up the porch steps and into the living room. He was getting madder all the time, because when he stopped in the middle of the floor, his dirty boots shed caked manure all over Grandma's new Persian carpet. Then he threw Jessie down at Ma's feet and yelled at the top of his voice.

"There's your young whore for you woman. She'd rather be out nights bitching than fixing me my breakfast so I can keep her in lipstick and silk stockings. No doubt! I would have thought you'd taught her better.
No matter. Such baggage is no daughter of mine."

With that he upped and walked out, leaving Grandma sitting upon the couch without so much as a minute to answer him. It took a full three months for the two of them to make it up, Jessie and Grandpa. And then it was only after Grandma had made two trips out to the farm, bad heart and all, to talk to him.

I'm sure he loved her though. Just as sure of it as if Jessie and he were sitting here today. He was no wife-beater and never laid a hand to Grandma as far as I know. He was normally so very gentle.
On a cold winter's night I saw him carry sick lambs back to the house cradled in those two trunk-thick arms of his as if they were sackfuls of feathers that might be crushed. He was often given to tears when any of us were hurt or sick, and he never hid his crying. He had no sense of shame about his emotions.

No, he just believed in the family, in its oneness and wholeness. It was always the center of his life. And the love affair that he and Grandma carried on through all those years after she moved for good to the city would make a great novel. We were everything to him, and he must have loved Jessie a lot to forgive her that following winter, up there alone in that icy kingdom of is. I remember, later, it took him five years to forgive Alex for not enlisting like Martin and me when WWII came along.

Oh, he could be a hard one. But no harder on any of us than he was forever upon himself.

CHAPTER XIX
HISTORY VII

A word to the possibly wise. It is always necessary to lie a little. It is often necessary to lie a lot. And upon increasingly less rare occasions, as we grow older and hopefully wiser, it is absolutely necessary to avoid, if possible, telling the truth. If, indeed, we know what the truth is.

A first lover, whether it is in the flesh or a red and black, plaid jacket, will tell you that, "it will be this way forever." A second, more experienced, more cleverly judicious in his assumed humility and honest individualism will give and require of you wordless consent: adult, wholly private, and tactfully considerate. But take a third to learn the more abundant consummation of desire, the austerity upon which our lives inevitably fall, even if we grow not wise and therefore remain happy.

"It will never--be--the same--again. "Never!" And this he will whisper to you in awful silence, filling the room with the dry cotton of old, old wine upon your lips, muting the floor with the thick, dull texture of worn Persian rugs, the walls hushed in darkness, the ceiling muffled in darkness, the flowered plants upon the windowsill, unseen, quivering behind the curvilinear solemnity of silken drapes. "It will never--be--the same! Never! Never again!"

And this when we are most alone. Unutterable within the dread stillness that follows love.

We pay for our pleasures always, and so surely Kate had solid precedents and did no wrong in expecting good Arthur to do the same; to take up his load and bear it manfully. "After all," Mother used to always say, in jest often, most often after two martinis before dinner on late, lazy summer afternoons when it was too hot to eat at five, or six, and the only civilized thing to do was invite the Rogers over, and the Fryes and Snooks and enjoy an eight o'clock dinner, begun at six, with chips and dip, hot sauce and shrimp (when you could get them), scallops, cold cuts, and hot mustard; beer for Hank Snook but Michelob, only the best. "After all," she would say, tittering a little by the third, the top button on her blouse tastefully askew but her lipstick as yet without a smear, "a wife's only a high class whore."

"Better paid," she meant, in the less obvious but more solid and longeval compensation of Eastlake Victorian beds, Picasso prints decorating the living room, sandstone fireplace rising into the ceiling, a well-stocked mahogany bar with inlaid leather, and Norman Rockwell in the kids' rooms.

Mother forever read The Saturday Evening Post as did Kate, late in her life after Arthur was gone, read it, leafing over the pages, always carefully, one by one, never too fast but never too slowly either, pausing upon the short articles, or those that looked short, often beginning, sometimes finishing the short stories or serial novelettes that happened to be well-illustrated. And Kate never gave one away. She died with them, dusty and spider-ridden, piled high in the northwest corner of her room, near the window and so yellowed from the light, to be thrown away by Martin because he failed to realize their more intrinsic value once the old Post was gone.

"Joined to me," Arthur states with bold masculine pride. And this along with Arthur's most enduring fantasy that all women are not to be trusted. Not to mention or pursue the obvious fact that all things are at all times an inseparable mixture of pleasure and pain. Thus the chemists are forever defeated, and Sir Thomas need not have written his lengthy discourse and so allowed so many generations to misunderstand not only the nature of a pre-Lapsarian wonderland but, misapplied, the nature of the true Christian Kingdom.

Sex is coeval with pain and more profoundly so, not because the first kiss can never be recaptured, but because it can never be taken back. In the end, power manifests itself as a protection against loneliness, not the pleasure of company. Trust is not born out of faith in love but out of the fear of losing it. Such is one of our many necessary lies.

Arthur put such quaint kisses on his letter, an act designed so ostensibly to express the undying and unflagging character of his own seemingly quite ruthless love (if sarcasm be any measure). Ruth Ann, and Jessica Bailey, and Esther would have been openly amused and inwardly proud of such a fine young lad, a good husband no doubt, or at least good material to be molded. Safe, secure, relatively docile among the women, except in bed upon sanctioned occasion, yet strong, a leader, hard working, dependable, and before marriage even a bit naughty. (To show the boy's got some spunk and the girl a good head on her shoulders after all, you've got to have somebody around the house who's a bit practical).

The letters show it! We make the past a pattern of our imagined success not our forgotten failures (unless we are sick of course and need help, thank God for Freud), and then build the future upon the oh, so, solid granite of their truth.

Life is movement. The definition-perceived fact. Just as Arthur warned Katie of his abject poverty so had Father Martin before him, while kneeling, this time upon grass, freshly cut but newly wet with the remains of a late afternoon, April shower (the song describes only the faint hope in northern climes), out back of the Schoonhoven family residence in Loudonville, north of but near to Albany so old man Schoonhoven could each day make his hegira to the customs house on Broadway just below North Pearl, up from the river and next to the Post Office and Court House, there to oversee the business of the colony. And there Martin pled his troth promising to love his dear little Esther with all his heart and work hard to deserve her, even though unworthy, his humble demeanor, muddy kneed and breathless, woebegone for lack of conjugal affection, belying the one farm already gained from Alexander Washington who increasingly stayed at home or visited each afternoon at Tom Aul's grocery in Dunedin to play checkers with

173

the boys, the old boys who remembered the big one, increasingly weak and incapable of a full day's work, increasingly arthritic, reminiscent, and woefully sorry for himself and his young'un.

And Joseph too. Arthur's oldest, this time upon wall-to-wall, an innovation newly arrived from downstate, the carpet itself from Amsterdam up-river, a fact unknown to Joseph, good quality at a cheap price being not his line just then, the rich, textured, broadloom surfaces of it cushioning his trembling joints knee-deep in bone-dry Carastan. It was an act oft repeated; by Alex to shy-eyed Dorothy the cute little blond from Haynersville who once during their courtship pushed the big lummocks off the spoonholder on the Frear Park Lake in Athens because he got too fresh and free one morning after the prom. 'Forward' Katie would have called it and not pushed quite so hard (oh those Russian arms and Roman hands). By Martin also, first before Susie, a lamentable mistake well-paid-for in grief, and then Beatrice a homebody (everybody said) more suited for her role if not for Martin; and then to Lillian and to Anne and to cute little Jessie, heller that she was. All made it into the lap of conjugal felicity before Korea broke and thus, again by definition, led prosperous and successful lives and proved the eminent good fortune of their father.

Joseph was the best likeness, even if he did marry the young jewess who was a bit short-waisted and over-hipped, physically suited for country-life but spiritually of another ilk, the couple thus moving to Athens early on to be near her folks and the synagogue, often leaving the kids on the farm during the depression while both of them worked in town, her in the shirt factories because she'd always been good with a needle and he as an assistant store manager for A&P because he knew his produce right-well.

Control: physical, spiritual, and intellectual. It was all the tradition. Kisses on letters, young women to be trusted, spotted lambs, hungry wolves, and the grey, spookish tom whining every night in Athens when Joseph would come to town to court Abigail with his more muted endearments which were nevertheless deeply felt and proof of quite real agony on his part, the dark-haired beauty having easily the most lovely and delicate countenance that he, trembling Joseph of the frenetic cat, a victim and uneasy instigator of many like scenes, had ever discovered. Thus Joseph married

174

back into the old law from which neither he nor the rest of coy and hapless Anne's generations had ever truly deserted and so described the closing of a circle in his capricious sojourning. The cat, on the other hand, merely howled to get a little, his spiritual sense, on bottom line, being at the bottom of his belly and his intellect unworried over the niceties of distinction.

I love children, I really do," old childless Albert was often wont to say while pushing a thin wisp of prematurely grey hair back from his high forehead, "but I just can't bear them."

The cat, of course, bore on, as did Joseph in well-mannered (if not at least for a while discrete) fashion, the joining being at the discretion of females in both instances (many times but one cat) and either case the pattern of pain being equal to and abiding with the pleasure.

I imagine Dionysus a lover of pain, like the cat and Joseph and De Sade. And old Arthur, for all his tears, was a violent man. Myth and legend are the true records of civilization's descent, as the literary historian well knows. Prometheus did not desire rescue. Dionysius searched only for springtime death. The Inferno is the only dog-eared part of Dante's trilogy. Beowulf is greatest at his leaving. And which young doe-eyed maiden, regardless of the cost, would love Galahad when given Gawain or Lancelot?

To be useful, Power must be manifest. Shylock knew that well and Portia even better. It is lying that saves us from the unacceptability of truth. Old Henry knew too, gouty and bedridden, unable at the end to even walk, but married still to young (and relatively pretty) Catherine, thus playing his lost but not forgotten role like some huge, ungainly actor upon a cardboard stage. There are no Iphigenias--not then--not now. You get what you pay for and pay you must. Sacrifice is only the more subtle and devious way by which we buy our greatness on earth and supposed entrance into heaven.

Henry knew, and was no mean user of the lamb if such an instrumentality presented itself to him, his appetite ever beyond the lesser self indulgence of humility. And Alexander Washington so discovered it, in Brooklyn after enlisting, when basic training presented him with the first unexpected fruits of honest, forthright, and unforgiving competition, later in more furious, brutal (and later

175

still more poignant), and capacious fashion at the Wilderness and Cold Harbor before he, too, in humility, learned the limits of our more powerful human affectations while surrounded by pickets and watch towers.

Arthur was right, of course, women are not to be trusted. But then who is? What's the saying, "all's fair in ....?" The D.A.R. would understand. And whatever the mystery of what Agnes did (with whom?), that Katie must not repeat, we can be equally sure there are no bastards among the holy daughters.
Indubitably!

So young and so somewhat foolish! Arthur attests to the inevitability and efficacy of competition, of cats howling in the night, and the great American tradition which grew to make us grow greater. Of our inevitable mortal scars.

Money on the barrel-head will get you a dollar's-worth every time. The war ended. Alexander Washington came home. Martin never left. Arthur came home, though not from as great a conflict. And Jessica, Esther, and Katie waited dutifully, or at least ostensibly so.

We pay the price, all of us. The physical records diminish to mitigating paper, and, like it or not, we are left with what remains.

And finally there is only Prometheus, fire-seared and wasted away in his craggy, storm-rent isolation, looking far-off, in wonder, at the horned apparition which stumbles toward him from below.

CHAPTER
PORTRAIT VI

Really, Dad lived a long while without a farm. He and Mom married and stayed only that winter up near his father. Then in the spring, the two of them packed up and moved down south of the Centre out on the north end of Lake Lane on the Perrysville Road. Old Jud McCochrane had a big farm there, and for three years Grampa hired on as a worker.

He hadn't wanted to, especially he hadn't wanted to live so near Athens, but things didn't work out as he and Ma had planned. The money they'd both saved wasn't enough and as if to make all Ma's worst fears come true, she became pregnant with Lillian almost immediately. If nothing else, she said she wanted to be somewhere where there'd be good doctorin' close by.

Dad scoffed at that first off, I'm told. Don't really understand why. He never really seems to have understood the dangers involved in cousins marrying. God's will was God's will to him, and if he ever swore, it was ever to insist that worryin' did no good. What came came, and it was a man's job to face it, whatever.

They stayed at the McCochrane place for three years. Lillian was born there the first winter. And it did no good that the Athens doctors were only three miles away either, down the old Mill Hill road or across the Lake. It snowed up a storm that morning, and by evening there was a full eleven inches on the ground and more coming with a fury. When the pains started coming in the afternoon, Ma wanted to be driven into Old Doc White's down on River Street, but Dad wouldn't hear of it. "Too dangerous!" he said. And besides, Liz McCochrane was just down the road, and she'd had seven of her own, all birthed alive before she was thirty. What could some city doctor know that Liz didn't.

And that was an end to it. As much as Ma cried, and she did, and as much as Liz McCochrane bitched about damn unfeeling husbands, and she did, and as much as old Jud McCochrane laughed in the living room everytime Ma let out a yell upstairs, and he and she did, Gramps remained adamant. His son would be born in his own house. And by his own hands if necessary, he bellowed to Liz when she threatened to leave and take no part in the affair. In the evening old Jud finally sent Peter, his eldest, to fetch Doc White when the two of them, Dad and Jud, suddenly realized what a sensible thing that would be to do, but the responsibility for a healthy, squalling and kicking child lay squarely upon Liz's shoulders all through the night. It was three in the morning when White showed up, his coat and shabby broad-brimmed hat whiter and thicker with snow than the stubbled beard which he habitually left unshaven even when attending picnics and church socials. Lillian had been born at one and was sucking by two thirty. For weeks thereafter old Doc wouldn't believe Liz, and he always swore with a smile that the baby must have been born in the afternoon to have been so active by the time he arrived.

"Just like a man," Liz would sneer back at him, "to think he's the only one with a right to hang onto a tit every now and then."

It didn't happen that way with young William though. He was born the next winter, at home and at night, but with Doc White right there to see him into the world as gently and lovingly as if Billy had been an evening song.

He never cried.

"Never cried!" Mom said later, "not him. He was too gentle and good."

Doc White knew though. Little Williams hiccupped to begin breathing, held his eyes tightly closed, screwed up his tiny, red face, clenched his withered fingers, and remained alone and silent, refusing to give the whole outside world a second notice. And old Doc was not really surprised, too, when less than 48 hours later little Billy left us, quietly, without ever sucking, as if the world, none of us, had ever been worth his love - or him of ours. He just hiccupped-twice, White said--and then chose to stop breathing, or so it seemed. He had been small for Ma's kids, only six pounds even. Yet not that, nor anything else Doc White could discover, was enough to kill him. Living was just too difficult and distracting I guess. He refused the bottle as well as Ma's breast. Even old Mrs. McCochrane's and her eldest daughter Marsha's.

Dad never talked to me about it. Only Ma would bring it up and not often at that, speaking with a touch of acid in her mouth as if little Billy, himself, had somehow treated her ungratefully after all she'd done.

Sarah Anne came a year later, even though Ma swore she wanted no more, and then I came in the fall of '18. After that the two slowed down a bit. Alex, Martin, and Jessie took another twelve years to come along, and it wasn't until 1930 that Grandma gave up having kids and settled down to nursing her heart condition, weight, and high blood pressure. By that time they had moved from Lake Lane to Hawk's Farm when old Tom Terrel took sick with cancer, and then after he died and was rightly buried for a good spell, they sold Ma's portion of the farm to Mattie and Lillian and moved onto the hundred and ninety acres that great-grandpa had always insisted was theirs. Of course the fact that old Martin was slowing down a bit had a lot to do with it, but Jessie was born here upon the farm, and Grandma swore that was the last. And she finally held to it.

Cousins! And none of us turned out Mongoloid, or simple-minded, or what else. That's always seemed remarkable to me. Only little Billy. I remember the winter mornings when Pa would take me with him on the maple route, all 5 miles of it. We would trudge out along the old maple trees, Pa with two empty covered pails, one in each great gloved fist, and I with a third which was to hold the overflow if we came up lucky. After an hour of walking and tending those broad, naked, spigoted trees, Pa always carefully emptying the small oaken buckets into the new aluminum pails and then replacing them upon the notches, we would pass the cemetery where Billy lay. Pa wouldn't say a word, his weathered, red face displaying the same disciplined gravity it always acquired when he stood before the conclusions of his life. Still--his strong, measured walk would be measurable slow, then stop, supposedly for me to rest. Most times he would take out his old red handkerchief and wipe his forehead and nose. When he thought I wasn't looking, he would stare silently across the field of stones, his eyes abstract, his jaw taut and rigid, eventually staring far beyond the little, wrought-iron enclosed graveyard to the oak and maple covered hills above it. Then he would wipe his face again, his eyes and cheeks, stuff the handkerchief into his back pocket, pick up his half full pails, and motion me to follow along.

Only when tending the maple route would Grandpa pass that cemetery casually. He was not a man of habit but of reasoned practicality which others often mistook for habit. When out hunting rabbits we--Dad, Alex, and I--would always bear north and west, down along the reach of piled, stone wall which Martin and Alexander Washington had built and where on lazy summer afternoons I could invariably be found. Then we would turn down Stoffer Road toward the Quakenkill and up along its banks toward home. It was perfect rabbit country, and I never remember coming home without at least two or three, even on our worst days. But Ma was always sure he went that way to avoid the cemetery.

"It's better rabbit country straight north, and you know it!" she would lecture me with bitten lip when we were alone. "After all, up along them fields by Aunt Sussanah's and over toward Shaver's? You know it is. He's just afraid to go up there more'n he has to. He's in a rut that's all, and he don't want to remember."

Maybe so. Maybe, the old man didn't want to remember, but I'm sure it was always in is mind. The possibility of sin, I mean. Sin and retribution. The harsh judgements which he suspected were full recompense for his vanity and lack of obedience to an even harsher law. He read little in his later years. Eyes couldn't take it, he insisted. But when he quoted you the Bible, as he often could do with hardly a moment's reflection, it would invariably be Ecclesiastes, or Ezekiel and the prophets, or Lamentations. Often he would quote Psalms. He admired the quiet humility of their rhythms a great deal and always spoke his lines in a low, reflective whisper.

> What is man, that thou are mindful of him? and the son of man, that thou visitest him?

He always preferred the King James, and throughout his life would read from nothing else.

There is a story that Benjamin McClennahan, the Dunedin Reformed Baptist Church minister who married all of us, save Alex, once publicly lectured Sarah Anne for wearing lipstick to church. It wasn't a severe calling out, evidently hardly more than a casual, pious reprimand administered to her in passing as the high-school Bible class let out one Sunday at twelve. But Sarah's friends were there, and it was enough to send Sarah home in tears, her crocheted handkerchief wet with them and the lap of her new green cotton dress crumpled and stained from where she had been wringing it all the way home in the buckboard.

When Ma and the other kids arrived home, Sarah was afraid to tell Pa because she knew he didn't approve, and she was double afraid that sick in bed as he and I were with the croup, he'd really give her a tailin. He found out anyway, though. We all knew he would, what with the way everybody acted all day, and besides Ma could never keep herself quiet.

Pa didn't say a word. He just lay in bed coughing and gaggin' with the croup, the smell of the Vicks on his chest so heavy none of us could stay in his room for more than a few minutes. The next day though he got up and talked to Sarah Anne alone in the front room before she left for school. She never did tell us what he said, but that night she went straight to her room, and at supper she gave Pa a small bag full of things that clinked like glass bottles and the like. That was the end of it. Or at least we thought so for the rest of the week.

For Pa, that was never the case. The next Sunday, left-over croup and all, he was up as usual before us all and ready for church by nine, his frayed, white cuffs protruding well below the sleeves of his worn, black suit coat to clearly display the gold cufflinks Ma had given him. We left for church half an hour early. "To be sure and be on time," he said. But when we arrived at the hall and no one was there, we kids played outside with Ma watching us while Pa went inside. He was sitting in our pew, hands folded and head down, when we came in a half hour later.

But it wasn't until after church, when everyone was filing out for classes that we understood what Pa had intended all along. At the door, he stopped before Minister McClennahan, shook his hand, and complimented him on the sermon.

"And what was that you said earlier," he questioned, "I liked it very much. About the quality of mercy?"

"Oh," McClennahan responded, "I'm so glad. It's Portia's speech, 'the quality of mercy is not strained but droppeth as the dew from heaven upon the earth below.' Shakespeare."

"Yes!" Pa agreed sententiously, "Twice blessed, Minister McClennahan, and two blessings you'll need if you ever call down a Countryman again before this congregation or any like it."
The minister's smiling affability turned to chalk, and he remained unmoving, staring incredulously into Pa's red face.

"Ill reprimand my own, Ben McClennahan, before man and before God. But by God don't you ever try such a thing again unless by casting the first stone you've prepared to receive what you give tenfold. Now good day to you."

With that Pa walked out the door, Ma worrying behind him, us kids giggling in high pitched squirrels of laughter as we straggled along, McClennahan still open-mouthed, and half the congregation buzzing with the excitement of it all.

It wasn't long after that that the whole family became Methodists. Ma convinced the old man of it. But every so often he would go back to the Reformed, usually alone, sometimes on Sundays, and sit for an hour in the family pew, gazing at the bare altar and white, opaque windows. He always loved that church and the people in it. He was never really content with any other.

CHAPTER XXI
Love Story VIII

the farm letter is here somewhere. actually there are a number of them, but this one mentions it most prominently. at first, he wasn't too sure. it seems strange for a farmer to think of working in a laundry as he did. i can never imagine him that way. taking another man's pay i mean. he was always too free. too bold and certain. i always remember him standing alone, perhaps with the barn in the background or the sheep ringing their way home in the far pasture, up the hill from the perrysville road.

he was always alone to me. always standing tall in the field, sun-burned, weather-raw and red, the neck of his red and black, plaid shirt open to the white hair on his chest, his suspenders frayed over the shoulders, his boots scratched and caked with mud from the pig pen. he was always like that to me, he lived and walked and spoke differently, not even in the city did i ever see him change.

he should have been named peter.

* * * *

Dunedin, New York
March 20, 1913

My Darling, Darling Katie, xxxxxxxxxxxx!

I am too sleepy to write much, but I will do my best for you.

Agnes sent a postal to Ida the same morning I sent the letter you did not get. If you do see Ida, ask her if she received the postal. That would prove that Don mailed them both. If she did not, I will get after Don for not putting them both in the Post Office.

Father asked me tonight when I would want Aunt Sallie's place. He has a chance to hire it out for a year. I told him that if I took it, I would want it sometime next January. He asked me if I could not get along some way until next April. If he does not let it now, he figures he might not get another chance, and if it were vacant this year he would have to lose the insurance, which naturally he does not care to do.

I told him to do as he pleased. If he lets the farm and we move somewhere else, he will have no fault to find except with himself.

Father was to Athens today. He stopped at your house to leave some butter. Your folks took one jar and two dozen eggs. Dunhards took a jar and three dozen eggs.

Father asked your dad what he was going to do with me coming down so often, and he said that he got out the gun to shoot us yesterday but decided not to use it.

Father asked, "Do you know that Arthur and Katherine are engaged?"

Your father said, "No! Is that so? Damn her! I'll have to give that young girl a talking to. She never told me a thing about

184

it."

Father then told him that he did not really know if we were
engaged but he supposed it so. Your Father said that I was all right,
that he liked me well enough but that he wanted to be told.

So look out for squalls if you see your Father. I guess he
will not be too bad, but it will do to be prepared for anything.

I suppose we should have told him. In the last letter I asked
you if we shouldn't. He may as well know now as anytime, but I did
not mean for father to announce it. Now it looks as if I were afraid
to speak for myself.

Don't feel hurt about this. I never suspected Father would
speak out so, and I am in no wise to blame. Let come what will, I
shall always love you. Nothing shall ever part us.

By the way, Lillian told Father what time we left last night.
She went to bed at eleven.

This has been a fine day to wash? I suppose Poultrie was
mad if you washed today. I don't blame him if he was. Whatever
you planned, it has not been fit to wash one's face up here. I guess
that is why I have not washed mine.

No, I think it is because I hate to wash those kisses away.
Especially when I can get them only once a week. Then I cannot
afford to lose them so carelessly.

I have been at work in the woods today. If the snow lasts a
day or two longer, I'll have all my wood and logs out. I shall not be
sorry when the job is done.

If Father does hire out Aunt Sallie's place and gets a year's
rent in advance, I shall hit him up for my half. He promised me half
of all the rents if I would stay at home this year. So we may have a
little money before long. If I don't get my half there will be music

but no band.

    I will close now with all my love. I am and always will be your loving, loving,

xxxxx Arthur xxxxx

xxxxxxxxxxxxxxxxxx

   * * * *

    he must have been very rich, at least in land. at other times, however, he pleads such abject poverty. much like a farmer, i know. you've told me that often.

    still, one can't help wondering what the truth really was.

    how could he, for instance, really try that washing bit. not even then, do you think? too corny and obvious?

    oh, i don't know! maybe he really meant it. kisses were seldom, and we all know what fools we make of ourselves when we're first in love.

    at least it seems so when we are denied so much and know so little. i remember the deer head, years later, all shot up in the empty hallway after some crazy red-necks had got in there when the old farm was empty. at least—i think that was it?

    i suppose the economics of love are much another matter, but i can't help but hope that he meant it all, without forethought or premeditation. knowledge often spoils things. takes away the good and gives us, at the very best, no better. lovers believe what pleases them and who's to say that's not the best of ways?

    the next two letters are a bit different. they never lived on aunt sallie's farm, but the necessity for a farmer to be ready for a wife must have been very great. life demanded preparations then, didn't it?

i wonder. is all true love before the fact?

* * * *

Dunedin, New York
April 5, 1913

My Darling, Darling Katie,

I received your letter tonight. It was left down at Ray Terrel's. I guess Don was drunk again last night. He left two letters of mine.

I have a different pen and new ink, so I will try to send you a better letter than last night's. Please forgive me for writing you in such a way. I was also so sleepy that I could not think straight.

I thought that I would have a day of leisure when I woke this morning and found it raining. I took Agnes to school and then went to the Centre to buy a new pen and ink. But when I got back home it had stopped raining so I went to work splitting logs. Oh well.

My raccoon is still alive. He's been in someone's trap before and has lost a forefoot. Needless to say he must not be a very bright raccoon. I have him chained up to the dog house, and they have learned to give him plenty of room I'll tell you. He's a pretty fellow and pretty mean too.

Mother's pigs are all dead but three. They began to die last night, one before dark and five more during the night. One today. I don't know how long the other three will live. They are smart now, so maybe we will be lucky.

A fellow telephoned from Twin River to Art Countryman's asking if father's place was rented. He wanted to know if it was for sale and how much Dad was asking for it. It is already rented for one year and father said he did not want to sell it now. So I guess we are sure of that if we want it.

If I do not get as much as I suspect by staying up here this year, I shall move next. But I am sure I will have as much at year's end as if I had worked by the month. I do not wish to get married until I can get nice things for you. If I find I cannot, I will leave as soon as the fall work is finished.

When I told him that I would stay at home this year Father said, "If you wish to go some place to work next fall, I will sell off the stock and you can go."

If I cannot make a go of it here, I will let him do it, take my part, and work some place else. But oh Katie I do wish to stay here, to work on a farm and be my own man. I wish to stay as we had planned, and I will find a place for us to stay for the three months until the farm is ready.

I would even wait another year should I not be able to make enough and it be necessary. I should never cease to love you if I had to wait ten years. But I do not like the prospects of traveling down and back to Hawk's Farm another year you bet. I love to be near you and see you, but it is some tough on a zero night when I must leave you and come up here all the way alone.

Don't misunderstand! The fun hours I have with you are well worth the suffering, but I do not expect to have to do it after January if I can stay well all year and work steadily. I may not be able to furnish a house as well as some, but I do not expect that you will have to want for anything that a young couple of our means might want.

I suppose I should have rather extravagant ideas for us if I had all the money I might wish. But you will have a chance to get what you need. I shall let you do the choosing and I the paying. So you can have things as you like. You must, however, give me some idea of what you want so I can figure on how much I will have to raise.

You must also doctor your old lady up down there so she will not die on you. You must have your hands full if Mrs. Poultrie has left. If you find it too hard, be sure to make them get a nurse for the old girl. I do not want you to chill yourself, for then I would have nothing to live for.

I also think you must practice what you preach before you tell me to be good. Ha! I don't think we need watching, and it would not be lucky for me or the other fellow if I heard of anyone doing it. I will try and be better though if you will help me. It is in your hands to make me good, so if I am bad do not blame me entirely. I was never bad with anyone else, so am I to blame?

I think I will close now so as to save some paper for next time. All my love will ever be your, and my hugs and kisses too.

Your love, loving Sweetheart,

x Love x x Arthur x x x x

* * * *

he encloses a short letter from little agnes as well, who closes with, of all things, "love."

well, there are worse sentiments.

* * * *

April 5, 1913

My dear, dear, Darling Katie,

How are you, we are all well and hope you are the same.
Uncle Len had ten pigs and gave them to us but all except three are
dead. Perhaps they will be in the morning.

You are an April fool I guess, by what I hear you sent a
couple letters the first--did you? Uncle Len and Aunt Ruth wishes
to be remembered to you.

Will you please answer this for I want to hear from you so
bad. Do you like the place? How is Grace and Arbie? When do you
suppose I will see you again? I hope it will be soon.

Now I will have to close with love,

Yours as ever,
Your cousin
Agnes Countryman

P.S. Please answer soon.

* * * *

there is a note from gramps on the outside of the envelope. he must have regularly read aunt agnes' letters.

* * * *

If you have time you had better write a few lines to Agnes so she will not feel so bad.

Arthur

* * * *

gramps used to take me out walking on summer evenings when i was a little girl. he was older then, much older it seems to me now, with long creases of weathered fat hanging loosely along his neck and down the backs of his bare arms.

then he had a far away look in his eyes as he would tell me about the farm--which i visited all too seldom for my own good, he would say. there were the sheep, and horses, and cows and chickens; all more trouble than they were worth what with the chickens not laying properly and the rats after what few chicks did hatch, or worse yet weasels and raccoons and foxes after the hens.

he often told me of the bastard bull he got from old man ricketts. "old crazy charlie ricketts," he'd chuckle, who once burned down his whole barn because he couldn't get his rhode island cock down from the rafters where it had flown one morning while fleeing from a weasel who had laid waste to the hens because of the rooster's cowardice. "burned the whole barn he did," and grampa would begin to laugh, his face turning as red as his hair with each wheeze, "damned horse's-ass burned the whole barn just 'cause he was afraid to go up into those rafters as his cock was to come down. dam horse's-ass. charlie never was one for thinking much, never should have been a farmer. not born to it."

of course, charlie always maintained he burnt the barn in order to build a new one without rats and weasel holes, and there was no doubt he got the better of gramps with that bastard bull who tore through barbed-wire fences as though they were ripe kindling, tearing himself up as well as the fence so that he was no good at all to the cows until gramps electrified and finally put a stop to the whole business. one try at the fence after that, and the bull had to be clubbed through the open gates both morning and night. and he never again came within ten feet of knocking down a post.

horses and sheep were easy in comparison he'd say. the sheep were just dumb and the horses too fragile, and quick to take a chill. as for pigs, he kept them to sell and eat but paid them little attention. they ate slops and more often than not laid on their own young. that was a sin for which gramps could never forgive them.

he'd tell me, too, about the crops: the buckwheat and barley, the oats and wheat and corn he grew. they were mostly his cash crops, although he never planted much wheat and kept a good deal of the oats. "the garden," he'd admonish with a stroke of his big hand over my hair, "the garden" fed the family with its potatoes, peppers, beans, tomatoes, peas, berries, and what not. that was what kept the body and soul alive and saved him from the city bankers through the winter, that and grandma's canning, and his own hunting and trapping, and the maple roots, and berrying, and wood cutting and fishing, and all the other things a man could do by himself, he would say with pride. no, there never was a reason a man had to go in debt for anything. not when a living was always out there on the land just for the taking.

of course you had to be willing to work hard and take pleasure in simple things. he never forgot that. let me read one more short letter. i'd forgotten how disingenuous he could be when he wanted to.

* * * *

Dunedin, New York
May 31, 1913

My Darling, Darling Katie, x x x

I am not going to write a very long letter tonight. I thought I would tell you so you would not be disappointed.

I have a visitor tonight. I won't tell you his name, but he prefers to stay outside and cry Bob-White, Bob-White. He is shy like you and almost as pretty.

We finished planting our field corn today. It's eight o'clock now and, I have been up weeding onions since seven this morning. When it got dark I could not tell an onion from a weed, so I stopped. The garden is well along also.

Victor Bundy and Miss Grammy are going to be married next Tuesday. There will be a party on the school house lawn, and Agnes says I must take her. How I wish it were ours.

I arrived home last night after twelve and then did not get to sleep. I can never sleep after having been with you.

Now, I have one chicken. My hen has just begun to hatch. The other is due to begin tomorrow.

I hope you have a good time at the festival. I wish I could

be there but don't see how. Don't look for me, but I may surprise you if my legs and back hold out.

Don't be angry if I go to the party with Agnes. I don't care to go anywhere without you, but I suppose Agnes should not have to go home alone at night.

I must close now and catch up on some of the sleep I missed last night. All my love is yours no matter how far away you are. Take my kisses to the festival with you. My heart will follow them wherever you go.

xxxxxxxxxxxxxxxxxxxxxxxxxxxxxxxxxxxxxxxxxxxxxxxxx

Your loving, loving, loving Sweetheart

Arthur

* * * *

and so he ends a day among the onions.
how beautiful those walks were that he took me upon, far down the maple-corridored, dirt road during those long summer evenings.
how beautiful and how sad.

CHAPTER XXII
PORTRAIT VII

You don't remember Dad when he was young. Well, not young perhaps but youthful in his middle age. A mountain with red hair still thick on his freckled forehead and washed blonde along his chest and over the heavy muscles of his back and shoulders.

I think he was always young, young and always sure of himself. A bit headstrong, I guess, not quick to anger but never afraid to come down on us like thunder if he thought we needed it.

He loved us kids! Loved us more than life itself. Or maybe it was that we were his life, and he was forever looking out for us, to make us more what he felt we should be - could be if only we'd let the best in us get the upper hand. He never coddled any of us. That's for sure.

I remember how I used to love playing by the old well pump across the road. Until '48, it was the only water the farm had, and Ma would twice walk daily out the front door of the kitchen, over the lawn, past the great rose bush that mastered the wide expanse of grass in superb idleness, past the hollyhocks and soporific lilac bushes that she loved almost as well, and then across the road to the pump to fetch water. She never seemed to mind it, even when she got older and her heart began acting up on her and Gramps would increasingly do the chore for her--morning and evening, two great pails without fail.

Gramps was a stickler about the responsibilities he felt toward other people. And besides, he worried a great deal about Grandma's angina during those years before the war. He loved her a great deal.

Loved me, too, I think, though he showed it in a different way when I walked to the pump. I remember that waling he gave me as though it were yesterday. I'd always loved the great pump across the road, and often I'd go over there and spend long stretches of time just pumping water out of the well onto the bare ground underneath the rotting wooden planking which Gramps had put together as a level base for Grandma's buckets. That wasn't a smart thing to do, because the well regularly ran dry in the hot summer months and Gramps was always at us to husband our water very carefully. He never did put in "city water," even when the lines ran through in '47 and they offered him a real cheap price.

"Don't want none," he growled, "can get along by myself. Why'd I want just another bill." And he went ahead and dug another well and ran it inside to Grandma's kitchen. He was right proud of that little pump, and always told us afterwards how smart he'd been to accept electrification when it came around in the thirties.

But lack of well water wasn't the only reason Gramps got it into his head that the old, dirt, state road out front of the house was terribly dangerous. He didn't want his son crossin it and "gettin hisself killed." After I'd disobeyed him often enough it became a problem of authority.

Anyway, this one day I'd done it again. I'd crossed the road, looking carefully, more for Gramps than the few cars that passed down the road every day delivering bread or mail, or to see one of the five families which lived down the two mile stretch of dust and mud which ran away from and back to old U.S. 24 before it began the long climb toward the Taconic, and then I'd run quickly to the far side of the pump so as not to be seen from the house, and I'd begun pumping with all my might, watching the water gush out after the first three or four thrusts of the pump handle and spill crazily under the grey-slivered wooden planks below. Lord it was such fun, the water shimmering in big globules in the air then splashing wet and cool over me and the pump, changing it to a dark shiny black from the grey-rust color of its dry paint.

I had such fun that I completely forgot to look for Dad. Never saw him, as a matter of fact, until I looked up from the playful spray of water in the afternoon sunlight and there he was, switch in hand, striding across the road like some huge colossus let loose, his red hair blond at the edges and matted with sweat, his wide red checks burnt raw by the summer sun, his bushy eyebrows knotted in anger beneath the long gashes across his forehead.

I'd never seen eyes so angry before, and I knew then that I was in big trouble. I let go of the pump handle as though it were a hot iron. I must have been scared because I let out a little scream as he marched toward me and for one short, unfortunate moment I remained rigid and glued to my spot. That was all Dad needed. He was upon me before I could run, and then no matter how much I ducked and stopped, changed directions and slid at angles to that always stinging switch, I could not get around him and across the road to the safety of your Grandma and the house.

"How many times have I told you boy," he yelled at me in a remarkably calm voice above my wordless terror, "Do you want to get run-over and killed? Better the switch than that. Let me tell you." And then he would flick it irritably out across the back of my blistering, red-welted legs. Each time I'd let out a yelp and try even harder to outflank him and get a clear path to the porch. But I couldn't do it. Gramps was too good, Bless him, always too good.

Finally, though, he let me go. After I was well switched and crying. Crying so hard that the tears felt hot and cakey all over my face. At last he let me have one across the back of my legs and failed to stay between me and the house. That was all I needed. Lickety-split, I let out a whoop and made for Grandma, running like lightning, I thought. But Gramps managed to keep up, and every few steps I'd feel that birch across the back of my thighs. Gosh, how it hurt.

He stopped at the kitchen door. That was Grandma's territory and Gramps never violated her ground. Course, he'd never meant to follow me further. Ma's skirts were sacred, and he was pleased that they should be.

Later that night he sat in his big rocker by the fireplace and from across the room watched me rubbing liniment over the back of my legs. Every once in a while it would sting terribly and although I didn't want to give him the satisfaction, I'd hiss or grunt in spite of myself.

"Hurts, does it," he called across the room after a time.

"No!" I yelled at him. But I winced and he knew better.

"Don't add lyin to disobeyin," he grumbled, "Course it does. And I meant it to. Every bit of it."

"I'm not lying," I cried, and tears welled up in my eyes.

"Well, at least I know you're a son a'mine," he considered sententiously. "I've never known a real Countryman not to try and call black white at least once. Bull-headed and proud, by God. A family curse," and he began to smile through the day's stubble of his beard.

"I'm not lyin, I'm not, I tell ya. It don't hurt at all. By damn it don't hurt. It don't."

"That's enough Joseph," he thundered at me all of a sudden and stood up out of his chair like a giant. "No son of mine'll curse in this house you hear. No son of mine."

"I'm sorry Pa. I'm sorry," I squealed and crouched away from him on the floor.

He just stared at me for a moment. Stared long and silent. And then he began to cry. Not loud, but quietly as a man often cries when he's very much in love. I'll never forget that time. Never.

"Well it were your own fault," he whispered. Then he walked toward me across the bare oak floor. "It were your own fault. You've got to learn Joseph, and it looks like you're bound and determined to learn the hard way." Then he reached me, he bent down and gathered me into those great arms of his, still crying and still whimpering, as though he were hoarse and couldn't talk anymore. "I won't have you disobeyin me Joseph. And what's more I don't want you dead out on the road from some crazy city-folk's car. It's for your own good you know, don't you? It's always for your own good. Everything I do."

And still cradling me in his arms, he carried me up to bed, gently and carefully, still crooning softly as though I was some little hurt bird he had to protect and care for.

The last thing I remember of that night are the crickets, chirping insistently over the warm night air. Crickets and the great gentleness of his hands as he laid me down upon my bed, kissed me, and tucked me in for the night.

That and the stinging on the backs of my thighs.

* * * *

I remember, too, later, years later, Gramps living on the second floor of the second town house. I remember him then, too, on hot summer evenings playing canasta, his huge shoulders slack and gaunt inside the over-large, white T-shirt he always wore to keep cool on those terrible city nights. I remember him peering endlessly at the great fistful of cards he always held as if some exotic secret was hidden within them. Of course, there wasn't. Gramps was just not a man to lose easily or win timidly. He either went out or went up, and how he loved to watch you kids when he'd pick up a huge stock of cards and lay down a hundred points or more at a single turn, his red arms and knotted fingers reaching across the table in leisurely display, magically leaving threes and fours and incredibly long runs behind them.

He only stayed in the city for seven months. They were his last with Grandma, and he did it only to please her. But it wasn't his way. He knew it and Doc White knew it. Gave him only six months if he went back to the farm. And he went back, only to be dead within a year. Finally, with that strange smile upon his face.

How he loved to play canasta and drink lemonade. How he loved to watch you kids squeal with delight when he won. And then he was gone, and young Minnie was whimpering in her kennel with the loneliness of it all.

CHAPTER XXIII
History Lesson VIII

No one! No one who truly requires love ever receives it! This is dogma! Unapproachable! Absolute!

Passion is never dictated by inferior need.

My Father! My Father! Why has thou deserted me?

Want something badly enough! Bite your lip! Reveal your want! And you will most surely lose it.

Old Henry's Annie was one such. As a whore, she reigned supreme. As a wife she was found ordinary and an awkward possession. Dead, she was infinitely more valuable to her living child than she ever had been alive to her dying dreams. And once dead she would be remembered for all time not only for her dying but for the manner of her living which led so inexorably to it.

Fine living demands finer dying or we fail before all history. It is, finally, a matter of style, history's pattern a manner of learning and choosing from the past what we would desire the future to become. Style, that capricious and singular nature of our vanity projected (usually with more than common wit and always with less than superior thought) upon our unlucky and immediate environment, both spacial and temporal.

True love is never born before the fact. In any kind (or 'type') of human action, altruism is secondary to will. Contrary to popular, unlearned opinion (or should we say unstudied and therefore ill-informed, the cliches of the hoi-polloi being what they are) love cannot be given unless it is first received. For every Christ or Buddha there are countless Hitlers or Stalins. We live after the Fall, and abstractions of rejected or unaccepted commitment produce only nominal apparitions in a real world. Luckily, our medieval fathers could afford the luxury of slow and laborious argument, their delightfully protracted and imaginative forms of torture always displaying, and most often proving, their point.

Lucky Arthur? We create the apparitions which we choose to worship and use them as the excuse for our more desperate responses. Love? It was a bargain for the strong, young lad, and like all bargains it required immediate payment. No checks. No credit cards. In those days, there were few of the former and none of the latter.

Still, 'true love' is always before the fact. At least we like to think of it so, and so by definition alone insure correct answers to our questions. The old deer loved the bear, although they never met. We can be sure of it. Such is the nature of mutual dependencies in our world that what we hate and fear the most we find ourselves most in need of. Death was the bear's irreplaceable gift to the deer, the most obvious and unshakable example of the truth.

Of course, Demeter brings back the Spring, but Dionysus manifests the long awaited issue in its only promised abundance. Girls forever know this, but for the sake of manners and good order ignore its more unseemly and coordinate implications until society's more pressing business has been accomplished. The acts are cultural distinctions as is the state of mind, necessary and desirable at the proper times but in no clear way allied to clear genetic causation, though we might dimly suspect its dim intrusion.

Arthur's lot was Adam's. And like all the Countrymen before him, he wrestled with his master both in good times as well as in bad. His father finally gave him a farm, the fabled 190 acres of good upland topsoil, timbered-over and rock-strewn, good for milk cows if cows were what you wanted at seven cents a quart. Good, too, for sheep and horses and chickens, the latter if you could keep the weasels and foxes away. Good for buckwheat and barley and oats and corn, but wheat was very difficult and the plains were proving better at all such onerous tasks which utilized great expanses of untrampled honey-sweet loam, fair and level as far as the eye could see and often up to thirty feet deep before bedrock proclaimed the resurgence of a more profound relationship between man and earth. So Arthur and Katie built their fair domain, full of walnuts and beechnuts and maple and birch trees. The bull, as all bulls do, even good King Henry, learned the limits and extent of his power and the proper channels within which to breed his vanity and insure its continuance. In short, the farm grew, and it prospered. Katie canned food, and Arthur supplied it. Together, they went about the business of building modest riches, so that after they were gone (hopefully many years hence) the spring might return. Katie bore her children well enough, even if in fear and with foreboding. Arthur "managed." And in managing he bought up some not insignificant portion of Dunedin's (and Athen's) prosperity for himself and his own for decades to come.

Like Anne, Katherine had acquired and chiseled out her sphere. The General Federation of Club women had only 50,000 members in 1898. A mere sixteen years later it had grown twenty fold to over a million before the war, and working for the boys at the front hardly diminished its swelling ranks. Katherine just "could not find time." A marriage was bad enough what with housework and kids and gardening and canning and, yes, Arthur, too, but with literary circles and social service organizations and women's equality groups (again in Athens, early and late), the like of it Kate had never seen nor hardly imagined.

The marriage discovered itself, its level and its value. Arthur loved and protected. Kate provided and comforted. The Montgomery Wards furniture, shipped all the way from Chicago with (understandably) a few chips, was duly displayed, admired, and cared for with a solicitous and prudent eye well into the next forty years before time and age, both advancing, took first Arthur and then Kate to abide with their maker. A short and direct story for two very direct but far from short lives.

Arthur built three castles (Henry's must be admitted to be countless) if the two townhouses be considered together one property. And, of course, those two beneficent and somewhat halcyon two-story walkups don't really count at all since they were really just rental homes, bought as rentals, leftovers from North Athen's more prosperous days when Herman Melville (as a boy) walked the slated streets singing dark songs of huge white whales to himself and of white jackets and maybe white-sepulchers (only that was to come later, much later, beyond mud-filled trenches 300 yards (sometimes four) forward, always forward never to go back, over cratered, moon-scarred earth where summer never returned, never returned even years later when the sepulchres were all full and the houses--thus inevitably--empty).

Bought, the houses were, after the Great One and before the Second in the "l'epoque entre la guerres" when dying was "pro patria and pro domo" but certainly never "dulce et decor." The old man knew too well. Mortgaged to the same simian knights his sons were to fight for, perhaps unknowingly but none-the-less with missionary zeal (as all the young boys did), on the seas (as Melville did), in search of heaven (as he suffered), or at least a better part of hell (which they all too often found, not among Jews but still with them, profoundly still in all cases and always knowing of what was saved if anything at all).

Before the flood, the earth was full of disquietude and anger. It pleased God not at all.

The other two were more mellifluous abodes of peace and love, homiletic citadels of foretold prophecy not burnt and scarred by the money-lender's incendiary touch (like candles in the muted night, filling the blue-penciled sky with unwanted light and washing the soiled ground in untempered sheen). Arthur's and Katie's first home (long before the child's war, their children's, to which they went and were sent, young Martin first, followed shame-facedly by Alex, then Joseph last because, already married and fathered he had more to lose and be responsible for) to be saved, at least implicitly by America's proud sons, was a rough log cabin, built down on the new 90 acres of upland cobble and slate chips, away from the state highway and with only two rooms and a loft.

Arthur made it all himself, after Martin and Edgar gave out and couldn't help him anymore. Family land was family land, true enough, but hard work demanded strong hands and a stronger heart. The old man helped with timber and joists, Edgar the same, when time permitted from his more pressing duties with his line of elixirs and new medicines which he sold in Dunedin, Perrysville, Stumps Corners, Ashokan, Hawks Farm, Twin Rivers, and every other place upon the periphery of Athens in which he figured to make a buck.

The cabin went up though, within a summer, and after their fourth year of connubial bliss, Arthur took gentle Katherine, now pregnant with her fourth, one already dead, in the middle of a war, and hid her upon his newly made but already nearly outgrown habitation, in order to protect his family from the more prolific terrors of modern man: the city, drink, gambling, cigarettes, the railroads, non-baptist ministries, department stores, cosmetics, frilly underwear, modern dance, and, again, the city. Once moved in, he immediately began work on the 2nd, more permanent, retreat of his life, a monstrous, two story, 6,700 square foot, eventually two dwellings, farmhouse with three two-holer outhouses, two barns (one large and one small) a chicken house as large as the smaller barn minus the second story, an attached tool-shed, a smoke house, and large inevitably muddy and stinking pig pen with a great yard for the sows and boar.

In later years, when he tried living in the city because of his heart, Arthur went back to the old cabin, then silent within the fringing woods around the unused west-pastures, and walked silently over its dilapidated, mouse-strewn floors where ragged weeds were poking up through the rotting wood. Dust and cobwebs had settled thickly into the corners and along the cracks and crevices. It had served him well for seven good years. He always spoke of it as the "family home." Seven, a magical number, a house where all his children were born save Martin, the youngest and baby, named after Grandad Martin but always huskier, a troublemaker, yet good at heart and never seen without a smile upon his face; and Lillian, the eldest, after Katie's sister but more gentle and good, the first of two daughters, if dead William were not counted (two days was hardly a life); the second Sarah Anne, a heller but so lovely a face, her patronym now lost in generation, but how he and Katie both loved that name, Ann.

He walked the floor and bent over the old stove hearth, looked high into the now bat infested loft and remembered Joseph, after Joe Terrel, and Alex, after old Alexander Worthington, and

Jessie, after Jessica Bailey, and those seven good years after the war. They were, he knew, followed by the frenzy of the late twenties. Frenzy and folly, he knew it, a time of banker's greedy dreams, and worsening weather, and a telltale drop in a farmer's income, and a high city life that foretold the fall. Arthur thanked his lucky stars that old Martin had had so few debts before he died in '33 and that he, himself, had always distrusted credit and been able to live simply and keep to his own. It had paid off then and handsomely at that. What with prices low he'd bought for less--what little he and his couldn't make themselves; and with no debt he'd managed to keep all ninety acres left to him personally by old Martin. The others could do what they wanted with their portion.

And so he lived in a passion for the land, holy and enduring. Absolute and unapproachable, he and his family in their transcendent happiness.

CHAPTER XXIV
Love Story IX

i remember--why must the world be without reprieve?

the adjustment must have been hard for grandma, at least i would think so. a city girl, she shopped at denbys and peerless and bon ton. along river street in those days, there were fine movie houses and fashion stores and professional buildings. she must have often regretted, just a little bit, her move to the country. there were no stores in dunedin that could compare with the wonders of athens.

i remember her often going to that old, oaken, hope chest of hers that she kept at the foot of her bed, and bending over it, and opening it, and taking from it, oh! on so many occasions, she would take out her fine, old, city clothes and lay them lovingly on the coverlet and step back to look. then she would bend down and carefully smooth away the untoward wrinkle and step back again.

she never wore them, that i remember. they were special and couldn't be replaced if they were ever worn out. all the beautiful wool skirts and lace blouses and old, high, silk stockings. her good dresses always had lace bodices with white trim. i thought they were so beautiful.

i would watch her, unnoticed in the doorway or along the wall as i slide further and further in the room to get a better look at the treasures in the

chest. how wonderful they all were to me. not years old but decades and centuries i became sure. for no one would stare like that at just ordinary things, i knew so. grandma would look and sigh sometimes, and then she would bend down and pick up a pair of soft leather gloves or frilly underwear and replace them in the chest, slowly, ever so slowly and carefully, smoothing out the wrinkles once again before placing something else on top. and when all finished, she would close the old chest, her solitary chore finished for the day. and she would drag out from the pocket of her skirt the key and lock it tight. how that key squeaked, i remember, as she turned it ever so slowly til it clicked the tumblers sharply into place.

i was very small then, only four i think. but i would watch from the darkest corner of the room, next to the doorway, away from the window light, pressing myself ever smaller and smaller into the papered wall, away from the sun, grandma never looking. after all, i was just a little girl. what did she care? i didn't understand yet, and they were pretty things anyway. i always felt i was watching some fine enchanted ritual in which grandma spoke silently to herself in soft elfin tones and murmurs, and then all those scrumptous river street clothes would magically appear from the chest to amaze the world with their grace. and grandma, i knew, had once been a great, great, lady who walked on grandpa's arm, ever so tall and stately and serene, up and down river street. and everyone had stared and looked at them. and she had lived in a great house up on pauling avenue and grandpa had courted her every sunday.

years later, after she had just died, and we were opening the chest, i remembered exactly where to look for the letters that she had kept in it, under the half dozen scented, crocheted handkerchiefs on the left hand side of the second drawer down. and i rushed past everyone to get them, mussing the handkerchiefs that she'd laid down but never used for as long as i'd known her.

aunt lillian got mad at me for being so pushy a little girl and told me to mind my manners even as i was desperately reaching for the old shoe box that contained all of grandpa's letters, which she'd never let any of us read. most of us never knew she had them until later when i told you all. but aunt sarah defended me and called aunt lillian an old grouch, and aunt lillian turned around so that i was able to get away, at least for a while, until the rest of you stopped oohing and aahing over the clothes, and jewelry, and shoes and comforters, and undies, and things.

grandpa often would call grandma a very high class woman, in the evenings, before we went to bed, as he carelessly joked with her. and i knew he meant it, even if it wouldn't seem so. he loved her a lot. i'm sure of it. and she knew it too. but at first his ways must have seemed rough and severe to her. like this letter.

* * * *

Dunedin, New York
January 30, 1913

My Darling, Darling, Katie,

How I long for you tonight. It has been a dreary old day and the same kind of evening. The wind is whistling around every corner and through every crack and niche. If only you were here there would be one bright spot in this dull old house.

Each time I must leave you I feel the loneliness of these woods and this farm more keenly. It gets harder and harder to bear. If you were only here where I could get you in my arms and give you a good long hug (say from now until midnight, that is only 4

209

hours) and a kiss (a small thing for so great a pleasure), then I should be happy. No! A million kisses if I could get them in that time. As it is, I suppose I will have to content myself with the knowledge that I love and am loved.

I guess I must hurt you many times with my unrefined ways. I don't mean to, and you will have to forgive me when I do so. I know how it must have hurt you when I referred to you as 'this' the other night. If it hurt you then, the thoughts of it and the way you looked at me when you asked why I spoke as I did, have since hurt me enough to repay with interest. I am so sorry. Every time I think of you I remember the way you looked--oh, that confounded word. Sometimes I do not think of how I sound to others when I speak. You may never fear of my using that word in such a way again. Please, always tell me if I ever hurt you. I would not have it so and will remedy it in any way possible.

I have finished that book of Edgar's you let me take. I have read most of the day. It is the only way I can pass the time up here when I am not at work. The book is good, rather sad at times, but that serves to soften the bloodshed and roughness of its other parts. I will bring it down Wednesday night, hopefully before I freeze stiff and blow away, as cold and windy as it is up here.

It was half past one when I arrived home last night. I only met one other team along the road and came near running into it on the Hawk's Farm bridge.

Please excuse me if I do not write a long letter tonight. The fire has gone out by now and I am nearly frozen up as far as my knees.

I hear that Jimmy Manard and Tina West are going to get hitched when Jimmy comes back from out west in the spring. That's coming east to get a little of the west. Eh!

I am your loving, loving, ever lonesome Love,

210

* * * *

how unlike him. or so it seems to me. about the "this" remark. although i'm sure no one would like to be called "this" in our day, i'm not so sure about then. okay! it's not really good, but he does show some pride of possession doesn't he? grandma's not property, like a cow or a horse, but--well, he hadn't known her very long then. he hadn't! it is only his seventeenth letter, and there are well over a hundred of them in all. he was a devoted lover, in his own way.

* * * *

Dunedin, New York
February 2, 1913

My Darling, Darling Katie,

I arrived home at three o'clock. It was cold, and the snow was blinding in my face all the way back. But I could stand much worse weather than that to see you, I bet.

Actually, I have been very fortunate in regards to the

weather. If last night had been like last Monday, I might have thought twice before starting down, but I should have tried to make it no matter what the storm. I should never promise you anything without trying to keep my word, and you, I know, would warm up my coldest of nights. Funny, but if anyone had told me four months ago that I would be engaged now I would have laughed at them. Love works wonders.

Tell Edgar I have been hunting today. I got four rabbits and should have had many more but just did not shoot them. I wish he could have been up today. He would have enjoyed it very much.

I did not get up until nearly eight this morning so you can imagine who did the chores. I will have to get up early tomorrow to mail my letters and postals. I have four letters and two postals, mother just one letter. I suppose Don Bennet will think we had better start a mail route of our own. He has become used to stopping mornings since I began writing to you.

I wonder if Charlie Finks has it figured out how he can gain his pints and still have his cake, or how a woman really can cure a man of drink? He and Don have been living it up lately, I hear.

Speaking of good times, we are having another snow storm tonight. There may be sleighing Sunday.

A fellow up here who saw me come down toward your house last night said to me when I was hunting today, "I should not think you would be hunting rabbits today, Arthur, especially after having your ferret in the hole last night." God! I was mad. And he got out of my way right quick, you bet. It seems that people think we are bad just because we are not dead.

Well, Agnes has gone through her fifth reader and erased all the pencil marks in it already. She said this morning, "Gee, the sixth reader is almost as good as new." I don't know what she thought about the one she's been erasing. She is mad at me because I will not stop writing you and play dominoes.

I hope your father does not move down toward Piney Creek just to get rid of me. It would be a mistake, for I would come once a week if I had to drive all Saturday night to get to you.

I guess I will get some sleep tonight unless you waken and think of me too hard. I always wake up whenever you are thinking of me. Of course you could not think of me more than I do of you unless you lie awake all night to do it.

Oh Katie, you are my very life. If you were taken from me I should not care to live. All I do I do for you, and one day I hope I can make you the happiest of women as you have made me the happiest of men. If I fail in this, I shall count myself a failure. But if we love each other truly, then I can see only a home where happiness shall reign supreme. For that, I am content to wait the year.

I left the keys to my trunk under my pillow when I dressed last night and did not think to remove them this morning. Bad luck, mother found them when she made the bed. She said she did not open the trunk, and I believe she would not lie to me, but I will be more careful in the future. She said, "When is Katie coming up again?"

I told her I did not know and she said, "I guess the old gentleman will not let her come up again." So you can see that none of them understand us yet.

The rest of the folks are going to bed and the clock is striking eight. I am tired and cannot think of anymore to tell you so I will close.

May the love I give always be ever as true as it is now.

Your loving, loving

Arthur xxxxx

* * * *

how crude! "ferret in the hole." "warm love" indeed. i
wonder. some things should never be repeated, and, yet some
things we should, perhaps, never know. because not knowing them,
they aren't. how i dislike all those who are so positive of the truth
that they insist upon repeating its inconsequential facts. greed,
brutality, and vulgarity are not love, need not be if we choose. there
are certain blessed ignorances that prove themselves i think, no
matter what the necessities of science. and for which all the world is
more beautiful and no less real. no sententious righteousness. he
should have been kind. at other times he was. remember . . . .

* * * *

Dunedin, New York
May 31, 1913

My Darling, Darling, Katie xxx,

I will not write a long letter tonight so don't be disappointed. I would tell you that now, because if I were to write a letter a thousand pages long, still, silence could tell you more clearly of my love for you.

I have a visitor tonight. He and the coming spring remind me of you. I will not tell you who he is, but, he prefers to stay outside and cry 'Bob-White.'

We finished planting the corn field today. It is eight o'clock, and I have been weeding onions since seven. I stopped when it got too dark to tell an onion from a weed again. And I heard Bob-White, Bob-White.

* * * *

wait! this is that other letter i just kind of summarized a little while ago isn't it? well, no matter. gramp's writing isn't the easiest to read, especially after so many years. it includes all that stuff about victor burd, or bundy, and miss grammy. remember? he tells her to take his hugs to the festival and all that.

* * * *

I hope you have a good time at the festival. I wish I could come down, but I don't see how. I am as lame as my horse from that cold and rain last Sunday. Don't look for me, but then don't be surprised if I try.

I will try and take Agnes to the school party. Don't be angry with me. I don't care to go without you, but I shouldn't make Agnes stay home just to suit me.

I must close now. All my love is ever yours no matter how far away we may be. Take my hugs to the festival, I would be with you always wherever you are happy and gay.xxxxxxxxxxxxxxxxxxxxxxxBob-White

Think of me. You loving, loving, loving Sweetheart,
Arthur

* * * *

see! that's better. we have the right to choose, and in not exercising it, we most truly lie. silence. in it there is remediation.

i remember.

CHAPTER XXV
PORTRAIT VIII

Old Dad was a great reader. No doubt. I once found a copy of the *Jungle* and one of The *Octopus* in his bedroom while I was opening drawers one day when he and Grandma were out to town and Lillian and Sarah Anne and I had been left with the younger kids. I knew I shouldn't have been in there, but I was curious and sneaked a look when Lil and Sarah were outside.

They were in the top drawer under his shorts, the books I mean, like he didn't want them read. That seemed strange to me because he always encouraged our reading and for years kept a copy of 1907: The *Panic Recalled* next to his big chair in the living room. He could even quote Frederick Marryat who had visited Athens way back in 1837 and called it "a city full of lumber and pretty girls."

Of course I don't think he really read very much after he got married--too much to do what with a wife, the farm, and then a growing family. Not, at least, the way Edgar did before he went to war in '18. Edgar was a real reader, make no mistake. Wanted to be a preacher, Dad told me. To make good his brother's wandering from the fold, he'd always joke to us in later years. But he didn't manage it. The war changed him, and when he came back married to Bessie Saeder in 1920, he got himself a piece of old Martin's hard-scrabble holdings and began to make a farm out of it. No thought of ministering ever crossed his lips again. Hardly could, swollen as they were and his voice so weak and splintered what with the gas he'd taken at Cambrai.

That wasn't all of it, of course. I've always thought that some of those books of Dad's were Edgar's first. They weren't Dad's kind of books, really. And then Edgar never really smiled during all those years I knew him. The war left him a lonely man, harsh and strict, with all that upland granite straight along his spine. He attended church every Sunday whether he was sick to death or not, always limping up the aisle exactly five minutes before call to worship, his left knee locked in place from German machine guns that had got him as he was scrambling back from his attack and our own gas, which had turned back on the Regiment before they were barely through the first rows of barbed-wire. After that he prayed a lot but always with a grim determination it seemed to me. And Bessie had to toe the line at home or she'd get the hell beat out of her just like the kids. Dad never approved of that much, not the whippings themselves but the frequency of them. Always said that Edgar's kids got their meanness from it and that Bessie looked like hell for weeks after one of those beatings, all black-eyed and bloody-lipped. Yet Edgar must have loved her and at least thought he did right, because he never cheated on her and never drank or smoked. He worked hard and played little, rose early and went to bed right after dinner, fell in with Dad on the milk route for a while, and when he died left Bessie a small fortune and the three kids a clean and prosperous farm which they proceeded to sell and forget about.

He was a hard man and never went to town during the twenties unless he couldn't help it. He died in '49 of cancer after getting thinner and thinner over those last two years, his teeth greying, the gums shrinking and whitening above them, his white, unshaven face progressively more scraggly toward the end, and his pencil-like arms and legs weak and wobbly beneath the slack skin, until finally he couldn't work anymore and took to bed, refusing up to his last hour to enter the hospital until finally his kidneys stopped, and Pa took him down in spite of himself, only to be too late when he up and died along the road. They buried Edgar two miles from his house at the Centre Cemetery. Bessie cried and protested how much he loved her, and how good and simple a husband he'd always been, her clutching young Jamie and weeping into his tweed cap. Until she joined him twelve years later after running afoul of a January chill, Bessie always maintained it was the gassing that gave Edgar his cancer. "Yep," she'd say, her hand passing abstractly over her mouth and her brown eyes set in a knowing country stare past us all and out the window toward the cemetery, "it was that gassin did it. No doubt! He weren't never the same man I knowed as a girl, when he got back. A good man, mind you! A good country man. But it were that gassin done it. Mark my words."

And then she'd begin to rock in her old shawl-covered chair, and we'd know enough to leave, while its rhythmic squeak troubled the bare oaken floor behind us, her Bible upon her lap, unopened and hidden within the folds of her dress.

CHAPTER XXVI
History Lesson IX

But Arthur grew old and tired before his time. All knew it
and brushed their chins sagely, even the whiskerless women who
knew but seldom spoke, knowing, too, their place, but worrying
each other with downcast glances and sad (but wise) eyes which
told all they did not say over pious and flickering hearths. Arthur
was growing old.

There is a song which the Dunedin men sang back in '18,
joyous and grim, cavalier in its mockery, full of the desperation and
despair of proud men who know their pride to be the only answer
to a world without mercy, and thus no answer at all if hope remains
its covenant, but still they proceed, and therefore the song shines
beautiful in all its mockery:

The 105th went over the top--parlez-vous.
The 105th went over the top--parley-vous.
The 105th went over the top,
Didn't stop to piss or even fuck.
Hinky-Dinky Parlez Vous.

Good lady Anne is in there and Katie too, her
latterly-lusting cousin-in-crime; and sin, which was no sin at all and,
therefore, all the more frightful and hideous since not only did no
purpose come from it but no pain either and so no heroism, thus
(ironically enough) no point, the poignard sheathed in melody.

Anne, and Katie, and Lillian, and Sarah, and sweet Esta, how many more were at his dying--too late to join his friends, not out of love of life (for his was not the age) but surely so not out of (knowingly) an equally impassioned love for honorable death as did his brothers and all the brave boys, so proudly rewarded for their virgin lust never to be repeated and, therefore, never to be sullied. The D.A.R. understands and appreciates (with piety) the pity, poignancy, but necessity and inevitability of such stasis within action.

Arthur built castles, riches, and made the students of the little stone schoolhouse (built in '42 out on the Perrysville Pike Road and in which great cousin Mary Countryman was the first schoolmarm) proud of him. At $5.00 a day he was making a good living, and though old Henry VIII might have scoffed at it, John L., and Hanna, and Gompers knew its unequivocal value all through the teens, and twenties, and into and out the other side of the thirties. If Sinclair and Norris neglected to deal with the more obvious but less certain ambiguities of summer drought and early fall frost, still the country owed the Pure Food and Drug Act (among others) to them as much as to Teddy, and Arthur steeled himself in good Democratic fashion against the trusts, and himself continued making money, even in Dunedin (or just a mile and a half to the S-SW of it, to be accurate) by preaching the then newly heralded gospel of social justice through legal reform.

The Salvation Army had come to Athens in 1900, a leftover from, or a benevolent growth out of, the body politic of British humanitarianism that wended its way westward, over the great ocean, away from the cancerous decay of a dying and incestuous continental society. It was Arthur's favorite charity, by 1900 a benign and intemperately joyful institution that counted 3,000 officers and some 20,000 privates among its dedicated battalions, called forth to war against the disease, poverty, and iniquity of a fair and newly innocent nation, awash with its more newly found progress, mercifully structured and hardened through Teddy's Progressivism from 1900 until a more surely progressive and celibate war was to begin and end not in the vernal maidenhead of a generous and philanthropic, Springtime godliness but in the exact and uncompromising certitudes of sputtering Rolls-Royce engines

222

and staccato Hadley-Vickers machine guns beating to the marches of, not thousands but, millions who wandered both East and West, endlessly, over ground made holy by the staunch, red flow of their freshly won maturity.

Arthur's inarticulate love consumed itself on 90 acres, on sheep and pigs and chickens, on oats and potatoes and beans, but this diffident greed of a simple man affianced to the land was overshadowed and beggared by the more implacable and acrimonious idolatry of, not a nation or even a continent but, a world freely rapacious within its own incendiary dissolution. All this while honest yank farmers lived piously well on record wheat and corn profits as they supported the boys "over there" and ruminated in quiet and tasteful cynicism about the mortality of man and the wanton caprice, not of Anne and her ilk but agricultural markets. Henry, good German hock in hand, would have understood and appreciated both.

There is a legend of love and death, given marginal validity by its recorded presence in a strictly limited number of local volumes, called the Legend of Diamond Rock. Predictably it is about love lost and love long-suffering and, equally certain, about war and love, enduring and rewarded. Long ago, 'once upon a time' if you wish, there lived near Athens, then not Athens but a Mohican (or Mohawk) fortress along the forest trail beside the flowing waters, two brothers Taendora and Onasqua beloved by their kingly, or more correctly chieftainly, father and more especially by their queenly and chieftainessly mother Monitas. The story is long but its sense short and to the point. The Mohawks (or Mohicans - what's the difference?) were attacked by northern tribes above the St. Lawrence. A fierce battle ensued and Onasqua was carried off, leaving his father to die some few years later unavenged, his brother alive but unfulfilled, and his mother in tears, constantly, for her lost child. The rock itself, not diamond but hard granite inexplicably outcropping amidst a chaos of slate and shale, became the lonely retreat of Monitas, bereft of both husband and son and able to think of no better and more satisfying occupation for her remaining comfort than to send him off on his own solitary journey to find and return his untoward and only brother who so unkindly left the bosom of his loving family, and thus hopefully rectify loneliness, love, pride, and revenge all at once.

This a charge which Taendora accomplished overly-well while his devout and ever-plighted mother sat on the rock, crying lonely tears which transformed its so indurate granite to diamond specks (miraculous transfiguration) and was, finally, propitiated by her son's return, four decades later, worn and haggard, an old man with a young boy's heart (supposedly) who presented to his joyful and proud mother not the children and grandchildren of his loins, dropped, perhaps unwillingly but in the end gratefully, from the womb of some fine, greasy young squaw, but the expected and clearly wished for baggage of Taendora's love, his brother, Onasqua now only a heap of bones dug up from some northern burial place, equally and blessedly anonymous in the greater course of human events but no less sacred and revelatory, at least of mankind's greater devotions.

Thus ends the story, or at least all of it that partakes of true legend and myth and so matters here. Some do come home to those who never leave. And some never return, except luckily in some wooden caskets (or threadbare bags) which bore them away (in time rather than space--the two are one in mystery).

Monitas was overjoyed at now possessing both her sons, or at least what remained of them, and one may imagine, without disregarding the need for historical accuracy, the great council fire which burned in the camp that night, with dancing, leaping, yelling, and the like over the remains of both dead and near dead brother. The legend thus began and lives on. Its history both amuses and teaches, the latter often in spite of itself and its intention.

But where are the young lads, the lost ones? How do we memorialize their living? Arthur and Katie lost no time and no sons to war or its consequences. He grew old and sold his crops, supported the effort in '18 and '19, visited old Doc White when he was sick with the croup or the ache, but old Doc never mended his bullet shredded thighs or pulled shrapnel from out of his bubbling chest and heard the deep, immutable rattle of men's (wild and wide wild-eyed) awestruck worship of the ever-returning Spring's passion. Arthur grew heavy-legged and thick-waisted, like Henry who boasted at 50 (or so, and with venereal gout), that he could still sit 36 hours on horse and lead an army across all of France if need be to save the Angevin, albeit Plantagenet, albeit Tudor Kingdom from its enemies. And Katie with him, growing old in peace and plenty, but not cut short, abruptly and unkindly so. She was his helpmate and he hers. He and she, and their brothers and sisters in the Athens and Twin Rivers factories worked for the nation's dream, and the railroads hauled the long and short of it: their produce, their creative genius, the root and cause of Arthur's calloused hands and reddened neck, and the long withering creases across his brow. As his bank book grew fat, Arthur grew old, though he would not admit it to himself nor to his sons. He became town assessor, finally winning an election from the "sneaky" Republicans. The milk route prospered. The town houses proved fair investments, especially in the twenties and forties when all the boys returned. Katie learned to accept her country life, especially when six living children gave her adequate reason for not grieving over (and above) the social pressure of a repressive decade that followed. Arthur bought a used truck and two years later a new car, a Chevy-without frills of course. When the Depression came, he put them both on blocks in the barn and went back to his horses for a while. In due time Roosevelt saved him from the worst of that.

But at what cost? And where are all the fine young boys who moldered without growing old and never found young sweet girls to provide them with their promised resurrection through eternal bliss? The boys from Dunedin and Hawks Farm and Perrysville? Where is little fuzz-faced Jackie Burden, who went off to (and never came back from) a third and lesser war without ever kissing goodbye the sweet, young thing with the silly, sharp tongue who would have knelt and kissed his feet and wept in the cuff of his trousers had he but closed his eyes and no one else been looking?

Where?

CHAPTER XXVII
Love Story X

hush! listen!

there are letters which support history, and if carefully edited display its more unique flow as if a river in ceaseless motion carried its eddies in center stream rather than hidden along the bank.

grandpa knew of grandma's sacrifice. it was always on his mind. in a march letter he says this.

* * * *

My Darling, Darling Katie,

xxxxxxxxxxxxxxxxxxxxxxxxxxxxxxxxxxxxxxxxxxxxxxxxxxxxxxxxxxxxxxxxx

I hardly know how to write you tonight. I feel so guilty for causing you pain that I am ashamed of myself. Katie, please don't ask me what I am thinking about all the time. Like a fool, I'll tell you. I should keep things that don't matter to myself. I had rather suffer all my life than cause you to feel as I know you did last night. And to think I should tell you when you were sick.

I do not know why I thought you meant as you did after all I know you have sacrificed for me. I realize what it must have meant to give up your most cherished desire when I could not promise you what you asked. I realize, too, the great sacrifice it is to come up here and live away from your old friends and acquaintances. After all this I know myself most ungrateful to question whether you cared for me enough to follow me wherever I asked....

I know I am not the son mother and dad expected of me nor the brother Agnes might have wished for, and God knows I always seem to make it all worse and may never make what any woman would consider a good husband.....But if I prove a failure in this it will not ...be for want of loving you....I will do my best to overcome all our problems and to live as a good husband should.....If you think we can do better in Athens or Albany or anyplace else, I am willing to go and try it for a while. I should be happy and contented to be wherever you are even if it were a thousand miles from Dunedin.

I have an idea of what we can do. It may not suit you, so I will wait and tell you when I see you next. If you do not like it simply say so. I will not insist upon your doing anything you do not wish to. I had thought of it even before I received your last letter. If you can think of any way we can be together earlier than we had planned or anything you wish me to do so that we need wait no longer, only tell me. I am ready to do it--I do not wish to set my will in opposition to yours in anything.

* * * *

228

perhaps a trifle overstated, but what was it gramps said about preferring the ebullience of youth to the dullness of wisdom? or it was at least to that effect.

and then there were the babies. as cousins, it was a serious problem which concerned them both, although he often seems confused by grandma's worry and pronouncements. for instance, in another letter he notes:

* * * *

My Darling, Darling, Darling, Katie,

xxxxxxxxxxxxxxxxxxxxxxxxxxxxxxxxxxxxxxxxxxxxxxxxxxxxxxxxxxxxxxx

You must be letting babies worry you to be dreaming about them. I suppose you will tell me before long why you take the stand you do in regards to them. If I felt as you do I should never marry for I do not see how one can be happy living in suspense all the time.

I know I can be happy if only I have you. But how are you going to enjoy life with the dread that something terrible is liable to happen at any time? I can tell you that if I did not love you as madly, passionately, and fondly as I do, there would be nothing to life. I would never have thought of marrying you after you let me know what you thought. If you would only give me a reason for why you think as you do I might feel different.

Don't think I blame you for not wanting to have children,

but I don't think you should blame me if anything should happen after we are married when you now hold sole power in your own hands to decide upon your way. Even if it cost me my life's happiness itself, I could stand it for your sake rather than to always have you live in fear of the unknown for the sake of making me happy.

I knew you loved me when you consented to marry me even though I could not make the promise you asked for.

I hope I have said nothing to hurt you.

Your loving, loving, loving Sweetheart,

xxxxxxxxxxxxxxxxxxxxxxxxxxxxxxxxxxxxxxxxx

xxxxxxxxxxxxx Arthur xxxxxxxxxxxxxxxxx

Hugs and Kisses

* * * *

a bit much at the end, but he's given grandma some tough talk. even love has some clever and practical side to it. still, i can't see why he protests such ignorance of her reasons which seem transparently clear. in another letter, i believe a july one, he develops a very interesting image of a "rubber man," and yet i remember him as anything but such a person.

* * * *

My Darling, Darling, Kate,

I received your letter tonight. Why didn't you tell me Betty Kidder was going to a party so I could go? Maybe I could satisfy her desire for a man. Be sure and tell me next time.

I guess I will have to turn into a little rubber man so you can bend me any way you wish. Then you can put me in your pocket and have me with you all the time. It will cost you nothing to keep me, and you would not be afraid of me then would you?

I guess you will have to have a house made to order to suit you. The only thing to do so that I can be with you all of the time is to live up here where I can work for myself. Then I can be home nearly all of t he time. If I worked on a farm for anyone else, I could not be home more than twelve hours a day. In Athens, I would be home no more. Perhaps you will have to make a job for me that more nearly suits your taste.

I don't know what to do. You know you cannot have me tied right to your apron string all the time. I would be satisfied with that, but I will eventually have to work at something. We cannot live on love we both know, but I am willing to die on it if you wish to tie me tight until I do.

I guess I will be able to get a house with two bedrooms. If not, I can sleep in the barn or get a cot and stay in the kitchen. I know there is no other way, and it was settled long ago that we were to sleep apart. Any old way will suit me as long as I can see you every day. I guess I will sleep downstairs if we get a house with a room upstairs and one down. For then you know, I might be able to sneak in a bedfellow once in a while. If you won't let me do that, I will have to get a rope ladder.

231

If I turn into a rubber man will you let me have room in your bed? All there would be danger of then would be a pair of rubber boots or a macintosh. Ha! I don't think I ever told you that story and am not likely to since I am going to be good for your sake.

What is to happen just six months from Sunday if nothing happens to either of us? Have you thought carefully of it? I wish I knew how I was going to be able to do as you wish and yet live, but I suppose time will tell.

You don't want me to stay around here. You don't want me to work in Athens. You don't want me to go to New York. You will not want me to work on a farm where I will have to be away from you half the time. What am I to do? Can you tell me? I can see no way clear but to lay down by your side and die. I would be willing if you wish it.

I'll be down the afternoon of the fourth while you are waiting on tables. I suppose the Hawk's Farm boys won't have life enough to start anything that will keep a fellow awake. Maybe I can get some of the girls to keep me going so that I will not have to go to Athens. There must be some girls who won't have to work.

All my love (and hugs and kisses) is yours now and forever more. xxxxxxxxxxxxxxxxxxxxxxxxxxxxxxxxxxxxxxxxxxxx xxxxxxxxxxxxxxxxxxxxxxxxxxxxxxxxxxxxxxxxxxxxxxxxxxxxxxxxxx xxxxxxxxxxxxxxxxxxxxxxxxxxxxxxxxxxxxxx Your loving, loving loving, ---------------------- xx ---xx Sweetheart, xxxxxxxxxxxxxx Arthur xxxxxxxxxxxxxxxxxxxxxxxxx
Sweet Dreams

* * * *

well, he might protest to be pliable, but he certainly doesn't show it. betty kidder and all the hawks' farm girls might attest to that. how clever he is sometimes, so unlike what i imagine love to be. it's a duet--so ready to sacrifice himself--though not without some obvious misgivings and complaints.

in that letter, too, he speaks of going strawberrying, the possibility of a hot and dry summer, and wilbur and matilda. there were so many marriages that year it's hard to complain at all--lillian and web, wilburn and matilda, allen and tommie, grace and the new schoolteacher. seems there must have been others, too.

if you'll excuse the expression, there's hope for us all, with separate bedrooms and long ladders to boot.

here's another from that month.

* * * * *

My Darling, Darling Katie,

We began haying today but had to stop when it started to rain. We had one nice shower and are hoping for more. The hay is about half a crop. We did not think it quite so poor until we started cutting it.

* * * * *

here he talks about berries, grandma coming up on sundays, and his mother making a quilt for them. then comes the old problem again.

* * * *

I suppose you are disappointed in me lots of times. I know I am as bad as the next one, and what is the worst of it, I know it at the time too. If I were not aware of how I was bad it would not trouble me. I think girl, you are in love with the man you think you can make of me rather that me alone. I hope you succeed, for I want to be good even if the bad is continually cropping out.

Confound this kid business though. I will tell you frankly that if there was no Katherine Terrel and I felt as I do at times, I would not marry the Queen of England. I love you so deeply, though, that it would be of no use for me to try and give you up. I would only pine away and die.

Katie, I can see no way clear to escape what God has a mind to send us. Nor would I meddle with his will in any way.

Still, in spite of myself, the more I see of those little devils the more I hate them. I think I know your reason for not wanting them, but I can't see for the life of me how you ever got it into your head that I would hinder God's will.

I guess you do not understand some things about men just

as I do not understand certain things about women. Only you know why you could not tell me for so long that you did not want any children. I guess the same reason kept me from asking you what I wanted to know.

We will find our way though Katie. I promise you. With all my love to my own darling Katie xxx

 Your loving, loving
Sweetheart,
 Arthur

* * * * *

    and yet i remember grandma's home filled with dozens of children and grand children, all of us dirty-faced and yelling around the christmas tree or playing too near the kitchen stove and eating homemade doughnuts fresh out of the oven, dipped in confectioners sugar when they were still hot and so sticky and gooey--all over the house.
    and he seemed the soul of patience. i remember that the church fathers once argued that the only justification for marriage was children. they assumed that the only excuse for sex was marriage, i guess.
none of that was on grandpa's mind though. he was in love, and that wasn't theology, sacred or not. how practical he seems. consequences are important to him, yet the questions and answers come so late in the courtship. he loved her. and she loved him. i know it...
    of course, they were cousins.
    listen.

* * * *

Dunedin, New York
September 20,1913

My Darling Darling Darling Katie, xxx

I am glad you are feeling fair this week. There are no stormy days now to keep me from work, and there's so much to do that needs doing all at once that I am kept busy, you bet. I have the buck-wheat nearly raked. It has been a tough job because father could not stand to help, and I had to do it all alone. In another half day the buckwheat will be ready for the threshers.

Father did cut some corn today. He says we will have near a hundred bushels, but most of it is soft from that freeze that caught it about two weeks ago. Two weeks too soon, but I guess we will not have much trouble fattening the pigs without buying them any feed. Father is also talking about selling all our hens. If he does they will bring a lot because we bought $30 worth off Charlie Fouks only last month.

I have put those two rugs on our bill. They make $87.14. The bill is full to the last line so I guess we will have to send Mr. Ward his order now. I guess we can get the rest of what we want in Athens even if it costs a little more. I did not think you would get cold feet so soon, though. I guess bare boards in January is enough to give anyone cold feet.

I am not going to worry anymore, though, Katie. I know we will be able to get started some way. You must not let it worry you because I do not like babies. If any ever come to our house how could I help but love them? I will promise to bear my part if any of the little meddlers come along. I sure don't want any though. Not for a few years anyway.

I know you will never be like Aunt Lillian, but it makes me shiver to think what might have happened if you had ever kept mixed up with that clique. I know Agnes would never have worried if you had gone wrong, and although I have nothing against old Jim, I think I could live forever if I never saw his family again.

It sure got on my nerves when I saw how dirty she let those children run. I think I could tolerate a clean baby, but one that you could smell piss on a mile away was too much for me. Little Earl was a nice fellow, but I was afraid to touch him or have him touch me. How you could kiss and hug them and make to-do over them, I just don't understand. I had just as soon hug and kiss a toad as a kid covered with sh-t. I don't wonder you were sick afterwards, I'd have been dead if I did as you did.

Darling, I can stand a lot, but if you should ever go for me as Lil did for Jim, I don't know what I would do. I think I could stand the swearing better than the dirt though. I am not worrying about that with you, however, for I have had a trial of your housekeeping and am content that you will clean at least as well and also be tidy and neat.

I guess I will beat many of my chums yet. Nig and Nina may not make it by next month. I am sure the luckiest of them for they could never find a girl half as wonderful as you.

All my love is yours, my own darling. Love, love, love, love, love. Your loving loving loving loving,

xxxxxxxxxxxxxx Sweetheart xxxxxxxxxxxx xxxxxxxxxxxxxx

Arthur xxxxxxxxxxxxxxxx
xxxxxxxxxxxxxxxxxxxxxxxxxxxxxxxxxxxxxxxx

* * * * *

    what a complete and astounding change he makes there.
now he is the one who wishes for no children, and grandma, for all
her reticence and delicacy, is worried about him. he's tough about
it, too. and speaks his mind very directly.

    i wonder if it's all so clear, or could he be doing all that for
her? we can't know, and clearly he seems disgusted by great aunt
lil's household. yet stranger things have happened for the sake of
love.

    and eventually we kiss with our mouths.

CHAPTER XXVIII
Portrait IX

Uncle Web, Lilian's husband, couldn't swim, but that didn't stop him from fishin with your Grandpa every spare spring and fall morning out on Long Lake. He still talks about it to this day, his long, good-natured jaw gone slack now without teeth, his mouth caved in but still cherishing the remains of a smile which goes well with his blue eyes, which at 89 are as full of life as ever. Like Gramps, Web never went to war. Instead, he married Lillian when she was only 15 and had her carrying young Herb at the same time Grandma was heavy with little Lillian. "A right good man," big Lil would always say patting her stomach and smiling devilishly when way into her seventies, "a right good man, quick and swift about it and no funny business."

Web always laughs, too, and still seems proud of it all. He's hated water all his life and didn't even like to wade with us kids when the two families would go swimming on Sunday afternoon picnics during the thirties. Still, he'd never let Pa back him down when it came to fishing, and many's the morning at 4 o'clock you'd see him through the mist out on the lake with Pa in the old, leaky 14' row boat that we meticulously sanded and painted every winter, but never managed to caulk all the holes dry. Web would sit, straight-lipped and level-eyed, terrified but always mildly amused at his own temerity, while Gramps stood up and cast lazily in toward the trees as the boat drifted southeast along the shore. It was only with Web that Pa cast rather than still-fished. He used to say that teasing Web so was good for Web and a harmless enough a sin for himself. He knew how the boat rocked when he stood up and how it leaned lazily over with each long cast into the fronds. He would smile at me as I sat, small and quiet in the bow of the boat, and he'd wink toward Web's hands as the knuckles whitened with each roll of the boat until it seemed there wasn't enough blood in Uncle Web's body to bring them back to color again.

But Web would stay there, even upon occasion getting up enough courage to let go and light his pipe, that in spite of the dunking that Pa had once given him when they were younger in 4 1/2 feet of carefully selected gravel-bottom cove, just for the fun of it. Web hadn't known that, and he'd cried out like a fried goose when Gramps suddenly stepped to one side of the boat (as Web lit his pipe) and laughed uproariously, throwing his rod where he knew he could find it again as the boat's off-side lurched upward and both men tossed dizzily into the cold September water. Web still smiles about it.

"Jus couldn't resist a trick or two--yer Pa," he croaks over the white merschaum we bought for him on his 75th. "Nope, he was always a kidder. And the best fisherman in ten counties. That's why he did it. Jus' like those fish so much. There wasn't a Brownell or a Phalan or a Wager could compare with him. Course I made him pay for my pipe, and he never done it again, no matter how much he laughed at the time. He sure looked like a skinned rat and never did find that lure he'd mistaken and let loose in the bottom of the boat. Served him right, but he sure was a kidder. He sure was!"

Web's oldest brother died in the flu epidemic of '18, same year my great Grandma old Jessie Bailey died, just a month after Edgar went to war. He'd courted your Grandma some when she'd gone to visit her half-sister Mattie up in Berlin, but not much had come of it other than Pa getting jealous and Grandma being flattered but bored. Mattie'd already gotten married by then after having lived all those years with the Whaley's after old Tom Terrel and Suzie split up for a time. Suzie, of course, died when Grandma was only 5 years old, and Tom had to raise Lillian and her all by himself. It wasn't any wonder then that he never really pressed the suit to get Mattie back from the Whaley's, especially after they produced papers saying Suzie had signed them and given up all rights to Mattie and that their adoption was therefore cold legal. Grandma always swore she never heard about her half-sister until one day when old Tom got a colored letter that smelled good and had little birds and flowers along the edges. Then he had to tell them.

Web, he just laughs and says any one of the Terrel girls were good-lookin enough for him. "Lively bunch, too," I've heard him whisper, more publicly than privately, in front of Lil. "Ayh--Lively bunch at that."

No, Web was always a winter man. He used to ice-skate a good deal up at Countryman Lake before the state took it over and made it part of the Taconic State Park for the down-staters. Now, Dunediners hardly ever go there. Too crowded, they say, what with the camping trailers, and clotheslines from every tree and the smell of kerosene so rank in the air you can hardly breathe. Web met Lil one winter when he was out bobsledding with Mark Hilty and his gang up on Birch Mountain out near the Corners.

Aunt Lil had a thing for Mark, to hear them tell it, and she'd gone there especially on Saturday to catch his eye, but it didn't work out like that. To hear Web tell it, Mark got to drinkin more than he should've that morning, and when he went to the hill with the boys he was kickin up his heels and swearing so that no decent girl would get within a ten foot pole of him. That left things open for Web, and while Mark was betting the other boys on how fast he could make the ride down without tipping over or hitting anyone else, Web strode right over to Lil and offered her a ride on his brand new four seater with a deluxe double-padded cushion.

Well, I suppose no girl could rightly resist that, for Lil went, especially after Web told her he'd promised himself that only the prettiest girl in the district was going to ride in it first with him, and the two set off down the hill, Lil firmly tucked in front between Web's patched knees and beneath his mother's new quilt. Screaming with delight all the way down, Web still, insists.

Or at least with delight until they met up with Mark Hilty's flyer bucking crosswise in front of the tobbogan. Up and off they flew, Web somehow keeping hold of her and landing hard underneath, his hand clutched firmly around Lil's waist and bosom. Lil's knees were skinned from the front of the toboggan, and Web had a sore shoulder for a month afterwards. But it wasn't until Mark stood up, shakey and snow-covered but without a scratch, laughing, pointing at them with a, "My God Web you sure 'nough know the position don't ya," that Lil realized what a state she was in. She turned all red right through her snow suit Web says, pushed Web away and got to her feet. Though before she managed it, she slipped on the hard-pack twice and fell on her dignity both times. She told Mark Hilty that he had the foulest mouth in town before limping away with her hands on her hips.

It was another month 'til Aunt Lil consented to see Web again, and then only after he'd asked Ma out and she'd refused him because she'd started to date Pa. Lil never did see Mark again. Never let him come too near the house even.

The Terrels, they tell me, are French, Canuck and European both. Old Tom's folks met on some boat coming into Ellis, fell in love, and moved upstate the minute they were let loose. Fell in love with the place up here, too, I guess. Maybe that's why Lil, and Kate, and Mattie never left the place no matter where us kids roamed. A country can get to a man, or woman I suppose. Even if the Dunedin air was bad for Ma toward the end, and I doubt it, she still never left Athens. Web and Lil still live on that little place of theirs out near Hawk's Farm. They'll never die. Not for me they won't.

CHAPTER XXIX
Love Story XI

here are some letters and excerpts--orally edited but without comment or conclusions. this time. they are in temporal order which should serve as an at least capricious judgement upon the courtship itself--and its various trials and tribulations.

* * * *

Stumps Corners, New York
April 17, 1913

Darling I wish you would give up working out. I am afraid it is too much for you. You have always had what you wanted when at home and can now....

I have enough to get your teeth fixed, and I can get along if

I do not get it back....

I would rather wait a while longer than to have you where you are, half worked to death....

Of course you will do as you like no matter what I say....

I cannot hinder you, but I would rather have you at home....

We will have your teeth fixed as soon as you are ready....

Please keep well and take care of yourself. You have not taken time to get over your sickness before you are back at work. I can hardly keep from crying when I think of what might happen to you.

Katie you little realize how my life is wrapped up in you or you would be more careful. You know why I did not go to the necktie social. I did not care to go without you. All the girls who were there could never fill the vacancy that is ever in my life when you are not near.

Your love, loving
Sweetheart,
Arthur xxxxx

* * * *

Dunedin, New York

September 6, 1913

Glad you are coming up. Mother says for you to be sure to bring your pear recipe....

I have a notion to get hold of a bushel more....

There will not be much to do up here next week. Tomatoes won't be ripe for canning and only a few peppers big enough to stuff....

That's lucky for us....

Darling, you must not think by anything I wrote in that other letter that I am not satisfied with you. You are the sweetest girl in the world to me. I could love no other and would suffer any torment rather than marry you and have you unhappy.

Perhaps it will be as you say. We will be happy when we are together and have each other. I hope so. I will do my best to be a good husband. I should love to have it so I could get you anything you might want....

But you know I am only a poor farmer.

You knew that when you promised to marry me, but I thought your eyes may have been blinded by love....

That is why I wrote as I did in my last letter. I did not want you to be dissatisfied when you saw what you were getting.

Your loving, loving,
Arthur
xxxxxxxx

* * * *

Dunedin, New York
September 29, 1913

My own Darling, Darling, Katie,

I suppose you will call me down for not answering your last
letter. I could not until I got some stamps....

I worked up at Herb Rawley's a day and a half this week.
He was going down to get his wife today if it had been fair
weather....

I am going to see if I can sell my wood and lumber to the
company that is putting up the new dam for the reservoir. If I can
we will not have to worry about having enough to get the rest of
our goods next spring. If I don't sell it now maybe I could later next
year. Only difference would be that if I had the money now it could
draw interest in the bank....

I will have to go to the Sandlake Democratic Assembly
Convention the 1st week of October. Oh, it would be so nice to
have you by my side....

I will come down some day next week and we can send in
our order. Then you can see about when you can get your teeth
fixed. -- On second thought, why don't you make a telephone call to
whoever you want to do the work, and then we can get it done
when I come down about the furniture and things. If you're too
scared to have them fixed then, I will wait until Pa and I go down
on our last peddling trip two weeks from next Friday.

Aunt Susannah hired a girl that got all loused up....

I'm going down to help Wednesday afternoon. Looks like there will be lots of time to get our furniture in for the mice to eat up before we are ready to use it....

How would you like the little horse than Lena and Ruth have?...

I think you could drive him after a while. He's nothing fast....

Don't think I am sure of him. It is only a game of chance. If Len can get another horse that he has his eye on ... he has offered to give old Frank to someone who would use him good before killing him. He said he'd as soon I have him as any....

I am not worried about how you will use me next Sunday. You could not be unkind to me unless you got angry....

I don't know if Nig goes to see Nina or not. Nina was up to see him yesterday, and he's due to go back to St. Louis week after next. Maybe it is better for Nina to know now then later. If Nig deceived her until after they were married, think of the life they would have then....

It seems impossible that two others could love as we do. It seems as if no one could love as I do you....

I am glad you have decided to make me be good. It is about time. I have tried myself and failed.

Your loving, loving,
Sweetheart,
Arthur xxxxxx

* * * *

Dunedin, New York
October 4, 1913

My Darling, Darling Katie,

It rained so this morning that I did not go to Sandlake! I wouldn't have driven over there in an open wagon for the office of President, to say nothing of just acting as a delegate....

It may cost me my chance of getting on the ticket but I don't care....

It stopped raining this afternoon, and I went down and finished fixing Susannah's house....

Have you told Eddie Poultrie yet that you are leaving?

You need not worry about me burning your letters up. I will leave that to you when you get so you don't want to leave any evidence that you ever loved me....

You must not put so much stock in what I say in letters you know. I could lie in those, and you could not tell when I did it by looking at me. I don't think you will find many lies in them though. I try not to lie to you....

You know how easy it is to be good as well as I, if I am not mistaken. I guess we can be good if we help each other though....

Aunt Lil is down here. She and mother have your quilt almost set together....

I am going to send two dollars to Mt. Union in the morning

to pay one of my debts that has been alive for over a year.

Your loving, loving,
Arthur
xxxxxxxxxxxxxx

* * * *

Dunedin, New York
November 3rd

My Darling, Darling, Katie,

I guess you do not intend to hurt yourself about writing. I have gotten one letter in almost a whole week....

You're not angry because I took that load to Perrysville night before last are you? They had no other way to get there, and father was feeling too poorly to do it himself....

I went to Athens today and got our things that were at the freight house.... The glassware is fine but the clock takes the cake. The chairs are not exactly what I expected.... That is, what I could see of them. They may be better after I get them unpacked. Some were scratched a bit....I did not see your rugs, they were rolled tight.... The knives and forks and spoons did not come... I put the chairs and rugs and parlor table down to Susannah's. The glasses and dishes that are here I will take down when I go again.

I'm keeping the clock here....

If I don't get a letter tomorrow and you are well Sunday, you will catch a deuce of hugs and kisses. I have wanted to hold you so bad since I saw the other fellows hugging their girls night before last....

Father bought another horse today. I will drive it down Sunday.... I suppose you'll want me to come even if you don't write....

The clock has a dandy half-hour strike.

Father will stay in Athens tomorrow night to try and sell some of the pigs and to see the doctor. ...

I suppose you will be ready for the dentist next week. If you want to go and need some money let me know.... If you want me to go with you, I wish you would wait until I get the rest of my wood over to the dam. I want to get it drawed and pick up my check before they shut down the tenth of this month or I may have to wait until spring for my money... But if the teeth are bothering you, I will go anytime....

Has old lady Poultrie got home yet? I don't know about trusting those old bachelors alone with you. Ha!

The clock has struck again, so good night. I hope you will like all your things. If you are not pleased I will try and get you some others when I have the money.

Your loving, loving,
Sweetheart, Arthur
xxxxxxxxxxxxx

* * * *

Dunedin, New York
November 6, 1913

My Darling, Darling, Katie,

I suppose you think me mean, not wanting to wait until
night when we are ready to get married. I am not ashamed to be
married in the day...I think though if you happen to ride up here in
the night two or three times in December you will be willing to
arrange it so that we can arrive home before dark.

Girls don't as a general rule realize what they ask of a
fellow. If they had to ride ten miles once a week every winter
Sunday night with the temperature anywheres from zero to twenty
below they would hate the sight of a winter night.

After this I am dumb on this subject. I will do as you wish
even if you want to make it unpleasant for us right from the start.

You must not do too much these last days. I would rather
you quit and let me supply the money we need until January....

Please do not let me go another whole week without a
letter....

When you really do get ready to have your teeth fixed, let
me know and I will go with you. I suppose you'll want me to go. If
not, say so and I'll not come down. I don't crave the job.

I'll have to stop writing now. I suppose I'll have to stay up
till midnight or after watching those sneaking Republicans to see
that they don't cheat us out of our just dues.

All my love is ever yours in life and in death if earthly love
can hold in the beyond.

Your loving Sweetheart,
Arthur
xxxxxxxxxxxx

* * * *

Dunedin, New York
November 8, 1913

My Darling - xx - Darling Katie,

I guess you will hear of the awful news of the defeat of the
Democrats in Dunedin before you even get this. We were all
defeated by a small margin, but the Republicans were certainly
scared for the first time in years. The supervisor was defeated by 25
votes, and I lost by only 3....

We have some consolation though. We did not buy votes as
they did. It cost the Republic Party $500.00 to win from us
yesterday...I don't care about being beaten half as bad as I would in
a ball game....

Our Parlor suite is at the freight office. I will get it when I
take the pigs down. We are going to kill six....

I suppose I deserve a call down for saying you had no
feelings. I know you are very sensitive and hurt easily....

I have been drawing wood all day today.... Then I had to
come home and do all the chores.... Father continues to feel poorly.

I guess I will get my work done before January. If so I am going to have a week's rest if it kills me. The more I do, the more there seems to be to do.

Your loving Sweetheart,
Arthur
xxxxxxxxxxxxxxx

* * * *

Dunedin, New York
November 30, 1913

My Darling Katie,

...suppose a scolding will be ready for me Sunday...not writing this week.... You will get only two more this week....

have to go to the Centre tomorrow....Should have gone last night, but it was -15 degrees....

I banked the house this afternoon...won't freeze tonight.

You talk about my lonely evenings...have had nothing to read all this fall.... You will have to read to me next year....

Just think...only six more weeks to stay single...six months just a little while ago...wish it were only six days....

...won't get tired of you....love you..careful you don't get tired of me first....

...can have your teeth fixed anytime then. ...if not, do as you see fit...if...mine...try to save them now....Telephone...come down with you if you want...that's an end to it.

...your father want his mittens soon?...

...Pearl have any advice to give you?...

...have not for the money for the wood yet...Mac Donough has been up ... that I know...will get it when he comes...not worrying...he's good for it.

...hunting yesterday...dog had a fox running...all I saw was its tracks... Ha!

...don't worry over my gun....carried it for years...ever since eight...should know by now...haven't ever shot myself...yet...

...want me to make a wall ornament of it...with a mat of moss...far from my intention.

...except...some hunting in the spring...if...work caught up...not had time to trap...if only for rats...haven't caught any yet...

...need gun...

Your loving, loving,
Sweetheart,
Arthur
xxxxxxxxxxxxxx

* * * * *

see! history has its moments in the flesh. have we learned
any more by paying attention only to subject sentences

CHAPTER XXX
History Lesson X

Guns!

The River never stops flowing. Interminably, in endless procession. And once-upon-a-time there was a great river of men flowing ceaselessly over mud-soaked and rat infested trenches for over 5 years over a greater river of water which merely flowed ceaselessly forever, and therefore across its seemingly unchangeable face there appeared not the poignancy that comes to all hideous and grotesque actions when movement stops and purpose (supposed or otherwise) bears no essential relationship to being. Young Arthur knew, as must have his namesake when creating heaven's earthly kingdom, and certainly Henry knew when not loving Anne, but saving it (the lovable kingdom of earthly splendor) from heaven (and France and Spain and the Papal States in their virginal lust, etc). They all knew the glory and the glory.

In October 1914, just before the fall of Antwerp, a fact then unknown in the allied soul because unadmitted to, out of love and desperation, but prepared for and accepted beforehand in the trenches, pillboxes, and staff-meeting, general or otherwise; the Athens Times, dear old herald of national opinion and worldly fact, noted in a three column 36 pt head in the upper left hand corner of the front page with subheads galore (it was the practice of the day)

257

that the Philadelphia Athletics, then 3 times world champions (in '13 over the favored Giants in six after a week of rain delays) were being defeated, ,inexplicably, in four straight games, by the upstart Boston Braves. Perfectly balancing (it was again the style of the day) this holocaust of sportive life (with two single columns in between for suitable local news) was an equal 3 column, 36 pt, upper, right-hand front page head (with subs) which for two weeks told of Antwerp's possible, then imminent, then actual fall within the, as yet, infant war before the Entente stopped the Huns at Ypres in the first little battle of the great battles. Upon occasion an applicable sub-head would note that things were going much better on the Eastern front, the Russians as yet not having forgotten the fearful and evangelical love of their Cossack ancestors for the more manly arts.

It was to come. Arthur would have read the left hand column first, we can be assured, and its writer, in clever and slightly wicked parody of the seemingly temporary disaster an ocean away (thank God--and weren't they all so lucky to have so wisely avoided European politics, etc, etc,), shrilled before the last inglorious defeat of Connie's (Mack) invincible battalion (and equally, left or right, appropriate line or two) "Battle Formations Drawn. . .the Athletics. . .Fight in Their Last Line of Entrenchments." The Athletics, it seems, were not found (or felt) as resourceful as their European brothers who found and built lines of entrenchments which stretched from torso to torso, mountains to sea, and infinitely deep into homeland and wasteland, forever and forever and forever.

Tinker to Evers to Chance, and let's start a new inning. Arthur, the newspapers attest, played ball with the best of them at Athens and Albany before the former went to the Giants and into history (Tink never could hit a good curve, Arthur always protested from centerfield where he played his own game, free to roam), and the young Countryman stayed home at the behest of gentle Katherine (how unlike Henry) to care for kith and kindred. Yes, there's nothing like a pitcher's duel, 0-0 in the 19th when Casey, or the Babe, or Joltin' Joe, or Arthur C. can step up there (closed stance, a grim lip, pointed finger, and metal heart) to explode one over the fence and so more perfectly end a perfect game.

Arthur wanted to go, just like his sons in the second of the

258

double header. Wanted to go in the first inning, too, before the Somme, before Verdun, before Pachendale, and even Belleau Wood. But they wouldn't let him. "We're not in it yet, Mac," they said, in early '15 after Antwerp but before the East Prussia defeats, and they sent him home. "You've got three kids," they reminded in '18 with due deliberation and then sent him home again to wait a more critical moment in history's unfolding which, happily in the long run, never came (thus the doctrine of the Trinity, evident and unspoken, proving an ultimate defense in an ultimately defensive war).

And Arthur had foreseen it, foreseen it all, when the Chinks reveled in Hankow October 12 and the (damned stupid) missionaries refused to leave.

"Them Manchus deserve their heathen end," he lectured his pure, young Kate, retold down throughout generations, "but that Suny-at-sin is no better."

Knew it, too, throughout those weeks of 1911 when the Tripolitan Blockade displayed the proud Turk's rotting carcass and a year later when the Spics in Mexico rebelled even while old Uncle Sam was thinking about raising the remains of the Maine from the bottom of Havana Harbor but gave the cost a second thought and so had no thirds. It took, of course, four years for the foolishness to work itself out when Pershing, in a prep for the big one he knew, went down across the Rio after Pancho and showed them what a little American ingenuity could do. That, of course, was during Verdun and the Carpathians, and before the Ardennes and the Carpathians (which to be sure never did end, the Austrians afflicted, it seemed to the Germans, not only with a sinful lack of skill but an absurd love of their homeland mountains). No knockout blows on the field boys, and in the center of the ring the Great White Hope was to be no more. Taft, of course again, had already gone West.

So Arthur became one of the unwilling, lucky few. Athens boys fought in them all, the county histories parade the proud accomplishments before us, "at Wallomsac and Ticonderoga, Fort Stanwix and Saratoga" (the feminine rhyme unintentional and unjustified for certain).

In the brother's war, the Athens Iron Work forged the great metal plates of the Monitor, felicitous vessel of future greatness, and Dunedin and Athens boys went off to battle, 37 officers and 725 enlisted men strong, in the 2nd Regiment of New York State Volunteers, then a year later in the 125th N.Y.S. Volunteers, and six months after that in the 169th and shortly later in the 181st to be followed again by the 1st, newly outfitted and up to strength with clean, pressed, unshaven, pink-cheeked, young boys with the clear, blue eyes and smiles for Mom and Sis, and a special way of laughing for Lil or Kate, only to return, (a precious few of them) later, old men, weary and leaden-gaited (like Edgar, even though he'd never laughed before-hand), never to again find their youth.

Sergeant Burton Julian Wellington, who failed to make, with Tink and Art and Evers and Chance, the Athens Bobcats, was the first in '16 to sacrifice himself to save democracy on the Somme, Sept. 9th on a routine patrol in no-man's-land, to be buried at Potieres. He left no parting words.

But some men did, like the Leathernecks at Belleau Woods. "Lafayette...." Or if not Leathernecks it should have been. One Dunedin boy screamed (is said to have) as the medics bandaged the stumps of both feet outside Bellencourt, "shit, another pair of shoes gone to the devil," and fourth cousin Nehemiah (out of someone by old Ebeneezer the legend goes) Countryman is supposed to have bitched in the Ardennes when the four fingers of his left hand were blown off, "ain't it hell, there goes seven years of violin lessons."

Then, too, there was Katie's 1st boyfriend, little Himmie Schyler with the 105th Expeditionary, who stood up before the trenches at Cambrai and cried to the advancing Bosche "wait till my Macaroni benders get up, you bastards, and then we'll show you." Henry would have liked him too, we can all be sure.

Even his sweet, little, sharp-tongued Jewess could not entirely disclaim the artless courage of it, the candor of the young before dying who knew no other way to live (and we are all bereft like she of hers). And certainly the historical thread would not be complete without a reminder that the Katmai volcano blew its top in Kodiak in June 11th. The year irrelevant. It was within the decade. Like, too, was the Black River which overflowed its banks in Minnesota on October 9th and engulfed the entire town of Black River Falls. During that week the Methodists held their Ecumenical Conference in Toronto and prayed mightily for world peace and

Godly mercy--to no discernible effect.

In later years, after the bust of the Depression, which lingered after the boom of the Twenties (all of which was the vainglorious attempt of a lost generation to rediscover its own lost youth so unkindly stolen from it on the Marne) and just before the Commie menace gave rise to the frenetic forties and fifties, young Martin, Arthur's youngest son and Katie's "little boy", enlisted in '42 of his own freewill, just after Arthur had gotten a letter from the Selective Service addressed to Martin Countryman which he assumed to be senior rather than junior and so answered it without telling young Martin, and informed the good men that "little" Martin was lately and incontestably dead. A second letter then arrived disputing the fact and requesting that said Martin appear before the board for further inquiry.

The records show it, and the fact is unquestionable, although the fun of it may be in the motive, that old Arthur (then nearing Henry's age at demise) journeyed down to the draft board, letters in one hand and death certificate in another and a smile, courteous enough but maddening to behold, across his face, and presented to the Athens selectmen incontrovertible proof that Martin Countryman was dead, of heart disease, among other things, such as a failing liver and finally weakened kidneys, and that no such man could possibly serve in the expeditionary forces, a mistake which the good men were at pains to note was at least one full war removed from the truth.

"I thank you," replied Arthur, the same affable smile spreading in good humor even further across his face, "but I will agree you've a good idea there. Be a damn sight better if us old fellers, and old Martin there too, might take care of this business on both sides. We'd be a mite slower, I admit, but we'd be a good deal more careful, too, and we'd all come out of it better off. Give the young fellers a chance to kick up their heels a bit and enjoy themselves." And then the grin disappeared, or at least in later years when he told the story it would, "seems as how they need it some. War ain't a place to grow up in. Gives a body the wrong ideas and always sets you searchin' for things you never can get back."

The selectmen were, to borrow a phrase, fit to be tied, but the records were the records, and it was six months before old

Martin and young Martin Jr. were separated satisfactorily. By that time Jr. was already in the Navy, well on his way to the big one in the Pacific to serve with Halsey and the fast carriers and watch the Nips make a damn fool out of his commander far north of the Phillipines. "War's not always for the young," he would later parody his father, "but its always for damn fools."

If not Henry, at least contentious Mars understood that one, when caught with fulsome Venus by her hubby. Martin solved the problem, although a wencher in his own right, never as lacking in class as Alex or Joseph. The former's line from behind the wheel while patrolling Athens streets was, "Hey chick, you put out?" A handsome and athletic man, it is rumored that he got a surprising number of acceptances, or at least tacit admissions which thus gained the lucky cutie admission to the front seat. And so he quietly married to a young catholic girl with demure face but wickedly joyful eyes who managed one child and uncounted years with him.

All three sons joined up for Pa and country eventually. Joseph in '43 to Europe and Alex in '45 when, a kid in hand and one in the oven, he could no longer avoid it, thus happily making the occupation force in Tojo's capital for 12 glorious months in which he taught the josans how American boys do it and gathered more war stories than both his brothers, much to young Martin's chagrin.

But Uncle Edgar knew, and Arthur remembered, that war was no place for remembered dreams. "If God Almighty, and I bless his heart," he would almost shout through the room in those days after he returned "if he were truly Almighty, and mind you I'm not callin' him a liar, he would never have unleashed on us, old and young alike, the Hell he did in France. T'was no fit way for a lovin' God to treat people." Later still he would repeat the admonition, "It was a Hell, never to be remembered."

So thank the good Lord for Alex's war stories, Arthur insisted. Some good ought to come of a hellish occupation. And everyone stared in wonder at what the good Baptist, who'd never told a lie, had said. And buxom Kate just smiled in her rocking chair, waist-full and hips astern, and thanked God that all three of her boys had returned. "Never a Countryman killed in the forge of war," she'd insist in later years, not a physically accurate or defensible statement but all knew what she meant. And so probably would Teddy, and Howie, and Woody, and Teddy II, and even Henry and old Alexander Washington. And the family to the sixteenth generation, or thereabouts, from poor Anne's great folly, weathered through two wars, another and even stranger union of bedfellows in which Vulcan lay in his wife's used, empty, and still bloodied bed not to surprise and throw down the callous, case-hardened cuckolder, but to marry with him and from their unnatural union forge the true and tempered furnace for a third and last arbitrament of the sword which lay between them.

Yes! Subject sentences do tweak the imagination. Don't they?

CHAPTER XXXI
PORTRAIT X

I remember the sack full of treasures Martin brought back, too, from over the river. Pa wasn't there when we divided them. Like kissing, he never really participated much in public greed, and although he always said he'd sooner trust a thief then a liar, I think they ran a close race.

He'd always tell the story about the retired Athens banker Jacob Burdick and his 19 year old wife Becky. Seems Jacob courted her late in his sixties and threw every young man in town into an uproar, because Becky Swift was pretty as a picture with sky blue eyes and promising red hair. And to see something that good wasted on a 67 year old lecher just naturally went against the grain of young bloods. Well, old Burdick got her, or his money got her, for Becky liked fine jewelry and frilly things, and Jacob knew how to satisfy at least that craving. And for a while things looked all right. Becky prospered, at least outwardly, and attended all the big Athens social functions. Jacob even got her an invitation to Theodore Roosevelt's last governor's ball in Albany, and although he was indisposed, Becky had a wonderful time what with all the attention she received. Still, everyone admitted, she came home to Pawling Avenue at a decent hour.

Oddly enough the marriage didn't break up, though after 5 years when Becky still wasn't pregnant and evidently hadn't even come close, there were persistent rumors that old Jacob, now 72, just couldn't perform no matter how much he might want to and that Becky must just be the most frustrated young girl in town. At parties the bloods vied unashamedly for a place on Becky's dance card and laughed over naughty jokes with her while Jacob sat close by nodding to himself, occasionally falling asleep, upon being wakened only to smile affably toward the windows, laugh across his heaving waist, and ask if Becky were ready to take him home now. The entire situation was a town scandal.

But that's what Becky Burdick did, took him home and was always in herself at a decent hour. The love of money does strange things Pa would always admonish, "sometimes it can even make you love the unlovable, both good and bad."

And strange it was when the whole town was breathlessly waiting for Becky to up and run off with some good looking stud, or at the very least show up pregnant with someone else's child, though no one had a likely candidate. Then both Becky and Jacob were murdered one night in cold blood by a servant who was caught with two huge suitcases of jewels and money that he literally had to drag, then carry, up the driveway.

Then everyone discovered why Becky always got home so early and how Jacob kept his wife. Seems old Burdick never did trust banks, though he always kept a large account of his own and an equally large general account in the Albany Savings. The old man had seen too many depressions and downturns in the cycle, however, and over the years he had begun investing heavily in stock certificates of only the best companies, jewelry and precious stones, gold coins as well as illegal gold bullion smuggled in from abroad, and large amounts of silver certificates, all of which he kept in a monstrous safe in his library. And it was there that the servant had chanced to see the two of them, Jacob and Becky, stark naked, cavorting through hoards of paper money, coins, jewelry, and savings certificates in an ecstacy that evidently left both man and wife breathless against the walls and on the couch.

The servant couldn't stand it, of course. Not 3 or 4 nights a week, what with him only able to pinch a stray coin now and then after breakfast while the two of them slept. So he plotted and killed them one night, while they were in the middle of it all, taking even Becky's wedding ring, a 7.6 carat diamond, to boot. He had to cut off her finger to do it. Pa said they all hoped she was dead already when he did that. They probably both were, because he slit their throats. Folks assumed Becky was dispatched first, by surprise, and then old Jacob who couldn't defend himself anyway and by then was so senile that he probably didn't even realize what was happening, sitting there naked amidst all that money, and no one else in the house....

Now, where was I? Oh yes.

No, Pa never liked to display open greed. He was up at the farm when Martin opened his G.I. bag and took out the real Japanese ceremonial sword for Pa and the geisha slippers for Ma. Then there was all sorts of stuff that we argued over: bar chips; oriental games; china saki cups; lacquered chopsticks; panted scroll of lions and tigers, and some with delicate flowers, birds, and insects; 3 kimonos, blue and white and red; 2 obis; a full roll of raw blue silk; the salary pay cards which Martin had stolen from a Japanese factory one night when he and some buddies were drunk; all sizes and colors of Japanese coins; four or five pairs of slippers; a number of little enamel figurines of some kind; an officer's uniform; and, best of all, a real Japanese officer's pistol with 30 rounds of ammo.

Oh, how we loved it. There was more, of course, but I can't remember it all. I just remember us, Ma and Lil and Sarah and me and Jessie, and some of you kids (Alex wasn't back yet, and he brought no bag) and Martin just grinning as good-naturedly as you could ask as we scrambled for all the treasures around us, oohing and aahing like damn fools. Oh, you couldn't help but love Martin. He kept only the pistol for himself (we'd all expected that) a kimono, a scroll with birds in it, and the bolt of raw silk for Susie. He was very generous.

It was a pity though. Even after they were married Susie never got to that bolt of silk, and it took little Beatrice to finally make a suit and sheath out of it years later. Of course Beatrice is a wonder with needle and thread, so maybe it was for the best.

Anyway, I guess we never really know what's good for us. Pa might not of cared much for money, but he was careful as all hell about it. I remember him saying that once he and Grandpa Martin herded some sheep all the way from above Dunedin to Athens back around 1900 or so, and when they found out that the market had dropped in the two days it took to get them there, the two of them just picked up, turned around, and drove them sheep all the way back up to the mountains rather than sell them.

"Damned," Pa used to say, "if I'd let the bankers and lawyers make all their money off of my work."

It was the same with old Uncle Edgar on the milk route, too. He came home from the war with only that blank stare on his face and went to work for Harry A. Owens at the 'Nuff Sed' Grocery Company. Then he married Bessie right quick, had a kid, and started drinking. At first it wasn't too bad, just a beer now and then and some loud talking at picnics when he'd get one too many down him. But a year or so after he went in with Pa on the milk business in North Athens, Edgar started drinking something terrible and not taking care of his customers at all well.

At the time, Pa was just starting out on his own as I remember it, with the two new town houses, and him trying to outfit a whole dairy in the bottom of one of them. So Edgar's irresponsibility became increasingly unacceptable. Finally, Edgar showed up 7 o'clock one morning at the dairy, staggering drunk and unable to go out on his route. That was enough for Pa.

"Get the Hell out of here, Edgar," he says, "or brother or no I'll knock you flat on the ground where you belong."

It was all over after that. Pa gave Edgar a small route as his portion of the company and worked from one in the morning till three in the afternoon for the next four years, worked a twelve hour day right up till the thirties trying to keep that dairy going, until the government stepped in with all those new regulations and put him out of business in six months.

"Never trust a civil servant," he always used to say, "don't know a damn thing and will lie to cover it up. Ain't a one of them that's worth the nickel an hour it should cost to pay 'em.

"No competition, that's the trouble. Anything that's worth havin is worth workin' for, and those damn civil servants never worked for anything in their whole lives. Just a bunch of misfits sitting on their sinecures. Tell you one thing today and another tomorrow. The only thing they love is their week's paycheck, and they get that by stealin everybody else's."

Lord, he could be crusty when he wanted to be. In later years, he'd read the war news every morning. He played ball way into his fifties before his legs gave out. I remember how he laughed one evening while putting on his cleats to learn that Edgar, who'd never been much of an athlete, had gotten drunk the night before and run his new Ford coupe into a tree. Edgar flew out the window and landed unhurt and uncut in an adjoining meadow, but for some strange reason, which none of us ever figured out, Edgar's boots had gotten hung up on a limb of the old maple and were still there, limp over one of the limbs, when the police found him the next morning curled up and sleeping it off near the trunk.

That's the God's honest truth. Dad swore to seeing it.

God, how I loved that man!

God how I loved him.

But you never could figure him out. Just didn't like liars. That's all. And he was hard as nails sometimes.

CHAPTER XXXII
Love Story XII

strange! well, on with it.

at times the letters are so much a part of his country. i mean the people and the past, the cold, clear, unlittered upland of our lost chilhood.

he was such a man's man. so often i remember him carrying me in his blistered and sunburned arms with all that wash of blonde hair on them. i can't distinguish him from sparkling summer days in the mountains, the cool, clean, fresh air; thc stone-filled, sheep-cropped pasture.
pastures that were far too full of trees and which always disappeared over the hill crest before you could get to the flock and turn it toward the barn.

when i remember him that way, he's not always obvious to me, not as he should be. but he's a bright cloud.

i never think of him in winter. yet in the letters winter surely comes. it is perhaps his most characteristic season. still i don't remember it.

* * * *

Dunedin, New York
September 1, 1913

My Darling, Darling, Darling, Katie,

I arrived home safe and sound and did not sleep on the way either. My luck. Oh, but it is getting cold though. I will have to begin wearing an overcoat before long.

It does not seem possible that the summer is gone and winter will soon visit us once again. I did not think time would pass as quickly as it has. I have been so busy, I guess, that I have not had the time to watch time leave me so lonely.

That, I think, is good. It really is a thief, but now I find it has stolen from me only those hours without you I would wish to forget anyway. I wish Winter were already here. It cannot come too quickly for me this year.

I went blackberrying today. I got enough for six cans. that makes eight cans in all. And that is all we will get, for they are very scarce up here this year. It took me near five hours to pick the six cans.

They threshed at Uncle Jerry's today while I was berrying. I suppose I will have to work a day digging potatoes to make up for my part.

I saw Herb Rawley, and he did not want to give $1.50 a day for a man to dig potatoes at his place. But he surely wanted me to help him Monday and Tuesday cutting oats and getting them in.

His wife wants to go to the hospital next week. Poor fellow. He certainly has had a hard time of it the last couple of years. I had to tell him that I had so much work at home that I could not afford to leave it. Perhaps I can help some other time in a few weeks, but it is work well worth $1.50 a day. Make no mind of that.

I am sending to Sears and Roebuck for a catalogue tonight. I don't think it will cost too much to get furniture from them or elsewhere. They have factories and warehouses located in the East, where they ship all their heavy furniture from, so it does not have to come from Chicago.

Edgar is fishing tonight out at Long lake. He wanted me to come and show him the good spots, but my new shoes made my feet ache so that I was glad to get them off and rest for a while. He caught twenty bullheads last night, but he did not get me or one good bass. Ha! Ha!

You, Katie, are the only one who has ever succeeded in hooking this bullhead.

Mother says to tell you that you will have to come up for a week if we want anything for winter because she is nearly flunked again. I think she has done more work than her share now and is very tired. Look at all that work, canning sixty quarts of berries. Do come if you possibly can dear for the more we have the more we will be able to save this winter.

All my love is yours, now and forever. Frank and Alex have come over just now, and we have a full house for the night. Looks like Edgar will have to sleep with me. You won't mind if I have a bedfellow will you?

Your loving, Loving Sweetheart,

XX Arthur XX

* * * *

winters came earlier, stayed late, and were always cold. it
was, then, only wisdom to prepare. surely, he knew his own mind in
these matters.
the letters tell their own story. don't they?

* * * *

Dunedin, New York
October 20, 1913

My Darling, Darling, Darling, Katie,

I suppose you do not expect a long letter from me tonight
and I will not disappoint you. The wind is whistling through this old
house and my chest hurts with its bite. Besides, I don't have much
paper left. Don't worry though, I will get some tomorrow at the
Centre for the next week.

Did you say only two more Sundays in this month? Often it
seems to me that Sundays will never come.

This has been a terrible, long week. They say the more rain,
the more rest, but I cannot take too much rest when every day that

it rains just puts me further behind in my fall's work and so with our plans. It will snow early this year, I'm sure. It seems the nearer winter comes the more I have to do.

I will probably need at least a week's rest after we get married. Do you suppose that I will get it? Ha! Ha!

I would like to go someplace for a few days if we could after we are married. Not to Mattie's though. We can enjoy ourselves just as much alone and perhaps go someplace later if we have to. All I want is you with me forever. There will be nothing to separate us except death itself.

Edgar said your father talked of moving to Berlin. He sure acts funny about Mattie, as if she were all there was now that she's made herself known to the rest of the family. If everyone doesn't do things to suit Mattie, he doesn't like it. If I were Lillian, I would never go to Berlin to be a waiter for anyone. If my father wanted to leave me for someone who was still almost a stranger after I had lived with him all my life, he could go alone for all of me. I know you love your father greatly, but it does not seem right that he should ignore you so and go away after all you and Lillian have done for him.

I suppose he feels a duty to her for forsaking her when she was little, but he should not forget the rest of you and leave home just to please someone he has seen only a few times.

I am sorry he does not like our getting married. I think he will be all right after a while when he sees there is no harm done. He knows as well as anyone what a person will do for the love of another, so he should not feel hurt that we love one another as well as he and your mother did.

He certainly must have loved her or he would never have taken her back after she left him. I don't think you would ever do anything like that, but if you did Darling I don't think I could ever forgive you. I guess you have will enough of your own not to be led

275

to any such thing by anyone, no matter how handsome they might be.

But I trust I can keep my own. If you were to be led, they would have had you turned against me long ago simply because fate caused us to be cousins. We will be happy in each other's love though, dearer even if the whole world turn against us.

I am glad you have a lantern now so you will have to be good. I am always good when I am not something else. Ha?

Father is going to Athens with some potatoes tomorrow if it does not rain. We bought six more pigs about as large as ours today for thirty dollars. We ought to make quite a little off of them when we sell them.

I am glad we have not many more weeks to be apart. We will manage someway in December. No storms must ever keep me from you now that we are so near to our dreams.

All my love to my own darling little Katie. Your loving, loving, loving sweetheart,

XXXXXXXXXXXXXXX Arthur
XXXXXXXXXXXXXXX

* * * *

well, mattie in berlin worried him. there was an earlier letter about that. he could be very possessive when he wanted something his way. i remember aunt lil once saying, " as careful of his emotions as he was his money. and a skinflint at that."

i suspect the same of all farmers, but can hardly believe it of gramps. if he was, he must have been afraid to let them loose.

* * * *

Dunedin, New York
July 5, 1913

My Darling Darling Darling Katie,

I hope you did not feel any ill effects from the Fourth of July. I got just two and a half hours sleep this morning. Such a headache. Wow!

I got the chores done and paris-greened one piece of potatoes by nine though. Then I went into the house, kicked off my shoes in a corner, and took a nap. But it was just jumping from the frying pan into the fire. I rolled and tossed and sweat. I didn't sleep three minutes though I lay there till half past eleven. When I got up I felt as though I'd been on a week's drunk.

I ate dinner then and decided if I couldn't sleep I might as well work. So I hitched up the team and cultivated for three hours. Sweat? I looked like a drowned rat, but it stopped the headache.

Wilbur was up today, and Mother asked him about Mattie and her husband. He said he was a good worker and a good provider, but a bit of a drinker. Father was the one who went down to tell Mattie that your mother had died long ago. He saw the

Cantwells though, and they said they would tell her. You see, their lie has made Mattie seem cruel to you. Actually she is not. Wilbur said today that after the funeral he was the first person to tell her. He met her one day and said, "Did you know your mother was dead?" She said, "No."

I will go to Athens Saturday, so if you wish to go to Tommie's with me you had better make arrangements. We want to go before haying; for I would not like to drive Billy down there after he has worked five days in the field.

If you can't get away Saturday, go up on the auto, and I will stay home. That would suit old Lillian just as well.

The Grafton boys won yesterday 10-9. I guess they won't be so mad at me now.

All my love is your forever. My Darling Little Dear your loving, loving, loving--------

XXXXXXXXXX Arthur XXXXXXXXXX

* * * *

the marriage plans came in midsummer, and there was a lot going on. here he seems abstract and fretful at times. grandma was so much her own woman. yet, i remember him as so strong and domineering. a man of his age, maybe, but the ages are always found in us, aren't they? why can't i remember gramps any other way than i do? why?

* * * *

Dunedin, New York
March 6, 1913

My Darling, Darling Katie,

I arrived home safe. The last I knew last night I was kicking my feet, trying to keep them warm on the way home, and thinking that you were warm as toast and fast asleep by then.

My first thought when I woke up this morning was that you were already up and flying around the kitchen as you always do. You are with me every hour of the day.

Of course I could not get to sleep again. It hurt me to think of you working for someone else while I am such that I cannot see you any longer on Sundays. I don't like you working, and it seems too much to bear that I should not see you for a whole week and then only for half a day.

Don't think anything was wrong with me if I acted queer Sunday. I had hoped you would stay at home this summer so you could come up and spend a day or two with me once in a while. You hiring out came as a shock to me, and all I could think about was how little we would see of each other in the coming months.

Before long I think I shall begin counting the days and hours until I shall have you as my very own. Then I will make up for the times we've been apart Katie. I swear it so, if ever a man loved with a true heart.

Don't overwork yourself. I wish you needn't work at all. It was not so bad when you were at home where you hadn't so much to do. But to have to let you go among strangers and work so hard is almost too much for me to bear.

Now you know why I acted strange on Sunday. I felt as if I were responsible for your hiring out. I know it was my fault. You wouldn't have done it except for us.

I meant to go hunting with Albert tomorrow, but if it is as cold in the morning as it is now I shall not go. It may be a waste of time anyway, what with so much to do around here and the prospects of so little snow to catch anything by.

It had not snowed yet when I got home last night, but there was 4 inches by morning. Mother asked if you liked your new place. She said they surely could not help but like you!

I love you, I love you. I love you so much I can never tell you.

Don't work too hard and for free. Make them pay you or quit.

Your loving, loving Sweetheart

xxxxxxxxxxx Arthur xxxxxxxxx

* * * *

and here are two other letters that show him a man who worried after his own, no matter how cold the nights.

i suppose.

* * * *

Dunedin, New York
July 21, 1913

My Darling, Darling Darling Katie,

We are having some more rain. It rained this morning until ten but began about half past six and should continue all night. I hope so.

This forenoon I made a hog yard for the little pigs, and this afternoon I picked twelve quarts of huckleberries.

When I arrived home I found things had been happening. There's been a fight at the dam, some shooting and some clubbing. Two men had been arraigned before father for lst degree assault and one for 2nd degree. Father committed them all to await the grand jury. The one who did the shooting got away, but he was cut on the head by a club, and I guess they will find him.

Darling, don't think I wanted to go away from you. It would

have meant losing many days of your company, and I would not have that for the world.

It would have been better in the end if you had been able to let me go, but I am glad you would not. As long as you are satisfied I suppose I should be willing to let you work yourself to death, but you will not if I can help it.

It will mean an uphill climb, starting about it again. I think the dam ruckus showed what city life gets to be. They trucked in some Albany boys and one of them had been drinking and started it all. It was for you that I wished to go, but it is settled now once and for all. I could not leave you knowing that you were longing for me so. I could never make you unhappy.

I supposed you cried after I left and you were alone. I hadn't realized what I'd asked you to share with me. I know you would not say anything unless you were hurt, but I read the pain in your eyes.

Oh, those tell-tale eyes. You could keep nothing from me as long as I could look into them. We shall do as we intended and you shall have your home as I promised.

I hope you don't have a headache today. I feel fine, only a little sleepy.

All my love is yours as it ever will be.

Your loving, loving sweetheart,
xxxxxxx Arthur xxxxxxx

* * * *

a few days later, mrs. poultrie must have gone into the hospital, for this letter of his clearly shows his nervousness and concern. he could be downright possessive. not a modern lover at all. right sis?

* * * *

Dunedin, New York
July 27, 1913

My Darling Darling Darling Katie,

I suppose you are having lots of fun with all those old bachelors now that the old lady isn't around to help. Ha! Don't work too hard. I wish I were one of them. I would make things interesting for you. Okay?

We hayed a little today before it rained, and we had to leave some of the fresh-cut out to get wet. I picked sixteen quarts of huckleberries yesterday, one four quart pail in just an hour. I bet you don't beat that Sunday. I have not picked in one whole half of the swamp. This is for your folks, but you had better buy a bushel basket if you intend to pick all day.

As long as no one picks before you, it will be a fine day. If I see anyone, I chase them out, and I pick on the farthest side from the house so I can watch the rest better. I do hope you can come up, for I want you to see the fine pickings. Okay?

It is the best year ever, and we've already canned 47 quarts with berries for at least six more. Mother gave out before she had them all cooked. She would have quit long before except Aunt Jessie came down for a week and helped out.

I would like to get time to pick six more quarts of raspberries. Then we would have twenty quarts of them and fifty five of the huckleberries. That's a good start on the winter I think.

Darling I did not want to go to school any worse than you wanted me not to. I knew it would be best for us, that is why. Now, I would not. I know how you feel, I think.

But for God's sake, please don't talk about your working in the shop or anywhere else. It was that thought that made me want to go back to school. We can can get along some way without you working. If not, I will go back to school just because. That's all.

If you have to work, then we will cross that bridge when we come to it. But we will not plan on it. I shall try farming for a year or two, and if that doesn't work out maybe something else will turn up.

I hope you can come Sunday. Look out for all the old b_____. I don't want to have to take care of any of them. Ha!

All my love to you my own sweet Darling. Your loving, loving sweetheart,

xxxxxxx Arthur xxxxxxx

ps. Lots of kisses and hugs, although I guess you can get enough of those without me, now the old lady is gone. if not, send for me. xxxxxxxx

* * * *

the pickings, i take it, were really good that summer. how
can he be so jealous? but then, she probably wouldn't have had it
any other way. i can't ever imagine her sleeping around. if she had,
i'm sure she would never have allowed him to get so jealous about
it.

well, aunt mattie was still a thorn in the berry bushes, and
the city was a place to sell your pickings. though easy pickings
could have been through wet swamps at times i imagine. yes, sis,
even in the northlands. calvin knew about sex, too, you know. most
certainly, and who knows, maybe kinky at that.

he seems so foolish. gramps could never have been anything
but a farmer. i'd like to pick berries like that. he is so sweet in the
letters, yet jealousy can bear such bitter fruit. oh dear, i'd better
stop. he writes this a week or so later.

* * * *

Dunedin, New York
August 4, 1913

My Darling, Darling, Darling Katie,

I guess I will write a few lines even if I did tell you I would not. We did not cut oats today but picked huckleberries instead. I picked four quarts after supper last night and twenty-four more quarts today. Now, we have seventy-two quarts to take to Athens to sell. If we cannot sell them, woe unto you for coming up here and telling us we could sell all we could pick in the city. But I hope you are right. There are lots left yet in the swamp.

I have got a man to cut hay in the upper field. He will get one-fourth of the hay and will furnish a team, so we will have two teams. We'll get out of it nearly as cheap as if we hired help.

I'm going to Athens with Father tomorrow. I'll not be able to get over for we will have all those berries and some potatoes to get rid of.

Dear, if you get a two weeks vacation, you will not go to Berlin and stay there will you? Go down for a week, but then let me come and get you on a Sunday and you can stay here with me for a week. If you stay in Berlin both weeks, I guess I'll know how much you really think of me. Mattie has said that if she gets you down there she'll not let you come back. You will not stay away there darling, will you, where I cannot see you once a week?

I stayed here when I could have done better for us both by going to New York. Now you will not leave me and go off down there to work? Please don't think of it.

I could come down Dear, so that we could go to Web's, but I think we had better stay at home as you said.

I half expected Mattie would have you coaxed up again before you get back home. I almost expected a letter Friday telling me you were going.

I will be down Sunday. All my love and kisses. Your loving, loving Sweetheart, xxxxx Arthur xxxxx

* * * *

he bought fifty hens in athens on that visit. that's a lot of
huckleberries, so i guess he had clearly decided that little katie
knew what she was talking about. of course what is clearly on his
mind is little katie and her doings without him. she did what she did
up in berlin, at least for a week.

i can't remember seeing him ever jealous. he did love her, or
at least love himself enough to be aware of what she might do
without him. he was not above guilt and bribery.

i remember once, years later, he kept her at home and away
from a shopping trip in athens just by telling her that he needed her
after he'd done a hard day's work, and he couldn't do without her
beef stew on a cold winter's day. she fell for it. of course, at the
time, she was old and long past her earlier feminine vanities. and he
so seldom gave compliments to anyone.

she had plenty of opportunities to deserve them. she was his
and he would have no other. he was not always a fair man. but not
always understanding. he kept what he wanted.

i was jealous of her too.

CHAPTER XXXIII
PORTRAIT XI

Dusty attics are good places for dusty memories. Often it's hard to recall those days and to weave them together. The pictures are so like old matting--tenuous and threadbare. Like Gramps always cheating the state game wardens out of at least one illegal deer every year because, he said, it was shot on his acreage and so his deer.

But when that amazingly tall, square-shouldered sixteen point buck appeared one cold winter to graze on the stubble of the west field behind the new house, he wouldn't let us shoot it. Grazed there all winter and two more before it disappeared late one March in '32 or '33. We were sure someone else had taken it, and we complained bitterly, but that didn't carry no weight with Gramps. He'd often stare for hours at that old stuffed buck on the livingroom wall, counting the horns over and over, even though he had such bad eyesight by then that he'd taken to wearing glasses when he hunted. Most beautiful animal he'd ever seen, the one that got away, he said, and if we didn't kill him, he'd live forever.

I remember how mad he got the time Martin shot a doe out of season from the front seat of the old pickup. Wouldn't eat the meat. Wouldn't allow it in the house.

Ma always understood I guess. At least she seemed to. Does were not for killing, not even in an open season. Men

289

contested with other men, not with women.

He was always good with animals. He could stop a mule from laughing just by looking at him the right way, and I always knew it was a good thing that old Minnie the hound, died first.

There were three Billies, the horse, as I remember, and probably none of them were ever treated as badly as that first one that silently and without complaint pulled the old buckboard from Dunedin to Hawk's Farm Sunday after Sunday. 'Course in the winter he'd use the old sled we still have out in the barn and dress Billy up in a red and leather collar with Christmas bells on it, but it still was a mighty long ride. As much as he loved his dogs, cared for the sheep, and put up with the hogs, he had a special way about him with horses. Don't quite know why. Maybe it was because of all that time he spent with them behind a plow or on the way to Dunedin and back to sell produce.

Then too, there was the milk route. He got to know his horses mighty well at four o'clock in the morning. I remember those years he worked out of the old Diamond Rock Creamery, the cooperative that all the independents created to compete with the big corporations. He'd been in on the start of it, always a trouble-maker the town boys thought. Well, the creamery had a horse that would up and run a mile-a-minute at the first excuse of a noise. That horse was as fidgety as a bad light bulb. Nobody could handle it, and the creamery boys were all for getting rid of it as a bad bet and looking around for another.

But Gramps wouldn't hear of it. That horse was a fine animal on his route, and he'd make do with him. And that's what happened. Gramps took that horse, and there was an end to it. Everybody laughed, even crusty old Ed Matteson who swore up and down you couldn't train such a dumb, ornery animal as that one no matter how hard you tried.

Gramps tried, too. Tried real hard. He learned to double knot his reigns whenever he left the milk wagon because that animal'd take off down the street even if its head was pulled all the way back over its shoulders. He learned to stack the milk cases carefully so as not to lose a dozen quarts every time the horse bolted at the sound of a horn or train whistle. And still half the time most mornings Gramp was cleaning up broken glass and milk.

At first, some of the boys went out every so often and followed Gramps around the route, hooting and hollering just to see the old dray start up. Weren't anything Gramps could do about it because he never saw the pranksters. So he'd just trot after the wagon until the horse got tired and slowed down. Then he'd walk up to it, take a hold of its muzzle, stroke the horse's head way back to its neck over and over, and then patiently lead it around the block and back on the route again, over and over. I couldn't guess how often he must have done that. Thousands I suppose, and how much milk and cream he must have lost in the process I couldn't tell you. But he believed in the horse, and he wasn't going to let any tom-fool pranksters get to him, even if it did mean an extra hour's work every morning before the route was finished.

And after a few week when they saw that Gramps wouldn't be swayed--well, the boys finally gave up. Besides, there were enough horns and whistles and bells on the street anyway to keep him busy for a lifetime they thought. Gave up that is until the next Fourth of July about eight months later when Eddie Poultrie and Herb Rawley's son Jud decided to have a good time at Gramp's expense. Poultrie bought some fire-crackers, and that morning the two of them followed Gramps out along the route, on foot for an easy getaway should they need it, paralleling the wagon by one street all through North Athens.

Well, it wasn't but an hour or so--with Gramps was out on the route--before the boys let go with a fire-cracker on a side street around a hundred and fifth. Up bolted the horse and off at a quick trot with the loaded wagon. And off ran the boys, snickering all the way north for about ten blocks before they settled down and waited for Gramps to arrive after chasing down his wagon.

You can bet how surprised they were when Gramps comes along about ten minutes later, cool as can be as though nothing had happened, calmly delivering his milk house by house, the horse stolid and sleepy in front of the wagon.

Jud thought for a minute and decided Gramps must have gotten lucky and caught the horse accidently while coming out of the alley gate down at the Dorfman place, so this time he lit three fire crackers while Gramps was in Tom Potter's house and watched from between houses as the horse bolted upright and took off down the street and around the corner at the fastest trot the heavy wagon would allow. Then the two of them, barely able to run for laughing, took off lickety-split up to the Fifth Avenue Diner so that they could see Gramp's face when he came in to deliver and have a cup of coffee.

Just imagine Poultrie's red-nosed beak when twenty minutes later, before Eddie had even gotten his hot cakes served up, in walks Gramps with twenty four quarts of homogenized, twelve hanging from a wire carrier in each hand. He slides nonchalantly through the kitchen door to deliver, then saunters out, sits down right next to Eddie at the bar, and orders up his usual coffee just as if nothing had ever happened. Eddie was flabbergasted. He'd expected Gramps to be chasing that horse for at least an hour if not the rest of the morning, and to see him calmly gulping down boiling hot coffee as he always did, just took all the taste out of those hot-cakes and sausages. Eddie put fifty cents down on the counter top, and he and Jud got up and staggered out, wide-eyed and talking to themselves. Gramps called after them that their flap-jacks had arrived, but when they didn't answer he just pushed the fifty cents toward the counter girl, pulled the plate over his way, and had a good hot breakfast on Eddie.

Gramps knew what was going to happen, but he stayed and finished off the hot-cakes anyway. Before he was well into Eddie's plate a whole string of fire crackers went off out in the middle of Fifth Avenue, and two men took off like rockets toward River Street because there was no doubt that Gramps would know who did it this time.

Up reared the horse and off it took, neck half askew to the left and hardly able to see. Everyone in the diner jumped up to see what had happened. Everyone that is except Gramps. He just calmly pushed Jud's easy-over eggs onto Eddie's plate and had himself a forkful of white and soft yolk along with the hot-cakes and maple syrup. Nothing he knew of, he often said, ever tasted better than flap-jacks, eggs, sausage, and real maple syrup.

The horse? Well it came back at a slow jog about three minutes later and stopped exactly where it had started. Seems as how Gramps never had been able to stop it from bolting and running at the slightest unusual sound, so he'd done the next best thing. He'd taught it where to run and when to stop. Every time the horse had taken off, Gramps had caught it, made three left turns around the block with it back to where it had begun, and then given it a cube of sugar. For six months he'd done that, and the horse had finally learned its lesson. For the next ten years whenever that animal took off on him, Gramps would just stick his hand in his pocket, pull out a sugar cube, and wait at the curb for it to come around the far corner in a minute or so. Then it would stop dead in front of him and wait for the sweets.

Gramps wasn't a man to give up easily on anything. He'd threatened to quit the cooperative if they sold that horse, and his reputation was on the line. He always had one motto about his beasts. "Never," he would say, "try and make an animal do what it shouldn't." Eddie and Jud were the best of creamery jokes up 'til Christmas as I remember it. Gramps ate up the last of breakfast, went out and fed the horse, and then finished his route. After that it was all over Athens that nobody could train an animal like Gramps.

He never did go after Eddie and Jud. Said they looked too much like damn fools to bother with them. Then he'd just laugh. I remember too, it was a charlie horse in Dad's leg that stopped him from playing ball a few years earlier. That was about the time he lost his last election as a Democrat in Dunedin by one vote for the city clerk. They counted that vote five times to be sure. The next year Gramps registered Republican for the first time in his life and was voted in as county assessor by a landslide. People'd always thought he was pretty smart. Smart and honest they would say, and he never lost an election after that day.

CHAPTER XXXIV
Love Story XIII

whatever happened all those years, he never lacked love. neither giving nor receiving. of that i am sure.

the letters show it.

how is it? dad, sis, how is it that we are so lonely in such a small world. they lived much farther away back then. traveled by horse and all of that. and yet he never lacked for those things most absent in our world. she loved him, and he knew it even when he protested the most. he used to laugh at me so and play cards he knew i couldn't use or match. he would laugh and by doing so command my love when i was most angry at him. he would laugh at me, and i would love him so. he knew himself.

what is it we've lost?

* * * *

295

Dunedin, New York
May 15, 1913

My Darling Darling Darling Katie, xxx

I arrived home about twelve. It was cold for May, and I wrapped a blanket around me. Hiram Hulder was just going home. I guess he must have some little Queen up to the Centre.

I have been plowing all day. By tomorrow the potato ground should be finished.

I guess Wilbur has changed his mind about Matilda again since last Sunday. He is going to take her horse home this Sunday. I don't know if he will stay there or come back here. He had the cast taken off his arm today, and he can raise it to his head.

Some of the boys were inquiring of Wilbur as to where I was keeping myself. I guess they want me to play ball Decoration Day. But if you say no, I shall not. I don't play much ball these days as I would rather please you.

I am sorry I caused you to cry yesterday. If you had only told me why you were angry, I could have saved us both a great deal of pain. It hurts me to see you cry. I knew I was the cause, I did not know how.

I am a blundering jackass at times, the very opposite of your nervous high-strung nature. But I try to please you. If I make blunders do not lay it at the door of my love but of my ignorance. I could never love anyone else.

The whole thread of my life is wound about you. Do not break it. Please! Never speak to me again as you did yesterday. And tell me of your dissatisfactions. I can feel the sting of your words still. Edgar could not see how your words cut me. I think we will forget this little trouble and try to do the better next time.

Though the clouds may fall, all my love will be yours,

Your loving loving Sweetheart,
xxxxxxxxxx Arthur xxxxxxxxxxxx

* * * *

see? he never doubts himself even when he pretends to be
most abject. he knows his own mind. i wish i did.
his style has weakness though. the thread metaphor pushes
things a little too far, maybe. but he has a flare for imagery.
i wonder if she ever explained. listen !

* * * *

Dunedin, New York
June 19, 1913

My Darling Darling Darling Katie,

297

Would you believe it is after eight, and I have just finished the chores? Agnes and Father are not back from the circus yet, and Mother and Edgar are out rocking on the front stoop. The day has become quiet and tired.

Don't look for any meanness in this letter. I said enough in that other one to last a lifetime. I should never have sent it if I had stopped to think about how I would have felt if you had said those things to me. Thank you for forgiving me, but you will never be able to forget how cruel I was to send it. I did not realize what you meant to me until afterwards. You are all the world, and nothing is good without you.

Oh, Darling, if you had ever gone away or done anything to harm yourself after that letter, I should not have wished to live. All the good in life would have been lost to me.

I don't know what came over me. I simply felt as though everything-- you--were lost to me when I read in your letter that you were going away from home to work. You were going among people whom I did not know. I had decided to keep still, but when you began going out without me I could not restrain myself. I could not ask you to stay in nor could I be with you. You needed some time for fun just as anyone does. Still, I could not help feeling as though something terrible would happen to us.

It was in defiance of that feeling that I stayed away and let you go alone to the last movie. I could have come down as well as ever, but I wished to prove to myself that my fears were wrong.

I could not find the words to tell you all this, and so I wrote that letter last week. But it was a poor show. Then, I wanted to tell you what I have tonight, but I could not. I began to blame you for my own state of mind, for going out without me when it was my own fault.

From this I began thinking about that other thing and

everything you had ever said in connection with it. Suddenly, some of the things you had spoken were too hideous for a human mind to even contemplate, much less alone do. You turned from the darling of my dreams to some monster without feelings, heart, or love. Than I penned the letter, read it, sealed it, and sent it off.

What a tragic decision. The next day I know I had done the most cruel and heartless act of my life, but it was too late to recall the letter. What was done was done, and not all my regrets would help. If I could have had my choice Sunday between death and facing you, it would have been a toss-up.

I did not know but that you might send me from you with a scorn. I would not have blamed you. I never realized the full love I have for you until I realized how much my letter hurt and frightened you. Had I known before how you loved me, it would have dispelled all my fears.

Katie, I am a foolish and fond man. Now I know that nothing can part us but death. I love and appreciate you even more. Perhaps the letter accomplished more good than bad, even if it took two heartaches to do it.

I am going to ask you to burn it. Forget it and try to realize that I love you more than ever before. I will try not to let you go out alone anymore now that I realize no one can ever take my place in your heart. And if you should go out without me I know that no harm could come from it.

Agnes and Father have just come in the house with Albert. They are chewing the fat, so I cannot write anymore. Father says to tell you they are all drunk and Agnes is the worst of all.

Edgar and I have been hoeing the garden all day and Father must go to the dam in the morning, so I guess he's got a right to howl a little. Edgar will be back down to work before the week is out.

Mother is going to bed. It's a very warm night so I think I'll stay up a bit and rock. The crickets are chirping. Maybe I'll fall asleep in the chair and get a crick. Ha?

All my love is yours, forever, no reserve. Love, love, love, all to you my own Darling True love. Your loving, loving, loving,

xxxxxxxxx Arthur xxxxxxxxx

xx good night & sweet dreams xx

* * * *

what a very long letter. and what sly style. it was a "poor show" because he didn't go to the movie with her. do you think he meant it? yes, i'm sure he did. it must have been so much fun to get letters like that. i mean, one likes to be loved, no matter what the situation.

for a little woman, grandma certainly was able to get her way wasn't she. look at gramps! he's apologizing for living. it's hard to square that with the big, dominating man i remember. true love does those things, just as much as hate or jealousy or boredom for that matter.

don't look so. there are knights in armor at all times and even among the most prosaic of us. gramps will forever be that to me.

he asks her to burn the letter. that's why we don't have it. he would die without her. and he would have. i'm sure of it. what's within us is hardly ever what shows on the outside.

there are no more may letters. she has had her way with him and he sees with the eyes of the buck. i know. women civilize us all

300

you know. we are the future.

　　　look at the next letter. apologies are what define the nature of civilization, itself, i think.

* * * *

Dunedin, New York
June 28, 1913

My Dear Darling Darling Katie,

　　　It is nearly half past eight. I have just finished setting out turnip plants. Now they will not wilt so bad, but it was hard work you bet. I have been cultivating, hoeing, and harrowing all week. We are going to sow our buckwheat tomorrow if it does not rain.

　　　We had a fine shower last night that is sure to help the new plants. Lightning struck a tree in the village near Victor Burden's and stunned Meggie Sims. She will be all right, but she is the second woman to be shocked by lightning this year. So stay in during storms Dear. I wouldn't want you hurt so.

　　　Yes, next Sunday is the first of our last six months wait.

　　　Yes, I will try to be good, even though it always seems that the bad in us is bound to come out. I see no answer but that both of us give up everything that had the least bit bad in it. Then we can trust to God for help. As long as we cling to any bad at all we will have to trust to our own strength, and that must surely fail us.

　　　In fact, there is no way to be good without the help of the Almighty. I have known the power of a Savior to cure sin, but having turned from my calling as I did, I can hardly expect help from him now.

I used to swear terribly, but after I was converted I hardly swore at all and sought forgiveness whenever I did. I had tried to stop before, but my own strength was not enough. Now, that I have stopped going to church and taking part in God's doings, the Devil has returned, and I am as far from a Savior as ever I was.

There is but one way back--to acknowledge to the world that I have fallen and to ask His forgiveness. It has been my mistake, but a man hates to acknowledge a failure more than anything else.

Dear, you wished that I was, and said I must become, as good as I was two years ago. If I were to become so, you might have to give me up for a while? Ha.

You know, too, that I should never marry until I finished college, if I felt as I did then. It is best that I am what I am if you can help me be good after you get me. If we could have each other and I finish school, then I might reach the heights of my past ambitions, but I will not give you up for even as short a time as four or five years. No matter what comes.

You ask if you have made me be bad. You have only done but one thing, and you know I would never yield to that. No. It is my own love for you that stands in the way of my services to God. But my mind is made up.

If I cannot be of service to God and have you then I shall not serve him. Nothing shall come between us. I don't see why we cannot serve together after we are married and accomplish as much more than I would have done alone, no matter what my education. I am not finding fault with you. You are not to blame any more than I that we love each other. God endowed us with this gift, and he must accept how we use it to his service. Well, I guess I have preached long enough haven't I?

I don't care how soon you leave Berlin for home. I will try to be good and be bad no matter where you stay. I guess your father would be glad if he saw you traipsing home bag and baggage. As for me, as long as I can't have you here, I don't care, but I shan't press the matter much.

I will be down Sunday if it doesn't rain. If it does I can't come because Wilbur and Matilda are going out, and Wilbur came and took his wagon today. He and Matilda get along all right, but I guess he and her Ma don't jibe very well.

I will have to close because I can't think of anything more to say except how I love you. I could say that forever, but now you must be tired of it.

All my love and hugs and kisses are yours my own sweet Darling.

Your loving, loving, loving
Sweetheart,
Arthur
xxxxxxxxxxxxxxxxxxxxxxxxxxxxxxxx

* * * *

what a long letter! and all because of a little petting? so sententious. he sounds like a rochester or heathcliff. it's hard to believe, but that was granps. would she have liked him if he'd been more diffident? he cannot service god and her? and the choice will be hers. certainly he doesn't mean it. a ploy. that's what it is. to be in love is always to be a little bad, whatever bad is. Hypocrisy is to be expected of lovers, else what's a titty for?

o' now i'm embarrassed. i don't mean to seem pretentious, but neither did gramps. did he?

* * * *

Dunedin, New York
July 19, 1913

My Darling, Darling, Darling Katie,

I received your letter last night, and I was sorry to hear that you are sick again. I don't think you can blame me for that though.

I am glad that you were pleased with your long missing sister. I hope, Dear, that you may never have any of the trouble that she has had. I hope, too, that your father knows where his responsibilities, as well as his heart, lie.

We have been trying to hay it this week, but have not succeeded very well. All we have in is the meadow around the house. We have the last of the hoeing done though. Finished that today.

I don't know whether Father is going to Athens Saturday. If I go alone, I will drive over and see you when I return.

Agnes wanted me to go to the center to hear a missionary lecture on Western Indiana tonight. We just got back. All they had was a prayer meeting. The missionary spoke Tuesday instead of tonight. Well, I guess I needed the prayer night right much.

Hattie asked me if the church was going to fall. She said, "I can see the shingles going already." It was the first time I had seen the new minister. He makes one think of faded pumpkin skin.

I have one of Edgar's books read and hope to finish the other before Sunday. Then you can bring them back home.

I suppose you will be ready to go into swimming Sunday. If you don't go this time, I shall not be fooled into bringing the clothes down again.

It does seem too, that your sister was much in love with her husband. I wonder, does he love her as I do you? If he does it must cause him great pain to know that she thinks so lightly of him. I know how you love me, and I hope to be deserving of that love. I could never again care for anyone as I do for you. True, it makes some things harder to bear, but we will love each other until the end. Won't we?

I have been having some serious thoughts lately. It seems a silent struggle between passion, love, and duty. I will tell you of it in good time, but it may cost us more than you think if love and duty conquer. I believe I know which should prevail, yet if I were to see the future I might think differently.

There, there, Darling I did not mean to trouble with any of my foolish thoughts. But there are some hints of them down the road and I cannot erase my concern. I may ask you to decide some things for us Sunday when I come down. I am at present unable to.

All my undying and passionless love is yours.

Your loving loving Sweetheart,
xx
xx

xx xxx Arthur xxxxxxxxxxx

sweet dreams
& good night

* * * *

     maybe long letters come from being so near the end. why is
he so argumentative though? great gramps evidently fooled around-
-at least at one time in his life. don't most men, at least if they're
worth the having? oh now, don't get so upset with me. i'm no more
a preacher than you sister, with all your supposed honesty. but duty
over passion, and equal to love? i wonder how old her sister was? i
think he means it. he's a thinker as well as a lover. he knows what a
woman wants, especially grandma, and that's not just sex. he's a
solid, stable kind of guy. that's sexy too. we all go to church. we all
want to believe, to be safe. the most telling quality of a culture is its
choice of amusements, and church was theirs.
     how about that sis? and don't tell me i "risk cynicism." your
syntax is as outdated as you pretend he is.
     i like him. he's sweet.

* * * *

Dunedin, New York
July 24, 1913

My Darling Darling Darling Darling Katie,

"Such a headache." How is your head? I hope you feel
better than I today. If you do I bet you will not enjoy your trip to
the city, especially as hot as it was today.

I arrived home last night about twelve o'clock and got up at
five. Thank you so for understanding. Probably in all our life
together we will never again be called upon to make such a decision
but if we are, we will need the same strength and love which you
displayed last night.

Oh, my head! It feels as if I have been on a week long binge.
The calf ate up my old straw hat the other day. I sent to the Centre
by Agnes & Mother for a new one. They got one today that was big
enough for me to crawl right into. I guess they thought I'd be
getting a big head soon & they were right. Ha!

If the weather is fair, we will finish haying here tomorrow.
Then we will begin haying up past the woods on Wednesday, so if
you people come up I will not have time to see you unless you wait
until I return at night. You had better come up and get some berries
though, even if you don't want to wait for me.

Mother wants to see your sister in the worst way. If you do
come and have time after you get this letter, let us know when to
expect you.

I suppose too, it would be better if you not let me visit but
once a month if you cannot get me to behave. I don't see why I
cannot be good, but I am always giving you trouble. I know I
should think you would get disgusted with me and send me home,

but you don't.

Darling, I guess we have got to stop fooling around when we are out nights or we will be caught one of these times. Then you know what a story would go around even if it were not true. The next time, I want you to get cross with me or say something to make me behave when I get cutting up as I do.

It makes me so d-- mad at myself, to think that I can't behave. Perhaps, if you would let me, I could punish myself by staying away from you for a month. That would be the worst torture of all. What do you think?

Dear, I don't know what plans I can make for us until I see what the settling-up is this Fall. Before I can put our plans into action I must know how much we will have. Don't worry though, we will arrange some way so that we will not have to wait longer than we have planned. There will be time enough for us. I will see to it.

Until then and forever after you can rest assured of all my love.

Your loving, loving, loving Sweetheart,

xx Arthur xx

(All my kisses and love, but no more hugs, for five months then! Ha! Ha!)

* * * *

the paper is lined, school writing paper. he must have borrowed it from his sister. it is a hastily written letter. he's home late and so blames her by implication. how like a man--and how endearing. and she has a headache too.   i can't believe it.

he's more casual, the headache must be just a simple pun, though his exaggerations become more profound as the letters proceed. i bet in private he used to tell her she had doe eyes. every man who deserves the title knows to do that. yes, i do believe he loves her--deeply. he's emotionally mature though and knows enough to temper reality with exaggeration and vice-versa. gramps was no dummy. after all, he slept in the belly of the bear, didn't he?

perhaps the "problem" was nothing: a desire not to live in the city again, a growing distrust of mattie, his mother weeping again at heaven-born incest, katie's evident liking of good times, gossip, home, or the lack of it, or some other mystery of which we will never know.

five days! he misses a full five days. perhaps love can only endure so long because it must. he feigns worry over a little petting. certainly not, but what a nice compliment to her. passion is desirable especially for the virtuous. and what should grandma understand? after all, she didn't send him home nor does he ever expect that she will. he's so wonderfully transparent. even our illusions are real.

love is a quiet job.
the long, hot, still days in the hills must have gone very quickly, and the nights very slowly.

i remember aunt mattie as small and round, her face reddened by an unusual snubbed nose, her eyes darting here and there, always suspicious, always ready to take offense, the brain in back of them forever thinking about what you might be thinking as everyone took tea or coffee in the living room with canapes and little pieces of bread and butter with the crusts cut off, neatly arranged in rows on sunday china atop soiled tables.

she never married again. never dared divorce! isn't that right? even when uncle jeb had left for good, never to be seen again after she had told us she was through with him. she never slept with a man after that. in her old age, she used to boast of it to us kids.

history, sister, is always creative. reality is most often what we have lived and failed to remember. lord! i sound like you. the difference is that i am content with what is left. with the bear and the haying and the squirrels and building dams. i don't think, however, that i would ever have been happy with a man who behaved himself.
let's hear one for gramps.

by the way. that thing about getting a big head. was it another pun do you think? a dirty one at that?

CHAPTER XXXV
PORTRAIT XII

There are bits and pieces. All of which fit, I guess. But I think the pattern is woven differently for me than for you two. And what designs we buy are inevitably a matter of taste.

There is a story about three Welsh coal miners who came over on a boat. But they came to New York, I think, through Ellis and all that riff-raff, then stayed in the city for a while, up around 125th somewhere when Harlem was still a pretty respectable neighborhood. Then they wandered north because there wasn't much work in the city. One eventually wound up over near Scranton and Wilkes-Barre. Good anthracite there, and I imagine he felt at home. The other got lost down around Poughkeepsie and married a little Polish jewess who sewed lace on all her panties, went to Temple every Saturday, and wouldn't move north and leave her father's beard - or something like that. Anyway they eventually moved back to Brooklyn and got lost there too. It's a side of the family we know little about and good riddance.

There's a book of family generations somewhere, a kind of history your great, great grandfather Alexander Washington worked on, but I don't know where it is now. Everybody knows about it though, and if we ever find it amidst all this clutter, it'll tell some strange tales you can bet.

He really did play with Evers and Chance, you know. That's

the God's honest truth, no matter how strange it sounds. I don't know about Tinkers. He could have been a great ball player! I remember once up in North Athens, young Martin was playing ball in the field kitty-corner to 110th Street. Dad was in center field, and a long fly drove him all the way to Third Avenue before he caught it with Jake Snooks' kid on Third. Well, the dads were all playing with their sons, and the Snooks boy was a little, raw-boned, smart-alec, no bigger than a weasel, who picked his nose and was always boasting that he was the fastest kid in town. When Dad caught the ball way out against the Third Avenue sidewalk, Snooks took off. Fast as the kid was, though, Dad had that ball out of his glove and on a straight line to home before the kid's trail foot was off the base. I'd never seen anything like it. The Snooks kid was like lightning, and your Gramps threw on a line with one bounce past the pitcher's mound from the middle of Third Avenue to home plate at the corner of 110th Street and Fourth Avenue where young Martin was waiting without his catcher's mask on. The ball came up, hit Martin in the nose, and knocked him flat on his ass just as young Snooks came roarin' into the plate in a cloud of dust.

Never saw such a mess in all my life. Martin had kept his eye on the ball as he went down and it ended up in his glove. Snooks was called out even though he swore up and down that Martin had never touched him, and he was probably right. Martin just sat there, bloody-nosed and teary-eyed, holding his face with his throwing hand and his ribs with his glove hand, the ball still in it, and moaning like a sick calf.

Dad saw it all and rushed in from center field lickety-split. He got to Martin, bent down and felt his ribs, and decided there was only a bruise. Then he wiggled Martin's broken nose back into place with his fingers, after wiping most of the blood away with his bandana, pulled Martin to his feet, told him he was all right and would feel better by Saturday's game, and sent him home to Ma. Damnedest thing I ever did see. Dad just straightened his cap, picked up his glove, and trotted on back to center field. He wasn't one to give sympathy unless he thought it was absolutely needed, and that was almost never. Martin just walked on home, trailing his glove in his left hand while his right held tight to his ribs. Countrymen always took care of themselves from the very beginning. There's the story about Great Grandpa Alex once beating up a bully in Dunedin with three punches; the first blow knocked him down, the second knocked him into the middle of the road, and the third knocked him into the gutter on the other side. When Dad once asked Grandpa how he did it, the old man said, "Well it was all done like it should be with one punch, but when that silly feller was dumb enough to get up again, I just couldn't leave him out there in the middle of the road so it took me three."

Dad eventually had an answer that was just as good. Once young Alex asked him how to win a fight and he replied. "Ain't much to it, just hit the other guy first." 'Course he never really meant that. He just prided himself on being practical.

He never really disliked Jews either. Both of you must always remember that! Not really.

Your Grandpa on your Mom's side, old Sam Bentman, knew that. He came to Dunedin back in the Twenties to nurse a heart condition and asthma. Wrong place to come, but that's what he did, and there was no telling old Sam anything. Stubborn as Gramps and twice as mean. Ran the local grocery 'til after the war, always wearing that cap of his and never shaving. Always in those old beat-up, baggy block pants of his with suspenders, a white dress shirt, and black bow tie, even in the summer, no matter how hot. He was a strange one, coughing all the time and so mean he'd never give a dime's credit. Always busy. Always taking notes on that little white pad of his.

But he cared for his own, just like Gramps. Lost a lot of money closing that store down on Saturdays just to travel into Temple at Athens. Long about '31 Gramps convinced him to let Billy Benchman keep the store open for folks from 10 till 4 on Saturdays, but Sam wouldn't have anything to do with the accounting until 8 o'clock Monday morning. Wouldn't even come into the store or even look at the register tape. 'Course on Monday morning he was all hell-a-fire, but not until then.

All that was after the huckleberry incident, when Sam caught some of us boys picking berries out back of his property near the pond. Sam was a real bull about property rights, and he always sold those berries in the store every summer, so it wasn't unexpected that once he saw us, me and Alex and Billy and the

313

young Fouks boy, that he was gonna sic the sheriff right on us. That's what he did, too. Had all four of us arrested one Wednesday. Had the sheriff right there beside him as he stormed out the back door of his house across the road into the patch where he knew we'd be because old Mrs. Bentman had seen us there the day before. The sheriff had to arrest us, what with the warrant sworn out and all. And not one of us over ten I don't think, trying to run away with half a day's huckleberry picking bouncing all over our arms. We finally dropped the baskets to high-tail it for the woods, only that was too late to escape Sheriff Kilmer's arms as they caught us up and carried us back to the beat-up Ford truck he used as a patrol car.

What a time of it we had at the sheriff's office, too, which wasn't any more than the winterized front porch of his house on Tinker Lane. Boy, did we feel small, all four of us, sitting there in that beat-up dirty, blue and white, vinyl coaster lounge, not even daring to swing it a little bit with our heels for fear the sheriff would add that to our time, too, and we'd never get out of jail. It wasn't until Dad came that I felt at all better about things and then only because when he came in with two days beard on his face, manure from his work boots tracking up the sheriff's front hall, sweat from his bandana running down between the white hairs on his chest, and a look of doom itself stamped across his forehead and eyes. I knew we were going to get a lot worse from him than the sheriff ever could give us.

Dad just looked at us without a twitch in his face, and our eyes all flinched to the floor. Then he turned to the sheriff and talked in the hallway so that we couldn't hear well. All the while old Sam Bentman just stood in the doorway on the hall runner looking first at us with the smile of the righteous written all across his mouth and then at Dad and the sheriff out of sight behind the doorway. Sometimes the talk got loud but never enough so I could hear much.

"But, dammit, he had to, Arthur," the sheriff let out once.

"And only kids, Daniel," was Dad's reply. I didn't take any comfort from it though because I knew that the way Dad talked to other adults had nothing to do with the hiding we'd get later on if he thought we deserved it.

Well, after a bit the two of them brought old Sam into the conversation. Then there was some shuffling and groaning, a couple of muted epithets here and there before they finally reappeared from behind the doorway, Sam all beaming and happy and Dad reaching into his torn, black wallet for two dollars, it seemed, to pay Sam for all the berries we'd took. The evidence, what was left of the berries after we'd run all over the field, was sitting on a little table next to the porch window. Dad just looked at it after he finished paying Sam, and he motioned to us to get out the front door.

"Yep, that's it Arthur," sheriff Kilmer answered as we skedaddled across the porch, "Guess it's rightfully yours now."

"Believe it is Daniel," Dad replied, "but they sure are sickly lookin berries. Besides, don't think I could stomach 'em, seein' as how I came by 'em an all."

With that Dad picked up the largest quart basket, turned, and dumped all those berries square over little Sam Bentman's head. Then without a word he walked out the door and took us kids all home.

Well! We got one hell of a tannin that night after we got home. Dad wasn't one for pickin' on other people's property, and he let us know it. But it didn't seem to hurt as much as some of the others. Just to see old Sam and the sheriff standing there so popeyed and befuddled was worth it all. Dad looked out for his own. If he couldn't teach us to be good citizens and obey the law, he didn't figure anyone could.

We never did go in Sam's patch again. That goes without saying. But Sam came to respect Dad a good measure after that. All Dad had wanted him to do was to try and work the matter out between the adults in the families first. Then if we hadn't obeyed, he was as ready for the sheriff as any. But he sure hated people going over his head.

Yes, I think they came to respect each other later on, when things started going so badly over in Europe and the Clan painted effigies on the new Esso gas pumps Sam had installed out front of the store. Dad didn't take to that a bit. He went to who he suspected had done it and the very next day those pumps were painted over in a glossy red, white, and blue. Painted over the very white wash that old Sam had used to hid the figures the morning he had discovered them. And when a few months later they painted slogans all over Sam's new Desoto, Dad did the same thing. Only this time he got the money to have the car repainted at Sheftel's Auto Body Works down in Athens.

I think that's when the two of them really became friends. Dad never did tell Sam who or how many did those things. People, he always insisted, often did things they didn't mean just because they were scared, or bored, or mischievous, or just too downright dumb to know any better.

Sam didn't quite agree with him, but Dad held that pranks were no reason to break up a community or to bust up friendships. The pranks got worse during the war of course. You girls know that. And maybe Dad never did see how dangerous the Clan really was. They weren't really big up here, and he never had any trouble in Dunedin after that, no matter what was going on in Athens. When the war came he was all for us doing our part, though he hated it like a high fever.

Oh, I remember so much. Like when he caught Alex and me smoking down behind the Camels billboard on Fifth Avenue in Athens. We smoked four more packs and drank a gallon of water before the night was out. Lord, was I sick. But only young Martin has ever taken up the habit in the family, and we all know why.

I remember your Grandma frying doughnuts for us on cold, November, Saturday mornings, standing there over the old woodburning stove and when the fire burned so low that the kettle cooled down and the doughnuts became all greasy, swearing low under her voice so Gramps wouldn't hear. She bought a new stove sometime later. On her own, in spite of her habitual reluctance to ever do anything without Grandpa's approval. But he had gone out the week before and loaned a hundred dollars to Ed Hatterson who had gone through a good deal of sickness over the winter, what with his wife's pleurisy and both his boys with the croup. It wasn't so much the loan that bothered Grandma, country folks stuck together even if they were tight-fisted, as that Gramps had never consulted her about it. And there she was, never complaining--at least not much, she said--while even Hattie Benchman had a new bottled gas stove that just make cooking a pure joy. So she just went out and bought one. What was worse, she charged it. Gramps spent six months paying that bill off, but when he came home, saw the stove, then saw the look in Grandma's eye, he never said a word. Only time I ever saw him stared down.

Oh, I remember how he hated F.D.R. and worshipped Teddy. For him the thirties were a big change, and he always told us how lucky we were to be on a farm with no debt so's we could grow our own food and live right there off the land if we had to.

Then there's Alex, bloody nosed and crying, after Dad gave him a boxing lesson with real gloves because he'd let Sandy Fouks beat him up at school and had run away when he saw Sandy in the village the next day.

And I remember Dad early on cold winter's mornings, boots on with yesterday's overalls tucked in them, holding onto his suspenders and shivering in his grey, woolen undershirt, standing at the back door hollerin', "Here Min, Min, Min, Min, Min, Min. Heere Min, Min, Min, Min, Min, Min, Min, Min.
Lord, how he loved that dog.

CHAPTER XXXVI
History Lesson XII

Poor Henry!

The mistake of love is its desire to possess totally. This is love's culminating, most extravagant, most inevitable, and most inexcusable truth. It is the thorn in the flesh more surely than sex can ever demand of men. Once committed, it is irrevocable, and it is always committed.

One loves and becomes joyously happy, in will if not in fact, and therefore we must love too, in the same manner regardless of our taste, and thus be joyously happy, too, a fact which can only be determined by the assumption of will and intention.

As the century progressed so did its mores and morals, two words--separate and equal concepts--which young Katherine often took as one and so confused, most naturally with "morale" which was what the boys had when they went over in '18 and so clearly lacked when they returned in '20 and '21, thus in part accounting for the young nation's confusion, though certainly in no way an apology for such appalling ignorance no matter how benignly protective.

Skirts went up ("and panties went down" snickered Joseph to his two demur Jewish daughters in later years) hats lost their brims, the galloping ghost tore over the turf, garters became profoundly decorative and in many cases blessedly cosmetic, the suffragettes had lost in Illinois in 1912 only to win the nation later,

319

the prohibitionists won the nation later only to lose it again--for good--much later, after the boys had come home, and Hemingway and Fitzgerald became the rage of the college crowd.

Not all things changed though. The Little Hossick River at Perrysville remained an open sewer straight through the next war and beyond, the local kids forever taking July and August dips in its tired, brown and green pools which huddled discretely in all the many crooks and turns the stream took as it wound its way past the tanning factory, newly built in '22 out on Humphries Lane above the village, and thence past the innumerable wooden pipes which emptied into it from the town's antiquated sewage system. Because the town had no "steady" doctor willing to suffer its economic privations for the sake of a greater good, old Doc White interviewed a steady stream of Perrysville children in September and October, all of whom (Jessie's, too, when she finally moved out there) complained of eye trouble and earaches and ringworm and various infections around their mouth and under their finger nails. Up 'til Thanksgiving, the River Street office where Doc hung out when not making house calls was forever crammed with bawling kids, their more fortunate runny-nosed brothers and sisters, and nervous moms always in a hurry to do some shopping while they were in town and thus get some use out of an otherwise wasted day.

For a few years, "Uncle Sam" was all the cultural rage: born in 1812, popularized some fifty years later, and come of age "over there." He was plastered on every poster that a proud and grateful nation could conceive, telling the boys where to go and when to come back, but never mentioning the cost, since no cost, at least not imagined, so far away from the unimaginable mud and rat filled trenches--away from smooth, young boys who retched from chlorinated lungs only to lie still, directly so, before tangled and rusting bellies and gangrenous arms and legs which had lain untended for days in rain filled shell holes that pocked an unnatural, Springless land; no cost could measure the value.

And that stream, too, wound its way home.

The age saw Bix Beiderbeck display his rare golden horn and equally rare fingering, not to mention a providential and prodigious set of lungs (and, unhappily, and equally inauspicious capacity for booze) to an adoring public. No band could sing as well. Louis of the strong arm/lungs was to come along a bit later, right after the West Point generals and Annapolis grads had fought and sacrificed through the second holocaust, Glenn Miller sacrificing his all.

In Athens in '25 a wild steer broke loose on the street and stampeded into the R.C. Reynolds Furniture Company on Lower Front Street, destroying the otherwise imperturbable calm of plush Drexel sofas, Stiffle lamps, and walnut antique love seats. Terrifying the best of Athens' gentry, among them Katie who was there enjoying Arthur's lately won but not yet assured prosperity by choosing a new mahogany dining room suite to grace the first floor apartment at 107 3rd Avenue in Lansingburgh, the terrified animal attempted to escape its tormentors by mounting the grand double stairs in the center of the first floor, ascending by them (its owners in hot but cautious pursuit--the animal in question a Texas longhorn on its way to New York for exhibition) from the level of living room furniture where Katie was busy tucking herself away behind a corner cupboard that stubbornly refused her adequate protection. Thence the animal ascended by a second and then third flight of stairs to the boudoir and finally through the lesser kitchen furniture before breaking out at last, through a closed door, onto the roof of the building, there to so manfully and stubbornly guard its keep that it took sixty (they were counted) bullets to bring the animal down as it circled the roof, bellowing to the sky before rushing back to check the broken door and stairs from which it had so miraculously appeared.

Katie always maintained afterward that it was a lucky thing she had not made her purchase because the animal destroyed a terrible amount of fine things on its ascent to the roof, among them three chairs from the oaken Edwardian living room furniture she had just about set her mind on. Later she was to buy a beautiful modern suite at Mooradian's six blocks up along the river, this in spite of all Arthur could complain to her about dealing with such people and how you never, at least mostly never, could trust them.

Tammany Hall came to control the state, as it had for so long but not so obviously. Teddy left (the darn luck of it) and Cornelius G. Bustard was elected (and re-elected and re-elected, etc.) Mayor of Athens, much to Arthur's continuing disgust.

For a time in the early Forties before he went to war, young Joseph, then newly married, tended a parking lot on Fifth Avenue across from the city park, a pathetic newly-bricked-in rectangle with hand-painted 8 foot maple trees sprouting amidst the dull red patterning which occupied fully one quarter of a block halfway down Fifth to Turabian's clothing outlet and halfway across Canal Street to St. Augustine's Catholic Church. There, late one winter Friday, Joseph was privileged to witness the rape of a white woman by a big Nigger who took hold of the poor young thing, held her mouth to his by pulling her short hair backward until she could do nothing but relent, then threw her down against a maple tree, without so much as a look to see if anyone was watching, pulled it out (it was huge of course), tore off the lady's panties and took his pleasure while the poor thing, skirts up to her neck, could but groan in muffled protest (I suppose). That not enough, the animal then turned her over and lay on again like a dog, all the while the poor young girl too frightened and beaten to do much more than moan (one would hope).

Joseph thought later that he had seen her often in that little park. It was a terrible place to be, even in broad daylight, and you never saw a cop there. In the sixties it became famous for a large Dodge Camper van that would pull up to the park by the back alley every hour or so to "let a few guys out only to wait four or five minutes for a couple more to hop in" the back to the delighted squeals of what seemed to be four or five long-haired, hippy, teen-age girls who would quickly close the doors before the truck drove off (the park, thereafter, to Katie's mind, always associated with moral decay and the corruption of big city life which had swarmed up the river from New York after the war, having as she knew, originally fled the millennium in Europe in droves). Much to Arthur's delight, Katie became and remained a good, liberal Republican.

Up Fifth from the park and Joseph's part-time job, Peerless East opened in a thunder of monumental Roman arches and Victorian pillars, eclipsing in their obvious significance and storied luxury even the five floors of Denby's Downtown which stood across Front Street on the river side in garish, modern, apparelled, black and white windowed architecture and dispensing its supposedly superior opulence not only to the superior hill folk, the Killmans and Laceys and Hoyts and Kramers and Tyndalls that so clearly and justifiably deserved such consideration, but also the Weingertens and Welchs and Zaleskiewicys and Reismans and Houlikans and Walters and Pangburns whose money, come-lately as it might be, nonetheless deserved equal condescension and patronage in that a buck was a buck no matter how dirty or where it came from and, of course, the business of buying and selling kept the economic wheels turning and in turn made the Killmans and Hoyts and Laceys, etc. even richer. "Pax" at least in the cathedral.

Amidst and within the orgy of growth, success, and contentment, Arthur's wealth grew, as it was supposed to by all sane economic laws, until the depression duly interrupted sanity with the insane mortification which so inevitably follows champagne swings on the veranda until three, chickens in every pot, a million more bucks to be made on the market for even the most naive of secretaries, and speak-easy parties easily spoken of to even the cop on the beat. In due fashion Arthur pulled in his economic nets, so to speak. He prided himself on his good fortune in being a seller (and grower) of food and the like (for him and his family first, he admonished during the really hard years). He rented both the houses in Athens after sectioning them off into four apartments, two up and two down, and even dared to take out a bank loan to do the job in '33 ("ah, the hell, if we lose 'em we lose 'em. Its not like they were ever our real home. I never did like the city"). Then he retired once more to the country around Dunedin, which he had never really left, with his milk route still intact on Mondays, Wednesdays, Fridays,--and Saturdays (to collect and tide people over the weekends) and the ninety acres of upland Ducalionial rocks still strewn comfortably, never changing.

By the '50's though (just before the old patriarch died, Athens' houses intact and a good bit of money which inflation would eat up but left for dear Katie), even young Trish, Liz's little sister out of Abigail by Joseph was to be horrified down to her teenage, lacey drawers when she came upon, by mistake in the fading light of a Friday, shopping night in Peerless and Denby's and Sunukjians Woman's Apparel--Father Martin and Sister Ruth Ann

323

from St. Thomas' on Fifth Street making out in a 1937 Chevy in the alley next to the little park that had been the scene of so much of father Joseph's distress a generation before. The good Father Martin, obviously untheologically or unchastely much in love with the said Sister, this made clear by the sweaty kisses he bestowed so aggressively upon not only her lips but her neck and arms and back and (not by choice clever Trish surmised) covered bosom, all the while his hand and arm, wrestling with some unseen obstruction underneath the good Sister's robes which though voluminous still were happily loose, thus allowing ample room for imaginative problem solving. Little Trish stood horrified and unnoticed by the ecstatic couple for ten minutes before, increasingly hidden by the darkening night. Finally, she kindly left Father Martin to his clearly successful connubial ministrations (he was after all, she thought years later, married to the church, and the Sister to Christ) and caught the Fifth Avenue bus home before it really got too dark and Mom Abigail would become worried, and thus angry, that little Trish was out so late and in so much danger of rape and the like. Upon arriving home she told the old Dad in strictest confidence, who nodded sadly and admitted that, yes, he'd always thought it to be an unnatural way to live, and yes, the Catholic Church sure wasn't what it used to be–both wise speculations, after the fact, which were given greater evidence and significance when six months later both the good Father Martin and the goodly Sister Ruth Ann were duly separated from the mother church for cause of conscience and thus duly joined to each other in questionably (for some), holy matrimony for cause of love (carnal et. al.).

Yes, there sure were changes. Katie saw them all from the parlor (front room) window while sitting behind the fading Chinese drapes in her rocker, increasingly old and increasingly fat, especially, finally, even with the gout (a royal disease avoided by husband Arthur not because he refused to drink as his wife wished {Henry would have been appalled}, but because he kept himself active and busy, thus assuring a heart attack, quick and clean, at the expense of the long, messy, more luxurious disease which Katie suffered with admirable courage). She rocked into a wizened, butterball of a woman, lonely for the farm and her lost youth and old Min and the Dunedin Baptist Church and finally even her

324

husband, most of all.

The kids took care of Katie and right well at that. The houses down on River Street and 2nd Avenue grew rich asbestos, false-brick shingling which looked dreadfully like false brick and so assured the ultimate decay of the street and its neighborhoods. Esso, later Exxon; Atlantic and Sinclair, later Arco; Mobil; and Pennzoil stations arose overnight on street corners deserted by people like Charlie Slick and Audrey Tanner whose neighborhood groceries couldn't make it when the Grand Union, A & P, Central, and Albany Public super markets pulled into town during the forties and fifties. (On the less traveled street corners) Bars joined the gas stations and developed a more distinct and more or less catholic neighborhood clientele.

After the lesser war, when he returned home from Japan, young Martin married, took to managing the Athens houses, and was smitten by the fever to asbestos shingle them as well. He did, and years later he was enraged when, after Katie's death, the family could get little more than $10,000 for the two of them, in the downtown, a piddling sum he knew, due to a general decline in the neighborhood served by old P.S. #12, the old brownstone elementary the city had closed down six years earlier thus determining (he determined, pounding his fist on the brand new stainless-steel table top in his new but boxy 3 bedroom 60 ft. trailer set on the old hill farm outside Dunedin) the eventual dissolution of the area, and the fact that folks no longer took pride in their property.

The shirt factories moved out of town (but Cluett and Peabody stayed) and all the men (at least) looked across the river to the Bendix, Republic, and Allegheny Ludlum plants for work. Schenectady grew on the strength of G.E., Chrysler and assorted high-technology. Albany prospered, in singular fashion (and Johnny-come-lately with peaceable Nelson R.) as the seat of state power and city corruption, and Athens grew sleepy in benign change, equally corrupt and equally pacific.

And so it was that the thread of Arthur's life which had wound itself so profoundly into the pattern of the city he so profoundly distrusted, disentangled with unconscious ease and found its way back the 12 miles to Dunedin, now post modern

325

suburbia, from whence it had begun, the way being full of shopping centers, suburban banks, MacDonald's and Wendy's roadside miniature gold courses. We love what we see and we see, unfortunately, all. Great tragedy is totally visceral.

CHAPTER XXXVII
LOVE STORY XIV

pooh!
and just who doesn't rise to the roof through the wreckage on the
lower floors. there's a well-earned symbolism in it all. what, after
all, was the poor bull supposed to do. you're tiresome. living is not.

grandma and gramps had their own problems, however, and
"being good" seems to have been a relative concept. i love it. he
always thinks of her, he says. and who or what might the poor bull
been thinking of?
when you are alone, at night, in a strange land, you have only
memories to comfort you. at times like that the bull or the bear or
the stag, or even the chicken might protest a little. it's all right.
'possessions' can always be replaced. i don't know whether the
getting there or the being there is preferable. but there is no doubt
that the getting is always done for the purpose, desirable or not, of
being.

here's a little letter about little or nothing, but he really
doesn't like his lack of control. "am i english," he asks and protests
not to get the joke. i wonder. winter is cold and lonely. she, too, he
intimates, likes sex a bit. by the looks of their children, you would
think so, but wit is no guarantee of fact, i know. still, i imagine her
coquettish and greedy too. such hypocracy is supposedly most

327

attractive to men and is often called charm.
great tragedy is totally visceral, if we understand the human nature
of it. really!

he sends a note to someone else, he says. do you believe the
gay cavalier? do you desire to? do you desire not to? i do. he
doesn't know what he's saying. she wouldn't have married him if she
thought he did. reality is what you perceive it. and it is only
acceptable if you desire to make it so.

so listen, and tell me the truth.

* * * *

Dunedin, New York
January 26, 1913

My Darling Katie,

Albert and I were out hunting today. We got two Mr.
Ringtails, one in the morning and one in the afternoon. The skins
brought three dollars tonight at the Centre.

Of course I care if you see Matilda without me. You know I
would like to see her too.

Yes, I will be hurt, but please don't look daggers at me
when I tell you I sent a postal to Miss Katie Terrel is good enough
for me.

You are not the only one who tries to be good you know. I

have so much to be good for that it does not take much trying. I suppose you have so little that you must try harder.

Katie, you know I love you. I think of you all the time. Even when I am working or hunting in the woods on these cold, lonely, winter days. It seems that whenever I am most lonely and far away from you then I am truly most near. If anything should happen to you I should be the most miserable of men.

It's nearly ten o'clock. You will have to excuse me if I don't write much more. I am alone and very tired. A big group went down to the donation tonight.

Am I English? What is the joke? "Grace says you have chicken enough." I cannot see the point. I would like to laugh, but there is no one to tickle me. Ma and Pa are asleep so there would be no one to make fun of me even if I did laugh.

Agnes has a letter for you. She put it in my box for me to send, but it is too mean so I will not. I suppose I say mean things enough, but I mean all I say when I tell you that I love you.

The clock has just struck ten. Now I will write no more. But I will go to bed and dream of you. And sweet dreams they will be.

You will always remain my Darling Katie. With love, love for you I will always be yours,

Arthur

* * * *

see! agnes is never to be trusted, yet he feels compelled to tell even the most irrelevant of facts. it must be love of some kind. lovers do that. nothing
can be left out of the day, and even manipulation has to confess itself.

father martin, i'm sure, was the same. they are so close now. he wants to make her feel safe and secure, yet he, himself, needs some comforting. who cares what happens in the rest of the world? they don't need it. time goes very slowly for them, and they must endure it. they must repeat the days every night. how i wish we had her letters. she seems very lucky from what he says. i wonder if grandma was ever aware of it. when i knew her she was so old and fat. and she wasn't that friendly anymore. she was old and deep in memory, i think, even when she smiled at me.

here's another from february.

* * * *

Dunedin, New York
February 13, 1913

My Darling Katie,

We arrived home about one this morning. It was not cold

but the snow was soft and we had to drive slowly.

I received your postal tonight. Father noticed the "love, much more mutcher" on it. He came home with the new horse tonight, and if he does drive it tomorrow you can expect me down about eight o'clock. If he does use it, Edgar will tell you not to look for me.

Do not stay home on my account.

Edgar and I hunted all day and shot only two rabbits. Fate seems against us every time we hunt. There was snow enough, but it was so tracked up we could not easily find the fresh ones.

I suppose you and Lillian enjoyed your walk. Did you get her a pair of "Jew" shoes? Tell Lillian that if I had feet like hers I would wear boots to hide them. That will get a rise out of her.

You have not cried since I came away from you have you? I think I know why you were upset, but I am not sure. In any case I will not again give you reason to be so sad and angry about it.

Don't think I love you one iota less for getting angry. I would be mad too if I had a cause, even though I pray to God I may never have a cause if it is what I think it is.

I told Agnes I would drive Headlight down tomorrow if Father did not return in time. She got mad and said I should not use her horse but that I would have five or six in a wagon behind it. I said I should if I wished for they were all Father's horses until we divvy up.

I was not as upset about her getting angry as I was when you were mad. I would rather have the whole family upset with me than you. If you ever left me, I would never trust another woman. And I would rather have your love than be John D. with all his millions. I would not mind the millions, but if I were forced to choose it would be you.

I would also choose to have you here, where I might give you a hug and a kiss.

I must close now with all the truest love a soul can give, your loving, loving sweetheart, Arthur

* * * *

        i wish we could know the background to so much of what he says. so much of history, sister, is personal and so lost to the rest of us. right? why does he plague her so? seems he's afraid she is angry all the time now, but at the same time he's not overly worried about it. she's most important to him, and the family is going to "divy up." what a strange division of subject matter. love eventually becomes the ordinary, i know. great loves die young, and we are the luckier for it sometimes.
        no! no! i didn't mean that. not exactly.
        lord, i can be a bitch. listen to this one.

* * * *

Dunedin, New York

February 16, 1913

My Darling Katie,

I was looking for a letter tonight. I had thought it Friday
when it was only Thursday. I guess I wished to hurry the week
along. If you shorten the years when I am with you as you length
the weeks when we are alone, I shall lead a short and happy life
indeed.

Mother will have your quilt finished. She had to piece
twenty more blocks to make it long enough. I will bring it down
Sunday, and you can use it for a parlor carpet.

Did you get the cloth Mother asked of you when you went
to Athens? I told her I had not heard of it.

I had a nice cold ride up Tuesday night. I came near
freezing my nose and cheeks. I would have frozen my ears if I had
not tied my handkerchief over them. It was a still cold that pierced
to the bone. I arrived home at half past three and was up at six
thirty to draw wood in the north forest all day. I was rather glad
that night that you did not insist I write until now. I went to bed at
seven.

Father went away again today and we do not expect him
beck before Saturday. He has changed his mind about moving over
on the Snooks' place. He looked at it and decided there were more
rocks on that land than here. He said it would cost a fortune just to
get the Snooks' house cleaned so it was fit to live in.

Albert is coming up tomorrow to go cutting logs with me. I
have about half of our cord out now. If the snow would stay
another week, I could finish it.

Tell Edgar he will have to come up and help clean the
shotguns. He should be staying up here anyway. I have not had a
spare minute. Of course he could let you come in his place, and I

should be better satisfied.

I suppose you and Lillian have been to Schenectady by now. How did Cyrus like it when she let Web come home with her?

I suppose the blooming red-head has peddled that story all over town. We will see what we can do to stop it when I come down Sunday.

If it were just us, I should laugh it to scorn, and for your sake I hope we can before your father gets a hold of it. As it is, I would rather have almost anything happen than for it to become public.

It sounds bad the way they have reported it. If it came to facts, we could prove it all false, but we will not have that chance. Remember Grace and Arbie?

Never mind, it is always darkest before dawn. Hope for the best and trust to providence. Next year we shall be married and laughing at them all.

They took in about $20 at the Valentine social up here. They say the girls would not accept the valentines and take their chances with them, so they had to let the valentines go and the girls went with whatever boy they liked.

Tell Edgar and Austin that the fellow he hunted with on Valentine's Day shot and killed two foxes and had a third running only to miss him because of the dark.

Oh, my Valentine, my Darling. How can I express my love for you. It is more brilliant than the red of my heart and deeper than the unplumbed ocean. I love you.

Your loving, loving Sweetheart.

xxxxxxx Arthur xxxxxxx

* * * *

      a short and happy life, indeed. he always has style. he plays at words and things. shorten the days, shorten the weeks, shorten the years - but only if she's with him. and what has been said about them? they're cousins, but that's hardly worth all the fuss at this point. does someone think she's pregnant? i doubt it. more likely, they all think the two of them have "gone too far" and the like. as though no one else ever had? well, let's hope they have a bit.

      i've forever dreamed of an abstract lover who would not worry about what others said or did. we'd live forever in a sweet half-dream, between waking and sleeping. he'd love me as my one true love and never leave me. we'd die together and never know a loss. it can--it does happen. it happens in the letters. they remain like this always.

      i don't like history. it lies and makes up things. only the flesh endures, finally and without comment.

* * * *

Dunedin, New York
March 8, 1913

My Darling Darling Katie,

Don't talk of crying any more. I could cry as easily too when I think of how little time we have together if you stay at work. If you had cried Sunday there would have been two of us.

You should see me. I have a cold, and the sun shining on the new snow has burned my face raw. I look like an Indian. My eyes were so red that Father and Mother would not let me go into the woods today, and so I sit abed, and Mother keeps yelling at me to sleep.

Father has traded horses since you were up last. He has a bay now instead of a grey. Father says to tell you there never was a Terrel who could box his ears. He said, "I don't think there are any of them who would care to try, even as old as I am." I know I wouldn't. Pa is tough.

Are you lonesome? Mother just said, "I bet old Trot (another new name) is lonesome. It wouldn't be so bad if she were just down the road someplace, but no." I don't think it will ever end.

I suppose Ida and Freddie called us fools when they climbed up to our place last week. They will probably ride us, too, about it. But I guess Freddie is all right to send letters by if you have to. I received your other one unopened.

I know I have blotted my paper again. I am such a poor writer, but if I blotted paper as much as I think about you there would be no writing.

Katie, the more I think of you the more I love you. I believe there is no limit to love. It is boundless I have found my love for you to be so.

Sleep well Katie I will dream of you.

Your loving, loving Sweetheart,

xxxx Arthur xxxx

P.S. Here is a letter from Agnes addressed to Eddie Poultrie. It's for you though. I don't know what the devil she is up to now. I suppose she wants to plague us.

* * * *

To Eddie Poultrie

Hawks Farm, New York
March 6, 1913

Dear, My Darling Katie,

Are you well? Do you like your place? Do you know it?

When do you think you will be able to come up again? Miss Cramps is or was asking about you.

Have you ever got the cloth for my underskirt? I need it as I have a new dress and apron.

Do you know Nettie Martin? There were 14 to school today. How many folks are there where you work? Does Lillian like to do the work too?

Eveline Bulson is worse today. Arthur got home safe and sound around half past twelve last night. I hear my teacher is truly going to marry Victor Burden.

Can you play Shine On as well as ever? I guess I will have to close now with much love.

I remain your cousin,

Agnes Countryman

P.S. Answer soon.

* * * * *

and so an end to it. agnes is hardly prolix. they cry often, one to another. eddie poultrie is everywhere. they are loving fools. this is all what they say. nothing more. not even being there would really help. we'd have to be in the skin. yet, something says "i know."
i remember something i have not lived.

338

CHAPTER XXXVIII
Love Story XV

and there is more, so much more. and we don't have to read between the lines or deeply. so much of experience is open to us if only we refuse to be afraid.

here are some letters. long and involved ones. i'll read them without comment. it is important not to be civilized sometimes, not to reflect upon things.

only then can meaning display itself.

* * * *

Dunedin, New York
May 19, 1913

My Darling, Darling Katie,

It rained for about an hour today. The grass has grown an inch. The morning everything was turning brown. Now there is a cool, green dye over all the hills and pastures. It makes a fellow feel good to be out here at a time like this.

I don't think it was seeing that girl that made my head ache. I saw her Tuesday night, though, and could not write you until Thursday.

Tell me, how are you and the old lady making out with your new job? If it has a bad effect on you to sleep with an old woman, what will you do with me? Maybe I will have to sleep in the guest room.

All kinds of bad luck this week. Mother's Teddy hen failed to hatch a chick. Mr. Ringtail pulled his chain loose from his collar and exited through a hole in the chicken wire. Then Agnes' lamb that had just grown horns fell in the spring and drowned. I found him and buried him before she could see.

Father has a chance to sell old Bob for $50. He is going to see if he can get another.

On Decoration Day you had better let me come down and get you. Then you can come up here and watch while I play ball and help Dunedin wipe out that old score of last fall. I could take you home again that night, but let me know if you will. I had rather play ball than anything, except being with you. I would like us to go to the circus a week from tomorrow night, too, but that is Father's day in Athens so I guess we will not get the chance.

I hope to get most of the planting done by next week. My potato ground is ready and had it not rained I would have begun tomorrow. As it is, I will plow my corn ground tomorrow and not plant it all until next week.

You are not the only one who can make posey beds, by the way. I have two ready but do not know what flowers to put in them. Mother has put some in and will not tell me what they are. I guess I'll have two surprises next month. You should see the titties on the old sow, she is due to drop a litter about the middle of June.

They have a piazza all along the front of the Snook house. It really gives it a grand look.

Don't scold me for not writing long letters. Especially when I write three to your two. If you believe me naughty, I will take care not to see any more girls than I must. My love for you is endless and true. I cannot say it in any other way.

I think I am worse to myself than to anyone. I try to please you regardless of the cost.

Love, love, love to you my own. Darling little Katie,

Your loving, loving, loving, Sweetheart,

   xxx Arthur xxx

* * * *

My Darling, Darling, Darling Katie,

It has been gloomy and rainy today. It seems a week since

last I saw you.

We need the rain though so I guess I can stand it. I put my rubber coat on and passed the forenoon putting pumpkin seeds in the corn hills we planted last week.

This afternoon I cleaned my guns so I would be ready to shoot crows in the morning. The old pig is still alive but just barely. She is a very sick animal even though I have doctored her three times and she seems a bit better.

Mrs. Burden is teaching school here now. Miss Gramps and Vic jumped the rope Saturday night. Agnes said she had to go to school today for examinations, and Father replied that Miss Gramps had her examination Saturday night. Some people say she and Vic are going to live in Perrysville, but I've heard they may trot off to her home in Erie, Pennsylvania, and set up house.

Darling, don't worry about what I say when I am with you. I know I say things I should not, but it is only to tease. Wilbur is to be married inside two weeks, so you need not worry that I will run away with him.

I love only you and would never leave. You are too very dear to me, whether in Hawks Farm, or Dunedin, or California. I shall love you even if we must wait another year. No danger of that, though, unless I am unable to raise two or three hundred dollars. And even then, no suffering is too much to bear for your sake. I am going to have enough though, even if it takes a leg.

I suppose you washed today. If it rained down there as much as it did here, the clothes on the line would have washed themselves.

Old Minnie is out in the swamp making music after a rabbit. How lonely she sounds. Remember old Mose? He used to make the same run.

Well it's after nine and everyone is abed so I had better high-tail it there myself. I'll have to rise about three in the morning if I am to have much of a chance at those crows.

I send you all my love. No! You already have that so I cannot send it. Instead I shall think of you and send you my dreams. Except that will make the night go fast and I will feel in the morning as if I had not a wink of sleep.

I am your loving, loving, Sweetheart,
 xxxxx Arthur xxxxx

＊ ＊ ＊ ＊

Dunedin, New York
June 12, 1913

My Darling, Darling, Darling, Katie,

Even if I did stay all night, for once I found everything going smoothly when I came home. Wilbur was getting ready to go out to Matilda's. They got their license yesterday.

I have been plowing all day and it will take a day or two more to finish the buckwheat ground. When it is finished, there will be ten full acres.

We have not heard from the people at the dam, so we will go to work.

Albert went to Athens and put six hundred dollars in the bank today. I wish we had that. What would we do if we did? I don't suppose you would leave Mrs. Poultrie's even if we had.

Don't look for me Thursday night. I would like to be with you, but I think you can enjoy yourself as well if I am home. You can give Edgar one of your tickets. He would enjoy the show more than I would anyway.

Don't think that I hold you less dear because I cannot come down. But put yourself in my place for once and see how many times you would drive all the way from Hawk's Farm to Dunedin just to be with me for, at most, a few minutes. I notice you like your sleep as well as anyone since you have been at work.

I know, too, that it is as hard for you to be away from me as it is for me to be without you. I should like to have you where I could see you every day. It will be soon.

Oh, say, can't you get away once a week in time to take a ride up in the stage or auto? I will take you back.

Oh, I don't know what is the matter with me. I can't seem to stop plaguing you even in my letters. You will have to stop getting angry at me, then I will stop teasing. I don't do it to be mean. I just can't help it.

I will close knowing you care for me as I love you. No matter what I say all my love is always yours,

Your loving, loving, loving Sweetheart,

xxxxx Arthur xxxxx

P.S. I hope you have not thrown the ring away again.

* * * *

Dunedin, New York
August 9, 1913

My Own Darling, Darling Katie,

    I received your second letter tonight, and I can tell you it makes me feel some different from the one I received last night. I have been trying to decide all day whether to write tonight or wait for another letter to see if you had not changed your mind about a vacation in Berlin.

    Sunday you felt I had no right to be hurt. I wish you could know how it seemed when you decided without me that you were leaving for three weeks. Let me reverse things.

    Suppose you had been coaxing me to come and stay a week with you, and I had refused because I had to work. Now suppose Arbie had come up and asked me to visit him, and I accepted right away. The next time I saw you, I told you that I was going but said nothing about visiting you. The next time I see you it is with a crowd, and I tell someone about going to Arbie's and then say I'm also going to Hoosick for a week to see Benny and then maybe over to Schenectady for another week, but I say nothing about you.

    How would you feel? Would you say, " How dearly he loves me?"

    Darling, I am sorry I acted as I did, but I love you. Forgive me. At the time I wanted to get away and cry, but I knew it would do no good so I hid my feelings. I suppose I made a mess of it. I will try never to show off so badly in a crowd again.

345

You know how dearly I love you. And you little goose, to think you were jealous of Mable Norton. Ester maybe, but Mable? Not if she were the last girl on the earth. I love you! When you are done with, if I haven't grit enough to find my way out of this world, I'll get in a row with someone and let them butt me out. I would have nothing to live for without you.

Thank you for not leaving me. I know now how dearly you must love me.

I want you to have a vacation. You need a rest and though I would like you near me, if you want to go to Mattie's I am satisfied.

Don't go to Tommy's though. The further we stay away from them the better. I saw them have one row and that was enough. There isn't any danger of our being like that dear. It would kill me to have you use me as Agnes does Tommy.

And don't try to make me lie anymore Dear, as you did Sunday when I told Mattie I did not want you visiting Tommy. How I hate to even think of lying. I came the nearest to being angry with you than I have ever been.

Had you not talked up at Sarah's and then to your father. You only did that to hurt me didn't you? You never intended to go to Berlin, did you? Not after you knew I did not want you to go.

Please don't stay at home because of what I have said. If you wish to visit me a few days I will be glad to have you. You are always welcome by one when you come here. What do we care about how the rest act?

Take part of your vacation now Dear, and then about the first of September you could come up and spend a week with me. Then I would have time to take you fishing and go on lots of rides. Now I would miss you because of the haying. But if you can't get away later, take your vacation now and visit Mattie's.

We begin haying up above tomorrow. I finished cutting oats yesterday. Today I drew wood to the school house. I also picked enough huckleberries yesterday for six cans. Now, we can have thirty six in all.

And don't worry about Mable Norton. She could not hold even my thoughts a single moment. I love you more than I can ever tell. I don't know how much. We must never argue again.

...is home again, drunk as usual. I am glad I do not drink. If I did, I would never let you throw yourself away on me. You are too good for me now, but I can never give you up.

Your loving, loving, loving Sweetheart,

xxxxxxxxxxxx Arthur xxxxxxxxxxxxxxxxx

* * * *

there. what do you think of that?

CHAPTER XXXIX
PORTRAIT XIII

The children grew up. The war came and went. Then he left and traveled one winter, I remember. It was the second after Ma moved down to Athens to be with Martin and Suzanne and to take care of her 'ailing condition' as she put it.

It was the only time I'd ever known him to travel a lot. Up in Vermont for a while I guess, to see Clem Haskins, one of the boys he'd studied with at Mt. Union, a great steel-haired, bone-whiskered man who drove sheep and cows in the same pasturage outside Bennington and loved to play pinochle at five cents a game. He had a stub left thumb that had been partially bitten off at the first knuckle when he was twenty-five by a year old ram he and his brother had been castrating. After that he always maintained that sheep were plenty smart. It was a testament to his genius that his angular wife, who had bore him seven boys and two girls, all of whom lived, and whose stomach was still so tight that her hips protruded like a saddle on either side of her pelvis, would sit in stony silence when her husband noted that he'd never understood why we didn't treat women like a mob of sheep because they were just as stupid and dropped only one or two in a litter. Clem would sit with his stoggie fire red as he drew on it and turn his head toward Marion who wouldn't honor him by looking up from knitting. Then he'd laugh and cry between coughs and phlegm

"Oh that's all right Artie. Don't mind her. She's been that way ever since '23 when I broke her nose. Damn good wife ever since." Then he'd laugh and cough some more. He was a hard man. But honest, and Pa liked him.

After that Pa wandered over New Hampshire way, I think. Maybe Clem didn't agree with him up close. Maybe just had to work the loneliness out of himself. Or maybe he just wanted to wander some, finally, before he died. I don't know. But it was the only Christmas I ever remember him not at home. He really didn't know about Martin and Suzanne having trouble early on, and I'm sure he thought we kids could handle everything. After all, we were all grown up now, he used to tell us.

There were those who thought old Art Countryman a fool for taking off at his age just to chase the women in New York City. I never believed them. Uncle Albert had died there, and I think Pa just wanted to go down and see what it was that had killed his brother and left him childless and without a family to boot.

By that time, Edgar's wife Bessie had started to turn nutty as a fruitcake, too. We'd all come home from the war safe and sound. Agnes pulled up stakes and trotted off to Athens with the rest of the family. There really wasn't much left up on the farm that had to be done in the winter except for feeding Min and the stock, and I did that every morning or two, as well as cleaning the place out real good every other Saturday. He probably did some ice fishing, too, because he took all his rods and tackle. I remember there was a great empty spot in the kitchen corner near the window where he always kept them. No telling where he took that old Ford truck of his. It wasn't long after the war, and Pa hadn't worked up the courage to pay what it cost for a new one yet.

So much had happened by then. Alex had stolen my car back in '40 and taken it on a joy ride all over Athens, Rapidston, Twin Rivers, Hawks Farm, and the Corners before finally doubling back at the Centre over the old brick road onto the turnpike and, with three sheriff's cars on his tail, missing a left hand turn on Shore Road and running axle deep into the clay and mud of Ashokan Dam. He'd had a hell of a time of it, used up almost a full tank of gas, outdriven the entire North Athens Police Department through alleys and side streets for over an hour and a half before taking off up Mill Hill and then on across Lake Lane lickity-split, horn blaring, cigar in his mouth, Tillie Walsh by his side holding a bottle of beer in one hand and giving the cops the finger out the window with the other. Blessing them out all the time. And that was what finally sent him into the mud (right in front of a 'Smoke Camels' billboard that bent precariously over the car when he broke one of its supports). Not a cop that could have caught him otherwise. Even Eddie Kilmen admitted to that. It cost Alex $72.50 to have my car dragged out of the mud and towed back to young Vic Burden's to be made fit to drive. That was a hell of a lot of money in those days. That and the speeding charges that he was socked with all along the way cleaned out his bank account, especially when Pa cut his allowance for working on the farm in half.

Lord, those were times. Took me a year to forgive him. But Alex was always that way, a great football player of a man who just had to tower over a girl for ten minutes, leaning with one arm bent with extravagant carelessness against the wall, before he'd have her talked into a ride out to the reservoir and a hustle in the back seat before going on home. He was good at it, and no real girl could ever resist that smile. Why--he was even smiling eight months later when I saw him in the hospital after the motorbike accident. Everybody always said that was why he fathered only five girls and never had any boys when he married Dorothy. I never believed it. Still, you can't help but laugh to see him lying there in bed, his legs spread wide apart under the covers and him trying to smile in spite of how much it hurt.

He'd gotten himself a motorcycle after he'd been grounded for 6 months by Pa as well as the police, and that fall he'd race all over the countryside with Betty Felar on the back, her skirt hiked halfway up her backside as she set astraddle, her white socks wet and brown from the cycle's spray. Alex had bet Tim Hanson ten dollars that he could ride from Athens to Dunedin in fifteen minutes, beginning at Mill Hill and ending at the Post Office across from the flag pole. He lost the bet at Stumps Corners on a wet bridge across the Cedar Kill and ended up wound half around a small oak and the bike in the creek.

Seven months later, when he'd been out and walking some five months, Alex up and married Dorothy and then joined up the next year. You never could pin that man down. Never knew what he'd do next. When he came back from the Pacific he worked the milk route for a while and then moved on to the Allegheny-Ludlum plant over in Twin Rivers. The girls just loved him. I guess Dorothy knew that though when she married him.

And Jessie was just like Alex, one hell of a fighter. I remember during the war when she was six months pregnant and Art hadn't come home yet from the gravel pit down near the Corners where he worked. Jessie knew! He was in town hanging out with the boys at Judson's just as sure as she was breathing, and six months pregnant or not, with stockings barely rolled up above her knees, two year old Alice in her arms and that little calico maternity dress so thin it could hardly hold her bosom in, she tromped off in their little Chevy station wagon that had so much rust on the fenders it released a film of brown dust whenever she started the car. Art always left it at home, and Jessie went to get him before he might drink up all the family's eatin' money for the next two weeks.

What a storm she was. Blew into Judson's like a Baptist preacher on damnation day, nose red, belly bouncing, and baby bawling. Art hid in the back room 'til she broke so many glasses and knocked over so many chairs that men started bailing out of the place left and right and Ted Hansen began thinking that Jessie might just be bad for business. So they got Art out, and Jessie took him home, drunk as a loon but still with most of his paycheck, which Jessie confiscated as she half pushed and half steered him through Judson's front door and into the car. God, she was a real spitfire - always was.

Good thing Pa never saw that one. He was still alive, but we all kept it from him. How he would have liked it; to know that Sarah, Alex, and Jessie all have got religion in their old age and now go to the Baptist Church and sit in those same hard oaken pews listening to the preacher with their blind eyes and carrying on their "ministries" to every part of the county. A 'ministry' of puppets for Jessie, a 'ministry' of words for Alex, and cooking and sewing for Sarah. 'Ministries' here and 'ministries' there, and Alex's wife hardly ever inviting guests in anymore because she's so embarrassed.

Dunedin sits on the side of a hill, and I suppose that's one of the reasons it never did grow much even after they paved the U.S. highway some years back. Now, all the kids seem to be going back there after so many years in the city. Maybe they never left. Maybe the country with its rickety, back porch doors, hunting dogs tied to fence posts in the front-yard, rusty horseshoes hailed beside the doors on swinging sidewalk gates, a post office where you ask for your mail by the first name, and the war memorial is a simple gravestone with a flagpole behind it alongside the highway, maybe things like that never really let you leave.

But it's a different town now. I'll have to say that for it. The Perrysville Rock and Gravel Company's gone and so is Art's old job. Now he sits in a slight, grotesquely fragile body, far too small for the farmer's overalls which balloon away from his spindly legs and hips, heavy jowled and toothless, staring at the TV and occasionally speaking in a country accent so thick an outsider cannot understand one word in ten.

There's a Catholic Church in town, and it's accepted right well. The schoolhouse out on the Taconic Road, though, now has sliding glass doors across its once serene white front, and there's a 25' by 15' swimming pool fenced off beside the new addition in the back. There are even a number of new grand brick homes out along the highway with round swimming pools and two car garages and people who commute 15 or 20 miles to Athens or Rapidston to work in the factories and mills.

There's a new state park on Long Lake. The old store across from Jeremiah's Hotel is still there, but a dozen ears of corn bring $1.39 in peak season and the homemade macaroni salad you get from the back room kitchen where Nina Brimmer makes it isn't nearly as good as her Mom's. Of all things, the veranda of the hotel is a liquor store, and no one seems to mind. Have to have one to serve the tourist crowd, and Grant Hollins admits that there's an awful lot of city voters in the district now.

------------------ah-------------------.

Ah, like I say, we missed him at Christmas that year for the only time I remember. He wandered around well into March, I think, and we all got worried he might not come back at all, because half the time we never rightly knew where he was or wasn't. But April came, and suddenly one Saturday there he was at the farm when Martin showed up on Saturday. The stock was fed, the plows cleaned and the old Massey-Ferguson tractor turned and ready to go.

He came into town with Martin and saw Grandma. They talked alone a long while, and we could see later they'd both been crying. Then he went back up to the farm and planted a crop. And after that he never missed coming down to see Grandma every weekend, even during the terrible blizzard back in '47 and that hurricane that came up the coast in '51, the winter before he died.

He just stayed on the farm and worked it. And when he died, there was a big funeral in spite of us all. Too many people knew him and too many cared. He'd left his mark upon these hills, and I don't think they'll ever forget him walking along the village streets, big and slow as a bear, but with fine gentle eyes and that tough red face of his brighter than the sun.

CHAPTER XL
HISTORY LESSON XII

Tick, tock, tick,tock. The clock in the basket keeps the puppy happy if not warm.

A syllogism, justly won and poorly paid, the middle unstated though distributed, in parts, equally, to the just.

Great knowledge is final loneliness. And, therefore, love is unbearable for the finally wise. Certain honesty is certain pain, surely deserved and most assuredly visited upon the ... To care too much is to ... only repetition and redundancy may ... Save us from ... Our scars of mortality ... or mortal scars ... To be without hope
....

I shan't continue.

Great knowledge, ripped to the tit.

Henry had his burden, at least in theory. Though burdensome as love is in the affairs of state, it is also ubiquitous and thus suggestive of our ability to carry great burdens more easily than we would have our kindred believe, as it suits our vanity, which is indeed the most honest of loves and therefore absolute loneliness.

A Mary Countryman was most surely the first teacher in the little old schoolhouse in Dunedin along the Taconic Trail, but then her sister Sarah taught for 51 years up in Hoosick Falls along the river (always to be crossed over--small gods being what they are), and she left a record never to be broken, if one believes what the old hands in the town still say, giggling out of the sides of their mouths, looking toward the windows while spitting tobacco juice into the now antique spittoon which still occupies the center of Zedo Hamill's Saloon and Bar, the present owner being misnamed for his profession and misplaced for his name and tradition. Fifty-one years and she never missed a day, unlike good King Henry carrying her burden in continuing chastity and peaceful equanimity all the days of her life, having visited Athens only twice after being educated at the Ladies Country Day Academy there-- once to see her uncle buried, a hard, small red-eyed man who made his fortune selling various religions icons, ornaments, and trinkets to the Italians and Irish of the city and thus retired well onto Pawling Avenue, and the other to buy herself a red taffeta underskirt, which no one ever saw until after she died and then only after pulling it almost by accident out from behind the piles of dollar twenty five, 42D brassieres and reinforced 42" rayon girdles in which she forever incarcerated her increasingly ample body over the 67 of her 75 years in which it was worthwhile for her to bother with such things. Only, the youngsters of Hoosick ever thought and then only toward the end when she became mean and cranky, that she was much of a load to bear at all.

Of this we can be sure, Arthur Countryman didn't leave a lonely house (made so by the unfortunate necessity of Katie's relocation to the city) in order to take up with the likes of Mary's sister, though the aforementioned extended trip has always excited conjecture among the unlearned to the effect--not the exact same sister but the likes of her. What makes a man leave home, kith, and kin so late in life? Why did Henry decide to contend with the French king so late in life and while suffering gout (a sorely postulating leg--sex crimes being what they are) at that? Clear, factual history has little need of motive. It happened! And that was (and is) that.

Things had changed for noble Arthur. They'd been changing since Joe Terrel's father (among others) tore up Athens from Constitution to 110th in seven bloody and frothy hours of glorious St. Patrick's Day riot in 1838, an accomplished fact by 8 P.M. that night which was for a hundred years to keep the Irish in particular

356

and Catholics in general out of the better sections of North and South Lake Lane as well as Pawling, only the elections of '32, disaster that they were, turning the tide and proving, finally, the efficiency of a truly democratic system.

Arthur, as well, knew nothing of the founding of the Athens Club in 1817, although old Alexander Washington had once thought about joining that group of 'public spirited citizens', the town's best who built the community's first private golf course (for the club) out past Pawling and almost into Greenbriar, because he thought the second floor billiard room might be a nice place to relax when on his increasingly frequent trips into what was clearly a growing, nascent industrial metropolis, benignly situated at the confluence of two great rivers and, therefore, destined to become a major force in the affairs of state and carry its more solid citizens along for the ride--so to speak.

The classical literary irony, though clearly with no historical significance whatsoever, is that soon Martin did, for a short time, lend his name and finances to the support of the New Horizons Club (circa 1855), a rival organization of young Turks (without national affiliation) who, still with money in their pockets, wished to be something more than the "hollow shell of landed wealth and privilege" which they considered the Knights of Athens. Although exactly what they wished to be, other than significantly younger and louder, remained a mystery throughout three generations and almost a century until finally no significant differences were discovered. The war (both) ended with their union in 1920 in the ballroom over the Athens' Masonic Temple to the tune of "Battle Hymn of the Republic" (for the old boys) and "The Tables Down at Maury's" (it was football season), young Arthur never seeing fit or having the interest to test his own luck and see if he could make the grade.

Other changes are clear and important although never mentioned in the letters, Arthur not, evidently, a news buff, at least it not intruding in his love life --or he being careful not to let it. The Baltimore Explosion took place in January 1913, the Athens Times being all agog with the incendiary nature of it and the great tragedy. Later in the year the Kanawha Coal Field Dispute tore through West Virginia and the Northeast. But the West Virginia mines were shut - they were - so why should Arthur worry, such burdens properly relegated to the weighty affairs of state and both Henry and Teddy were not there to shoulder the load.

For a cultural epi-center: Pulitzer had died in '11 thus gracing upper 5th Avenue and lower Central Park with a bit of nice statuary. The "Titanic Disaster" occurred in April of 1912, the loss of so many great leaders of world commerce seemingly having absolutely no effect upon the future course of world events, even in the short run. Disaster visited Athens that year with almost poetic redundancy as the spring floods came early not only in New York but everywhere east of the Mississippi. There was $2,000,000 damage in Athens itself as the river surged past flood stage and left half the citizens of Twin Rivers and Rapidston without homes at all. It was a major disaster matched only by the 500 dead in Ohio from the same swollen rivers and unexpected thaws which left the center of Dayton awash in debris, corpses, and broken American dreams.

Good Arthur never bought stock. Didn't trust it. So the more direct nature of that not-so-singular American tragedy was not visible to him for several months when falling wages and the discontinuance of industrial activity left the farmer without a ready market for his goods. In October of 1911 (a capricious date for an equally capricious set of figures), the Athens Times reported that General Electric sold on the New York Stock Exchange at 148 3/4, Republic Steel 22 1/2, Canadian Pacific 225 1/2, Southern Pacific 107 1/4, and Dupont not listed. Westinghouse 62 3/4 and General Motors 38 1/2.

On September 2, 1929, before the crash the figures were: General Electric 395 1/2, Republic Steel 129, Canadian Pacific 232 3/8 (splits), Southern Pacific 153 3/4, Dupont 215, Westinghouse 288, and General Motors 72.

On September 1, 1933 the figures were: General Electric 24 3/4, Republic Steel 17 1/2, Canadian Pacific 16 1/2, Southern Pacific 30 3/4, Dupont 80 3/4, Westinghouse 45 3/4, and General Motors 33 5/8. How the mighty do fall. And all this essentially unknown to then middle-aging Arthur.

The age had come and gone. And poor old Teddy, God Rest His Soul. Arthur paced the living room floor on his Whittel Rug bought out in Quackenbush, "at discount" as all good merchandise was in the thirties, and wondered how things could get worse. But at least (he knew), there was the garden and the stock and winter hunting and the maple routes and milk to be sold in Athens. The farmer had a living. At least there was that.

And there were other tragedies; even Great Henry's great hock was not always green (or too green if you are a connoisseur, but such culture came with the cork in the 1800's). The dried plant collection of the Athens' Botanical Society, gathered over 83 years of careful, loving, and meticulous labor, was inadvertently burned by a young janitor who used it as kindling to start a fire in the old Franklin stove that had stood for decades because the society had taken to meeting in private homes as it grew into its well-deserved, although unsought for, senescence.

The kids were actually townies during the first years. Arthur grew in stature and wisdom at first on someone else's farm then later his own. By 1917, there were two townhouses and a thriving milk route. Arthur worked for three dairies; Schiffer's in Albany, Boronskill in Athens, and the Scarlatti Dairy in South Athens before moving his own business into the lower floor of the larger 4th Avenue house and announcing his independence by stealing over three-quarters of the customers from his former master's routes. The Diamond Rock Cooperative was created as a last resort and self-protection after the depression and increasing government regulation drove Arthur and 26 other independents like him to increasingly profound bankruptcy, both the concept and reality during the thirties discovering in itself a possibility for comparison to which until then (and beyond) the academic world would not admit.

For a while Arthur even took to breaking horses in order to make a living, but then his back went out on him, and besides he'd managed to pay all of his debts and still keep the townhouses (and the 90 acre farm and the milk route), so he really "didn't need the exercise after all."

By then Arthur and Katie and the kids were "back on the farm" where they belonged, and Albert had moved south to Scoharie to a farm of his own on sweeter (and less obdurate) land. Mattie had joined the Salvation Army after marrying a 120 lb. Italian from South Athens with blue lips, an almost hairless mustache, and perpetually dirty fingernails who had become disenchanted with the priesthood but not a good Valpolicella, and Katie then lost again, but for once or twice a year at the holidays, her previously long-lost sister.

An Arthur Terrence Countryman came home, eventually to die, but with his burden, if not lightened, at least more comfortably distributed, Katie being secure in the now mature hands of lovable Martin; Lillian, Sarah, Joseph, Alex, and Jessie--all adults and all seemingly well placed or close to it; the farm built and its various boundaries established; corn here, potatoes there, the south pasture for sheep, the north for horses, hogs behind the small barn with a trough the length of the roadside fence, chicken coup north of the house, hay barn out back next to the corn field; and a new tractor to replace the horses for most work.

The growing season had been completed before he knew it had begun, and now was the harvest time.

Oh say, Old Henry and William Clarke and Teddy and Howie and Woody and most especially Franklin; how do you harvest the decades with the victory yet to be won, the journey not finished?

And all the banks are closed.

Tick, tock, tick, tock.

CHAPTER XLI
LOVE STORY XVI

no! no! no! there are many things that are not solved by thinking.
this is one of them. why must i always be repeating the obvious?
who are we talking about anyway? they loved from the beginning.
they said so. what if it's hidden or obvious? we might, we can,
never know unless we feel it all.

     listen to these. just like the others, we are summing up, we
are ..., my god! we are--aren't we? we're summing up. we're telling
the last from what we've seen of the beginning. and what they said
then, what they felt and what they thought and what they did? I
mean, ever since we came up here among the cobwebs. sis, dad,
this is us. what we are and where we came from. no arguments.

     people never die, do they? and the past is only real if it's
lived in the present. that means it's always changing, the past i
mean. it's always whatever we make it. gramma and gramps made
their present our past, and now we make it the their present once
again.
it all is what it is to us and only to us. i know them by what i accept
as left to me. sis, remember that, and listen to these last letters.
there are times when i feel so close to them. i don't even need the
words.

361

* * * *

Dunedin, New York
September 1, 1913

My Darling, Darling, Darling, Katie,

I hope you are feeling better. I arrived home about twelve o'clock. It was not as cold coming up as it was at Hawks Farm. If it had been I would have been frozen. But I shall hope for better next time. I do understand and am only joking. Ha! Ha!

I have just put that glassware on our list. It makes a total of $89.18. I'll finish making out the bill and the next time I get to the bank in Athens I will send away for the goods. I guess we're really going to get married now that we have begun to spend money. When I was trying to save and not spend, marriage seemed only a happy dream I might lose. Now it seems we will have a real home.

And the sweetest of girls will grace my home with her presence. My wife! Oh, may that day come soon. We will not be unhappy, but when one sees so many unhappy unions it makes one think. We will have to be strong Darling and work for the love that we have.

I cut some buckwheat today...and tomorrow will dig potatoes some.

I did not get much sleep last night so I will close.

All my love and kisses are yours. Be sure and be well next Sunday.

Your loving, loving, loving sweetheart,

XXXXXXXX Arthur XXXXXXXX

* * * *

    sometimes he uses too many words and not enough silence.
to spend money is to really love.

    how about that? i think he's right. a stingy man is never a
good lover. i'd rather worry about losing something i had than
regret what was never given to me. i'll bet she liked the petting a
lot. i don't care what will happen. this is too good.

* * * *

Dunedin, New York
September 22, 1913

My Darling, Darling, Darling, Katie,

    I thought I was only to get one letter this week. Imagine
my surprise when I received two in one night.

    I cannot send for our furniture this week. I cannot get the
$17.50 for the wood just yet. I will have Edgar put our money in
the bank until we are ready for it.

    Arbie said he heard we'd set the day soon. I told him not till the middle of the winter. He and Grace (he allowed as how) could not have been engaged until he got older and appreciated a girl more. He said he never went with a girl but that he didn't think she was all there was at the time, but he soon got over them all. He also said that eventually a fella had to get over the puppy love.

I wonder if poor Grace only got some of Arbie's puppy love. She certainly thought enough of him or she would not have written to him for two years.

I got a postal from Albert saying not to write again until I got his new address. He's going to Schenectady to work and take off maybe for New York, but I think I can get him to come over and stand up with us if we want him to. I think I will ask Edgar first though.

I suppose we will have to tell your father before long. It may as well be one time as another... he is expecting it....

I have my corn all cut ... and beans picked. Herb Rawley wanted me to come and help him again this week, but I could not ... I'll help him next week if he still wants me.

Darling I don't see why we cannot live like pigs in the clover once we are settled. How could we help it when we love one another as we do...I am afraid I do not fully appreciate the love you give me. You have all of mine but I am afraid it is not as warm as yours. I don't know why it should not be since it is my only love. One's first should be one's strongest.

.... How will you keep your plants when you move from Poultries, especially that Passion one which is so pretty? We must bring them up in the middle of winter ... and if we have a cold day they will freeze. They are nice to have, dear, but I am afraid you will find them some bother this winter. Maybe we could put them in the cellar when we are away.

We will not be able to leave for long once we get settled

and get the hens in,--and the cow.

        Don't worry I am not going to over work anymore and don't
you either.

        All my love

        Your loving, loving, loving, Sweetheart
        XXXXX Arthur XXXXX

P.S.
Wasn't I good last night? I hope you will not have to find fault with
me any more because I do not know how to behave. I was good,
wasn't I?

        * * * *

        "like pigs in clover," i think little pigs can be cute. and they
are very intelligent aren't they? think how young the two of them
were. i always think of him as a wild animal though, and evidently
that's how grandma must have felt. just look at the first few
sentences of this next letter.
        you get away with what you can. and we all like it that way.
how she must have tortured him. and how such torture is forever

the beginning of love.

* * * *

Dunedin, New York
October 11, 1913

My Darling, Darling, Darling, Katie,

I suppose you have some fault to find in me for being naughty again. Don't be too hard. I am only human. Flesh and blood as anyone else.

We went to Athens today, and I got our money for the furniture. I will go to the Centre tomorrow and mail the money order.

Darling, you must not mind if I tease you. I don't mean what I say about other girls. There's only one for me. If they should convert you into thinking it was wrong to marry me, I should never marry for the rest of my life. I don't see that we are doing any harm. We can love each other as well as anyone if only other people will mind their own business and let us attend to ours ...

I am glad I did not read Mattie's letter Sunday. If I had I would have never gone down there with you...I would have had an answer for her and that would have been to mind her own business...She just makes trouble for us both.

If you want to listen to someone else and not use your own mind, you have the liberty.

But me Never! You know, myself, too, and never did I have much use for people who try to run other's lives for them.

Never mind...we will have each other, and if we cannot

mind our own business perhaps we can hire someone to do it for us.

If I was ignorant, I might truly believe there was something wrong in marrying ones cousins. But I am not.

Your Loving, Loving, Loving, Sweetheart,

XXXXX Arthur XXXXX

* * * *

and mattie appears a bit later as well.

* * * *

Dunedin, New York
October 18, 1913

My Darling, Darling, Darling, Katie,

I know you would not pay any attention to what anyone said...Mother expected what Mattie said in her letter. If you will bring that letter over Sunday, I will read it just to see what I think about how she treats us. If I had read it last Sunday, I'm sure I would not have used her well, knowing that she tried to get you to give me up.

I sent for our furniture yesterday. It cost $87.14 and should be here in three weeks. The express will be five or six dollars. I drew sixty five of mine besides the interest in the bank yet. I have another five in my pocket so I guess we will have enough.

...this has been a beautiful rainy day...It makes me lonesome...The man has not brought my money yet. I guess he has forgotten me.

I bought two grey flannel shirts, a cap, and a necktie when I was in Athens.... Father bought me a new plush robe and a lantern for the wagon. The new law makes it a five dollar fine not to have a lantern on the wagon at night.... I guess that means we will surely have to be good now.

We will go to Athens with a load of potatoes this week. Father will drive down later with some apples.

Don't worry about what I said earlier in the week. I love you, and we shall spend some time together this winter, you can bet.

Your loving, loving, loving, sweetheart,

XXXXX Arthur XXXXX

* * * *

so? what's next what are the first flowers that will bear, pardon me, the final fruits?

* * * *

Dunedin, New York
October 25, 1913

My Darling, Darling, Darling, Katie,

I arrived home about 4 A.M. It was a peach of a night. The road was wet and slippery and rutted. Billy had to wade through water up to his knees sometimes. I had two and a half hours sleep and have dug eleven barrels of potatoes today.

Darling don't think I am mad over last night. I was sore at myself for letting you make a fool of me by kicking me out in the rain when I had thought I was to have one more evening with you.

I know I snapped at you when I told you to get out of the wagon. But Billy had his head down and the wagon was cramped, and I could not get down without climbing over the wheels, and you had the parasol in my face so I could not see. So you see, you must forgive me for whatever I said. Won't you?

I suffered enough in the rain before I got home. Not so much as poor old Billy suffered though....Old faithful Billy. He plodded through the mud and water where sometimes there was no road in sight at all. I pulled under Bonen's shed and stayed from twenty minutes of eleven until nearly half past two. Then the wind shifted and it rained as hard as I've ever seen it...Joel Arden came by and invited me in...but I decided to try for home anyway. I couldn't have gotten wetter.

... Please don't be angry about how I used you last night....

Apples are $1.50 a barrel in Athens now. Some week. They're selling Northern Spys, Baldwin, Delicious, and Jiffy Flower. The Macs should go well....

Did you enjoy yourself any better at the Poultrie's than you would have if you had let me stay down to the house with you? I suppose it was all for the best. I finally got home safe and sound, and you got some sleep rather than staying up with me all night.

Darling, please promise me not to meet with your Aunt Lillian...I am glad there are not many more weeks to wait. I know, dear, she never could turn your love from me any more than Mattie or your other friends, but I've heard she is a mean woman. She might injure you if you made her mad....If she should ever harm you, I would have my revenge. But that would be no good if she killed you... Please have someone with you if she comes. If you are alone, lock the door and let her think no one is at home....You might not be afraid of her...but do this for me please.

At least, hear her address in silence and let it go in one ear and out the other. She is mad because she planned for you and

Lillian to marry some rich men and then she could come in, make trouble, and get the money...

Please darling, forgive me for saying everything to hurt you last night because I could not stay...I know I am a brute at times. I fear that part of my own human needs more than all the rest...If you ever have trouble from me, it will be that.

Your loving, loving, loving, sweetheart,
XXXXX Arthur XXXXXX

* * * *

she did, of course, forgive him. love forgives everything doesn't it? even death, itself, can, should, must be forgiven if it is to be love.

right sis,--dad?

yes, i know i'm editing a little. so? i've been leaving little things out for a while now.

* * * *

Dunedin, New York
November 1, 1913

My Darling, Darling, Darling, Katie,

It was just as well you did not come up for the husking. It will be Tuesday rather than Wednesday night as I had thought....

You should be up here this week...I had an invitation to a birthday party. They sent word for me come along and bring a friend...I did not...There is a social at Burden's tomorrow night. His name has been linked with the Snoop catastrophe. It is said Miss Annie has been seen coming out of his house at all hours of the night.

I pulled turnips today and finally put some wood in the school...I was getting ready to go trapping tomorrow, but the man over on the dam came tonight, and wanted to know what I would take for the twenty cord of wood down by the new mill, and me to draw it. Four dollars a cord, I said, and that city fellow agreed...I have to draw it within a week though, and I will have mileage for it when I get paid. I think we still owe $15 on it.

Still, if I get eighty we will have sixty-five left and will not have to worry when our furniture gets here. You need not work anymore, and I can let you have what you lack.... With this and what I get for the pigs, we should be able to start housekeeping in fine shape .... We will get that bed you wanted...like pigs in clover. Darling, I will try not to be cross anymore. I certainly will not have too many times.

Your loving, loving, loving, sweetheart,

My own little Darling,

XXXOOXXX Arthur XXXooXXX

XXXooXXXXXooXXXXXooXXXXo

* * * *

i'll speak a little about this. let me remember.

CHAPTER XLII
HISTORY XIII

The course of history moves from loneliness to loneliness in endless cycle as the prayer wheel spins. Peopled with clowns, tricksters, and magicians, all of us, Henry and Teddy and Good Arthur, who to be saved must lose the name of action or be lost in lesser movement regardless of their former and complete devotion to it. The ambivalence of all energy is its great, and possibly only, attraction. That in it we lose ourselves and so are saved from certain and continued anguish.

Love is the desperation of the gods before loneliness. Love, to be love, must be absolute, in laughter as well as in tears, or else it is without substance. Augustine with an empty cup; gross Henry, his mouth full of bitter fruits; dear Ann without the privilege of sacrifice, unsought and undesigned until possibly the end; Teddy with no hill to charge, for at least a moment without self-delight; Woody without a grand dream; the bear without a belly; the hart without its quiet eyes; another Countryman without his ninety acres within which, upon which and from which, all great heroes (and heroines and child martyrs) are born, mature, and clasp tragedy to their bosom.

All love is pain or else not love but self love, indulgent to the end. To avoid such pain is to be without courage or humanness. It is the magic garden --for us bereft, without the passion plant--no flowers of wondrous delight.

No river flows forever quick and fresh but that it gathers its own salinity in the turbid, churning, paradoxical distention of its own death and (therefore inevitable) resurrection. And the roads beneath the liquid surface are paved and repaved by every storm that strips the stillness from the sky and remits down into that pathless vortex only subdued light. We pray between the flashes and remain forever unaware of the slow, sempiternal architecture forever changing in the dark beneath the waves.

Oh! Where are the headwaters in the hills? In pain the vocative is our only mode, and the future is forever past.

We picture action and so excoriate the past to palliate the present: dear Osta in her overlarge hat never laughs, old Jebediah and Ebenezer and William Clark never cross rivers, Arthur never cracks a slightly off color joke to his 'dear little girl', and Henry's greasy hand never stuffs mutton into a mouth already drooling good hock. In pictures, all that is ever left us, there are only fine roman noses, long-tapering fingers, delicate and palpitating breasts, and the supposed accomplishment of actions long since disassociated from the flesh. And so we should not weep for smooth, young boys who leave for springtime shell-holes and cross barbed-wire only to find the clear and startling consummation of their quest.

Ah! Arthur, dear Arthur, lost mountain man pacing within violent, modern shoes. The hunt never ends, and the quarry is never known. We were or become what we are.

All history is momentary. A summer rose in December and so an end to it.

CHAPTER XLIII
Love Story XVII

i don't want to say anything about these last letters. there must have been more, but gramps and grandma should be allowed to speak for themselves, sometime, i think. this is their beginning, their new world. they made it. we make ours.

* * * *

Dunedin, New York
November 14, 1913

My Darling, Darling, Darling, Katie,

I did just as you told me by not writing. I would have, but I missed Vic Bunden when he went through and so I had to go way down to the house to see if he brought our goods.

They were there. I uncrated them in the house and took the wrapping off one chair. It was rubbed a little but not bad. If they are all as nice, I won't find any fault. The covering is the most beautiful I've ever seen. The wood is rather light, but I guess they will hold to look at. Ha! I was going to try it but thought the seat too nice to dirty, so I only looked at it for a long time.

I am glad there are only three more weeks for me to ride down there and back there and back this month. I can't get any more things into Aunt Suzannah's until you come up and straighten around what is already there. Two rooms are so full, I can hardly find my way, and I bet there will be a cord of paper by the time we get through unwrapping.

Did Mrs. Poultrie get home all right? If I had not found those mittens, I would have frozen my own fingers before I got back. I guess you did not feel much like writing last night? Hey!

I guess I will have to go down and see Miss Hanna tomorrow and put in the rest of the wood. I have it all drawed but have not got the pay for it yet. Gee, what a spree I can have when I get it. I can stay drunk for a week. Hey!

I am sorry to make you walk home yesterday, since I did not get the goods until today. You must not let Mrs. Poultrie work you too hard these last weeks. I will have work enough to keep you a week just cleaning up paper and string.

It will be too good to be true when we are together once more. I wish I did not have to wait so much longer. It seems now as if I cannot bear to leave you whenever we are near. I suppose you will have to commence getting things before long. You don't want to wait until it is too late.

I must close now. I will try and write more and better.

Your most and ever true lover,

xx Arthur xx

My love always

* * * *

Dunedin, New York
November 19, 1913

My Dearest, Dearest Katie,

I received your letter tonight. I suppose it will be the last I
get so I thought I would go you one better this week. I guess two
of my letters would only make one of yours, so we'll just be even.

I have been to the Centre and it is ten o'clock. I had to make
out a paper, stating how much I spent trying to secure the office of
Justice of the Peace. Ha! I guess I spent about a million.

Father sold his beef cow to Ed Hupp so I guess we will
have to buy our beef this winter. We killed another pig today and
are gong to scald him with the hog. Besides the old sow we have
only five left and I will have one of them.

Father and I divided the hens we bought. He brought his

home and I left mine over at the Snoop barn. I have thirty of my own and nine of Aunt Suzannah's plus four roosters, two mine and two hers.

I guess you will have your hands full next month, but you must not expect me to do much. I will have to have December to rest up and prepare for what is to come in January. Ha! Ha! I will have someone to warm the bed for me, but I am going to get some pajamas, or whatever they call them, so you can't put your cold feet on me. My feet are cold sometimes though and then I will make you squeal.

It will seem like being born again to have you near in such a short time, but I don't expect to take much comfort until we get our own home. You know how Agnes and Mother are when you are here. They make me so mad. We can manage through it if we can only be together. You won't get much time at home. If you stay a week so Lillian can go down to Mattie's with the news that will be enough. I want you where I can see you and, of course, tease you once in a while.

I have all the curtains drawn, so you won't fade when you get in the house. The cover on the parlor suite is guaranteed not to fade. I wish you could see them. Just think! I got some of them so long ago I've had to wind the clock three times.

Good things come slow. If you dream of being my wife, certainly I did not dream of being your husband. Even after I knew I loved you, I was afraid to dream, I loved you so.

You see, it took me a long time to realize my love. I had never loved anyone before, except my own folks and then not as well as I should have. So I did not even know what real love for a human being was let alone for the one love of my life.

Even after I found that I loved you, I thought there was no hope. You little know how you hurt me when you refused to tell me where you got that ring. I thought another held the heart I

380

longed for, and I was tempted to leave and never see you again. You told me I could not love you because you were my cousin, and I thought you would not change your mind. That I loved you and might not have you drove me wild, but when you kept making me come down every Sunday I took hope in spite of the ring.

I determined then to make you love me or leave you, and that was how I came to speak as I did last Christmas night. When you cried because I might leave, I knew you loved me. Had you not cried I would not have been in Dunedin this night.

I don't know how you came to love me when you could have had so many others. No other girl has ever loved me as you do. I must have loved you before you did me or I would not have let you know me as you came to.

I know we will be happy. See how well we get along with only ourselves to look after last year. You were only angry with me once because I failed to say, "Good Morning" to you. Soon every morning will be good.

I wonder if we will be like Wilbur and Matilda? Burt Snyder says they don't quarrel, they just suck tongues. The queerest couple he ever saw. Well, we can do our share of tongue sucking, but I hope not quarreling.

All my love to you My Dearest one,
Arthur, Your ever true lover

* * * *

Dunedin, New York
December 1, 1913

My Dearest, Dearest Katherine,

I love you.

I hope you arrived safely home. I have finished drawing all
the lumber from the mill and our future is nearly assured.

My throat is still sore though. It stormed this afternoon, and
I had on my old boots, and got my feet wet. I will be all right by
Sunday, so don't worry. Nothing could keep me from our meeting
then.

Dearest, you little knew when I bought you your locket,
why I did it. I supposed then that you loved another and that ring
stood between us. I wanted to give you a last thing to remember me
by. I never suspected that you would want my picture in it. I would
have been pleased enough if you had just worn my present. I loved
you so. I expected to leave you and my home and seek a new life
somewhere.

Don't think me soft or laugh at me, please! It brings tears to
my eyes to think of what might have been.

I don't know what was the trouble with me last night. I
could have cried easier than laughed. It seemed I could not stand to
have you leave me. It doesn't seem so bad when I have to come
away from you, but when you go away from me after we have been
together for a day, all the joy leaves my life.

If my throat is all right in the morning, I will go hunting
when the snow stops. It is so peaceful and quiet now. All the world

is still, and cold, and beautiful. Next year will be a fine year.

If it doesn't stop snowing, I may go down and straighten up a little at our palace on the mountain. I know it isn't much, but it's to be ours and so it seems like that, doesn't it?

Father wants us to go in his house, now, when we've married. He said we could clean it as well now as in the spring. I promised Suzannah we would go in hers and I ought to. I would rather go in our own, but I don't like the way things hang around here just now. I may quit Father all together and go someplace and hire out where we can have a house to live in after the first of April.

Oh, the time is so short now. It will come out all right. It has been a long year--all the times without you.

It is six o'clock and dark now. I must finish my chores. Oh, how I care for you, so very much my sweet little girl.

Good night. Sweet dreams.

Your ever true lover,

xArthurx

I do love you. It seems I always have.

CHAPTER XLIV

Elizabeth Terrel and Arthur Countryman were united in love under God on a sunny Sunday afternoon some years before the Great War broke out not many years later--to which Arthur never went.

Thank the Lord!

there is no more to read.

or say, not here, not now among the . . .

Nor I.

TICK TOCK! TICK TOCK! TICK TOCK! TICK....